The Well Deceived

Isaac Kuhnberg

Clink Street

London | New York

Published by Clink Street Publishing 2018

Copyright © 2018

First edition.

ISBNs: 978-1-912262-92-2 paperback
978-1-912262-93-9 ebook

For the dead friends

This is the sublime and refined point of felicity called the possession of being well-deceived, the serene peaceful state of being a fool among knaves.

Jonathan Swift, *A Tale of a Tub*

So the Angel said: 'Thy phantasy has imposed upon me, and thou oughtest to be ashamed.'

William Blake, *The Marriage of Heaven and Hell*

CONTENTS

PROLOGUE

Our investigation thus far confronts us with the following: the historical record (heavily redacted); the official explanation as to why any subterfuge was necessary; and last of all the subterfuge itself. Beyond this point, it would appear, we can go no further. Access to the appropriate archives is restricted 'for reasons of state security'. Essentially an official brick wall.

Where the historian's work is hampered by impediments of this description, her best recourse is to play the detective, using her knowledge of the period under examination, allied to simple common-sense, to plug whatever gaps appear in the narrative, demolish the occasional flimsy alibi, and dismantle the over-riding false premise. Her aim, as always, is not to contradict *but to* clarify *– to separate what I am obliged to term 'wilful prevarication' from what is manifestly true.*

Once the body of evidence is approached in this spirit, it becomes immediately apparent that the official explanation is so radically unsatisfactory as to constitute a further and even more perplexing subterfuge, operating in this case not against the subject peoples but against the Sisterhood itself.

G Bellairs, Unpublished Introduction to: *Separation and Divorce: Five Centuries of Anglian History, (fourth edition),* University of Evelyn Press, 481

ONE

In the Beginning

A'll nae forgee th' faither hen
Fa clepped me tae his brast
Ay aw th' fowk as e'er A loved
Me daddy war th' best.

'Loch Lonely-Heart' (Traditional) sung by Jock Lomond,
Heather & Thistle Music, 398.

1

I must have been five or six when I first came to realise that my
father was a distinguished scientist. By that time our family name
was already a household word, owing to one of his earliest inven-
tions: the Riddle Suction Cleaner, or simply, 'The Riddle'. Over time
the word has become synonymous with any act in which things are
disposed of quickly and efficiently, as in, "I had to be elsewhere, so
I riddled up my dinner in five minutes." A gardener *riddles* rubbish
from the lawn; the police *riddle* a city centre of beggars; the SS *riddle
out* troublemakers, and so forth. The word is also commonly applied
to a particular sexual act – you can puzzle this out for yourself.

At one time my fellow pupils at Bune College used to go out of
their way to air this usage in front of me, in order to rub my nose
in the fact that if my father was famous it was for something essentially ludicrous and un-Bunian. It was only when I made Praetor
that they stopped doing this to my face, though no doubt the practice continued behind my back. After that I only heard Purkis
using the word in its sexual context, but he was a friend, with a
friend's privileges, and he only did it to tease.

2

My nursery was a collection of humble stone buildings near Glenlockie on the western coast of Alba, where my father was based at the time. The landscape was wild and inhospitable – steep cliffs overlooking rough seas, flat plains of heather and gorse, with the occasional stunted thorn tree, and a few battered sheep cowering in the shelter of the odd low stone wall. No doubt the region enjoyed some kind of summer – I have some vague recollection of an unfamiliar glow on the skin, and the fields being transformed by sunlight and blue sky – but if so it no sooner arrived than it departed, leaving behind what seemed like a perpetual winter.

Most of the time it was freezing cold. I could never get warm all over. Even when I stood in front of a roaring fire (this was a rare enough event in itself) an icy draught would attack me from behind, and the moment I turned about to warm my nether parts it would blast me full in the face.

We slept on mattresses stuffed with straw; the sheets were thin and ragged, and clammy to the touch. Every evening we stood in line to receive our individual hootie, filled from an immense aluminium kettle that sat grumbling on the range. Although the hootie was an absolute life-saver – without it many of us would have died of frostbite – it was a good deal more than that. I thought of mine with the loving tenderness you might bestow on a favourite bed-mate. At first the fat rubber bladder, ribbed like a fishbone, would be too hot to touch. Swaddling it in my hairy sweater, I would carry it with me into the clammy envelope of the sheets. Next I would kick the burning package down to the foot of the bed; then once the fierce glow had abated I would untangle my heated sweater and apply it like a bandage to my frozen toes, while at the same time placing the precious hootie – now somewhat cooler – first on my chest and finally between my legs. Clamping tight, I would chew on a fingernail, and imagine myself to be a huge white bird, sailing over an endless landscape of ice and black waves into the region of sleep – and wake shivering in the greenish light of early morning with the chilly coolie, as it had now become, stuck to my tackle like a giant leech.

During the day we played with rough wooden letters and crayons and clay and sorting-boxes, and for recreation took long walks across the fields, heads bowed against the icy wind. Our nurses were inflexibly aloof; there was no profit in going to them weeping with a grazed knee or a cold. If you cut yourself they would bandage the wound; if you broke a bone they would take you (by cart and ferry and finally an ancient wheezing steamer) to the hospital, some fifty miles away; but if you wanted sympathy, you had to whistle for it.

My infant schoolfellows, being Islanders, were also prone to dourness. They used as few words as they could get away with, and dismissed any display of language that was in any way descriptive or analytical as 'fookin' blether'. Their name for me was 'mirren-tap', a reference to the colour of my hair; a designation I carried stoically throughout my early childhood. It was not regarded as much of a stigma, for red hair is a great deal more common in Alba than it is here.

Glenlockie Nursery adjoined Glenlockie Middle School, to which we seamlessly transferred at the age of three, staying there until we were eleven. The nurses were succeeded by schoolmasters: much the same sort of men, only even more disgruntled, and generally older, and inclined to lay about themselves indiscriminately with a knobby stick. Reading and writing and woodwork were the main subjects we were taught, together with a rudimentary form of Mathematics that went by the name of 'Sums' and mainly consisted of exercises in the addition and subtraction of pounds, shillings and pence – a currency formulation that even at that age I recognised to be complicated to the point of absurdity.

Lessons began at seven in the morning, and continued until three, with a short break for lunch: bread and soup, mostly, with some dry sheep's cheese and pickles if you were lucky. Dinner was at six, and generally involved potatoes, cabbage and stewed mutton, with semolina pudding for afters. During the autumn months our afternoons were devoted to digging up and washing the potatoes and turnips which formed a large part of our diet. In the early evening we would congregate in the Green Room, where

there were smelly sagging sofas and a log fire, and listen to pro-
grammes on the wireless: *Mark Martin, The Flying Detective; The
X-ray Man; News of the North; Sam of the Woodlands* were particular
favourites. Reception was unreliable; the wireless had an annoying habit of fading or emitting a prolonged burst of crackle at
moments of high suspense. Every Sunday there would be a wireless talk about civic duty, and personal responsibility, and making
the most of one's opportunities. ('What opportunities?' I would
often ask myself). Oddly enough the reception remained adequate
during these talks, or perhaps that is just how I remember it: the
talks gave us an opportunity for gossip and messing about; if they
had been inaudible no one would have cared or even noticed.

On Friday nights there would be a kind of party. Our schoolmasters would bring out the wind-up horn, and a collection of
heavy black platters worn smooth by constant use, and play us
long crackly renditions of Songs from the Island North – melancholy pieces like 'Laddie ay th' Heather', and 'Loch Lonely-Heart'
– while they drank their way through several bottles of what they
called 'Daddies' Ruin'.

The only excitement we experienced was when wee Dunca'
McIntyre (he was two years younger than me) had one of his fits,
which he did roughly every two months or so. This usually happened at suppertime, when we were passing the loaded plates
along the long refectory table, like items on an assembly line.
Sooner or later the relentless repetition of the movement would
trip some circuit in Duncan's brain, causing him to twitch and jerk
and fall to the floor, where he would lie, jerking to an impossibly
violent rhythm, like an industrial machine attempting desperately
to expel some obstruction jamming its natural processes. Foam
would gather on his lips. One of the masters would place a cushion
under his head; another would put a wooden spoon between his
teeth, to prevent him biting his tongue. The jerking and thrashing would go on for some twenty minutes, after which the mad
rhythm would slacken to a simple pulse, and then the occasional
twitch, and then die away, leaving him in a deep unquiet sleep.

Most of the time Duncan seemed more or less normal, but there was something worrying about his eyes: a disconnection; as if one of them was looking inwards on a vacancy, and the other staring out at a treacherous world. One day, after a particularly violent fit, a doctor was called, and he was taken away to hospital. He never returned.

3

For games we had kicker, sticks, and burly, none of which I cared for. I found no pleasure in charging about a muddy field in the freezing cold with snot flying from both nostrils, or being shoved and kicked and pushed over whenever the master's back was turned (and often when it wasn't). This earned me a reputation in some quarters as a 'wee jessie', an ancient term whose origins had been lost, but remained a pretty deadly insult all the same. I retaliated, then as later, by cultivating skills as a mimic. I was merciless, but I chose my victims carefully, targeting primarily the odd and the vulnerable, and anyone at all out of favour. At the time I saw nothing wrong in this, for I felt odd and vulnerable myself: persecuting boys more vulnerable than me was nothing more than a means of survival. My mastery of this tactic made me hated in some quarters, but it also made me feared, and won me a reputation of being funny, which in any school I have attended is the next best thing to being good-looking or good at sports.

A medical technician came every two or three weeks to check you over: he weighed you, he took a sample of blood, he peered down your throat, holding back your tongue with a wooden spatula; he wrapped a bag around your upper arm, and pumped it up until it squeezed like an Indian burn, he fondled your goolies; and when all of that was done he scribbled something on your record sheet. Occasionally a boy failed to thrive, and was removed.

We received no pocket-money, but this was not considered a hardship, as there was no shop nearby, and therefore no opportunity for making purchases. There existed a schoolboy trade in the sort of items schoolboys like to collect, such as stamps, or buttons, or badges, most of which had to be sourced from the local rubbish-dump, or stolen from the masters' private quarters. Sugar, salt and pepper were also a kind of currency; supplies of these had to be filched from the dining-hall, and smuggled out in one's underpants, wrapped in twists of paper.

No one was particularly good at lessons, but since the masters were themselves indifferently schooled, no one cared very much either way. There were a few shelves of useful guides to subjects like fishing and carpentry and boat maintenance. What we mainly talked about were other boys (particularly those who were gormless or especially daring), the masters, (particularly those who were cranky or especially cruel), our favourite wireless serials (most boys wanted to be The Flying Detective when they grew up) and the progress or otherwise of our sexual development – how many times a night you stroked your wullie, for example, and how long it took to bring the matter to a conclusion.

Sex was not of all-consuming interest. The schoolmasters chose for some reason to make a mystery of it, referring to the subject very rarely, and only then in terms of deep disapproval, as if there was something wrong with things that everyone did, whether openly or in secret. This strikes me now as pointless and hypocritical. We all – masters as well as boys, presumably – had the same equipment, apart from the odd variation in size, colour and shape. The usual acts were routinely practised by virtually everyone. Some boys preferred one thing to another, and concentrated more or less exclusively on that; others rang what changes they could.

The feelings we had for one another were practical rather than romantic, a matter of choosing a boy who could be relied upon to bring the business to a quick and pleasant conclusion. Luckily not everyone fancied the same few individuals. As a general rule, boys are drawn to the physical type least like their own. The slighter boys are drawn towards the stockier, and vice versa. The same pattern of attraction has applied at every phase of my life, and in every pocket of society I have visited: so much so that I suspect it of being a universal law of nature.

Of course there are always a small number of relatively ugly boys who on account of their self-confidence or some other individual advantage acquire a following among the sort of boys who are natural followers. (Intelligence, unfortunately, is not one of these qualities: if anything it tends to make an individual disliked by his peers, to much the same degree that it exceeds their own.) But there are always a small number of boys who are in every way too ugly and hopeless to appeal to anyone. At Glenlockie these had the choice of either finding their satisfaction alone, or with someone as unappealing as themselves. As a last resort they might purchase the services of a more attractive schoolfellow with bribes of collectibles or some other form of persuasion. This kind of negotiation was tolerated, as long as no one actually forced himself on anyone. Boys at Glenlockie disliked bullying, and if it was taken too far they would gang up to teach the bully a lesson.

The only time that sex became a problem was if one of the masters blundered into our world. There was one particular master – a man of about fifty – who was known to prey upon the younger boys, particularly when he was drunk. His victims regarded him with contempt, but seemed powerless either to refuse or report him to another adult. At the time I wondered why this was, but not being one of them, I didn't give the matter too much thought.

Like all boys we grumbled constantly, mostly about the food, but we didn't consider ourselves to be either deprived or abused. Glenlockie was all we knew – we had nothing to compare it with – and the truth is that most of us enjoyed our time there, the way that one enjoys a midwinter dip, or scaling a high hill in a fierce wind.

4

In Glenlockie the anniversary of a boy's arrival – November 9th in my case – was celebrated with an announcement over porridge, followed after lessons by a round of indoor games. These invariably degenerated into a bout of joshing, whereby boys and masters piled onto the anniversary subject, and let him know their true opinion of him – information transmitted by a variety of means, mostly good-natured, but occasionally otherwise. Since I had over the course of my Glenlockie career attracted a fair degree of enmity, my experience of the process generally involved a good deal of covert pinching, punching and goolie-mashing.

The morning after my fifth anniversary, I received a visitor. Immediately after supper I was called to the Headmaster's office, where a man was sitting, arms folded, on one of a row of low folding chairs, looking thoroughly awkward and miserable.

"Professor Scoolie, sair, here is yeer soun Weelum," said the Headmaster, Mr McNab. He was known to us as 'Smirkie', on account of the fixed scowl that permanently deformed his features, excepting for the odd unguarded moment when he was listening to the weather report or a gramophone record of a sentimental ballad.

The man addressed as Professor Riddle put out his hand. "Hello, William," he muttered, avoiding my eye.

He was very tall and bony. He had a ragged red beard – slightly unusual that, for a man of his status, although I didn't realise it at the time – and red shaggy eyebrows, and was bundled up against the cold in multiple layers of clothing, mostly a dull green in colour. Under a many-pocketed overcoat he wore a green tweed suit, a green tweed waistcoat, a green woollen shirt, and a green woollen muffler. These were just the visible layers; there were doubtless others underneath as well. His huge shoes were of orangey-brown leather. His red hair was curly and unruly, and had started to recede, drawing attention to an alarmingly high forehead crowded with large tawny freckles. A pair of gold-framed glasses with round lenses perched permanently halfway down his nose. A heavy gold chain was attached to to a bulky gold timepiece fattening the pocket of his waistcoat. A red spotted handkerchief overflowed from his breast pocket. It struck me that he might be dressing deliberately to fit a part.

His grasp was firm, the skin rough, the fingers contrastingly slender and tapering. After a second he released his grip.

"I'll lea ye twa alane," said Smirkie. "Ye dinna need mah hulp tae blether ower yer kinship."

"If you don't mind," said my father glumly.

Smirkie left. I waited for Professor Riddle to initiate a conversation.

"Well, William," he said heavily, "I'm your father, it seems."

"Aye," I said. "A ken sae." The exact nature of the relationship he alluded to was unclear to me. Some of the other boys had also received visits from their fathers, but the meetings took place with no one else present, and the various reports of what took place never struck me as authentic.

"Do you like games?"

"I do not," I admitted.

"Nor do I," he said, visibly relaxing a little. "Are you interested in science?"

"I canna say I am," I said slowly. "They dinna lear it here in Glenlockie."

"Is that so?" He sucked air through his teeth disapprovingly. "Well, they should. Can you read?"

"I can."

"That's right: I have a report here, somewhere." He fished around in his pockets for a few seconds, before giving it up as a bad job. "I shall be coming to see you every month."

I nodded. I wondered why this was necessary, and what he hoped to gain by it, but it seemed presumptuous to ask for information on the point.

"In the meantime would you like me to arrange science lessons for you?"

I thought it advisable to humour him. "Is that whit yi'll want, faither?"

"It's not for my benefit. It's you I'm thinking of."

"Aye, then."

"I shall speak to … what is his name?"

"McNab."

"See what he can do."

"Braw."

"Goodbye then, William," he said, putting out his hand a second time.

"Cheerio sur."

"Pa will do."

He had a private word with Smirkie before he left.

"Science!" said Smirkie, ushering me back to the Greenroom. "Who the de'il does he think is gang to lear that deft blether?"

11

I had a sense – it was to be the first time of many – that my father had unwittingly offended the powers-that-be, and that I was somehow implicated in his offence. But I had more important things to worry about. Thanks to his visit I had missed virtually a whole episode of *Mark Martin*.

5

After that my father visited me regularly every month, always in the evening during the Wireless Hour. Usually we sat outside, on a bench in the yard – you couldn't really call it a garden. He always brought a present for me, and it was always something connected with his own interests. The particular uses I found for these gifts, however, were rarely those he would have had in mind. A pair of compasses came in handy for pricking the boy sitting next to me in the thigh, earning me a pretty savage beating. A U-shaped magnet enabled me to perform a number of magic tricks of a rather obvious nature. The most impressive of these gifts – much coveted by my schoolmates – was a powerful magnifying glass, which I used for frying insects and setting fire to patches of dry heather on the rare sunny days when this was possible.

The first few minutes of his visits were a little strained, because he invariably made a point of asking me if I had found his last gift useful. Despite the need to prevaricate about these and other matters I enjoyed these visits, for he was an interesting and intelligent man, with a fund of opinions of everything under the sun; this being something of a novelty in an environment where people tend to hold their personal views very tight to their chests. He spoke about the history of Anglia and Alba, and the things to be seen in the great cities, and what it felt like exploring a labyrinth of underground tunnels just wide enough to take one man at a time, or launching yourself off a cliff-top with canvas wings strapped to your back.

He also told me about the projects he was working on. He was already by this time pretty famous for inventing the Riddle Suction Cleaner – you could find a Riddle in the broom cupboard of every decent-sized house in the country – but his real interests were of a more abstract nature. He was developing a theory of the nature and origins of the universe that required him to correlate his observations of the stars and planets with the examination of microscopic particles of matter, in order to determine whether the universe is either infinitely large or infinitely small, or both at the same time.

By this time I suspect you are losing interest, just as I did; but because he was my father I kept nodding and throwing out the occasional question to show that I was listening, and keen to hear what was coming next.

All this time he continued to press Smirkie to add science lessons to the curriculum. At first he was met with the standard response in bureaucratic situations: the sort of evasion that is tantamount to a refusal. That continued to be the situation for the next three years. But his growing fame as an inventor must have won him a modicum of influence with the Alban Education Authority, because in 471, three years after our first meeting, Smirkie suddenly capitulated, and informed us, during one of my father's visits, that a new teacher had been taken on specifically to teach me science.

"On your own heid be it, Professor Red-ill," he said grumpily. "Ye may think ye ken this laddie of yours, and whit fashion of instruction wad suit him best, but if he war a cuddie nae a wean, A ken the end *A* wad encourage fust, and it wadna be the pairt as leads the wee."

6

Timothy Butterworth, my new science teacher, was a nervy young man with a forlorn expression, whom I immediately identified as the type of immature adult who could be led all round the garden path and out into the streets, and left there to find his own way home, or not as the case might be. He was a recent graduate of the University of Gillie: obviously a competent enough scholar, but completely hopeless as a teacher of small boys. He was dreadfully in awe of my father – if there had been a Professor George Riddle Admiration Society he would have been its president – and to begin with he assumed that I too must be a scientific prodigy. Instead of attempting to interest me in experiments involving things like controlled explosions, where he might have had some limited success, he started droning on about theory A and theory B, and how Bibby postulated this and Bobby refuted it, and Buffer came up with the principle of inverse delineation and how space turned time inside-out, bum, double-bum, bum supreme: all fascinating stuff, no doubt, for anyone who had any aptitude for it, but in my case a complete waste of time.

I gave him every opportunity of correcting his mistake. I explained that I was completely at sea, didn't have a clue what he was bibbling on about, and would be glad if he would just start at the start and teach me something I could understand. He took this as meaning that I was finding his lessons too easy, and raised the bar even higher. Finally I was forced to retaliate. The next time we had a lesson I told him in confidence that my father had taught me a method of telepathic communication which enabled me to read a person's thoughts – his, for example – even when he was at home in his bed, and at the lesson's end I handed over an exercise book containing my homework: one enormous calculation taking up ten pages, peppered with brackets and letters and numbers big and little, and ending in an equals sign and the value b to the power of six. At which point he simply panicked, and sat in the classroom with his head in his hands, not saying a word.

The next day I was summoned to Smirkie's office. "Congratulations, laddie!" said Smirkie. "Ye'v gubbed yon fenless Jessie an nebbit' tway weeks. Thon'll be some kind o' warld record, nae doot." He cuffed my head lightly, his face red from stifled laughter. "An wadnae be tae vogie, mind," he said, as I rose to go. "Yer faither may no be blythe as to the efterclep."

7

Word of my deplorable treatment of Mr Butterworth must have got back to my father, because the next week he turned up out of the blue, and took me off to the Western Islands for a holiday.

I don't know if you have ever been to the Western Islands,

but if you have you will know that it is not the obvious place to take a small boy on holiday. Even in the summer the islands are windy and damp and deserted, and on some of them you can walk for miles without seeing a single soul, let alone a shop or cafe or amusement park or any of the things boys generally need to keep them entertained once they and their fathers have run out of things to say to one another. So on the face of it, the holiday could have been a complete disaster. Instead it was a dream come gloriously true: an idyll so flawless that no subsequent happiness has ever come close to replicating.

My father had acquired a somewhat antiquated steamer and a fat booklet of floritol vouchers, so distance was for once no object. Soon Glenlockie and all its works were far away, and we were steaming along a winding road flanked on both sides by glaring fields of yellow rapeseed stretching as far as the eye could see, with the wind whipping around our ears and the feedpumps going *thump thump thump* like the energetic beating of a healthy heart.

At the outset I was full of trepidation that my father would scold me for tormenting Mr Butterworth to the point of breakdown. I waited for him to raise the subject. The subject did not arise. I assumed that he was waiting for the right moment, and shifted the problem to the back of my mind, where it continued to fester for most of the remaining holiday.

At Poltraich we left the steamer in the charge of a friendly stuttering Islander, a giant of a man with a ragged black beard and one missing eye. From the same individual my father hired for the princely sum of ninepence-halfpenny a small motorboat smelling of oil and rotting fish; and to my surprise he allowed me to help him operate the craft. This is every small boy's dream, and worth a thousand rides on any corkscrew railway in the land.

We stocked up with bread and cheese and cans of beans and chocolate cake, and set off with no particular destination in mind, and what had started off that morning as a grey cloudy sky cleared the moment we got out to sea: the sun shone hotly out of a dark blue sky, and the boat tossed gently on the waves, and the engine chugged away merrily like a swiftly beating heart, and gulls flew round and round us squawking for bread, and I felt for the first time in my life deliriously happy in a way I had never thought possible.

And for the next three days it seemed that happiness was something that could be created magically, out of thin air, and that a limitless supply of it was waiting for me in the future.

We wove in and out of the islands scattered about the coastal waters like the jumbled pieces of a giant's jigsaw, and came to rest in the sandy bay of a small wild island which my father identified from his chart as Wyrd. A rough path wound up to a stone cottage overlooking the bay. We trudged up to it, expecting at any moment to find ourselves face to face with an angry hermit waving a hefty club. But the cottage was empty. We peered through the windows, and finally tried the door. It was unlocked. The cottage interior was furnished with a few rough chairs and a wobbly table. We lit a fire – the wood and kindling was already laid in the fireplace – then ate our bread and cheese at the wobbly table, sitting on two wobbly chairs. The fire crackled merrily. My father sang a comic song, then told me a story about a Time Machine. Things could not have been more perfect.

We slept that night on straw mattresses, and early the next morning went down to the gull haunted bay, and walked through the reeds and climbed some low sand dunes: and all this time, from the moment he arrived at the School to take me away, my father did not mention science or Mr Butterworth or my powers of application even once.

There were other holidays, though never again to Wyrd. That was the place to which you do not need to return, the secret place of memories, the place where we had first spoken together honestly, as father and son, and won some understanding of one another, and what we were together, as a family unit.

It was more than that. Somewhere along the way, and for reasons that are necessarily unfathomable, we had developed a liking for one another.

TWO
Crammer

"Every man," declared Rattle, making an airy gesture in which both pomposity and self-importance played equal parts, "chooses for himself a career that reflects his inner essential nature. For example, the man who lives with his head in the clouds will commonly waste his time on something perfectly useless, such as the production of vast tomes of fantastical fiction. Whereas the man who is more at home in the universe is likely to exhibit a more practical bent, like an affinity with the operations of complex machinery."

"May I take it," enquired Wisley dangerously, "that you place yourself in the latter category?"

The Jigsaw Man *by F R Trumper, Grubstop Press, 480*

1

When the holiday was over, and my father had gone back to his work at Gillie with the subject of Mr Butterworth still in abeyance, I naturally felt a great sense of relief. Nonetheless I was worried. I knew how important the science lessons were to him, because he had insisted on my submitting to them so resolutely and for so long. Presumably he will have been disappointed with me for refusing to take them seriously. Why in which case hadn't he said so? Was I now completely off the hook, or would he bring the subject up at some time in the future?

Over time I began to be first puzzled and then suspicious. All grown-ups have their secrets, my father no less than anyone else. Was the holiday quite so unplanned as he had made it out to be? Had he ever visited Wyrd before? Had he known that a simple

17

cottage would be waiting for us, empty but intact, and with the fire laid in the grate? All these questions remained unasked and unanswered, tainting my memory of our trip like a worrying blemish – an injured animal, a bloodstain, an onlooker's sneer – in the background of an otherwise happy photograph.

2

I had now reached that stage of life where one's voice alternately squeaks and booms, and hair begins to sprout in the patches of one's body that were formerly as smooth as the skin of an apricot. A light down of reddish hair had recently appeared on my cheeks and chest: portents of a coming maturity whose progress I followed obsessively, keen to see an end to a phase in which one is neither a child nor a man, but a creature drifting awkwardly back and forth between the two.

My schoolmasters took it for granted that like my peers I would be going on to a Vocational College, where I would learn useful skills like carpentry and welding and steamer maintenance. My father himself had attended such a college in Loath: it had been the best preparation he could have had, he told me, for a life spent creating new technologies. Leaving with a Diploma in Engineering, he had started work for a small company manufacturing machines for use about the house – lawn-mowers, carpet sweepers, etc. That was where he had come up with his idea for the Riddle Suction Cleaner.

From then on his rise was swift and inevitable. In quick succession he was made a partner in the company, a Government Advisor on Infrastructure Renewal, and an Associate Professor in Engineering at Brack, one of the colleges of the ancient University of Gillie.

I was a very different case. The only thing I really enjoyed was painting. There were courses offered in Art at a College in Gillie which I thought might suit me, but I hesitated to tackle my father about signing up to one. He had still never mentioned my treatment of Mr Butterworth – effectively my rejection of the career he would have liked me to have. But the question of my future could not be put on hold for ever.

I raised the topic in the Glenlockie Workers' Cafe, over a full Alban breakfast.

He heard me out with one hand lightly touching his temple, as if I were deliberately giving him a headache. Once I had said my piece he removed his glasses and brushed his forehead with the back of his hand. His eyes looked tired and a little bloodshot. "I don't really care what you do, William," he said. "That is to say," he corrected himself, "I do care, of course I do, but it can't be my choice. You have to decide what suits you best."

I mumbled something about liking to draw and paint.

"Yes, but are you any *good* at it? Is it something you could do for a living?"

The fact that he could ask me these questions, having seen a good deal of my work over the years, was tantamount to saying that I wasn't and couldn't.

"I could work in a gallery or a museum."

"Is that really what you want to do? The men I know who do that kind of work all tend to be ... I don't know: stuck in a box. Hobbyists, bird-watchers, collectors of medallions and portrait miniatures. Admirable in a way, of course, but deadly dull. I don't see you being like that at all."

Nor did I, when he put it like that.

"I've been thinking," he said. "You know I suppose that money these days is no object." He lifted his mug of tea to his lips. I waited for him to continue. His words, when finally they came, were something of a surprise. "Has it ever occurred to you that you might become a pupil at one of the great private schools: Barrington, Polchester, Belmarsh – maybe even Bune?"

It never had.

"Of course there is an entrance examination to get through. We would have to get you up to speed so that you could at least scrape a pass. Brush up your four Basic Elements, and maybe throw in this Art caper for good measure. That means a year's course at a Crammer, somewhere in the south – Cantleford, for example. I've been offered a post at Equinox College as Director of Scientific Research – I've been meaning to discuss it with you."

I mopped up some runny yolk with a piece of bread. "You really want me to go to *Bune?*"

"You don't sound too keen."

"They're all snobs there, aren't they?"

"Pretty well, yes. That doesn't mean you have to be one. The great thing about a place like that, for someone like yourself" – he looked down at the remains of his breakfast – "is the people you meet. The contacts you make. And of course the doors it opens to you." He looked up again, meeting my eye. "After six years at Bune you would be pretty well guaranteed a place at Falkland – one of the newer Colleges … studying Media, perhaps, or Journalism, or Business Management … And from what they say an old Bunian will never be without a job. A pretty good one too, certainly in financial terms."

It pained me to hear my father trotting out these platitudes – notions I knew he didn't really subscribe to – because it confirmed a truth I had known for some time. Although he was fond of me – that is not the sort of thing one can fake – he had no confidence at all in my abilities, not just as an artist but as anything whatsoever. Bune was being offered to me as an easy road through life.

But what really was my alternative? Artisan College? Gillie Art School? Waiting tables in a restaurant? I felt suddenly tired and deflated.

"Fair enough, pa, yes," I said. "You've convinced me."

"Really? This has to be your choice, remember?"

"Yes, and I'm choosing it."

"Good. William, that's wonderful! I'm so pleased."

He really was pleased. It was the best thing possible. One more problem solved, to everyone's satisfaction. Now he could get back to his work.

3

Cantleford Tutorial College was a tall red brick building overlooking the River Ajax and the Gethsemane Gardens. It had been built two centuries ago as a family house, and adapted for its present use about thirty years ago. Because pupils of the College were taught in small groups of three to five, they needed lots of small individual classrooms, which they created by partitioning every room into three or four. The partitioning had been done on the cheap, with heavy cornices diving abruptly into shaky plasterboard walls, and elaborate ceiling roses way off centre, and windows either non-existent or situated in odd corners, and grey electric cables running around the frames of the doors and along the skirting boards and then disappearing through further walls on their way to the rooms beyond. Since corridors were deemed a waste of space, many of the rooms could only be reached by cutting through one or two others, which meant that your lessons were constantly interrupted by people tapping on the door and asking if it was all right to pass through.

My Anglian teacher Mr Thatcher – a tiny desiccated man, with flaking skin, patchy white hair and a permanent crabby scowl – took these interruptions as a personal affront, and made it as awkward as possible for anyone to cross his teaching space: quizzing the unfortunate petitioners about what *exactly* it was they wanted, and whose class *precisely* they were going to, and was he going to be tormented with these constant interruptions *every single minute of the day*? This was all part of his ongoing war of attrition against the College establishment. He had previously taught at a reasonably well-known private school (he had taken early retirement for reasons that were never explained); his descent from that eminence to a lowly tutoring position at an institution as vastly inferior as the CTC was a personal affront from which he made no effort to recover. The contempt in which he held the owner of the College, a Dr Harvey Porlock Dip BS, was never stated in as many words, but we divined it nonetheless from a multitude of signs, such as the emphatic "Ah, Dr Porlock! To what do we owe the pleasure of your visit?" with which he greeted Porlock's frequent passage through our teaching space on his way to what passed as his office; the over-elaborate courtesy complemented by a narrowed mouth and furiously twitching eyebrow. The College itself fared no better: its teaching regime he described as "training ignoramuses to parrot nonsense". The ignoramuses in question, he made it clear, constituted the great majority of his pupils.

The two other boys in my Anglian Literature class, Simon Sharpe and Stephen Swift, as well as having similar sounding names, were also rather similar in appearance. Mr Thatcher affected to be unable to tell them apart.

"Swift," he would say, holding up an essay between finger and thumb, as if it was not only filthy but possibly infectious, "What is your excuse for turning out this exercise in empty drivel?"

"Actually, sir, I'm Sharpe."

"Oh, you're *Sharpe* now, are you? Then you must be the author of *this*" (holding up another essay in the same contemptuous fashion) "identically futile exercise in empty drivel."

"No, sir, the first one was mine."

"Is that so? Well, it hardly matters. Both pieces of work, like their authors, are interchangeably dull: possibly because both are slavishly reliant on the same collection of dull platitudes masquerading as *A Beginner's Guide to Anglian Literature*."

To everyone's surprise, not least my own, Mr Thatcher took quite a shine to me, declaring that I possessed an original mind, and blaming my near total ignorance of Anglian literature on the inadequacy of my early education, rather than any failings of application on my part. Having a teacher regard me in a favourable light was a happy novelty, and for that reason I worked hard at his subject: at first to please him and get good marks, later because I had actually begun to enjoy it. Until I joined his class I never once read a book for pleasure; afterwards I never read one for any other reason. As a consequence I became very knowledgeable in some areas, and completely ignorant in others: a condition which my father – a far harsher critic than Mr Thatcher – called "skating on thin ice with your nose in the air".

Mr Thatcher could recite great swathes of poetry by heart, and once he got started he was unstoppable: a recitation could continue for the best part of an entire lesson. Both Swift and Sharpe would sit through these performances with the glazed expressions of boys waiting for the end of the world – much the same look as I wore myself when a science teacher attempted to explain the nature of refraction. Unlike them I listened to Mr Thatcher's recital of choice snippets of Anglian literature with enormous delight. It was a revelation to me that words could fall that way, in such delicious and surprising combinations. Before long I was devouring the books of Mr Thatcher's favourite authors – Oldroyd and Peter Macclesfield and Lord Percy and WCF Collins and Gavin Kiddle – like a starving man who has stumbled across a larder full of every dish the heart could desire.

Mr Stacey, the art teacher, was a sensitive but untalented young man who also gave lessons in woodwork and something called 'Domesticity'. Rather than making any suggestions as to what I should do, he just let me get on with whatever I liked. My other teachers were young men recently out of University, who based their teaching methods on the same beginners guides that Mr Thatcher so deplored. This is probably just as well, because without that kind of help I would never have stood a chance of passing an exam in any subject other than Literature and Art.

4

My father had bought a house in Cantleford in an area of narrow fourth-century terraces that had once been mill-worker's cottages and were now the habitat of lesser academics and the better-off sort of student. Now that I had left Glenlockie this became my home.

Our house, like every other in the terrace, was small and rather cramped: a fourth-century mill-worker's cottage, with two rooms above and two below, and a built-on annexe housing the kitchen and bathroom. There was a decent little fireplace surrounded with old tiles, and some of the plasterwork was original, and the stripped floorboards were covered by cheerful rag rugs. My father could probably have afforded something grander, but he himself was not grand, and did not care to waste money on indulgences.

The only pictures on display were framed photographs of scientific instruments. Most of the wall space was taken up by sagging shelves loaded with works of science – precisely the sort of book I never read. My father also owned a large collection of scientific romances, mostly in paperback, which he kept in his own bedroom, adding a new volume every week or so. I tried reading one or two myself, but they were lacking in some dimension, and the writing, though efficient, struck me as plain and dull.

Apart from the usual pots and pans, our kitchen was equipped with various prototypes of machines my father was in the process of developing. There was, for example, an electric carving knife that tended to slip its gears and start smoking at a crucial stage of the carving process; there was a device for peeling carrots that shaved any carrot you placed in it to an orange cone the size of your little finger; and an electromagnetic casserole that could reduce meat and vegetables to a soggy pulp in a matter of seconds. Thankfully I was forbidden to handle any of these labour-saving devices in case I broke one of them or hurt myself or fused the lights: not unreasonably, since that is what happened whenever my father handled them himself. It was interesting to see that he was not entirely infallible. Also I was beginning to find his idea of design a bit old-fashioned. His Suction Cleaner, for example, looked like a robot out of one of his scientific romances, with a glass dome for a face, and a chubby round body, and a fat silver hose instead of a trunk.

Our daily routine was boringly dependable. I would get home around five in the afternoon, my father would arrive two hours later, then we would have our dinner, usually a baked potato served with beans and some kind of protein cooked in the electric casserole. Afterwards he would disappear into his workshop – a large shed in the back garden – leaving me with my homework and whatever novel I had borrowed from the College library. Around ten o'clock I would make a pot of tea, and carry a mug out to him. Although I did this any number of times, my memories of the act have become compressed into a single sequence, like an endlessly looped short clip of film. My father sits at the gate-leg table he used for a desk, bending over a complicated model made of wire and slotted metal. The light from an elbow-jointed desk-lamp illuminates his freckled forehead and the sharp bridge of his nose. The air is thick with the smell of resin and pipe-tobacco. A thin wisp of smoke curls from his soldering iron. A round screen pulses soundlessly in a far corner of the room, the green wave travelling from left to right with hypnotic regularity. The floor underfoot is deep in wood shavings. Rows of grey tobacco tins fill the shallow shelves that run along one side of the wall. A tottering stack of *The Modern Physicist* leans against a grey filing-cabinet. He looks up from his model, removes his glasses –they flash momentarily in the lamplight – and reaches wordlessly for the mug.

5

I had been quite taken with Cantleford at first. Left to my own devices, I would spend hours wandering through the narrow cobbled streets surrounding the ancient colleges, discovering a succession of imposing ornamental gateways through which it was possible to catch odd glimpses of an enchanted world of perfect lawns and regimented flowers and golden stone: a world seemingly redolent with the very essence of Learning and History.

Later my father took me for a guided tour of the enchanted world, at which point it lost a good deal of its charm. The entrance-halls of the mysterious buildings were guarded by uniformed wage-slaves with stained waistcoats and white-bristled jowls. Their interiors were the usual ugly mix of makeshift partitions and scratched furniture and shabby green paintwork.

Every so often we would encounter a skeletal grizzled Don surrounded by a fawning band of bespectacled students.

"Riddle!" the Don would croak, extending a withered claw. "How're tricks?"

"Peter!" my father would growl back, pumping the claw vigorously up and down. "Gervais! Cedric! Kenneth! Never better! Bloody marvellous!"

The town beyond the colleges was a disappointment of a different sort. The collision between the underclass and the University is generally supposed to be a dominant feature of Cantleford life. From my experience this is a delusion, a product of the self-important paranoia natural to those whose lives are with encircled with wealth and privilege. The town's natives had their own territories: the windswept estates on the outskirts, and the cut-price shopping-centre just beyond Crucifixion Green. By and large they kept to those, straying only very rarely into the ancient centre. If they came across a bicycle they would steal it, or puncture its tyres, or stamp its wheels and frame into the shape of a butterfly. But that was the extent of it: not so much rebellion as casual motiveless hooliganism.

6

I have not so far mentioned any close friends. The explanation is simple: I had none. Like my father I was inclined to find social intercourse boring and awkward. My sexual encounters at Glenlockie had been brief and casual; there was never any danger of them leading to anything more serious. The boys I knew at CTC – Swift and Sharpe, for example – lived some way out of the city, and hurried home as soon as the day's lessons were over. My closest relationship was with my father. For intellectual stimulus I had Mr Thatcher. To be honest, that was how I preferred things to be.

7

The following summer I took my National Grade One papers in Anglian Language and Literature, Art, History, General Science and Mathematics. My best grade (1.1) was in Art. I got a 2.2 in Anglian Language and Literature, and a 2.5 in History. I failed Mathematics and only scraped a pass (5.0) in General Science. In the same month I sat the Bune Entrance Examination. I dealt with the questions in my usual cavalier way, answering some at inordinate length, dismissing others with a few lazy sentences. To my astonishment I passed with flying colours in all four units, and was invited to join the College at the start of the Renunciation Term.

The only person not surprised by my success was Mr Thatcher. "These old schools know how to sort the hare from the hounds," he said, when I visited the College to thank him for his help. "Don't let them change you: that's the important thing. They like a boy to be obedient. But they value originality a lot more."

THREE

The Bunian Code

Ensor *and* Bune *are twin towns in the South East of Anglia separated by the River Flux and joined by Ensor Bridge.* Ensor *is a historic town famous for its castle, the former seat of the long defunct Royal Family of Anglia, and now the administrative centre of the Anglian Security Service.* Bune *is a smaller town, the home of* Bune College, *the ancient private school which educates the sons of Anglia's first families. Many ex-pupils of Bune College go on to become ministers of state, judges and stars of the media.*

A Visitor's Guide to Bune and Ensor (Gannet Press, 465)

1

I was not looking forward to going to Bune. Strictly for purposes of research I had dipped into a few school stories set in
private schools and was dismayed by much of what I had found
there. The oldest of these books, *The Education of Sam Smith*,
was written over a hundred years ago, and I doubted that the
fictional School of Bagley celebrated in its pages bore much
resemblance to present-day Bune. *Rupert Flame*, a more contemporary production, had as its hero a noble youth who rises
above a number of powerful but unparticularised temptations
to become a shining example to his fellow pupils, and ultimately the School's Head Boy. Despite affecting to be above this
kind of reading, Mr Thatcher owned large collection of books
and magazines devoted to the subject, and had suggested for the
purpose of comparison I get hold of a copy of *The Gymnasium*,
another recent book on the same topic, in which the temptations

in question (he told me with a chuckle) are particularised in vivid detail, and not only not overcome but indulged in with patent enthusiasm. Unfortunately Mr Thatcher did not have a copy to hand, and none of the Cantleford Booksellers would admit to knowing of this book's existence.

By way of compensation Mr Thatcher lent me some copies of *The Schoolboy*, a magazine which featured a series of stories about an obese boy called Barnaby Bumble who is heartily despised by all his classmates, on account both of his fatness and his objectionable character – he is lazy, greedy and dishonest, and has a disgustingly rich father who sends him a packed hamper every week. These stories afforded me many hours of not altogether innocent pleasure. I particularly liked the way in which Bumble, for all his father's wealth, served as the main target for whatever teasing and bullying went on in his immediate circle. This offered me a certain amount of much-needed reassurance, suggesting as it did that the strategies for survival at a school like Bune might not be so terribly different from those that I had already practised with some success at schools like Glenlockie First.

2

There were three Houses, named after the group to which each class of pupil belonged: Equestrians, Patricians and Scholars. I was to be admitted as a Scholar, presumably because this was the least inappropriate category into which a case like mine could be fitted. Unfortunately, as I saw it at the time, this meant that I would be lumped in with boys who were much cleverer than me; also that everyone, masters included, would expect me to be cleverer than I was.

That was one worry; another was the fact that the younger boys seemed to be treated as little more than slaves. In their first two years they had to serve certain seniors – they were called 'Praetors' – as their 'ticks', making them breakfast, cleaning their rooms, fetching coal, taking their washing to the College Laundry, and so on. A further level of hierarchy was the Bune Society, known popularly as 'Crow'. A member of Crow had at his disposition every tick in his House, and was encouraged to flog any of them who failed to come up to scratch.

In all the books I read this system was justified on the grounds that it reflected the structure of society at large, and that it taught boys that before you can command you must be expected to serve. To me it all sounded hateful and demeaning, though possibly a large part of my aversion stemmed from the fact that I was facing the immediate prospect of being a tick rather than a Praetor.

3

The night before leaving for Bune I had packed all the things I had been advised to take with me into two large suitcases. One was a cheap cardboard article purchased specially for the purpose; the other turned out to have a broken clasp, so my father secured it with an old belt. During the journey to Ensor I spent much of the time worrying about the impression that these two cases were likely to make on my new schoolfellows, whose luggage I was convinced would be in every way irreproachable. Every now and then I glanced up at the loathsome objects, swaying in the sagging brown net of the luggage rack: searching for some sort of reassurance, however flimsy. With each succeeding glance they looked shabbier and more disreputable.

It was raining when my father and I arrived at the station, so we engaged a taxi – a vast polished steamer with bright yellow doors and a luggage compartment as big as a horse-box. Perched in stiff twin thrones above the driver, we looped round the castle and over the bridge, then turned down a stately drive, past two iron gates; and there in front of me, suddenly, was the west front of the ancient school: now darkened with driving rain, but easily recognisable from the many photographs I had studied beforehand. Two elegant columns of chequered pink and yellow brick, topped with white stone cupolas like bakers' bonnets, rose on either side of a castellated facade, which featured in descending order, first a pale clock-face with golden hands and numerals, then a sky-reflecting vista of tall mullioned windows, and finally, at ground level, a sturdy ornamental archway.

We alighted. The driver left his taxi steaming quietly on the cobbles while he unloaded my two suitcases, glancing at them briefly with a face professionally empty of comment. They sat on the stone flags of the pavement, radiating inferiority like a beacon. My father hefted up the one with the strap, thinking to carry it over to my dormitory.

"Pa!" I said fearfully. "Don't do that. They'll think you're my servant."

"Nonsense. Don't be so sensitive, William!"

A college porter came hurrying up. Giving the suitcase with the strap a barely discernible double-take (it was, needless to say, discerned by me) he wrested it from my father's grasp, while at the same time reaching for the cardboard case at my feet. Balanced on either side by these two burdens, he stood swaying from right to left, waiting for instructions. He was small, and very old, and the suitcases were large and heavy.

"Scholars," said my father. "But hey, old chap, look – we can manage those ourselves."

But the porter, bending himself double in order to accommodate the weight of the suitcases, was already beetling over the stone flagstones, heading resolutely towards the stone archway. We followed him through it into a quadrangle bustling with boys, standing in groups, hands in pockets, their gleaming toppers tipped rakishly over their foreheads or tilted to the backs of their heads: angled in any way but vertical. I knew these superior beings must have spotted my suitcases, and were now identifying me as their owner.

"Pa!" I pleaded.

My father was pressing the needlessly large sum of two-and-six into the porter's leathery palm, who for his part regarded it with a look of astonishment. This detail, I suspected, would further ornament the tale of my suitcases, which in my fantasies was destined to inspire mirth in every dormitory for the remainder of my school career.

I tugged at my father's sleeve.

"What's the matter?"

I could say nothing: only stare at him with the miserable eyes of an animal that is marked out for slaughter.

"I have to go. I have to get back to Cantleford. Do you understand?" He said this, or words to the same effect, a number of times. I still could not reply. In the end he moved forwards and crushed me to his prickly tweed chest. "You'll be fine, William; you'll be fine," he muttered, and then rushed off before I could say or do anything further to prevent his departure.

<h2 style="text-align:center">4</h2>

Before we were shown our dorms we were given a short introductory talk by the Deputy Headmaster, Mr Williams, a giant of a man with a shining bald dome framed on both sides by wild clumps of greying woolly curls. Apart from factual stuff, some of which I knew already, Mr Williams – or 'Willie' – as the boys called him – told us that our group of Scholars would be under the overall command of a Praetor called Nevis. "Any problems you have, take them to Nevis," said Willie seriously. "Homesickness, special dietary requirements, bed-wetting – anything like that, he'll sort it out for you. A most capable boy, Nevis. He's a leading light of the Bune Society, better known to you as Crow, so you know you're in good hands. He may even ask one of two of you to join his personal army of ticks, if you're lucky."

The dormitory was a long white-walled room with small rectangular windows. It contained ten beds. We each had a small cupboard by our bed in which to store our pyjamas and washing kit, and any other possessions that met the school criteria – of which this Nevis, apparently, was to be the arbiter. The other boys milled round excitedly, asking one another the usual sort of questions. I sat with my face averted, hoping I would not be called upon to join in. I was afraid to let them hear me speak. Their voices were all so self-assured, so confidently Anglian, so effortlessly *posh* – like the voices of boys heard on the wireless. I did not speak like that. I could not speak like that.

There was a loud banging from the end of the room. A large mop-haired youth wearing a sporty-looking loose grey outfit– zippered top, elasticated wrists and ankles – was bashing the door-frame with a knocker stick.

"Got your attention, now?" he asked, nonchalantly raising the stick to rest on his shoulder like a firearm. "My name is Nevis, like the mountain. I am in charge of this dorm. My room is just down the hall. Your beds have each got a number. Come and see me one by one in that order."

5

I tapped on the door of Nevis's study. Nevis yanked it open. His stocky gym-built body was giving way to flab; he had large red hands and a dented snub nose one size too small for his face. In some lights he would be considered handsome.

"Come in, buddy," he said. "Which one are you?"

"Riddle, sir."

"'Nevis' will do. Riddle, eh? First name James, I take it?"

"It's William, actually."

"No sense of humour, then, Jimmy. Pity. Take a seat, while I attend to nature's summons."

I looked round for somewhere to sit. The most visible chair was a high-backed multi-wheeled contraption of black plastic and chrome, but I assumed this was Nevis's personal property, and therefore not included in his offer. Two moulded chairs of red plastic were stacked one above the other in a corner. I took one of these, and waited for his return.

The study was airless and uncomfortably hot, with a pervasive smell of something like yeast. Apart from the wheeled chair, it had nothing in the way of furnishings that could be described as elegant or even comfortable. The fitted carpet was grey and grubby. A dented white filing-cabinet stood in a corner. No books were visible. A shelf above the burning radiator held some silver sporting trophies and three framed photographs of episodes from sporting life: a bunch of beefy youths locked in a clinch like a giant spider with too many muscular legs; a three-tiered platform with a golden youth on top and a much younger Nevis poised, beaming, on the second tier; and finally another Nevis, younger still, standing bare-chested and bloody-nosed with his arm around the shoulder of a skinny boy with a badly swollen eye.

A ferocious splashy torrent was followed by the explosive crash of a flusher, and the sound of water gurgling into a sink; then the present-day Nevis emerged from his small washroom, shaking his still-wet hands, and dropped into his chair.

"What do you think?" he asked, swivelling from right to left.

"Of what?"

"The snaps."

"Oh, right. That's you, isn't it? Winning some prizes."

"Come again?" he asked, putting a hand to his ear.

"I said: isn't that you?"

"'*Isna tet yee...*' What kind of accent is that?"

"Alban, I suppose." My father had paid for me to have lessons in correct pronunciation, but they didn't seem to have taken.

"You sound like a savage. We'll need to change that or the chaps will rag you silly. Don't look alarmed: I'll school you."

This was unexpectedly gracious of him. "That would be useful. Thanks."

He acknowledged this with a swift nod. "My fees are very modest."

"Right," I said, wondering if this was a joke. His face gave no clue either way.

"Of course, you'll need to do something about your bags."

I went crimson. I had been hoping I had got away with the state of my suitcases, but now I saw that they must be the talk of the school. "Sorry," I said.

"Not your fault. I'll lend you a few bob so we can set you up with something a bit less remarkable. You'll need some new togs, too."

"Really?" My father had gone to some lengths to kit me out in what I told him was the correct uniform.

"'Fraid so. Your first week here is pretty crucial, if you mean to make a good impression, and that whole outfit is a bit Sam Smith, to put it mildly. I'll introduce you to my tailor – he'll sort you out. Don't worry about paying me back. I keep a tab here in my room for just that purpose."

"I do have some pocket-money," I volunteered.

"Oh golly, hang on to that. A chap's pocker is strictly off-limits. I said not to worry about these things. You can settle up if you come in for a fortune, or scoop the jackpot; otherwise we'll keep it on the tab until such time etcetera." He gave me a further looking-over, head-to-toe. "The hair's a bit alarming, but there's nothing you can do about that. Even if you dyed the bugger, the eyelashes would blow your cover. How's your trim?"

"My trim?"

"Are you dense? You do speak Anglian, don't you?"

I nodded wordlessly.

"Golly, this is hard work. Let's try again. Are you fit and able?"

"Oh, I see. Yes, I think so."

He screwed his face sideways. "You look a bit puny to me. Show me some press-ups."

"Press-ups?"

"Yes, press-ups. Do twenty for me now. I'll pace you. You can unbutton your waistcoat if you like."

I got down on hands and knees, and began self-consciously to perform some awkward press-ups, my face pushed up against the smelly carpet, blemished by stains of mud and coffee and fag-ash. He set an insanely fast rhythm, crouching down next to me with one hand pumping up and down on my bottom.

"Interesting," he said. "Right, fine, get up now."

I got up. My arms and knees and back ached from the unaccustomed exercise. He gestured towards the chair, and I sat back down, gratefully.

"I'll have to help you with that, too. We need to build up some strength in those arms of yours. Flatten the abs, firm up the buttocks. Tell us your name again?"

"Riddle."

"*Raddle*," he repeated. "As in the act that dare not speak its name?"

"Yes," I conceded, my face heating.

"Any connection with the inventor?"

"He's my father."

"No worries. Chaps get into Bune by one of four routes: by rank, by cash, by influence and by merit. Boffins like your pa are way down in the pecking-order, about the level of a ticket-inspector, so we can discount the first three of those straight away. That just leaves merit. So you're a Scholar."

Everyone in F block was a Scholar, so this was not a particularly astute of him. "Yes," I said.

He nodded knowingly. "No shame in it –- I'm a Scholar too. My scholarship was for exceptional sporting prowess. I was captain of my school at burly."

He waited expectantly. Burly is a sport that calls for skills in wrestling, kicking, running and subduing your opponent with your weight and bulk. Nevis, I realised, was waiting for me to express admiration for his achievement.

I have never been good at simulating sincerity, but I did my best. "Gosh," I said. "Burly."

"Burrily," he repeated. *"Gaush."* Taking a small black notebook from his table, he made a short note in a precise small hand. "Right," he said, looking up. "Starting tomorrow you can make my brekker. Normally I like my brekker-tick to have some experience under his belt, but I'll make an exception in your case. I'd better warn you, though: I can be quite fussy. If I don't like something you'll have to keep making it again until you get it right. There are other sanctions that may prove necessary, but we'll get to that when the hour arrives. All right?"

I nodded.

"Seven o'clock then, in my room. Sharp. Got it?"

"Yes."

"Nice. One other thing, Riddle, and then you can go. If anyone tries to give you grief of any description – I'm talking bullying, ragging, knob-jerking, under-blanket party invitations – just send the little buggers to me. I'll sort 'em out. Is that clear?"

"Perfectly clear. Thank you, Nevis."

That wasn't so bad, I told myself, going back to the dorm. He seemed quite a decent fellow, actually. My only reservation was about the issue of cash that had been a running theme in our conversation. If he presented a bill, how was I ever going to pay it?

But no doubt I was worrying myself unnecessarily. He himself seemed totally unconcerned about such matters.

6

The next morning was a Saturday, so there were no lessons. I turned up as required at seven, and cooked Nevis a breakfast of fried eggs and bacon. He was already up, and drinking poke-weed in a shiny red dressing-gown. Being a little nervous, I burned the bacon, and broke the yolk, and the rest of the egg stuck to the pan, so what I put on the plate was something of a disaster. He looked at it blankly, making no attempt to eat. I expected him to order me to do it again, but he simply made another note in his notebook. "All right," he said, "let's see what your domestic skills are like".

I set to work to clean his room. He sat back and watched, smoking several cigarettes, one after the other.

Housework is bearable if you have only one day's backlog to deal with, but when the grime is months old and ground into the carpet, and every surface is thick with dust, and the curtains stink of tobacco smoke, and the flusher bowl is stained all colours of the rainbow – these were only a selection of the problems confronting me – it is another matter. I did my best, but the result when I had finished was not much of an improvement on what I started with.

I was expecting an explosion of fury, but he remained weirdly dispassionate. "All right, Jimmy," he said, holding out his plate. The bad breakfast was untouched, apart from a cigarette end planted in the egg-mess. "Scrape this excrement into the dustbin, then you can buzz off. Call back here at two-thirty and I will take you shopping."

7

The town of Bune is arranged around a small square containing three public houses and four parades of shops and cafes. That afternoon it was full of boys from the school, lounging about, hands in pockets, staring into the windows of the tobacconists, or loitering in the doorways of the public-houses, drawn by the powerful smell of beer, redolent of the adulthood that awaited them in three or four years' time. Nevis and I attracted a number of curious glances. One youth blocked our path and accosted Nevis in a rather knowing way. "Hello Benny," he said, grinning broadly: "Taking the new tick for walkies, I see."

"Mind your own business, Know-all," said Nevis. "Cheeky sod," he muttered as we walked off. "Tony Knowle. Boss of Crow, you know."

"Really?" I turned to get a better look at this illustrious being, who on first sight had struck me as pretty nondescript, but he had already disappeared into the throng.

Our first stop was 'J. Swanson's, Bootmaker and Saddler', where the shopkeeper greeted Nevis very courteously. In a matter of minutes we had purchased two fine calfskin suitcases, each of which was discreetly priced at the astronomical sum of fifteen pounds and sixpence. "We'll pick these up later," said Nevis. No money changed hands, or was even discussed: Nevis obviously had an account and an infinite amount of credit.

Next we went to the premises of 'R. Sampson & Co, Made to Measure Tailoring,' where Nevis picked out half a dozen fine shirts in my size, and got the elderly stooping tailor to take my measurements for a new morning-coat, waistcoat and pin-striped trousers, while he himself tried on a variety of jackets and waistcoats. As before he was served with the utmost courtesy. He had an account here too.

"That's the basics, then," he said, recording the details in his notebook. "Now you'll be able to pass for a proper little Bunian, so long as you keep your trap shut. I think we'll nip in to Eddie's now for an afternoon tea."

'Eddie's' turned out to be a rather grand teashop which operated under the formal name of 'Your Obedient Servant'. Afternoon tea consisted of a plateful of scones stuffed with jam and fresh cream, some handsome wedges of cakes of various kinds, and a large pot of tea, brought to us by a portly uniformed waiter on a heavy silver tray. Nevis ate with single-minded concentration. I attempted to ask him a few questions, but he wagged a finger at me, chewing vigorously.

"Great," he said, slurping down a mouthful of the pale delicate tea. "I'm going to have to scarper now, Jimmy, I'm afraid. Got a try-out with another new tick, back in F block, late already worse luck. Stop by later, around seven, for your first school in Bunese. I'll leave you to settle up, all right?"

He was gone before I could explain that my meagre supply of pocket-money – I had brought all I had, which was about one-and-fourpence-halfpenny – was unlikely to be enough to pay the bill. Some minutes later our waiter came to the table with a small pad. Frowning, he wrote down a great number of items, muttering a description of each as he did so. He then totted these up, sniffing, and twisting his mouth sideways, as if extracting the very last pound of flesh from the exercise. Having checked the list and his addition several times, he tore off the bill, and placed it face-down beside my tea-cup. I waited until he had retreated to his post in a far corner of the room before turning it over. There seemed to be far more items than we had in fact consumed, but the man's handwriting was illegible, making it impossible for me to challenge the sum; which was in any case so large than no reduction would have made it any the more affordable.

I looked at it, covered it with my hand, then looked again. The handwriting might have been obscure, but the figures were agonisingly plain. The total was eighteen shillings and fivepence-halfpenny.

I sat mechanically finishing up the last of the cakes for what seemed an agonising length of time. Finally the waiter, who had been watching me sceptically all this time, came over to clear the table. Face burning, I explained the position. He listened with a face of stone. This was evidently a man who in his time had seen and heard everything, particularly in relation to the non-payment of bills.

"Name?" he asked, when I had finished my confession. "Which house? – Scholars I suppose. Father's name and address? Sign this chitty. I'm adding 20% administrative charge. The bill will have to be settled within the week. Otherwise I will have to call on your Headmaster."

I left the teashop in a state of panic. I supposed that in due course my father would get a bill, not just for the Afternoon Tea, but also the outfit and the luggage, and no doubt he would pay it, but his opinion of me would suffer in the process. And that would not be the end of it. Nevis, I felt sure, would not be satisfied with the plunder of a single afternoon. I had embarked without realising it on a disastrous and irreversible course of action. I had no control over what happened next, but Nevis did, and Nevis I now realised was not to be trusted.

The town was still humming with activity, but I couldn't stay a moment longer. I returned to my dorm and sat on my bed, unable to read, unable to do anything but observe the same terrible thoughts circling round and round like terrible predatory birds.

8

That evening, after a horrible dinner, made all the more horrible by my anxiety, I reported to Nevis as requested at seven on the dot.

"Enter!"

I entered. Nevis was stretched back in his black leather chair, studying his photographs. He swivelled around to face me.

"Are you prepared?"

"For what, Nevis?"

"For your first schooling in how to speak like a gentleman."

"Was I supposed to prepare something? You didn't say."

"I shouldn't have to. You are expected to know the drill in advance. In future I want you to find a new phrase every day, and bring it to me, word and pronunciation perfect. Is that clear?"

I nodded dumbly; I could not trust myself to speak.

"All right: first exercise. Repeat after me: 'Riddle is a shameless oik from the far shores of Oikland, who must either learn to speak as like a proper Bunian or be ragged without mercy.'"

Resentment flared in my heart, but I kept a wooden face, and repeated the sentence word for word. In the process I inadvertently replicated his tone of voice. By the time I realised that I was doing this it was too late to stop.

He looked at me disbelievingly. "Are you taking the piddle, Jimmy?"

39

"No, Nevis."

"You'd better not try that game with me. Do thirty press-ups."

I did them, sweating and panting, with his hand as before pumping up and down on my bottom.

"All right," he said, when I had finished. He resumed his seat in the leather throne, and took up his black notebook. "James W. Riddle," he read. "First report. Cooking: inedible: disgusting, poisonous, fit for nothing but the dustbin: marks out of ten zero. Housework: also hopeless. Leaves muck everywhere, the room stinks afterwards, and most of the stink comes from the 'cleaner' himself. Marks out of ten: minus four. Elocution: deliberately crap. Marks out of ten: minus six. Total marks: minus ten. That calls for ten strokes of the cane. Take down your trousers, Riddle."

I loosened the belt of my trousers, and dropped them to my ankles.

"Knickers too," he said wearily, as if this should have been obvious. "I have to make sure you aren't wearing protective padding."

I pulled down my knickers. Nevis took up a cane – he had a good supply of them which he kept in an elephant's foot by the door, along with a couple of umbrellas and a knocker-stick – bent me over a humble wooden chair, and loitered behind me, cane in hand, studying my bottom with great interest.

A fierce hatred was building up inside me. The anger was good: it kept me from feeling fear, and when the cane finally descended it kept me from feeling pain.

He stroked my bottom fondly, then struck again, in quick succession, nine times.

To my horror, the experience left me with an incredible erection. This was of course impossible to conceal. Nevis pointed to it with a squeal of laughter, and reached for it. What happened next was at first humiliatingly intense and then intensely humiliating.

"Dirty little beast," he said. "Bloody mop that up, and make sure you wash the towel afterwards."

I got a towel from his little washroom, and attempted to sponge all traces of sexual activity off his carpet. He meanwhile sat back in his swivelling chair and buttoned up his tight trousers. "All right, Jimmy?" he said, tucking in his shirt. "Enjoyed that, did you?"

"Yes, Nevis."

"In future you'll be marked for that, too. That was a two. Incidentally--"

I waited. He raised a hand to one corner of his mouth, and drew it across to the other corner.

"Sorry, Nevis, I don't--"

"Keep it zipped. Tight. Or else."

"Oh. Right. Yes, Nevis, I will."

"You'd better. Run away now."

As I turned to go he gave me a friendly slap on the backside. Following the beating it was already smarting unbearably. Oddly enough, this was the only part of the whole performance that actually hurt.

Safely back in my bed, I ignored the other boys, and took up a novel by WC Collins, *Reversals*, one of my all-time favourites. Supporting my weight with my elbow to relieve the pressure on my throbbing buttocks, I turned to the pages in which the narrator describes the tragic death of Nigel Flannery, his friend turned enemy, and my eyes welled up, as they always did at this point in the narrative, with uncomplicated tears.

9

Abuse is a complicated business. I soon learned that the best way of dealing with Nevis was to finish him off as quickly and efficiently as possible, so that he would have no further use for me until at least the following day. Once I had gained this amount of control, it was even possible to enjoy what took place, in a cold-hearted sort of way. This is something that may possibly shock those who have not been in that situation themselves, but I daresay it is a common enough experience. Since I had not initiated the abuse, I was not required to feel personally responsible for any pleasure I got out of it. The important thing was to refuse to let him damage me; or to be more precise, to refuse to admit that I was damaged, even to myself.

Every night, after I had put down my book, and closed my eyes, I comforted myself with fantasies of revenge. Some of these were very simple, involving my caning Nevis's bare bottom in much the same way as he had mine. When that paled, I swapped the cane for a variety of implements ranging from crutches to saucepans. I devised a torture involving straps and elastic bands and razor-blades. I pictured myself slicing off his head with a sword so sharp that it would pass through his loathsome neck without register-ing the jolt. I imagined causing him unbearable pain simply by the power of thought. I distilled my hatred into a small intensely potent pellet of acid, and fired it into his temple, then stood over him, rel-ishing his dying agonies. I laboured to think up some scheme by which he could be publicly shamed, as happens with the infamous bully in *The Education of Sam Smith*. I desperately wanted things to work out the way they do in books, where criminals are brought down by an excess of greed or by their own stupidity or ineptitude – caught in toils of their own devising. I constructed countless such scenarios in extravagant detail – knowing, of course, that I would never dare to put any of them into practice, since if I did the one who would be shamed and humiliated was me.

What Nevis was doing to me was in theory the sort of thing people got expelled for. But I couldn't tell the masters about it. I couldn't tell anyone. I was a small boy, surrounded by enemies. My chief tormentor was an older boy in a position of authority. He was part of a system of power that extended upwards all the way to the Headmaster himself.

The kind of pressure that is put on a younger boy to suffer his abuse in silence – ultimately becoming complicit in it – is some-thing you will only understand if it has happened to you. It is not something that the victim usually admits to, except in coded ways – complaining, for example of being 'bullied' in unspecified ways. The tick-master is a senior boy with considerable status in the school: in Nevis's case a member of Crow. He is very much a favou-rite of the system. To accuse him is tantamount to accusing the governing body of the school, since it is from them that he derives his authority. I made some discreet enquiries; it was a subject on which most boys held an opinion. Only once, apparently, had a tick made a complaint against his tick-master, and that was long before I ever joined the school. The tick was a scholar; the abuse involved his being offered for sale to a number of his tick-master's fellow Praetors. His complaint was dismissed for lack of evidence. After that he was treated like a pariah, even by boys who had been victims of the same monster. Eventually his father removed him from the school. The case became the stuff of legend; it was held out to us as an awful warning. You didn't whine and you didn't tell tales; you put up with abuse, just as you put up with beatings and other punishments. If you were given a humiliating task, you did it. That was the Bunian Code, and if you wanted to survive at the school you had to abide by it.

The masters, of course, were well aware of what was going on; indeed they openly approved of the Code, referring to it in morning pep-talks as 'The Code of Honour'. Privately I felt a better description would be 'The Code of Shame,' but I kept that opinion to myself, at least until I met Purkis.

FOUR
Love and Friendship

It was with considerable trepidation that Sam, looking out of the windows of his carriage, viewed his new domicile for the first time... Boys in top hats sauntered about the quadrangle, as if the school, the town, nay, the entire universe was their personal property.

One of these heroic characters approached his coach and four. "Are you Smith?" he enquired. "My pa knows yours – he's a lawyer chap, you know."

As Sam dismounted, the other boy surveyed him with a critical eye. "Must do something about your rig, old chap," he said in a tone in which the assumption of superiority contended with an innate and unaffected amiability. "First impressions count in this place. Can't afford to go around looking like a country-bumpkin."

The boy introduced himself as 'Hammond'; it would be some weeks before he admitted to the possession of a first name.

Sam's upbringing had taught him to be wary of fine manners and a taste for fashionable apparel. But his self-appointed mentor was of so open and direct a character that a bond formed between them in a matter of minutes; and within the hour Sam was adopting his new friend's comportment and turns of speech and opinions as if to the manner born.

The Education of Sam Smith by Philip Middleton, (London 394)

1

Much to my surprise I found a refuge from Nevis and all his works in my studies. My fears that everyone else would be cleverer than me were soon dispelled. The system at Bune is designed for boys of vastly differing abilities. Those who send their sons there do not expect them to fail, however stupid they might be; therefore the school makes sure that no one does. Scholars, for obvious reasons, are expected to be cleverer than boys admitted to Bune for reasons of family, wealth or influence, but their cleverness, far from being an advantage, is generally regarded as distinctly suspect. The important attributes for those who wish to succeed are charm, cunning and nerve. Science is for the brainy few who are destined to have to work for a living. Arts subjects are popular because it is easy for those with limited ability to get a decent mark. The masters want you to succeed, or at least scrape by, knowing that if too many boys fail in their subject they will get the blame. Even where a boy is utterly hopeless, he can still earn marks for 'effort' or the neatness of his diagrams. Boys who are genuinely gifted receive higher than average marks, but they are not feted in the ways that athletes tend to be, or those who have mastered the tricks of debate, such as sneering at anyone who thinks differently to oneself, or constructing a ridiculous argument in order to undermine the whole concept of rational thought.

Thanks to Mr Thatcher, Anglian came easily to me. I also did well in History, partly because it is such a simple subject: very few books are considered essential reading, and they always tell you exactly what to say about any particular event. As for Art, all I had to do in order to get high marks was enjoy myself with paints and paper, chat with Mr Trotter the Art Master, and clear up after myself at the end of the day.

2

During the first few weeks I made no friends at all. My schoolfellows saw me as an outsider, a curiosity, a freak. My accent was wrong, and if my clothes, following Nevis's intervention, were now passable, my way of wearing them was not. It might have been different if I had managed to stay on the right side of Nevis, but my inability to defer to authority had put paid to that. In essence I was incapable of pretending to enjoy what he made me do. I complied, but when someone disgusts you it is impossible to hide the fact.

At weekends I found myself a lot of the time alone. The usual thing, unless you were a sportsman, was to wander into Bune, and saunter about the town square with a friend. Sauntering about on one's own, I discovered, is a hard trick to pull off. To disguise my solitary state I generally ended up drifting into the Bune Bookstop, and browsing through its feeble selection of tourist guides and well-thumbed popular novels until it was time to go back to the dorm.

One Saturday afternoon, when I had been at the school for perhaps six weeks, I was in the Bookstop leafing through a novel called *The Case of the Missing Penknife*. This was one of a series by Sir Henry Morgan Carter, featuring a master-detective called Caractacus Wilson, whose adventures are chronicled by his rather dim friend, a dentist named Horace Stapleton. Whatever crimes they investigate, Stapleton invariably gets the wrong end of the stick, and has to be set right by the vastly more intelligent and perceptive Wilson. This was not the sort of thing I usually read – Mr Thatcher thought the books somewhat overrated – but it was efficiently written, and I soon became absorbed in the plot.

After some minutes a prickling sensation at the back of my neck alerted me to the fact that I was being watched by another boy. When I turned to face him he looked away, so I knew my instincts were right. I knew him by sight: he was in the same year as me, but because he was an Equestrian we moved in different circles. His father I knew to be Sir Roger Purkis, one of the senior ministers of state. The boy's awful raw complexion gave him the look of a bully and a thug. The only possible reason he could have had for singling me out for observation was to make fun of me. I returned to the mystery of the penknife. He approached me. I braced myself to hear something I would not like.

"Good book?"

"If you like that sort of thing."

"I do." He put out his hand. "Purkis," he said.

I took the hand, as one does, automatically, and shook it. "Riddle."

"Hello, Riddle." He kept hold of my hand a moment longer than was strictly necessary, then let it go, continuing to stare at me as if I were an interesting example of something he was keen on studying.

"I was just wondering," he said, "how this establishment survives. Commercially, I mean. They can't take very much on a few postcards and Gannet's Guides, can they? Say two shillings and sixpence a day – that would be a generous estimate, don't you think?"

An interesting idea occurred to me. "Perhaps they have a source of income we don't know about."

"Such as?"

"Oh, I don't know. A back room selling photographs of young men in artistic poses, for example. Or drugs. Or rubber teddy bears for fetishists." Nevis had recently shown me some photographs of fetish-wear, which is how I came to know about this topic.

"Do you know, I think you may be right. A lot of businesses in Bune strike me as being of dubious authenticity. Have you ever noticed how the flavour of the place changes after dark?"

"How, exactly?"

"Muffled squeals of pain – or pleasure – escaping from closed doors. Candlelight flickering in the windows of derelict buildings. Secret meetings of the crucifixion cult: that sort of thing."

"Now that you mention it, I have caught a whiff of something like that. Do you think the school is behind it?"

"Some of the masters are, undoubtedly. The Head in particular. Have you ever been in his study? It reminds me of a crime scene that's been tidied up by the perpetrator – body stuffed in a cupboard, bloodstains mopped up with a rag soaked in disinfectant, the whole place fumigated with lavender furniture polish."

This was a game for which I was by nature ideally suited: all that had been missing until now was the right partner. What began as a casual conversation swiftly turned into an act of energetic collaboration. An alternative Bune – a grotesquely evil place of comically wicked characters, all of whom had their counterparts in the masters at the school and the town's shopkeepers – took on shape and colour with a kind of supernatural effortlessness, as if it had been leading a shadowy existence for centuries, waiting for the alchemy of our meeting to expose it to the light. Its stories – a blood-bespattered sequence of vile crimes and ingenious deceptions that had been going on for centuries – demanded to be written down.

The other Bune, we decided, was in reality a much more ancient town called Malcaster, which had been a centre for depravity from as far back as the Stone Age. Its present-day activities were the responsibility of a sinister gang of grotesques called the Malcontents, whose nominal leader was Dr Porter, our Headmaster. The name 'Porter', of course, was a pseudonym: his real name – his Malcaster name – was Septimus Floater. Over the course of several years he had recruited the bulk of the school staff to assist him in his nefarious activities, chief among whom was the Deputy Head, Counsellor Peter Joyce, nicknamed 'Humpty' by the boys, but known to the Malcaster set as 'Belch'. Despite Porter's command of all the levers of influence, one or two masters continued to hold out against him, and he was continually contriving to lure these brave but corruptible souls into potentially compromising situations, in the hope of blackmailing them into obedience.

"The odd thing is," I said, "that no-one but us seems to have noticed the existence of Malcaster."

"It's not in the least bit odd," said Purkis. "Virtually all of our schoolfellows have the happy knack of being able to ignore what's happening right under their noses. You and I, unfortunately, are not so well deceived."

"I don't see what's unfortunate about it."

Purkis pulled a face. "No, you wouldn't. You weren't brought up to it, so you're constitutionally incapable of fitting in. If everyone was like you the system would collapse."

"You're making me out to be a kind of rebel," I objected.

"Well, aren't you?"

"Not at all. I'm a complete innocent. I never asked to be sent to this fucking school, to be mocked and despised by snobs and fools."

Purkis sighed. "You're not in the least bit innocent, Riddle. That's a pose, and it doesn't suit you. Try and see things another way."

"Such as?"

Purkis screwed up his face in a parody of thought. "Well, take Malcaster, for example. It's quite obviously a scene of multiple crimes, including rape and murder. Given that scenario, what sort of role do you see yourself as playing? And please don't say the victim. Unless you really want to end up strangled in a cupboard?"

"I'm not sure I have much choice in the matter," I said glumly.

"That's utter rot. You can do a lot better than that."

"All right. Perhaps I could be one of the criminals?"

"No no -- you're not ruthless enough for that. You'd only botch the job and have to spend the remainder of your sorry life in the jug with a tame spider and no proper flusher. That only leaves one role worth considering."

What he was saying was so obvious I was amazed I had not thought of it myself. "Do you mean some kind of detective?"

"Why not? Mind you, if you were working for the police you'd have to be a bit dim."

"That's true," I said. "Dim and a bit of a bully. Suits me down to the ground. And what part would you play?"

"I'd be your bosom pal, obviously. An entertaining mix of neurosis and perspicuity. We could investigate Malcaster together."

It was the insight we had been waiting for. By an extraordinary coincidence the models for our two protagonists were already to hand in the persons of Caractactus Wilson and Horace Stapleton, the investigating duo whose exploits had been chronicled in the works of Sir Henry Morgan Carter. As if by magic the figures of Detective Inspector Ernest Rattle and Mr Hubert Wisley appeared before us, emerging from the swirling filth of a Ludden fog: Rattle portly, short, and hunched over him ample stomach like a mole; Wisley tall and skeletal, with dark mournful eyes and sunken cheeks. Both of them were equipped with droopy moustaches, wide-brimmed hats and heavy black overcoats. In character they differed in line with their appearance. Brilliant but neurotic, Wisley possessed an intuitive grasp of both human and inhuman psychology. He had deduced the existence of Malcaster from the outset, concluding correctly that its chief figures lay behind every crime committed in Bune and its environs. Despite Wisley's efforts to alert Rattle to the existence of Malcaster, however, Rattle persisted in believing that the secret town was nothing more than a mad fantasy, resulting from the ingestion of the vast quantity of pills and potions which Wisley took to address his interminable digestive complaints. Rattle's general blankness meant that he was prone to falling into the traps set for him by the Malcontents, and endeavouring – often with some success – to bring the innocent to injustice.

This was the start of our collaboration on a series of tales about Malcaster provisionally entitled *The Infected Pistol and Other Stories.* Our pseudonyms as authors of this joint work were F R Trumper (Purkis) and H O Minty (me). I was initially responsible for coming up with the crimes and the cast of characters, Purkis for providing the scatological material which was his forte: detailed descriptions of inappropriate couplings, unthinkably bizarre perversions, mass orgies and unlikely feats of sexual acrobatics. As time went on, however, our contributions became more evenly matched, to the point where it became impossible to tell where one of us left off and the other began.

The process of defining and chronicling The Other Bune inevitably led to an exchange of confidences. Purkis had few inhibitions and very little shame, particularly with regards to sex; quite early in our relationship he made a habit of regaling me with graphic accounts of his escapades in this field, many of which portrayed him in a less than flattering light. I was less forthcoming, but however much I struggled to keep my own sad history private, Purkis refused to respect my boundaries.

"Tell me about Ben," he asked, a couple of days after our first meeting. "He's your tick-master, isn't he?"

"Yes, unfortunately."

"Aren't the two of you...?" He locked one hand over the other: the heraldic symbol for partnership; then followed this up by shaping his fingers into a configuration suggestive of a more intimate connection.

"What gives you that idea?"

"That seems to be the way of the world."

"Well it isn't in this case. I can't bear the hateful swine. He makes me want to puke."

"OK. Keep your wig on."

He regarded me keenly, with a look of sympathetic understanding.

It would have been all too easy to tell him everything. And yet I couldn't do it. I had already let things go on too long, to the point where I had become compromised. People would think I was complicit in what had happened – Nevis would tell them I was. He might even accuse me of initiating it. It was all too shameful, too dangerous. And yet Purkis – this was already apparent – was a friend, the first real friend I had ever known. He deserved to know something.

I settled for lifting a corner of the blanket. "He makes me do press-ups," I said. "And practise talking Bune. And I owe him money." I gave details.

"Nothing unusual there," said Purkis, sounding a bit disappointed. "Press-ups won't do you any harm. I don't know about accent – yours is a bit weird, it's true. That'll come right in time. The money's a bit more serious. You'll have to settle up, or he'll use it against you."

"I can't settle up. I'm stony."

"Write to your pa. Tell him exactly how much you owe, down to the last penny. Promise never to do it again."

Sensible as this sounded, I was reluctant to presume upon my father's good nature with fresh demands for money. He had already received the bill for tea at 'Your Obedient Servant', and had written me a short note expressing his annoyance. Asking for a further instalment so soon afterwards would be adding insult to injury. Nonetheless, a week or so later I wrote to him along the lines Purkis suggested. He contacted Nevis and asked for his account. I never learned how much it was, but I am sure Nevis made a tidy profit on the deal.

3

The first weeks of my friendship with Purkis coincided with a relaxation of Nevis's hold over me. The press-ups made me ache afterwards, but I was already getting stronger – I could now manage thirty without breaking a sweat. Even the lessons in Bunian were paying off. Thanks to his tuition my broad Alban accent had faded to a mild burr; I had picked up a good repertory of Bune catchphrases; I sometimes surprised myself by replicating the Bunian tone. Best of all, Nevis had found another tick he liked better: a boy called Lester who clearly adored him. They walked about Bune together on weekends, hand in hand and deep in conversation: pretty much (I told myself spitefully) like a circus animal and its trainer. Presumably Lester was accommodating in other ways too, for Nevis's demands had substantially fallen off. Eventually all he asked for was the odd quick riddle when Lester was nowhere to be found.

This was an immense relief. Perversely it was also a touch galling. It annoyed me that Nevis was able to drop me so casually, as if I counted for nothing with him. Briefly I was tempted to make a scene: accuse him publicly of neglect, rail at Lester for stealing his affections.

This was stupid: more the result of vanity than anything else. I soon got over it. Besides, by that time I was starting to have crushes of my own. Mostly these involved older boys I had never so much as spoken to – boys that walked in charmed circles I had no right to enter.

For the most part I kept these feelings to myself. Purkis, as I have said, knew no such inhibitions. He chiefly hungered after boys who were unattainable, unaware of their appeal, and completely innocent of anything to do with sex. In time these heroic figures became absorbed into the mythology of Malcaster and its denizens.

One of the earliest of the Malcaster stories, *The Innocent Boy*, concerns a youth named Percival Phillips whose startling beauty brings him to the attention of the Malcontents. At the story's climax Septimus Floater confronts him in the deserted swimming pool. He unbuttons his long black overcoat. Underneath, he is stark naked, his monstrous penis hideously engorged. Mistaking Floater's self-exposure for an unfortunate accident, Percival averts his eyes, dives in at the deep-end, and swims away to the safety of the changing-rooms, leaving the Headmaster too stunned by the boy's sublime innocence to press the point.

Malcaster and all its works became an obsession. Purkis and I met every day after lessons, and spoke of little else. There were two entwined trees on the eastern corner of Bellarby's which had been felled by lightning some half-century earlier, and were known for some arcane reason as 'David and Jonathan'. We often sat in the cradling hollows of their ancient shattered trunks, talking excitedly, putting on comic voices, slapping one another's arms and repeatedly howling with laughter. People seeing these antics naturally assumed that we were lovers. It was an easy mistake to make. But there was nothing to it. We were friends, and that was all.

Those words make it sound as though friendship were in some way inferior to a sexual relationship. That is not actually what I believe. A boy who is reasonably attractive can always find lovers, but friends – real friends, the sort who remain true to you unto death – are much harder to come by, and in the end they are infinitely more valuable. Whatever I might suggest to the contrary, I did value Purkis; valued him immensely – knowing nonetheless that what made this degree of affection possible was precisely the fact that we were *not* lovers, and were never likely to be. It is possible of course that Purkis saw the matter differently, but if so he did not say.

FIVE
The Bunian Tone

"What sort of plot?" challenged Rattle witheringly.

"The worst possible," said Wisley. "Floater intends to utilise the school's science laboratories for the manufacture of a hypothetical 'second- gender': a monstrous race of beings with sexual characteristics entirely different from our own."

"That is preposterous!" said Rattle flatly. "What conceivable purpose could there be in attempting something so unsavoury, so unspeakably perverse?"

"The number of sexual acts that can be practised is at present is necessarily limited, there being only one gender to engage in them." Wisley paused, examining his ragged fingernails, then continued with the air of a magician pulling a dead rabbit out of a hat: "Create another gender, and you double it – at a stroke!"

'The Second Gender', from *The Infected Pistol and Other Stories* by H O Minty and F R Trumper. (Privately printed, 1409.)

1

"I see you have acquired the Bunian tone," said my father.

This was during the long Festival break, ten months after I had started at the school, and I was back home with him at our house in Cantleford. Relations between us had seriously deteriorated following his receipt of Nevis's account at the end of Pagan. It was quite an alarming sum, swollen considerably by various extras like commission and tips and the cost of his stationery. This, coming after the bill for Afternoon Tea sent by the management of Your Obedient Servant, had convinced him that Bune was turning me into a wastrel.

This seemed unfair. He had no idea what I had suffered at the hands of Nevis, or what efforts I had made to avoid incurring any further debt. As for Bune, since meeting Purkis I had actually begun to enjoy my life there. Once you had mastered its mechanics it was an excellent school. Yes, it was changing me, but that was all to the good. Before I went there I was miserable; now I positively looked forward to returning. Hearing him speaking of it in his customary disparaging tone, I wanted to rush to its defence.

"Isn't that why boys are put in the school," I asked crossly, "to acquire the tone?"

"It's not at all the reason why I put you there, as you well know. Of course it was inevitable that you would pick it up sooner or later, given your aptitude for aping the ways of your inferiors. I'd simply forgotten how insufferable it is."

"I'm sorry I've become so insufferable to you. If you go to a school like Bune you're expected to fit in. I didn't ask to be sent there."

"What else was I to do with you? Enrol you in the School of Engineering?"

"Of course for you that's the only education worth having."

"Absolutely. Places like Bune are designed for parasites and poseurs; you'd learn far more at any common or garden Technical Institution. The only point of Bune is that it provides an automatic route to career advancement, even for someone as lazy as you."

"Pardon me for existing."

"I'm not sure that I can. Not when I see you handing yourself over body and soul to a set of values that you know in your bones is not only worthless but also profoundly *stupid*."

"All right, pa, I get the point. It's a stupid school for stupid people."

"Some kinds of stupidity are a matter of choice. You can take advantage of a system without actually believing in it."

"How do you know what I believe in?"

"I can't help knowing it. Look at yourself: your body language, your vocabulary, your pathetic bloody snobbery!"

"What do you want me to do, then? Retrain as a plumber?"

"Do what you like William. If you think that going to Bune makes you in some way *superior* to the rest of humanity, that's your problem, not mine. I can't help it if my son turns out to be an obnoxious little shit."

"You know what, pa?" I said. "It's you who thinks himself superior, not me." I left the room, and went out into the garden for a smoke.

2

Later that same day he received a letter addressed to both of us from Sir Roger Purkis, inviting the two of us to dinner at his house in Ludden. Purkis was to be there; also Sir Roger's close friend the actor Ronnie Tempest, and the celebrated Lord Haverhill, our Deputy Prime Minister. "Splendid chap, Haverhill", wrote Sir Roger. "Head of one of the oldest families in Anglia, but the most modest man I know … wonderful company … common touch … brilliant mind … great sense of humour … no side to the man at all."

Haverhill was also, apparently, a great admirer of my father's, and thrilled at the prospect of meeting him. They would, Sir Roger predicted, "get along like a house on fire".

My father brought the invitation into my bedroom (I was sleeping late) shaking with an emotion that was part rage and part something else.

"You don't seem too pleased," I said. Under normal circumstances I would have welcomed the prospect of seeing Purkis in his native habitat, but the thought of having my father in tow set off any number of alarms.

"Pleased?" he said, slapping his hand to his forehead. "I'd rather cut out my tongue."

"I don't see the problem. You don't have to go, surely?"

"One can't just refuse an invitation from someone like that. Not without a reason."

"Well, make one up."

"I know these people. In their eyes a refusal to join them for dinner is tantamount to being discovered exposing yourself at Balls Junction Green."

This meant that despite his misgivings he was going to accept. I wasn't sure what I felt about that.

"What is this all about, pa?" I asked. "It's only a *dinner*."

"Well I'm not sure that's so. What's behind it? Something is, otherwise Purkis wouldn't go to all this trouble. Of course he claims it's a purely social occasion. Fat chance of that! Haverhill's is up to something, no question of it. Wouldn't meet me in an official capacity; that's not the way that kind of creature functions. The man's a menace. Finger in every pie, foot in every door, nose in every backside, particularly when said backside is ten rungs higher up the ladder. *He's* not going to pitch up just to show willing. Having to dress up – there's another bad sign. Everything calculated to put you at a disadvantage. It'll be an absolute bloody disaster – bound to be."

For the next few days he prowled about the house like a caged tiger: jumpy, irritable, smoking heavily, and every so often clutching his head and groaning. I recognised what he was doing: dreaming up a series of ever more embarrassing scenarios in which he made a fool of himself in a hundred different ways. I did my best to reassure him that everything would be fine, but my words had little effect, perhaps because I had ceased believing in them myself.

As the day of the dinner drew near, I became as apprehensive as he was. I had seen my father in polite company before: only once or twice, but enough to know that his fears were more than adequately justified.

3

The Purkises lived in central Ludden, in Macclesfield Square. We travelled there in a tall black steamer like a hearse. Their house was an elegant flat-fronted terraced building, four storeys high, with delicate sash windows, a neat portico and a basement area protected from the pavement by a run of black iron railings topped with gilded arrowheads. We mounted a flight of steps to an arched doorway framed by four slim white pillars. The doorknocker was a heavy brass griffin. My father dolefully used it. After a long interval the door was opened by a crumpled balding man in his shirtsleeves. His shirt was purple and blotched with food-stains; over it he wore a too-tight waistcoat that was pulling apart over a small paunch. One of the buttons was missing; another was hanging by a thread.

"Dr Riddle, is it? You're very early."

This form of words seemed to be inviting an apology. My father said: "Our cab got us here quicker than we expected."

"No worries," said the man. "Don't expect anything to be ready, that's all."

Positioning himself behind my father, he divested him of his scarf with a single upwards motion of his arm, like cracking a whip, and hung it around his own neck; after which he wrenched off my father's overcoat. I removed my own coat and scarf before he could treat me in the same fashion, and handed them over. He draped them over a crooked elbow with a look of disparagement. I was wearing two recent purchases: a high-waisted green jacket with an abundance of buttons, and an elegant silk waistcoat in stripes of black and white. My father had abandoned his usual uniform of three-piece tweed for an ill-fitting double-breasted suit of navy-blue wool. In the harsh light of the electric chandelier it was all too easy to detect the presence of moth-holes.

Muttering to himself, the servant dumped our coats and scarves in a dark closet, then ushered us into an elegant, slightly dilapidated sitting room.

A tall sash-window fronted a walled garden cluttered with neglected pot-plants.The room's furniture was old with plum-coloured upholstery. The walls were panelled in pale green, setting off a number of gold-framed paintings: landscapes and horses, mostly, with a sprinkling of aristocratic portraits. One of these I recognised from my art books: a country nobleman and his son pictured in the gardens of a grand estate. The nobleman lounged with a gun and a whippet; his gorgeously costumed son perched on a delicate green bench.

"I'll tell Paul you've arrived,' said the servant, and left us to our own devices.

"Pretty room," I said.

"Apart from the cobwebs," said my father, looking up at the ceiling rose. "And that man of theirs is a bit too familiar for my liking. Doesn't matter how loaded you are, if you can't—"

He broke off: Purkis had just entered.

He shook hands with both of us simultaneously: a rather daring feat that could easily have gone badly wrong. "You're a touch early," he said.

My father repeated the excuse about the cab.

"That's perfectly fine," he said. "There may be a longish wait for dinner, that's all. The entire kitchen staff walked out this afternoon, so Ronnie and pa are doing the cooking themselves."

"Perhaps we should do this another time," said my father hopefully.

"Oh, you mustn't *go*. Lord Haverhill's coming to meet you specially. Anyway, Ronnie loves to cook; it's his favourite thing these days, now that he's 'ruminating', as he calls it. I think that's partly why the servants all walked out. He tends to be a bit imperious when it comes to dealing with his social inferiors. It probably comes of having no real status in the world outside."

"Ronnie – he's your father's partner, I take it?"

"They've been together for years. He paints as well, you know – kind of. Trouble is he can't draw for toffee, and flies into a rage when people don't praise him to the skies. Touchy, you know – about everything."

"Is that for you to say?" asked my father disapprovingly – rather hypocritically, I thought, since he allowed himself the luxury of criticising others whenever he thought it appropriate.

"Sorry – was I being indiscreet? I thought it best to prepare you, that's all. In case he makes a fuss."

"I'm sure that won't happen."

"I wish I was," said Purkis ruefully. "Can I get you some drinks?"

I had a glass of red, my father a whisky. Purkis already had a drink: a heavy tankard of something dark and oily. We made desultory conversation. Purkis seemed subdued: almost as jumpy as my father, though no doubt for different reasons. He replenished his drink, and ours, several times.

Presently the servant announced the arrival of Lord Haverhill. He waltzed in, all smiles: embraced Purkis, and pumped my father's hand as if he were a long-lost friend. All I got was a nod and a half-smile, but as the least important person there I assumed that was all I was due.

I disliked him on sight. He cut an imposing figure: tall and patrician, with a great mane of pale streaky hair brushed back from his noble temples, and one eyebrow permanently higher than the other, and the expression of someone who takes nothing very seriously. His get-up was flashy to the point of caricature: a wonderful suit of midnight blue flannel, set off with a pink-striped shirt and a broad silk tie with a bright floral motif.

"My pa will be out in a mo'," said Purkis. "He's with Ronnie in the kitchen."

"What fun," said Haverhill, one eyebrow shooting up.

Purkis got him a drink, and refilled my father's glass. After the usual polite enquiries, Haverhill began to praise my father's achievements in extravagant terms. My father received these compliments awkwardly, unable or perhaps unwilling to reciprocate. The conversation stalled. A moment later Sir Roger bustled in, wearing a red apron over a sober blue suit and pinstriped pants, and beaming like a lighthouse. More pumping of hands, more compliments, the only difference being that Sir Roger included me in both rituals. We had of course met before: he had treated Purkis and me to Afternoon Tea in Bune once or twice. He had always been extremely kind. He was perhaps a touch too practised a charmer to be altogether genuine, but I liked him nonetheless.

"Ronnie's apologies – he's still slaving at the ovens," he said. "Unfortunately we're still reeling from a servant crisis, so we will have to manage without an entrée, but I think the bird and the pud will more than make up for it."

The bird was some variety of large fowl. Sir Roger bore it in proudly on a large china platter, followed by Ronnie Tempest who was wearing a matching red apron, and carrying a silver tray laden with a variety of side dishes.

Ronnie set down the vegetables on the tablecloth. He was one of those men who occupy a kind of hinterland between youth and middle age that shifts according to the light and the time of day and the angle of view. He had an actor's face: disturbingly handsome, with heavy dark eyebrows and a floppy cowlick of fair hair falling over one eye. From across the room you might guess him to be not much older than Paul and myself. Viewing him at close quarters, however, you could not help noticing the fine parallel cracks in the surface of his forehead and at the corners of his eyes, and the first signs of collapse in the region of his mouth and cheeks and the underside of his chin.

"Wonderfully fine spread, Ronnie,' said Lord Haverhill. 'Don't tell me you did all this by yourself?'

'I had an assistant – of sorts,' said Ronnie, glancing at Sir Roger from under his forelock. He took a seat at the head of the table, and began carving the bird.

"Hear you had problems in the underlings department," said Haverhill.

"Not up for discussion," said Ronnie.

Purkis was seated on my left. "This'll go on for ages – you see," he muttered in my ear. "Ronnie drives everyone away sooner or later, apart from Thomas. That's the chap who opened the door, you know, and he only stays because he's basically unemployable. You don't have this problem, do you?"

"We don't have any servants, thank goodness. My father doesn't hold with the idea – he's of the egalitarian persuasion, as I must have told you already. Besides he'd never allow anyone to tidy up after him, in case they lost something. How are things going, anyway?"

"Swimmingly," said Purkis. "Picture of domestic bliss."

My father, at the end of the table, made a loud snorting noise suggestive of either mirth or outrage. I glanced over at him. Sir Roger had placed him next to Haverhill, and they were deep in conversation. He was drinking rather more than he was used to. I was afraid that Haverhill's compliments might be going to his head.

"How about yourself?" inquired Purkis. "Have any further tempting prospects emerged out of the slums of the Other Cantleford?"

I groaned. The writings of Robert Lord Percy had inspired in Purkis a romantic belief in the heroic virtues of Anglia's proletariat, and over time he had developed the notion that the men of Cantleford –- particularly those that were well-muscled and aged between eighteen and thirty-five – exemplified the type of being Lord Percy had in mind. Possibly I was somewhat to blame. While discussing my own experiences of Cantleford life and society, I had made the mistake of claiming a better acquaintance with its seamy side than in fact I possessed. Inspired by what had begun as vague hints and the occasional flight of fancy, Purkis had encouraged me to regale him with stories of ever more daring escapades in the night-time world of Cantleford bars and clubs – a world which in truth I had never had the courage or indeed the desire to explore. However insistently I had tried in subsequent conversations to correct the record, I had awakened an appetite that could not easily be diverted.

"You mean the underclass, I suppose?"

"If you must call them that."

"For want of a better term, I must. I'm afraid to say, Purkis, that you have a rather fanciful conception of what these people are like. They have no interest in the poetry of daily toil, only in beer, fried food, and cock-fighting. Their lives are less noble than mean and squalid."

There was a pause, while Purkis took in what I had said. "It's a funny thing," he said, in a priggish tone of voice, "but the very worst snobs are those who have the least right to discriminate against the working man".

This was a low blow, all the more hurtful for coming from that source. "What do you mean by that?"

"Oh, what could I possibly?" said Purkis.

"I suppose you're referring to my origins," I said stiffly.

"I'm referring to your politics."

I had drunk three glasses of wine, which for me was a fair amount. "At least my politics are based on experience," I said. "As opposed to the pretentious scribblings of a wealthy aristocrat."

Purkis shook his head sadly. "You, Riddle, are a fucking sight too cynical."

He was starting to sound querulous. "Too cynical for what, Purkis?"

"For anything. It's not pretty. You're like a dog pissing on a daisy. Why, for fuck's sake? Leave the daisies alone!"

"Why should I? What if I don't want to?"

Purkis was drumming on the table-top again. "These Cantleford youths..." he began.

"Yes?" I said wearily.

"I'm beginning to think you don't actually know any."

"I never said I did."

"Oh come on!"

"I told you what you wanted to hear. You weren't meant to believe it. Any more than you believe in Malcaster."

Purkis mulled this over. "So it was all a lie?"

"If that's what you want to call it."

"What other word is there?"

I shrugged.

Purkis shook his head. "You know what most annoys me? It's not the fact that you lied, it's the cowardice. You have all this amazing stuff on your doorstep, and you daren't even start to explore it."

"It's not cowardice. I have no interest in your mythical fucking working man. He bores me."

Purkis lifted his tankard. When he put it down a line of foam had attached itself to his upper lip like an old man's moustache. "Seriously, how much effort would it take?"

"To do what?"

"To engage with some of them. Man to man– as equals."

"You can't *engage* with the underclass. There's no point. There's a gulf, and you can't cross it."

"You could always try."

"What's the point? The minute they caught a whiff of Bune they'd smash me to a pulp."

"They might not," he said. "Let's say you donned a disguise

63

– rags and a cap and dirty gym shoes, say – and ventured into their night-time haunts, in search of comrades..."

He was quoting Lord Percy again. "Why don't *you* do it?" I suggested. "It sounds more your sort of thing than mine."

"I'd like nothing better."

"Come for a visit, then. We can venture out together."

"I might take you up on that."

"Do. I mean it."

I sat back, feeling exposed and bested.

4

On the other side of the table Haverhill was going on about the Riddle Suction Cleaner. What he was saying took the form of high praise, but the unspoken implication was that the labour-saving machine was my father's main claim to fame. I could sense my father's hackles rising.

"The servants couldn't manage without it," Haverhill enthused. "You must have saved me a fortune in cleaning costs over the years. As a matter of fact we have two: one for the East Wing and one for the main hall."

"That's very gratifying," said my father dryly. "Unfortunately the state owns the patent, not me personally. So the extra sale doesn't benefit me in the least."

This remark was received in silence.

"We have lots of reasons to be grateful for George's abilities," chipped in Sir Roger, smiling in my father's direction. "He also had a hand in designing the Fallon Cooker."

"I thought that was Percy Fallon's invention,' said Haverhill.

"It's no one's bloody '*invention*'," said my father crisply. "Only laymen use that term. Did the blackbird *invent* the wing? Did the mole *invent* the burrow?"

Haverhill made a scoffing noise. "Oh, come on, man, credit where credit's due, you know. Percy didn't just snap his fingers, and there it was."

"Actually that's pretty much what did happen. I know because I was there. I was building an electromagnetic generator at the time, and he was there in the lab with a bar of Caramel Cobbler in his pocket. Gives a yell, stuffs a hand into his pants, and brings it out coated with melted caramel like – well, work it out for yourself. The rest, as they say, is history. Today there's an e-mag Cooker in every restaurant in the land, with Percy Fallon's name on it. Couldn't get it much jammier than that, now could you?"

"Damn fine achievement, if you ask me," said Haverhill, in a tone that brooked no denial.

"It's a bloody monster!" exploded my father. "Big as a bank safe, and twice as heavy. If ever a machine was crying out to be redesigned, it's the Fallon. I'd take a crack at it myself, only the bloody NAC won't give anyone else a look in." He was speaking rather loudly, and making extravagant gestures.

"The NAC?" queried Haverhill. "You think they're to blame?"

"Who else?

Haverhill cocked his eyebrow at Sir Roger. Sir Roger screwed up his face in reply: an appeal for tolerance on all sides. He looked over at Purkis and me. "How are you managing down that end, boys?" he called. "Grub OK?"

"Fabulous," I said, rather exaggerating my enthusiasm. Thanks to the wine and my tiff with Purkis, I had neglected to taste what I was eating: just shovelled it down like stewed mutton.

"Thank Ronnie, not me. He's the chef!"

"Thank you, Ronnie. The food's delicious."

Ronnie leaned over, stroking back his forelock, which promptly fell back over one eye. "William, isn't it?" he said. "Or do I call you Billy?"

"William."

"Good friend of our young Paul's, I take it?"

I was keen to cancel out some of the bitterness that seemed, quite unaccountably, to be spoiling my relationship with Purkis. "Absolutely," I said. "Paul saved my life. I wouldn't have lasted a term if it wasn't for him."

"How touching," said Ronnie, with a knowing smile. "I'm rather fond of Paul myself."

"Hey, Riddle!" muttered Purkis, spearing me with his elbow. "Don't give him the wrong idea."

"What wrong idea is that, my boy?" asked Ronnie.

"We're friends, Ronnie," said Purkis crossly. "Nothing more than that."

"If you say so, Paul."

On the opposite side of the table my father and Haverhill were radiating hostility towards one another. The tone of Ronnie's remarks must have struck my father as sympathetic, for he now leaned across the table.

"What exactly do you do for a living, Ronnie?" he asked.

Ronnie stiffened. True to form my father had asked precisely the wrong question.

"I don't *exactly* do *anything*."

"Ronnie's an actor," explained Sir Roger. "Quite a celebrated one. I'm surprised you've never heard of him."

"It's not an area I take any interest in," said my father warily. "Pretending to be someone else, though: that must be fascinating."

"Frankly, it's not," said Ronnie. "As a rule it's bloody boring. Take the movies, for example. People imagine that's about the most glamorous job in the world. In point of fact it's about waiting around all bloody day in the freezing cold while the cameraman gets his tackle warmed up. Eventually, hours later, they start rolling, something isn't right, the light or the rain or somebody's damn shirt is the wrong colour, and you have to do it again. And then again, and again, and again … About as glamorous as queueing up to use a public flusher. Stage-work even worse. Same bloody thing night after night, with the same bloody crew. A bit like *marriage*, in fact."

Sir Roger looked up. "Another drink, Ronnie?" he asked.

"Trying to shut me up, Roger?"

"Wouldn't dream of it, Ronnie. Be a bloody fool if I thought I could do it that way."

There was yet another awkward silence, while Ronnie glared at Sir Roger across an expanse of tablecloth.

Ronnie turned back to my father. "What's *your* line of work, then?" he asked. "Some kind of boffin, is that right?"

My father looked a little affronted by this description. "I'm a Professor of Engineering at Cantleford – Equinox College."

"Ah, you're an educator then. Another worthy profession – not a million miles different from my own. Basically, performing the same narrow repertoire of tricks over and over again for the edification of a gang of ungrateful little beasts. Have I got it right?"

"Not in my case. Work in my own lab, mainly. Never go near a classroom."

"Good for you. Must be nice to do something useful."

"It would be – if I was allowed to do it," said my father.

"Are you not?"

"To say the least. It's nothing short of scandalous." He was starting to raise his voice again. "Obstacles to progress in every direction: recalcitrant colleagues, incompetent assistants, shortage of funds and equipment, incomprehensible assignments, unreasonable objections to the simplest of requests, constant wilful failures of communication..."

The volume of these remarks made them impossible to ignore. Haverhill leaned in with an expression of affront. "And who do you think is to blame for this regrettable state of affairs?" he asked dangerously.

"The bloody NAC of course! Who else?"

"The NAC again! Bit of a bee in the bonnet there, old chap."

"You'd have a bee in your bonnet too, if your work depended on their permission to go forward. The bloody meddlesome idiots spend more time obstructing research than encouraging it."

Haverhill gave him an icy glare. "In my experience the NAC always have a good reason for what they do. They can see the bigger picture – we can't."

"Only because we're not *allowed* to see it. Take communications. We have the scientific knowhow, right now, to make a portable telephone the size of a sandwich. Ten years from now and everyone would have one. But they won't allow it. That's ridiculous."

"Ridiculous, is it? It may come as news to you, Riddle, but not everyone in this country is as naive as you are. There has to be a measure of social control. People have to be *monitored*, okay? Either that or denied the means for making trouble – means which this portable telephone of yours would undoubtedly place in their hands. How do you monitor fifty million conversations? You wouldn't know where to start."

"I wouldn't want to. What's the point of all this secrecy? They call themselves an Advisory Council, but what *advice* do they ever give? Who even knows their names? Are they in any way accountable?" He flung open his hands, nearly knocking over a bottle of wine – Haverhill reached over and caught it just in time.

"That's rather a lot of questions," he said. "But I'll do my best to answer them." He set the bottle down well out of my father's reach. "The point of 'all this secrecy' is that in some areas of governance any sort of publicity is invariably counter-productive. The NAC is a dedicated and responsible body; it has to be allowed to get on with its work calmly and in a focused way, undisturbed by the intrusions of the yellow press, which if permitted would only lead to disruption of their proceedings and a distracting and wholly unnecessary scrutiny of their private lives. They prepare to remain anonymous – faceless, in fact – because they do not believe that their names or their faces are in any way relevant to what they do. Indeed knowing who they are would only lead to division and contention. That's certainly what happens to the elected body, as I know only too well. The function of the NAC is advisory for the simple reason that it theoretically remains in the government's power to reject that advice. In practice we invariably follow it, and for one simple reason: it invariably proves to be right.

"Lastly, you ask, are they in any way accountable? Yes, they are: in the most direct way possible. Their accountability resides in their achievements. They've given the Anglian people four centuries of peace and prosperity. That's good enough for me. Do you think they'd still be where they are if the system didn't deliver?"

My father sat through this lecture with his head tilted back, staring at the ceiling with an expression of glacial boredom. As it came to its conclusion he sat upright and placed his hands palm down on the table.

"Of course you would say that – it's what you're paid to

propagate. In answer to your question, I don't know where we'd be without the NAC, and nor do you. What I *do* know is that there's a lot more to this than anyone's letting on. The NAC is just the tip of the iceberg. There's a whole world out there that we know nothing of. You know what I'm talking about. Everyone knows. And everyone pretends otherwise. It's astounding."

Lord Haverhill glared. My father glared back.

"It's a fine wine you serve, Roger," said Lord Haverhill, turning away to look at Purkis's father. "Perhaps a little potent for anyone not used to it."

My father coloured. "Are you saying I've had too much to drink?"

Ronnie leaned across the table towards him. "That's enough, Riddle, if you don't mind," he said, wagging a tobacco-stained finger under my father's nose. 'You're being bloody rude. You're a guest in this house: have the courtesy to respect another man's opinions."

"That knife cuts both ways," said my father.

Another frosty silence.

Purkis stood up. "More plonk, anyone?"

"Good thinking," said Sir Roger. "Haverhill, what's the state of your glass?"

"Empty. Oh, thank you, Paul."

"Fill me up too, Paul, there's a good chap," said Ronnie.

"Dr Riddle?"

"I won't, thank you, Paul. It appears I've had enough."

"Shall we adjourn to the smoking room, gentlemen?" said Sir Roger, standing up and dropping his napkin on his plate. "Ronnie, shall we leave Arthur to do the washing up?"

"He'll grumble."

"Yes, he will. That's how he gets through the day."

Sir Roger led the way into the smoking room. It was furnished with red leather high-backed armchairs and a carpet the colour of dried blood. Around the walls were hung a number of paintings of theatrical subjects, including a portrait of Ronnie, skull in hand, stray forelock fetchingly employed, performing the celebrated soliloquy from Wagstaffe's *Tarquin, Prince of Antibia*.

Sir Roger passed round a lacquered box of cigars. Ronnie took one, and so did Haverhill; my father declined. A silver tinder-box was struck. By degrees the room filled with suffocating blue smoke.

"So, William," said Purkis. "Remember that book I mentioned to you?"

"On what subject?" I asked guardedly.

"*The Blissful Dawn.* By Lord Percy."

"Ah yes. You were going to show it to me."

"I have it upstairs. In my room."

"Lead the way."

Purkis's bedroom was every bit as splendid as I might have expected. There were two big sash windows, and an elegant bed of polished mahogany. A small bookcase held books by Sir Henry Morgan Carter and the complete works of Lord Percy. The oddest detail was the presence of a stack of jigsaw puzzles: the sort that comprise huge numbers of very small pieces, and take several days to solve.

"Fond of jigsaws, I see," I observed.

"They're my father's," said Purkis, looking embarrassed and annoyed at the same time.

"He keeps them in your room?"

"Everywhere else is choc-a-bloc. This is just the overflow."

"Obsessive."

"They help him to relax," said Purkis stiffly.

"Right."

Purkis produced a slim silver box. The cigarettes inside were slim and grey. We each took one. A silver statuette of a naked boy stood on a low table. Purkis reached for it, and snapped back the boy's head. A flame sprang from the neck.

"What about your old man?" said Purkis, lighting my cigarette.

I drew in a mouthful of perfumed smoke, resisting the impulse to choke. "What about him?"

"Bit of a card, isn't he?"

"Why do you say that?"

"No reason."

There comes a point in every relationship where you are faced with the choice of either quarrelling or agreeing to differ. The latter option is the safest, and often the only way of maintaining a friendship intact. There is however a cost. Declaring any subject off-limits will necessarily involve a certain loss of intimacy. In the interests of preserving a friendship, one settles for a lesser version. That is what happened here. For some seconds we remained silent, smoking the Flints and thinking our own thoughts. Presently we went downstairs, and joined the grown-ups in the smoking room. There was an atmosphere of awkward silence there too, with the frequent gaps filled with meaningless chit-chat. After a few more minutes of this my father and I exchanged glances, then he made our excuses and we left.

5

Back home, my father went quickly to bed. The next morning he avoided me. For the remainder of the long vac we operated at a distance from one another. We were particularly careful to steer clear of any discussion of the dinner party.

I did however broach the idea of Purkis visiting us for a few days after Renunciation.

"Of course," said my father. You arrange it. You'll have to entertain him yourself, though."

"That's fine."

I went back to Bune in September, for the start of Renunciation. Purkis was very welcoming, very good-natured and affectionate. He seemed on the face of it unchanged, but there was nonetheless a new coolness in our relationship, a limitation on what we could and could not say. In particular both of us avoided making any reference to our respective parents.

SIX
Life's Bonfire

Enough of these beautiful predatory boys
Who know too well how beautiful they are, and how desirable.
In future I will keep faith with the common working lad,
Who makes no bones about the price of love
And hands over his goods, like the florist or fishmonger,
Honestly, and without complaint.

Desire and Other Maladies by Robert, Lord Percy (401)

1

Renunciation Half ended on December 13th, and shortly before Gifting Purkis came to stay with us for a few days in Cantleford.

The visit began badly, with a row about Lord Percy. Purkis, as I have said before, was a huge fan of Percy's, and had based many of his opinions on sex and society on his writings. He liked to think that he modelled his behaviour on Percy's too, but for a fourteen-year-old schoolboy with a ravaged complexion this was more an aspiration than a practical proposition.

Mr Thatcher always said that Percy tended to attract the wrong kind of readers for all the wrong reasons. "Not that he isn't a lot of fun, even so," he would add, with a mischievous twinkle in my direction, "so long as one can disable one's moral compass for the short amount of time required to do him justice".

Personally I didn't find Percy's brand of wilful depravity any fun at all. His message is a simple one: life is tragic because it ends in old age, or death, or both together, and the only thing you can do about it is enjoy yourself as much as possible – "leap into life's bonfire" as he puts it – without paying any attention to the opinions of the prudes and the spoilsports. This sounds perfectly reasonable, until you realise that what Percy meant by leaping into life's bonfire was fucking boys, who because they were from the lower orders would do anything he asked for what was to him a trifling sum of money.

He was objectionable to me on other counts. Although he described himself as an ardent socialist, he never made the least attempt to dispense with his title, and the people he chose to mix with socially were all fellow aristocrats, including most particularly his closest friend, the famously snobbish Lord Alaric Willoughby.

Normally I would have kept my views to myself, but when Purkis started telling me that I could learn a lot from Percy's example, my irritation reached that critical point where something has to be said whether it causes trouble or not.

"You model yourself on Lord Percy, if you like," I said. "Personally I find your hero no more admirable than the repulsive Nevis. The only difference between the two is that Percy dresses up his disgusting behaviour in fine language. At least Nevis never pretends to be anything other than what he is."

"At least Percy knew how to enjoy himself."

"Well, he always got value for money, it's true."

"Don't be such a prig. What if cash did change hands occasionally? Percy had plenty, and they didn't."

"So what you're saying is, paying for fucking is a straightforward commercial transaction? Like for example buying a pair of socks?"

"Come off it, Riddle. They got something out of it too – not just Percy. A good time was had by all."

"Certainly that's how Percy wanted us to see it. I don't remember reading anything his rent-boys wrote on the subject."

"So for want of evidence to the contrary, you assume the worst? Poor logic, Riddle!"

"Fair enough," I said. "We'll agree to differ."

2

We got back to the house. My father had made himself scarce, which after his behaviour at the embarrassing dinner party was something of a relief. He was unlikely to hold the events of that evening against Purkis, or Purkis against him, but the prospect was always there, and for everyone's sake it seemed best that encounters between the two be kept to a minimum.

I took Purkis up to my bedroom. My bed was a sturdy wooden object, only just wide enough for one person. There was also an uncomfortable metal contraption of rods and canvas.

"I'm afraid we have to share the same room," I said, "I'll take the collapsible thing, and you can have the bed."

"Certainly not," said Purkis, looking around with a long face. "I wouldn't dream of depriving you of your little bunk."

I looked at him carefully. For all his famous perfect manners he didn't have one good word to say about our house. I found this annoying. Compared to his place in Ludden it must have seemed very cramped and plain, but it certainly wasn't a hovel.

"Sorry it's such a let-down," I said.

"No worse than Old House," he said lightly, which only added to my irritation. Old House – the block where we had our study – was a draughty monstrosity of a building with bulging walls and narrow creaking staircases and blackened floor-boards worn thin by countless generations of boys' boots: in many ways it resembled the dormitory of a public workhouse. I suppose all he meant was that he was used to a degree of inconvenience at school, so he wasn't going to let it bother him here. True as this was, it did nothing to alleviate the sting. He did not intend to insult me, but I was insulted all the same.

3

We lunched on some patties and fried potatoes in a Quickie-bar in the shopping-centre, and discussed the evening's entertainment. My plan was to begin by having a drink in a famously disreputable tavern called The Potter's Field, situated in a narrow alley on the far side of town – it was, I had heard, a favourite pick-up place for the working-class youth of the town. There was however a drawback: neither of us looked old enough to drink in public, so the chances were that we would be thrown out as soon we came through the door. At Purkis's suggestion we decided to blacken our cheeks and chins and upper-lips with charcoal to suggest a few days' growth of beard. We also bought two tight-fitting black woollen hats from a market stall, calculating that the less we showed of our faces the easier it would be to pass ourselves off as being older.

We went back to my bedroom, and rubbed on the charcoal. The effect was odd in a way that was difficult to define. We then put on the hats. Odder still.

As soon as it started getting dark we sneaked out of the house. For all my scepticism I was now as excited as Purkis. The experience was beginning, however shakily, to take on the elements of an adventure.

Soon after we set foot outside, it became clear that these 'disguises' of ours, far from rendering us less conspicuous, actually made us more so. A group of small boys in the distinctive yellow-and-black blazers of Manor Bar School rounded a corner, swaggering and chattering with that relaxed ease in one another's company which I have always envied but never been able to master. Catching sight of us, they stopped in their tracks, pointing and jeering. We pushed past them, turning our faces away and exchanging artificial remarks in overloud voices. Behind us rose a skirling of high-pitched pre-pubescent laughter, like the yawping of sea-gulls, accompanied by cries of "Sweeeeeep! Sweeeeeep!"

Our tormentors began following us, hurling abuse and pointing us out to every passer-by. We turned to face them, and stood shoulder to shoulder, doing our best to look threatening. Forming a warlike phalanx, they advanced on us. None of them can have been any older than ten, or any higher than our chins, but in a pack they were as threatening as wolves.

"Fuck off, you vermin!" roared Purkis.

His plummy tones made them scream with laughter. One of them darted out from the group, and kicked him on the leg, and suddenly they were all over us like rats, punching and kicking and biting and scratching, and emitting their seagull yawps: a dreadful sound which hurt my ears like fingernails scraping over slate.

Three small boys had Purkis backed against a wall, absorbing kicks and blows from all sides. The rest were doing their best to drag me to the ground. One had his hand in the pocket of my jacket, his fingers nibbling away at its contents like a mouse.

At this point two burly men rounded a corner. One of them shouted something. The next second our attackers had vanished into the darkness.

"Nasty little buggers," said one of the men. He looked closer. "Why the fancy dress?"

"It's camouflage," I said, with an attempt at dignity. "It's a Woodland Patrol exercise."

"Supposed to make you invisible, is it?"

"That's the idea."

"Doesn't work."

They went away, laughing.

"Those kids got my wallet," I said.

"Mine too. How much was in yours?"

"Ten bob."

"Mine was empty," said Purkis, with considerable satisfaction. "Apart from a few coppers. All my folding dough is in my belt. It's a tip Ronnie gave me for precisely this sort of occasion."

"Ronnie knows we're going slumming?"

"Absolutely. Ronnie is a big fan of misbehaviour. –I'm not surprised this happened," he continued. "We were targeted. You saw what those kids were like. They hate everything we stand for. *'The battle lines are being drawn,'*" he quoted – Lord Percy again.

"'The Faceless Demon rides to meet us: at his rear
Gallop the numberless ranks of the untenanted dead.'"

"So this is – what? Some kind of class war?"

"It's not about class, Riddle," said Purkis pityingly. "It's more about power, and respectability, and towing the line. Kids like that have been trained to spot people who threaten the natural order of things. Like us, going into pubs to meet working men. Or even just thinking of it."

"How could they know what we were thinking? They're not mind-readers."

"They could smell it. They saw through our disguise. They knew we were trespassers."

"Only because you gave the game away," I said.

"Oh really? How did I do that?"

"They heard your voice. One syllable was enough."

"What has my voice got to do with it?"

"The accent. Pure fucking Bune."

He shrugged. "At least it's the one I was born with," he said nastily.

4

I was all for giving up the evening for a bad job and going home to have a hot bath and nurse my bruises in front of the wireless. Purkis however was determined to press on, and seeing no easy way to discourage him I agreed, on condition that we scrubbed the charcoal off our faces. Purkis with some reluctance conceded the point, and we made our way to a large public flusher in the shopping mall, not far from The Potter's Field.

It was the usual underground dungeon, dimly lit, smelling to high heaven, with a row of monumental stalls of cracked white porcelain opposite a line of battered cubicles. None of the cubicle doors had locks. The walls teemed with a wealth of erotic material: graphic accounts of erotic adventures, times and dates of availability, details of the writer's sexual equipment, amateurish illustrations of various sexual acts, and so on, all penned in different hands and by a variety of writing instruments.

I had always avoided the Cantleford public flushers, so the look and layout of the place was something of an eye-opener. In the spare corner of my brain I reserve for such purposes I began to plan a work of art where the walls of the cubicles would be covered with heartrending accounts of loneliness, loss and abuse.

An elderly man with a battered face and an air of inexhaustible cynicism watched over the premises, seated under the unflattering light of the flusher's single naked bulb. He eyed us suspiciously when we entered, but Purkis quickly slipped him a small silver coin, after which he couldn't have been more helpful. He apologised for the fact that there was only cold water; he found us a thin sliver of purple soap within which several hairs were embedded, and offered us two squares of scratchy toilet paper in the place of towels.

We removed the charcoal as best we could. Purkis used the soap; I could not. Afterwards we still looked peculiar, but not remarkably so: more like vagrants than refugees from some fourth-century tale of chimney-sweeper's boys. Replacing our woollen hats, we proceeded to the door of The Potter's Field.

Although it was a Friday the tavern was half empty, so any hopes we had of merging into the crowd were dashed. As we walked over to the bar I was acutely conscious of eyes following our every movement, weighing up every detail of our appearance. I began walking strangely, with stiff jerky leg movements and clenched buttocks. Behind me I heard a low snigger.

The barman was a young chap with a meaty face and a pony-tail.

"Two pints of Kiddle," said Purkis.

"New to Cantleford are you?" asked the barman.

"I am – he's not," said Purkis. Surprisingly he had recovered much of his equilibrium.

"You realise of course that I can't serve you."

"Why is that?"

"Why do you think?"

I nudged Purkis: I was ready to go.

One of the youths standing at the bar turned curiously in our direction. He was large with long fair hair and a worrying smile.

"Hello matey," said the fair-haired youth. "Oliver giving you trouble?"

"Apparently he can't serve us," said Purkis.

"Why's that, Ollie?"

"Why do you think?" said the barman, just as he had said to us, only in a friendlier tone.

"Can you serve *me*?"

"What do you want, Jace?"

78

"Two pints of Kiddle – that was it, wasn't it – and a Gullenby stinger."

Shaking his head over the frailty of humanity, the barman began to pour the drinks.

"That's awfully kind of you," said Purkis, holding out the ten-shilling note we had reserved for the purpose.

The young man plucked it from his fingers. "Don't mention it," he said. "I'm Jace, by the way."

We introduced ourselves as Tommy and Hugh. Oliver placed our drinks on the counter. Jace paid with Purkis's ten-shilling note, then pocketed the change and picked up his slinger with the other. "All right boys? Come and join us. Bring your drinks."

Panic gripped my chest: every instinct urged me to flee. But Purkis was already following the youth over to the corner, where a group of his cronies were sitting, watching us like a kettle of hawks who have spied two defenceless mice advancing towards them across a barren plain. Flight was no longer an option.

"Lads," said Jace, "this is Tommy and this is Hugh. And this is Keg and Cal and Dibble and Gunner".

Purkis shook hands all round beaming. I followed suit, with rather less enthusiasm. My hand was crushed in one mighty grip after another.

The four youths made room for us. I was squashed between Purkis and the youth named Gunner. Gunner's thigh pressed against mine. I edged away; the thigh followed. I tried to shunt over a second time, but Purkis dug his elbow into my ribs. After this I had nowhere left to go.

Purkis was soon revelling in being the centre of attention. Where I endeavoured to mimic the vowel sounds and the conversational rhythms of the natives, hoping by these means to render myself invisible, he allowed his unmistakeably Bunian tones to ring out in all their plummy glory. Indeed if anything he exaggerated them. So much for our plan of appearing in disguise.

To my surprise, the Bune accent was quite a hit.

"Are you on the wireless, Hugh?" asked Jace. "You sound just like it."

"'Fraid not, alas," said Purkis beaming.

"'Fwaid not, alas," mimicked Jace. "That how you say it?"

"'Fraid not, old chap!" declared Purkis.

Roars of laughter.

"Here, you – Tommy," said Gunner. "You say it."

"'Fraid not," I said, without much enthusiasm.

"Go on – say the rest."

"'Fraid not, old chap," I intoned mechanically.

He stared at me. "Something bugging you, Tommy?"

"Got a bit of a headache," I muttered.

"Bit of a headache," repeated Gunner. "Ay say, what beastly rotten luck!"

"*You* haven't got a bit of a headache, have you Hugh?" asked Jace.

"'Fraid not, old chap!" said Purkis brightly, to further roars of laughter.

One of the youths came back with a tray of drinks. I was handed a Gullenby stinger. This turned out to be a small bottle of very strong brown beer with a segment of lime wedged in the top. Out of the corner of my eye I saw Purkis handing over some money. He had a stinger in front of him too.

The evening progressed along much the same lines. At some point Purkis disappeared. I finished up my stinger. For several minutes I sat in front of the empty glass, feeling foolish. Gunner glanced down, and pulled a face.

"Your shout, I believe, my Lord," he said satirically. He extended a large tobacco-stained palm, and waggled the fingers.

At that point Purkis returned, looking flushed.

"Purkis," I said, in an undertone. "Can you advance me a greenie?"

Sighing, Purkis dug into his money belt, and pressed a hot crumpled note into my hand.

"The power of patronage," observed Gunner satirically, waggling his fingers again.

I handed over the greenie. Holding it between finger and thumb, he split his face in an exaggerated grin, then twisted the note behind his back, and pretended to use it to scrub his bottom.

There was a chorus of guffaws. "Enough frivolity, lads," he said.

"Name your poison, if you please. Courtesy of the benevolent Lord Thomas."

The youths gave Gunner their orders. They all, I noted, still had full glasses in front of them.

"Lord Thomas?" enquired Gunner, stooping low. I asked for another stinger. He went to the bar.

"Having a good time?" asked Purkis.

"No. Are you?"

"Absolutely."

Gunner came back from the bar with a tray of drinks. There seemed no prospect of my getting any change.

I took a longish pull on the stinger. For some reason it seemed to have vastly improved in taste.

Gunner wedged himself in next to me. His thigh began to press against mine again; this time I made no effort to repel it.

"Where are you from, Tommy?" asked Gunner.

"Hibernia," I lied.

He leaned towards me. His breath wafted sourly across my face. "You don't sound like a bog-boy."

"What do I sound like?"

"I've been wondering. Are you perhaps a plant of some kind?"

I decided it was time to leave. I looked around for Purkis. He had gone again.

"What's nibbling, Tommy?"

"Nibbling?'

"You look frit."

"No, not at all," I said. "I was wondering where Purkis was, that's all."

"Who?"

"Hugh," I said, remembering our aliases.

"Left on an errand," said Gunner, placing his hand on my thigh.

"Oh, right. Will he be long?"

He rolled back his eyes. "Maybe," he said, taking his hand off my thigh, and began to speak to Dibble.

I sat over the dregs of my stinger for a good half hour. No one spoke to me. No one offered to buy me another drink.

At last Purkis returned, with Jace's arm around his shoulder.

"How's tricks, Thomas?" he said brightly.

"Tricky, Hugh," I said, standing up.

"Not going already? Have another drink."

I shook my head.

"Oh well ... Do you mind awfully if I stay? Just for an hour or so."

"As you please."

"That's awfully nice of you. Don't wait up for me, will you?"

"No," I said. "Enjoy yourself."

"Oh, I will. I will."

"Goodbye Tommy, goodbye," shouted the men as I left. I could see they were glad to see the back of me.

Purkis arrived back at about two in the morning, wearing a dazed expression.

"Are you all right, Purkis," I asked, out of politeness.

"More than all right, Riddle, thank you."

"Any money left?"

"Not a penny," he said merrily.

5

The remainder of his visit followed much the same pattern. My father kept out of sight. Purkis and I got up late, and ate a cheap lunch in a Quickie. We wandered around Cantleford for a few hours, then went back to the house, where we prepared ourselves an evening snack, usually involving toast and cheese. Around eight Purkis announced his intention of dropping in to 'The Gardeners', where he had agreed to meet 'the lads'. He invited me along. I declined, pleading tiredness. He spent some time sprucing up – no more applications of charcoal for him – then took off at around nine, leaving behind him a reek of expensive fragrance. He did not get back until long after midnight.

This was the regular pattern of events for the rest of his stay.

The time came for him to return to Ludden. At the station I apologised for neglecting my duties as a host.

"Don't be silly," he said. "I've had a fabulous time."

When I returned to the house my father was waiting for me in the front room.

"Where's that friend of yours?" he asked casually, pulling on his old pipe.

"He's just left."

"What, already? What a pity! I'm afraid you've had to look after him all on your own. I feel quite ashamed. I hope he had a good time here."

"He did."

"Good. Good. He's been no trouble at all. I'd almost forgotten he was here. Tell him from me, the next time you see him, he is very welcome to come again — any time he likes."

6

After Purkis had returned to Ludden I occupied myself by beginning a Malcaster story, 'Poetic Licence', which draws upon the many contradictions implicit in Robert Percy's life and works. This, as I see it now, was my way of getting back at Purkis for his over-enthusiastic embrace of the boys of the Potter's Field, and of Percy's views in general.

'Poetic Licence' took for its subject the adventures of a latter-day version of the poet's character. Percy Roberts is a senior pupil at Bune, who has contrived, thanks to a combination of bribery and blackmail, to remain a pupil well into his thirtieth year. A leading light of the elite club of seniors known as 'Raven', he is celebrated for his sadistic treatment of his numerous slavish ticks, and his savage attacks on the younger college servants. Despite his unabashed snobbery, he is also known for penning sentimental odes extolling the virtues of the underclass, and calling for a 'universal nakedness of soul.'

I read Purkis the opening passages when we returned to Bune at the start of Renunciation, fully expecting him to be incandescent with rage. Instead he roared with laughter, and insisted on embellishing the story with lurid descriptions of Percy Roberts's expeditions into the College's subterranean servants' quarters.

My plan, in short, backfired. I resolved in future to be less censorious, more understanding of my friend's needs. It occurred to me that much of my annoyance with Purkis might be due to envy: to my resentment of his popularity with a group of men I viewed with a mixture of fear and contempt. I briefly entertained the notion that jealousy – envy's evil twin – might also be involved, but quickly dismissed the thought. Purkis, was not, as I have said before, someone I had any desire to possess, certainly not as a lover.

SEVEN

Art

"It's all here," said Rattle excitedly, "in the good Dr's medical notes".

"Is it really?" said Wisley languidly.

"You can't miss it. Dr Floater is described as a 'thoroughly toxic personality'. 'Instead of blood,' writes his medico, 'what flows through his veins is pure vitriol.'"

"What of it?" asked Wisley.

"Well, don't you see? This gives us motive and murder weapon in one. Clearly the murdered man was a vampire who thought to make Floater his victim."

"Oh yes," said Wisley facetiously. "And I suppose you're going to tell me he died with a stake through his heart?"

"Not a bit of it," said Rattle triumphantly. "He was poisoned."

'Pure Vitriol', from *The Infected Pistol and Other Stories* by H O Minty and F R Trumper. (Privately printed, 480)

1

There isn't much to say about the middle period of my schooldays: 'more of the same' just about sums it up. There's a set pattern to any school story: you learn about the new boy's arrival and early experiences, then once he has overcome his initial problems of adjustment, and seen off a bully or two, and found out what subjects he is good at, and met his lifelong friend, there isn't much left to happen until he becomes a Praetor, and ultimately Head of Crow, or its equivalent (some of the lesser schools call things by different names). I imagine that much the same thing applies to the life of a man: he leaves school, and if he's lucky he gets a degree, and starts a job, and goes through a period of sexual experimentation, then he meets the love of his life, and the two of them form a partnership, and buy a house together, and acquire a son or two, and settle into a routine: and that's the story more or less over.

As regards my development in the sexual sphere, this remained at a standstill, stuck in some kind of unsatisfactory *cul de sac*. Before arriving at Bune my experiences in this area were pretty uninspiring, amounting to little more than mutual masturbation. At Bune certain sexual acts – specifically anything involving penetration – were debated obsessively, but the actual practice of those acts was largely confined to the senior boys. Nevis had already introduced me, very much against my will, to the passive version. He did his best to initiate me in the active version as well, but the mutinous behaviour of my private parts meant that this for me was a bridge too far. My sexual experience was in other ways remarkably limited. I had never spent a night in the same bed as another boy, and had no particular wish to do so. I had had crushes on other boys – everyone did – but these consisted of vague if intense fantasies that evaporated at the first contact with reality. As soon as the opportunity arose to consummate my wishes I would lose interest, and find an excuse to leave.

Whatever I did on my own account, whatever acts and experiences other boys told me about, whatever erotic descriptions I read, whatever illustrations I pored over, it always seemed to me that there existed, or ought to exist, somewhere, some other outlet for what I felt – a further and deeper and more fulfilling connection that anything that was available to me. The worst of it was the conviction, derived from I know not where, that until I was able to unearth this peculiar, unlikely, perverse, indefinable *other thing* I was yearning for, I would have no way of ever becoming *myself*: the person my nature intended me to be. I tried many times to discuss this feeling with others, including naturally Purkis, but none of them appeared to have the least idea of what I was going on about.

2

My first impression of the Headmaster, Dr Porter, was of a person who leaves very little impression. He was a man of unprepossessing appearance, small and slender, with well-oiled black hair divided by a central parting, a low narrow brow, a pencil-thin moustache trimmed low on the lip, and a mouthful of worryingly regular white teeth. He had no partner, and was commonly supposed to be a lifelong celibate.

My father already knew him in a professional capacity – they had often crossed paths at the sort of event where my father was a guest speaker and Porter a representative of the educational establishment. Not surprisingly, his opinion of Porter, which he did not hesitate to share with me, was unfavourable to the point of contempt. Intellectually he considered him mediocre, but that was hardly offered as a distinguishing feature, since in his opinion most men of his acquaintance, other than his fellow scientists, belonged to a lower order of life. The best part of his scorn was reserved for Porter's role as a widely respected bureaucrat, the advocate of a kind of nit-picking cost-cutting educational regime that placed the virtues of 'managerial efficiency' and 'customer satisfaction' some way ahead of the pursuit of academic excellence. At various times I had heard my father call Porter a martinet, a penny-pinching fool, a corporate sell-out and a brown-nosed bottom-feeder. The fact that Porter had risen to the headmastership at Bune by way of an academic career in what was called 'Business Practice' was further evidence of his absolute mediocrity, both as a man and as an educator. The antipathy, I gathered, was mutual, though the true depth of Porter's dislike for my father was something I only came to realise at the very end of my Bune career.

My view of Porter only took on definition after I became friends with Purkis. Dr Floater, his Malcaster equivalent, was a monster of perverted lust, who concealed his disgusting appetites behind a veneer of civility and charm.

One of the earliest Malcaster stories, 'Punishment and Crime', exposes him as a raving sadist who is in the habit of secretly filming the flogging of small boys by the members of Rook – the

Malcaster version of Crow. The sequel, 'The Mystery of the Locked Confessional', purports to be the transcript of a recording made in one of the narrow cubicles within the school's cloisters to encourage the anonymous reporting of transgressions, especially of a priapic nature, by the younger boys and junior masters. A further story, 'The Yellow Pool', has him arranging for a camera to be installed in the floor of the school's small unheated swimming pool, so that he can monitor the goings-on beneath the water level. All three of these Malcaster stories, like many others, follow the same pattern: what begins as a parody of the tale of detection quickly becomes a lurid and ever more grotesque fantasy in which innocent boys are subjected to ever more sadistic punishments culminating in an orgy of violence and rape. The fact that the real Dr Porter was to all intents and purposes the exact antithesis of the Dr Floater of these stories greatly added to our pleasure in composing them. It was, as I see it now, a form of revenge on the school for making us play its games and submit to its notion of order and respectability.

Acts of revenge, however, rarely escape detection and punishment, even when they are confined to the writing of stories. Sometime around the start of Renunciation I began to notice that the Headmaster had for some reason taken a dislike to me. When I passed him in the quad his head would swivel in my direction, subjecting me to a glare of disapproval that I continued to feel long after I had passed out of his ambit. If he came into our classroom his eye would invariably fix on me to the exclusion of anyone else. No words were ever spoken, but the antagonism was unmistakeable.

I sat on my suspicions for a while before eventually admitting them to Purkis.

We were sitting side by side in the blasted trees known as David and Jonathan. At one time they had grown side by side, a couple of feet distant from one another; a century earlier a lightning strike had fused them together in the shape of conjoined lovers. It was coming on for evening; the shrill melodious voices of young boys rang out in the blue twilight, singing without accompaniment in the Crucifixion Hall.

"I haven't noticed him doing that," he said.

"Well you wouldn't, would you? – since it's not directed at you."

"Oh I think I would. I do notice things like that, whether they affect me of not."

"So you think I'm imagining this?"

"Probably," he said. "Art is a risky occupation, you know. If you write about madness, sooner or later you start going mad. Perhaps you should step away from Malcaster for a while: throw yourself into a sporting activity, run until you feel exhausted. A good night's sleep works wonders."

This sounded like a claim to superiority. "That's a bit patronising."

"Sorry about that, Riddle. But let's suppose you're right – that Floater has taken against you, for no good reason. What's your explanation?"

I broke off a piece of bark. I had a theory, but I preferred not to go into it. "Maybe he knows about Malcaster. Or just suspects it. Like when you start talking about someone across the hall, too far away for them to hear, and they look directly at you."

"You're talking mind-reading," he said. "Not scientific, Riddle."

"Not mind-reading, exactly. More super-sensitivity, like picking up inaudible messages and gestures: a kind of vibration in the atmosphere."

"Mm. There's a story there, I fancy. Floater invents a machine that picks up hostile vibrations, with a view to expelling everyone who doesn't worship him. And then…"

"Then he discovers no one does." Where Malcaster was concerned, we had become adept in picking up one another's train of thought.

"Exactly. You could call it, 'The Mind Reader'."

"You can laugh," I said. "It isn't happening to you."

"Why not, though? If your theory is right the Good Doctor should be glaring at both of us."

"That wouldn't be convenient," I said. "Your pa's too important. Whereas mine is just nobody – a social inferior."

"So you're the whipping boy?"

"Yes. I suspect I am."

3

One afternoon towards the first week of Gifting Dr Porter sent a messenger to request my presence in his office.

I was in the middle of an Art class: something I looked forward to as the brightest spot in the timetable. By this time I had abandoned my early interest in creating compositions purely out of colour and shape (these had been a great hit with our art master, Martin Trotter, but no one else saw the point of them) and had started building things, or to be more exact, designing things that could be built, if only I could afford the time and money they would demand. My current project was a series of interconnecting rooms, each of them crowded with articles of furniture culled from various phases of my past. Once a group of people entered the first room – furnished to resemble the study I now shared with Purkis – the door to the outside would be locked, and they would have to keep wandering through the loop of rooms until they were released, exactly one hour later. The title of this piece was 'A Short Lifetime'.

In the three years I had been at the school, Porter and I had never so much as spoken to one another. Now, suddenly, I was being summoned into his presence. There had to be a reason.

All my recent fears came flooding back. My drafts of the Malcaster stories were kept in my locker, wrapped in several layers of brown paper. What if he had had the locker searched? I thought of his peeling back the layers of paper, opening the creased manuscript of 'The Locked Confessional', starting to read. I recalled my description of Dr Floater, watching the floggings, his tiny withered penis clutched in his skinny claw-like hand. I imagined his look of fury, his snarl; I saw him rise from his desk like a giant spider. Sweat sprang out all over my body, running down my chest and back, dripping from my face. I could hardly breathe. My guilt was already determined. Only one punishment was possible: I would be expelled.

Up to now my feelings for Bune had been ambivalent. A year earlier, when my father had criticised its elitism, I had come to its defence. My loyalties at that time had been less than total, based less on any fondness for the school than the feeling that his criticisms had been primarily aimed at me. Since then, without quite realising it, I had become a convert. Bune had won me over by stealth. It had convinced me in a thousand different ways that I was destined for a superior fate, that I could enjoy the good things in life without guilt, as a just reward for merely being myself. I had claimed to be a rebel, but my rebellion was nothing more than a pose. The truth was that I loved Bune. I loved the way it made me feel. I loved the privileges it gave me. And better things were still to come. Within a year or so, if I kept my nose clean, I would be made a Praetor. Beyond that beckoned the dizzy eminence of Crow. I would walk among the gods as an equal. There was nothing I wanted more.

And now, suddenly, I was going to lose everything.

4

I tapped on the door.

"Come!"

Porter's office was furnished with the kind of bad taste that passes itself off as good among people who have none: a reproduction antique globe that doubled as a sherry cabinet, a rather too immaculate rosewood writing-desk, a mariner's chest that had never smelt the sea – that sort of thing. Porter was standing with his back to me, looking through the tall mullioned windows which afforded a view of the playing fields, beyond which rose the golden pinnacles of the first-century Crucifixion Hall.

Porter rotated to face me. "Sit down, Riddle," he said indicating a high-backed chair with a narrow seat and high armrests – the interrogation seat, I thought. I lowered myself into it, and waited to hear my fate.

"We haven't spoken before, have we?" he said, distorting his features into a smile.

"No, sir."

"Pity. I make a practice, normally, of interviewing the scholarship candidates myself, just to make sure that they are the right material for Bune. Not everyone is, as I'm sure you know."

I could only nod.

"I can't think how you slipped through the net. Well, it can't be helped. You're here now. How are you finding things?"

"Fine. No complaints."

"Give me a bit more detail. What do you like in particular?"

"Well, everything really," I mumbled. "All the masters have been very helpful."

And the other boys? Have you any friends?"

"A few."

"One of them being Paul Purkis?"

"Right." I nodded, a few too many times.

"Paul's father's a great friend of mine – Sir Roger. I believe you've met him."

I wriggled in the uncomfortable chair. "I have, yes. Sir Roger. He's been very kind."

"Wonderful man. Sits on our Board of governors. Rising star in the government – Minister for Communications. A boy like you needs connections of that sort, given your origins. Role models too. You were a tick under Nevis, weren't you, in your first year?"

"Yes", I said warily. Nevis had left the school at the end of Pagan. I had been hoping I had heard the last of him.

"How did that go?"

I wondered where this was leading. Every tick-master, before leaving, had to draw up a detailed evaluation of those boys who had served as ticks under him. In my case, the report was almost certain to be damning. If so, I was done for. It was no use my protesting that Nevis had abused me. Porter would never believe my word against Nevis's, whatever the evidence. That would mean siding with me against the school: an impossibility.

I said nothing, just nodded stupidly, as if in general agreement with some proposition that had not been made.

Porter was studying me closely, his chin resting on his fists. "Excellent chap, Nevis, wouldn't you say? Considering his background. Came from nowhere, just like you, and made it all the way to Crow. He's doing very well, I hear, in the great world outside. Just shows what can be achieved, if you put your mind to it."

I went on nodding.

"He gave a very good report of you, you'll be pleased to hear. Very complimentary of your cooking skills in particular. Said you had made tremendous progress, both in manner and bearing. No longer the little street urchin he met on day one. One could almost mistake you for a proper Bunian, is how he summed the matter up. That's quite a compliment, don't you think?"

The sensation of relief was overwhelming. "Yes," I mumbled.

"What about your studies? What's your favourite subject?"

That was easy. "Art."

"Art." He grimaced, as if the word was in some way not quite respectable. "What do you think that means, exactly?"

"That depends on the artist," I said, a little vaguely.

"If an Artist makes it, it must be Art – is that the line?"

"In a way."

"Well, that's something I've never been able to understand, you see. To me a work of art – if we're talking about painting here – is a depiction of something I can recognise, and enjoy looking at: an attractive landscape, say, or a vase of flowers. Not the kind of 'art' you produce, if I may say so."

"Well … landscapes and flowers are not quite my thing."

"I understand that. From my own point of view," he said, lifting his chin off its prop, "I would have thought that art, if it's anything, has to be *everyone's* 'thing,' as you put it. Otherwise it's simply an indulgence on the part of the man who made it. Pretentious rather than useful, if you take my point."

"Kind of," I said. There was obviously no point in debating the question: anything I said would just be used as a stick to beat me with. The truth is, I wasn't that interested in theory, just in doing what felt inevitable.

"Well, Mr Trotter speaks very highly of your work," he went on. "It's his field; he ought to know what he's talking about. I just wonder whether you mightn't, once in a while, produce work that was rather more … accessible. Not just to me: to the world in general."

"Like what, for example?"

"Well, that's something for you to decide. I can't be proscriptive in a matter like this; that would be fishing in another man's pond. But it does occur to me that before an artist can allow himself to smash the mould, he should be quite certain that he knows how to employ it – in a more traditional way, as it were. Do you get my drift?"

"Sort of. Do you mean I should paint something recognisable?"

"That makes it sound terribly boring. But yes: that would at least reassure your audience that you have a basic measure of skill, as a draughtsman, shall we say. That you're not simply doing what you do just because you can't do the other thing."

"The trouble is," I said, "I'm not altogether sure that I *can* do the other thing."

"Now, that's very modest of you. All I'm asking is that you give the matter some thought. See what you can come up with. And if it's totally worthless: well at least we'll have established that, if nothing else. Well? What do you think?"

By this point I would have agreed to anything. "I'll give it a go."

"I wish you would. All right, Riddle, off you go. Just remember what I said. Make Purkis your example. And, among the older boys, Nevis. All right?"

"Yes, sir." The ordeal was over; the axe had not fallen. I could hardly believe my luck.

Returning to our rooms, I reported the gist of the conversation to Purkis. He was amused. "What did I tell you?" he said. "Porter isn't your enemy. All he cares about is maintaining order – making the school look good. Keep that in mind, my boy."

"I will, Purkis, I will. – Porter really hates my work, you know."

"Well, naturally he does. He believes in 'tradition': the sort of tradition which is basically just convention wearing a fancy hat. The ruling classes – or their slaves, which is what he is – worship convention, because convention is the dam that holds back change. That's why they hate art, unless it's the really boring sort: vases of lilies, portraits of stuffy old men, muscular youths caught in the act of labour, sugary landscapes without a factory or telegraph pole in sight. Art like yours embraces change, it makes the wheels spin faster. So it has to be smothered. Toe the line: that's what it all boils down to. A warning shot above the bows – nothing more than that. How I hate these old fools! Now what's for tea?"

EIGHT
Instruction

A well-balanced and humane society is a huge achievement, which deserves to be properly valued and protected. The only belief-system we as educators can safely endorse is one which offers us stability and security and peace: which allows man to live happily and harmoniously with man.

'Why Religious Studies?', a talk given by
Counsellor Peter Joyce to the boys of Bune School
on the morning of Sunday February 14th, 484.

1

When we returned to Bune for Vernal, Purkis and I began a course of instruction in preparation for our First Union. Our instruction was in the hands of the Deputy Head, Counsellor Peter Joyce, commonly known as 'Humpty', a reference to his enormous hairless dome.

Counsellor Joyce was renowned for being boring, a gift he possessed to an extraordinary degree, even among schoolmasters. He was skilled at expressing an idea in as many words as possible. He followed every statement with a rephrasing of the same point in other words, and then rephrased it a second time in what was supposed to be an encapsulated form. He had a monotonous declamatory delivery, matched with a fund of theatrical gestures and a fondness for quaintly outmoded idioms; he radiated a conviction that whatever he said was not merely fascinating, and to the point, but expressed in language that could not fail to inspire those subjected to it. Attending one of his classes was like being hit over the head repeatedly with a roll of wet newspaper. In the Malcaster

Stories he appears, under the name of 'Deacon Toadflax', in the role of Floater's right-hand man, tasked with executing his master's commands in such a way that no blame could ever be attached their true author. Floater had only to mutter, "That dratted X is such an *irritating* individual, don't you think?" for Toadflax to glide into action, first deploying his ability to lecture a man into a coma, and then despatching his insensate victim in such a way as to leave no detectable traces of any crime. A mid-period Malcaster story, 'A Victimless Crime', has him tasked with eliminating Magnus Bottery, an unusually inquisitive young schoolmaster whom Floater suspects of being a government spy. Unfortunately for Floater, Bottery's prodigious inquisitiveness renders him impervious to the numbing power of Toadflax's lectures: he continues nodding and asking ever more pointed questions until Toadflax himself succumbs to a fit brought on by nervous exhaustion. Tasked with explaining Toadflax's condition, Rattle develops the theory that the Deacon has been rehearsing a lecture in front of a mirror, and has bored himself into a coma.

Until we began our course of Instruction I only knew Counsellor Joyce by reputation: I had observed him on numerous occasions crossing the quadrangle – his gleaming skull made him impossible to mistake – but had never actually faced him across a classroom. The extreme prolixity for which he was famous I assumed to be, at least in part, a product of schoolboy exaggeration. I was accordingly unprepared for the true potency of Counsellor Joyce's speaking style, and the dangers of surrendering to it.

The session had begun at eight in the morning, an hour at which, in those days, I was barely awake. I opened my rough-book; Joyce began to speak. His voice rose and fell in a monotonous chant. I struggled to follow the first few sentences, then my ability to concentrate began slipping away from me like the life-force of a dying man. I remained distantly aware of my hand moving jaggedly over the page like the needle of a lie-detector, but my attention was occupied elsewhere, in a place of light and space and placid beauty.

Purkis jabbed me in the side with his elbow. In front of me, on the open spread of my rough book, taking up most of both pages, was a drawing of an erect penis. The head of this organ had taken on Joyce's unmistakeably pudgy features, wildly overgrown eyebrows and complete absence of hair.

The actual Counsellor Joyce was looking at me with the same eyebrows hoisted high on his forehead. "Well, Riddle?"

I turned the page, and held it down, as if the penis might have acquired a life of its own. "Sorry, Sir, I didn't catch that."

"Purkis, you appear to have the measure of Riddle's concentration, or lack thereof. Repeat the question for him."

Purkis twisted his mouth about, before saying, in a voice deliberately devoid of expression: "What, Riddle, do you understand by the term 'gestation'?"

I had never paid much attention to the Biology of Reproduction, which my father had said was unscientific twaddle. "Is it something to do with infants?"

"Of course it has something to do with infants. But what?"

I shook my head, mystified.

"Crabb?"

Casper Crabb was a fellow Equestrian, whom we judged something of a creep. "Gestation," said Crabb, with the serene certainty of someone quoting from a remembered text, "is the process whereby the raw material that is to become the child is nurtured in the hive until he is capable of independent life."

"Independent life?" queried Joyce. "Quitting his father's house, do you mean? Finding employment? Earning a living?"

"No sir. More like ... breathing and consuming food and things like that."

"The phrase I'm looking for, Crabb, is 'capable of independent existence outside the hive'."

"Yes, sir," said Crabb, carefully writing the phrase down.

"So enlighten us, Riddle, how long does this period of 'gestation' continue? Do you know?"

"Couple of years?" I guessed.

"Crabb?"

"About eighteen months, I believe."

"About eighteen months is correct. Back to you, Riddle. What needs to take place before any of this process can be put in train?"

I shrugged.

"No idea? Anyone? Yes, Purkis?"

"Something to do with Union, is it, sir?"

"'Something to do with Union' – thank you! Go on, Purkis. What precisely do you understand by 'Union'?"

"Well I don't really understand it, to be truthful, sir."

"You don't really understand it," he repeated satirically. "Tell me, boy: what do we call something we don't really understand?"

"A secret?" suggested Purkis.

"Not a secret, no. Find another word. Anyone? Crabb?"

"A mystery?" said Crabb, smirking.

"Thank you, Crabb. A *mystery*, exactly! The mystery of life; the mystery of how new life comes into the world. A matter that is, by its very nature, *the thing that cannot be known.*"

"So, Sir: are you saying *Union* is a mystery?" I chipped in.

"No, boy, you're putting the cart before the horse. Without Union the mystery could not take place. But Union *itself* it not the mystery – that comes after."

"So once we achieve Union, what happens next?"

"That 'we' is somewhat presumptuous, Riddle. *You* in person may never achieve Union. Those who do – the fortunate few – are permitted to contribute materially to the process on which society's continuance depends. Society will recognise their contribution, and reward it accordingly."

"What about those who can't manage it?" I asked, beginning to feel worried.

"Those who fail to achieve Union, Riddle, fail in everything. They are nothing – fit only for menial tasks. Porters have never experienced Union. Tailors have not. Nor have waiters. But certain of you boys – absurd as it may seem – do have that potential. Crabb: you seem to be rather more clued up than your two fellows. What rights and privileges are attendant upon the successful completion of Union?"

"Well, you get to be a Praetor, for a start."

"Yes, yes, for what it's worth you normally advance within the hierarchy of the school. But something else happens which is rather more important. Yes, Purkis?"

To my surprise Purkis knew the answer. "Fatherhood," he said confidently.

"Fatherhood, exactly. And along with fatherhood certain other rights and privileges necessarily accrue. For example? Crabb?"

"The potential to be a full member of Albion society," recited Crabb. "Along with the right to own property, and form a partnership, and vote in elections. Also the right to stand for parliament."

"Well done, Crabb. The right to stand for parliament, yes: a unique privilege. This is something you in particular might want to consider for the future."

"I already have, sir," said Crabb, cracking open a shit-eating smile.

"Good," said Joyce. "Keep up the good work, and you should have every chance of success." He turned his eye upon Purkis. "What about you, Purkis? Do you entertain any ambitions in that direction?"

"Why not?" answered Purkis lightly.

"Why not indeed? By rights, considering your lineage, you should be first in the queue. And yet –"

He looked pointedly at me. I bore down on the page of my rough book, hating the man like poison.

"Let me just say," he continued, turning back to Purkis, "if that is *really* what you have in mind, you would be well advised to heed the wise words of the illustrious Wagstaffe:

> 'Now I am grown a man, the seemly thing
> Must be to say farewell to roistering,
> And say farewell, since I am wed to truth,
> To all the fond companions of my youth.'"

I looked at Purkis, hoping for some answering look of reassurance, even just a twitch of the lip or a slight widening of the eyes. He looked away.

This was a bad sign. I didn't care what Joyce thought of me: he was a hateful old fraud, and his good opinion wasn't worth a fart in a bucket. Purkis was a different matter. He had opened doors for me, and I had assumed that he would go on doing so, at least until we had both left Bune. Now a further door blocked my path, as yet some way off, but drawing closer with each succeeding day: the door into the world beyond Bune. I pictured it in my mind: massive, made of blackened oak, with rusty hinges and an iron lock. This was, I suspected, a door that Purkis would walk through and I would not.

2

Union became for me something of an obsession. The more I delved into it, the more impenetrable it became. The whole point of Instruction, as taught by Counsellor Joyce, was that it depended on rote learning: getting certain responses off by heart, rather than forging any sort of understanding. If anything, his lessons seemed to be designed to stop you asking awkward questions – to throw you off the scent. The MHH leaflets he handed out were just as bad. They too rambled on in very general terms about the contribution Union made to society and universal well-being; at no point did they tell you exactly what you actually had to do in order to – in the words of the Union oath – 'facilitate the survival of the Anglian nation-state'. And oddly enough, none of the boys who had gone through the rite of Union were prepared to make it any clearer for you.

As a rule it was impossible in Bune to have any secrets: the moment after you confided in anyone, your confidence would become common property. But Union was different. Those who had been through it acted as if they had been allowed to join some sort of sort of secret society. Talking about the experience to anyone outside of the circle was strictly forbidden; and because those who had done it were all by definition seniors, and mostly Praetors at that, they had the power to make it stick.

To me the whole thing had the flavour of Malcaster. I relayed this thought to Purkis, expecting him to be delighted, but if anything the suggestion annoyed him.

"It's precisely *not* Malcaster," he insisted. "It's far too obvious for that. It's Rattle's version of Malcaster, not Wisley's. A trumped-up mystery with a ready-made explanation."

"What explanation?"

He shook his head impatiently. "Oh, patriotic duty, that kind of thing. It's all hot air."

"It's more like a smokescreen," I said. "What I want to know is what's behind it."

"Absolutely nothing. Look, Riddle: just do what Joyce asks, can't you? We have to make an oath of loyalty to the Anglian nation-state, and promise to dedicate our bodies to the NAC if they ever need them. That's basically all there is to it. It's like the bloody stupid initiation rituals of the stupid bloody Woodland Patrol. All you have to do is learn the words parrot-fashion, and turn up when asked, and everyone's happy."

This sounded plausible enough – it was very much the way Bune tended to function in other areas – but I wasn't convinced.

"It made Boxer horribly pi," I said. Boxer was a former lover of mine – the original of Fletcher, the 'Innocent Boy' in the Malcaster story of the same title. Despite being two years older than me, he'd been amazingly ignorant of anything to do with sex. It had taken me two weeks of assignations in Grape Alley to get him to under-stand what it was I wanted him to do, though once he did cotton on he couldn't let it alone. Unfortunately his far too public devotion became quite wearing after a while, as did his insane jealousy – if I so much as looked at another boy he'd go berserk, even threatening to kill himself on one occasion. Then suddenly he achieved Union, and dropped me flat. I didn't care, in fact I was quite relieved, but I was curious to find out why it had had that effect.

"Boxer was always pi," said Purkis. "He's too fucking dreary to live, that boy. He can't have been much fun in bed."

"Actually he wasn't that bad, once he got the hang of it. But the minute he achieved Union everything changed. He became another person altogether."

"It didn't have that effect on Nevis, did it? He just carried on with his old habits, only more blatantly than ever. No one was safe.

And Porter and his gang let him get away with it. The fucker even got elected to *Crow*! Is that jammy or what?"

3

I resolved to be awkward: to call Joyce's bluff. This was foolhardy, but I refused to think of what repercussions there might be.

The fatal lesson proceeded much as before, with Joyce inviting first Purkis and then Crabb to chant the Five Responses in the approved sing-song manner. Each of them was by this time pretty well word perfect. That Crabb should have contrived to master this rubbish was understandable; that Purkis had done so too struck me as a betrayal of our friendship.

Thinking back on it, it was no coincidence that Joyce had left me to the last. It was as if he had sensed that I was about to mount a challenge, not just to him personally, but the very structure of authority.

"Well, Riddle, enlighten us," said Joyce, leaning back in his chair and folding his arms. He studied me with a sadistic smile, as if about to witness a public flogging. "What is the first duty of the Citizen?"

"I don't know," I said.

"What don't you know?"

"This 'contribution' we're expected to make, for a start. I don't know what it is."

He sighed. "We've been into this. There is no 'one thing' that Citizens are asked to contribute. It varies from individual to individual."

"So what am *I* meant to give?" A current of undeclared anger was flowing beneath my words: the sense that I was being treated differently from other boys, for reasons that had less to do with me than with the circumstances of my parentage.

Joyce regarded me with disdain. "You haven't been invited to contribute anything, Riddle. Perhaps you never will be."

"Why not?" I demanded.

"Because –" He stopped himself. I wondered what he had been going to say.

"You'd better wait behind when the others have gone," he said heavily.

4

Joyce kept me waiting for several minutes while he made notes in one of his books. At last he looked up.

"Riddle: why do you think I kept you behind?"

I shrugged. "Extra instruction?"

"What would be the point of that?"

"Sorry?"

"You never pay attention to Instruction. Why prolong the agony?"

"I don't know."

"You are absolutely hopeless. The laziest, most inattentive boy it has been my misfortune to have to teach."

"I'm sorry."

"Sorry, sorry – that's all I hear from you. Tell me, Riddle, where do you see yourself in three or four years' time. What do you think you'll be fit to do?"

"I don't know. I was thinking I might have a go at getting into Cantleford."

"Cantleford? You mean the *University*?"

"Yes."

"The closest you're going to get to Cantleford University, Riddle, is the Cantleford Packing Factory! What are you doing?"

I looked down in alarm. Without realising it, I was doodling in my rough-book again. As before I had drawn an erect penis, only this time the penis had a low brow and black eyebrows, and was wearing a mortar-board.

Joyce took the book from me, and stared at the portrait. He paged through the rest of the book, scowling. Luckily I had torn out the drawing of him, but the remaining pages were crowded with grotesque caricatures of boys and masters, surrounded by thickets of interlaced vines and straggling foliage. He turned back to the penis in the mortar-board

"What is this meant to be?"

Fortunately I had not got around to adding public hair or testicles, and the presence of the mortar-board made the penis a bit less obvious.

"It's a doodle."

He squinted at the image, his forehead dividing above the nose-bridge into two vertical creases. "Is this meant to be Dr Porter?"

"Not specifically, no."

"Then why is it wearing a mortar-board?"

"It's meant to be a schoolmaster. Not anyone in particular. Generic."

"Generic." He tasted the word: chewed on it for some seconds, pulling a sour face. Clearly the flavour was not to his liking. "Why is the neck so long?"

I fumbled for a credible explanation. "Well, you know the expression 'sausage neck'?"

"No. What does it mean?"

"Kind of like: craning over people's heads. At the scene of an accident. So you can see what's going on."

"Being nosey, in fact."

"Maybe. More like: inquisitive."

"And this sausage-necked person in the mortar board: is he by any chance overly *inquisitive* about matters private to you?"

"Not *overly.*"

There was a malicious gleam in his eye. "I shall confiscate this book. I will show it to Dr Porter. No doubt he will discuss it with you himself."

"Oh. Yes. All right."

"That's it. You can go."

5

I spent the rest of the afternoon in a state of extreme anxiety – bracing myself for what was bound to be an unpleasant experience. When the day ended and it had still not come, my anxiety did not disperse. Why the delay? Could it be that Porter and Joyce between them were marshalling evidence against me; that instead of a rap across the knuckles I was going to face a full-scale inquisition, possibly with expulsion at the end of it? I envisaged having to face my father: having to explain yet another failure to come up to scratch. That would be the worst thing – apart from having to leave Bune, of course. I couldn't bear to think of it, and yet I did, constantly.

Back in our study, I confessed my anxieties to Purkis, but he was unsympathetic. "Let's face it, Riddle," he said, "you've been pushing your luck with Joyce for a good two weeks, and now you're having to pay the price. All you had to do was shut up and learn your responses. Instead you keep asking the sort of questions that no one wants to answer. I never thought I'd say this, but you're just like your pa – you don't know where to draw the line. Some areas are off limits, don't you see? You don't tread there, and you don't ask why you can't. Learn that and you'll be fine. Disregard it, and you'll be out on your ear."

This was a Purkis I had never encountered before. A disturbing thought flew up out of nowhere. Purkis knew something I didn't, and was pretending otherwise.

"What are you hiding?" I asked him.

"Hiding?" he said with unusual violence. "Don't be bloody ridiculous, man. Just shut up about it, right? You're in enough trouble as it is."

6

My summons finally came two weeks later, just as I was beginning to think that Porter and Joyce might have forgotten about me. I knew of course that they hadn't – people like them don't just let things drop – but I had allowed myself to be lulled into a false sense of security, like a condemned man whose execution date keeps getting put further and further into the future, as one appeal after another comes to nothing.

The tick arrived to escort me to Porter's office in the early evening. Purkis was out, for once – he had started cultivating a third-year called Rawnsley, and they had gone into Ensor for a drink. They had invited me to join them, but had been wise enough not to accept, pleading pressure of work. The pre-Union tests were coming up in ten days. I had to brush up on my Union responses, I explained, which seemed to satisfy Rawnsley, if not Purkis.

In fact I really did need to do some work in that area. It had been stupid of me to let things slide the way I had. Joyce already had it in for me. What if my test results were so bad that he refused to let me participate in Union? That would be a disaster. Without Union I could never become a Praetor, and I could never, never expect to be elected to Crow. I had been an idiot, I told myself. If they wanted me to learn something, I should have done so. Why had I been so stubborn?

A tick knocked at the study door. Sighing, I put aside my notes, and followed.

The tick led me to the door of Porter's study. I knocked.

After a second or two the door was opened by Purkis's father.

"William," he said, putting his hand on my shoulder. "Come in. We were expecting you."

I had always thought of Sir Roger as a friendly figure, so to find him here, in the lair of my enemy, was a nasty shock. Seriously confused, I let Sir Roger take me by the arm and guide me into the office.

Porter sat at his desk, his face a sallow mask of disapproval. Two chairs were placed side by side, facing him. One was an armchair upholstered in plum velvet; the other was the Interrogation Seat I had occupied previously.

Sir Roger settled into the armchair; I took the interrogation seat.

"I expect you're wondering why I'm here," said Sir Roger.

"Something to do with Paul, is it?" When in conversation with a friend's father we maintained the fiction that we identified one another by our first names.

"That's right." He hesitated. "It's something of a delicate matter."

"Has he done something wrong?"

"Not *wrong* exactly. But definitely, ah, *concerning*. –Headmaster, perhaps you should explain."

"What particularly worries us," said Porter, watching me very carefully from across the polished plain of his desk, "is this *writing* he's been doing."

"Writing?" I felt a jolt of alarm. "What sort of writing?"

"A short story," said Porter. "He left a briefcase in Mr Spelman's classroom. Mr Spelman opened it to ascertain the identity of its owner. He found the story and brought it to me. It's in Paul's handwriting."

My whole system was in a state of panic. I felt myself going hot and cold, both at the same time; my head reeled, my fingers and toes tingled with shock.

Amazingly, I remained outwardly calm. "What is it about?"

"Silly nonsense. Some sort of imaginary world, peopled by monsters and lunatics."

"How weird."

"There is a scatological element," said Porter, wincing. "Certain ah, *activities* are described in graphic detail."

"Oh. I see."

"We thought you might be able to shed some light."

I pulled a face. "He does write a bit, I know. Short stories, a bit of poetry. I don't remember any, um, *scatological* element."

"So it has nothing to do with you?"

"No."

"The title page suggests it is one of a collection of similar compositions, by two separate authors. It occurred to us that you might be one of them."

"Is mine one of the two names?" I asked, knowing it wasn't.

"They are clearly pseudonyms."

"Well, then…" I said, shrugging.

"I'll read some excerpts," said Porter. "That may jog your memory."

The excerpts he read were from a story entitled 'Alien Invasion', an account of one night in the life of Dr Horatio Floater, as told by the doctor himself. After an evening spent guzzling cheese and red wine from his personal vineyard, and gossiping maliciously about his pupils, Floater lapses into a drunken coma and has to be put to bed by two of his minions. Barely conscious, he hears them exchange derogatory estimations of his character and personal habits. He falls into a deep sleep, and has an extraordinarily vivid dream in which he is transported by aliens to a space-station orbiting around the earth, and subjected to an intrusive and very thorough physical examination. As the dream reaches its climax he wakes to find his sheets soaking wet, and his bedclothes stained with vomit.

"Well?" asked Porter.

His tone was icy. I shrugged, wondering if he had recognised Floater as a portrait of himself. To me the resemblance seemed unmistakeable, but schoolmasters are well-trained in the avoidance of inconvenient facts.

"Nothing to say?"

It seemed advisable to make a limited admission. "I think Paul may have read me something along those lines."

"And I suppose you both thought it was funny?"

Composing the passage in question some months ago, Purkis and I had screamed with laughter; now it seemed childish and spiteful.

"Not really," I said.

"Look, William, you know him better than anyone," said Sir Roger.

"Yes."

"What's at the bottom of this, do you think?"

I thought about this. "I think it's just nerves, really," I said. "I mean, he is pretty strung out about Union, you know."

"Union? Why on earth should that be giving him any problems?"

"Well, you know how it is. Not knowing whether one will, you know, shape up to expectations. I think that may be why he writes these things – to help with the...." I paused, and looked down at my hands.

"Carry on, Riddle," said Porter grimly.

"The thing is, Paul tends to take things rather to heart. He always has, for as long as I've known him, but lately it's got a lot worse. For example, he's got this idea that Union may have something to do with harvesting organs. Liver and kidneys and so on. For, I don't know: *medical experiments* or something."

The two men exchanged glances.

"Riddle," began Porter warningly.

"Of course I told him that was nonsense. I said to him: ask Counsellor Joyce. He'll put your mind at rest. But he wouldn't. So I had to promise to ask him myself."

"Ask him what?"

"Exactly what was involved. Which I did, two days ago."

"And what did Counsellor Joyce say?" asked Sir Roger.

"He wouldn't say anything, that's the trouble. Just kind of: clammed up. Than when I pressed him, he flew off the handle. Which made Paul all the more certain that his suspicions were right."

There was a long silence.

"I see," said Sir Roger. "Thank you, William. Where is Paul now?"

He's in Ensor. With a friend."

"I know his haunts," said Sir Roger. "I shall seek him out."

"You'll drop by later, Sir Roger?" asked Porter.

"Of course. I'll bring Paul."

"Good idea. We'll tackle him together."

Sir Roger said his goodbyes. I rose to leave with him.

"Stay behind, Riddle, if you please," said Porter.

I slumped back into the Interrogation seat.

Porter waited until Sir Roger had left the room, then he reached into a drawer of his desk and brought out my rough-book. He slid it across the table, open at the portrait of himself.

"Do you recognise this, Riddle?" His voice was silky with fury.

"The book? Or the drawing?"

He sighed. "The book. It's yours, is it not?"

"Yes."

"Is this meant to be me?" He reached across the desk, and indicated the penis in the mortar board.

Frowning, I examined the drawing. "I don't think so, no. It's just a schoolmaster. No one in particular."

"So you told Counsellor Joyce, when he tackled you on the subject. I believe you offered a specific phrase by way of mitigation."

"You mean, that it was just *generic*?"

Porter nodded. "Generic, yes. Would you care to elaborate?"

I gestured vaguely. "You know: not anyone in particular. A kind of comment on schoolmasters in general. Just, you know, school-boy humour."

Porter sat back. "You are sailing very close to the wind, Riddle."

I waited.

"Let me tell you this. If you think this display of obfuscation carries even one shred of conviction you are greatly mistaken."

"I don't—"

He raised his hand, silencing me. "Sir Roger is a man of consid-erable standing, both in the community at large and the national government. As you know, he is a governor of this school; any-thing he says carries a great deal of clout. I have given him my opinion of you, which concurs with that of Counsellor Joyce. We believe you to be a bad influence."

Here it comes, I thought.

"This *story* of Purkis's ... It may be written in his hand, but I have no doubt that the true author is sitting in front of me now. The turn of phrase, the contempt for authority, the personal spite, the unbridled vulgarity: the whole despicable performance bears your signature, and no one else's. This obscene caricature" – he gestured disgustedly at my rough book – "is further con-firmation of your guilt. That alone would be grounds for your expulsion."

My scalp tinged; Porter seemed to have receded to a great dis-tance. I waited for the blow to fall.

"Nonetheless–"

I waited.

"Sir Roger is of a different opinion. He thinks that Paul must shoulder some of the blame. He is worried about Paul's reaction if you are punished and not him. He has asked me to give you one last chance."

I nodded dumbly.

"One *last* chance, Riddle – do you understand? You will not get another. I shall be waiting to see if you put a foot wrong. If you do, I will know about it."

An involuntary grin tweaked at the corners of my mouth; I had to fight to suppress it.

"You are currently receiving Instruction." said Porter. "The question arises as to whether you should be permitted to join in the act of Union. I am inclined at present to say that the opportunity should not be offered to you. As an interim measure, I have asked Counsellor Joyce to suspend your course of Instruction. I will make my final decision later this term. In the meantime..."

My mouth twitched; I was on the verge of sniggering. I hung my head, not daring to look at him.

"Don't imagine for a moment that you have got away with this. I know what you are, I know the kind of influence you wield on the more impressionable of your companions, on boys that deserve to be shielded from the damage you cause to everyone around you. It would be useless to ask you to change your ways. You are your ways, your ways are you. Sooner or later you will slip up; and when that happens I will expel you in a flash. Is that understood?"

"Yes, sir. Thank you, sir."

He shot me a look of undisguised hatred, and gestured for me to leave.

7

As I left the Old House I saw Purkis and his father crossing the quadrangle, on their way to Porter's office. Purkis was in smarts, rounded off by a new purple flash – no one wears a topper when they go for a drink. He had his hands in his pockets, and was wearing a defiant expression. His father walked alongside him, glancing occasionally in his direction.

It was a good hour before Purkis returned to our study. He was fuming.

"What have you been saying about me?"

"Didn't your pa tell you?"

"I want to hear it from you, Riddle."

"Does it really matter? You were stupid enough to leave the story in Spelman's classroom. It was in your handwriting. They wanted to hear something that would let you off the hook, and I gave it to them."

"By telling them I was mad?"

"Come off it, Purkis. What was I supposed to say? That I helped you write it?"

"Don't be so fucking patronising," he said crossly. "It was all my own work."

I was starting to feel angry. "I don't see the problem. You've got away with it. You're not going to be sacked, are you?"

He was silent for a minute or two. Then he began to giggle.

"What?" I asked, beginning to grin myself.

"I wonder what Floater thought when he read it."

"I know exactly was he thought. He was livid."

"That's me fucked, then," he said, sobering up. "Never make Crow now – not in a million years."

"That's not true. And you know it."

"Oh, really? Why is that?"

"You know why."

I had a good idea by now of how the system worked. The last person who would be blamed for 'Alien Invasion' was Paul Purkis. Mentally I began sketching the outline of a new Malcaster story, based upon the day's events. I already knew its title. It would be called 'The Scapegoat'.

8

Purkis soon got over his little fit of pique. He told me that Porter had made his father read 'Alien Invasion' in his office (he refused to let the manuscript out of his sight in case it fell into the wrong hands). Sir Roger had been hard-pressed not to laugh out loud.

"Porter asked him what he thought of the story. He didn't know what to say. He wasn't going to pretend to be outraged, much as Porter wanted him to be, but equally he couldn't make a joke of it, or he and Porter would have ended up enemies for life. In the end he settled for being sorrowful – 'Poor Paul, what on earth could have possessed him?' – that kind of thing. Of course Porter just took that as his cue for laying into you – blamed you for everything, said you'd been leading me astray, filling my head with all the wrong ideas, all the usual guff ... He was more or less inviting pa to ask him to expel you. But pa wouldn't play ball. He saw right through it. Then when Porter showed him your rough-book, that was the last straw. Tears came into his eyes from holding back the laughter – he had to fake a coughing fit."

"He wasn't cross, then?"

"I wouldn't say that. He got onto me a bit. He didn't like it that he'd been dragged into the business. He didn't care about the story, of course – he thought it was hilarious – just that I'd been stupid enough to lose it." He hesitated. "He did say one other thing, though."

"What was that?"

"It was about Union. How important it was. He said you really had to start taking it seriously."

"*Me*? What about *you*?"

"I take it seriously already." There was a shaky tone in his voice, as if he was defying me to contradict him. "I always have."

9

Things went back to normal. Malcaster still remained a main topic of conversation between us, but some of the fun had gone out of it. Malcaster had been a private universe, designed to be explored by us alone. Now its walls had been breached, exposing the Malcontents and their doings to the withering air of reality.

As an antidote to this, I proposed that the two of us collaborate on a story that would be the summation of all we knew about Malcaster: a wholesale purgation of all its secrets, a resounding demolition of all the myths it disseminated about itself. The story, naturally enough, was to be called 'Union.'

"I thought we'd discussed this," said Purkis. "Leave Union alone."

"Why?"

"Riddle, Union is only a few weeks away. I can't afford to mess this up. Neither can you. Union is off-limits. Keep it that way, for my sake if not your own. Please."

I was silent. Porter had still not pronounced on whether I was to be allowed to take part in the culminating ceremony. The longer I was kept in suspense, the more certain I became that the judgement had gone against me. Purkis would be allowed to make Union, and be made a Praetor. I would not. We would drift apart. I would end up friendless and despised: the outsider I had been when I first arrived. It all seemed terribly unfair.

There was no point in my appealing to Porter. He obviously hated me too much to listen to any argument in my favour. That left only Joyce. However much I despised the man, I was going to have to swallow my pride and go to him and apologise.

I waited until his Instruction class was out, then tapped on the door of the classroom.

"Enter!" he sang out. I opened the door. On seeing me, his bristly eyebrows shot to the top of his head.

"What do you want, Riddle?" he asked grimly.

"I've come to apologise," I said.

"What for?"

"Everything My general attitude. The rude drawing. Not paying attention in your class. Not taking Union seriously."

"And what has brought this on?"

"Purkis gave me a good talking to. He pointed out the error of my ways."

"Don't fob me off with clichés, Riddle. In what sense were you in error? Because you were stupid enough to get caught and punished? Or because you did something wrong?"

"Both, really. The thing is, Union is a privilege; I should have been grateful that the school was offering it to me. I realise that now." My voice grew tremulous with emotion, none the less powerful for being feigned. "The school gave me a chance. And I threw it away."

Joyce regarded me for a few seconds, his eyes sharp under his bushy brows, his mouth turned wryly down. He shook his head. "I have been teaching a long time, Riddle: quite long enough to have witnessed every variety of misconduct of which a boy is capable. Over the course of a long career, I have become acquainted with every conceivable manifestation of human vice and human deceit. I've seen boys who lie so convincingly that their testimony alone, without evidence, would suffice to send a man to the gallows. And I've seen boys who can get away with nothing; boys whose every word comes over as a bare-faced lie. Those in the first category invariably go far in life. Those in the second go nowhere. I need hardly tell you in which category you belong."

"I'm sorry," I said. My voice trembled; I was ready to burst into tears. "Isn't there anything I can say to…"

"Nothing," he said. "A determination in your case has already been made. You will be resuming Instruction next Monday."

I struggled to make sense of this. "So I'll be allowed to make Union?"

"For whatever good it may do you, yes."

"Thank you, sir," I said with an ingratiating dip of the head.

Underneath the show of humility I was exultant. Yes, I had had to eat humble pie, but doing that is only humiliating when it fails to produce the desired result.

"Don't thank me," said Joyce curtly. "If it were up to me you would have been on your way home two weeks ago. But I am an optimist. I think that people by and large get what they deserve. In your case the Day of Judgement has been postponed. But I wouldn't get too comfortable, if I were you. It's not going to last."

10

"Good-oh," said Purkis, when I told him the news. "Perhaps now you'll start toeing the line, like everyone else. It's about time. You can't go on fighting the system for ever."

NINE
Union

Union is in essence an affirmation of the individual's oneness with the nation state to which he belongs. It is a declaration of faith in the values which define us.

'The Meaning of Union' a talk given by Counsellor Peter Joyce to the boys of Bune School on the morning of Sunday May 3rd, 483.

For young men everywhere the first experience of Union *marks the beginning of* maturity, *and with maturity comes* responsibility. *The time has come for you to put away your toys, and take your first steps as a man.*

'Union and You', Anglian Ministry of Health and Hygiene
Leaflets (Ludden, 474)

1

Pagan Half, May 6th, 483

Union was set to take place in a month's time over an entire weekend. A team of medical personnel specialising in Union procedures would be in attendance. The Saturday was reserved for physical examination. On Sunday morning we would be interviewed by an agent of the NAC. Union itself – for those of us who proved eligible – would take place in the early afternoon, and in the evening there would be a party.

Before any of this could happen we had to acquire a Unionist's uniform. Mr Jackman, the elderly tailor from R Sampson & Co, the Bune Outfitters, took our measurements in the school library, wheezing, and clutching painfully at his back whenever he had to bend low. "These Union pants have to fit like a glove," he said, running his tape down my inner leg. "A fraction of an inch, and you'll be in agony all day." He stood back to get a better look. "You cut a very fine figure, young man, if I may say so. Broad shoulders, narrow hips, upright carriage … It's a pleasure to cater for such a physique. I was in the theatrical business for years, you know, making costumes for the Conduit Players. You would make a perfect Tarquin, in my opinion. Just the right nobility of expression and bearing." He bent my arm and measured the distance from elbow to wrist. "Not like the Equestrian boys here at Bune: a crooked, shifty, round-backed lot, most of them: all blowed-up with grub and beer, and stinking of smoke and fried onions, which you can't help noticing when you have to take intimate measurements as I do." He measured my chest as he said this, getting me to take a deep breath so that he could determine my maximum girth. "You're a friend of young Mr Nevis, I believe: he's gone on to study Business Ethics at the New University of Cantleford, you know. I remember the two of you coming into my shop some years back, for a complete kitting out. Now there's another fine young gentleman: a little on the brawny side, perhaps, but that would stem from his many sporting activities, I imagine. Do you ever much of see Mr Nevis these days?"

"Unfortunately not. And I live in Cantleford – at least my father does."

"Well, never mind." He stooped, groaning, to measure my calves. "You may have the good fortune to bump into him again, you never know. Right. That's me done. I have your pa's address, haven't I? We have to ask for payment in advance these days, what with the woeful condition of the national finances. Thank you, sir, thank you," he added, as I slipped him a shilling for his pains. "It's been a real pleasure. – Next boy please!"

2

The great event drew ever closer. My Union outfit arrived, fitting as Mr Jackman had promised, like a glove. A little too snug, perhaps; the trousers were as revealing as ballet tights. Purkis tried on his outfit at the same time, then we pranced about the study in dandified fashion, making all the appropriate gestures and noises.

"This is ludicrous," said Purkis, dropping into a chair, and loosening the fastening of his trousers, which were even tighter, if possible, than mine. "I hate dressing up. It makes me feel a fool."

"You look very splendid, Purkis."

"Don't say that; you know it isn't true. What a ridiculous outfit this is! White pants, white waistcoat, white tunic … Anyone would think we were getting married!"

3

The day of the examination dawned at last. Purkis and I went down to the Medical Centre, and waited in the lobby for our name to be called. We had woken early that morning, to make sure of getting a hot shower (the hot water at Bune tended to run out around seven-thirty, and even earlier on the first of the two Union days) so we were both very fragrant and well-scrubbed. Purkis had blow-dried his hair into a white fluffy cloud, through which you could glimpse rather too much of his raw pink scalp. He would be bald within a decade, I surmised, and he would hate it.

We both had brought small glass bottles containing samples of our urine, which we had obtained, as instructed, immediately after getting out of bed. Purkis insisted upon comparing colours. His was much paler than mine.

"Have you taken a sniff?" he asked. "Yours is pretty rank, I bet."

"Fuck off."

He leaned over, and pressed his nostrils against my neck. "Secret of the Desert," he said appreciatively, that being the name of a fragrance habitually applied by Dr Floater before the weekly midnight congress. Prepared from a formula of his own devising, it comprised a mixture of crushed wormwood, skullcap, rose-petals, ginger, ear-wax and pure alcohol.

4

A nurse – a strapping fair-haired fellow in a green apron—called my name, and showed me to an examination cubicle, where he asked me to undress and don the cotton gown hanging behind the door. I did so. After several minutes the man came back accompanied by a sepulchral individual in a white coat with a stethoscope round his neck, who introduced himself as Dr Clapper. Procedures were followed according to a rigid protocol. First the nurse weighed me. After that Clapper listened to my chest, then took a pencil-sized torch and carefully examined first my penis and then my various orifices, including the most personal. He cupped my testicles and asked me to cough. I sat on the edge of the bed while he hit first one knee and then the other with a small rubber hammer. The nurse took my blood pressure and temperature and pulse, noting the results on a form attached to a clipboard. Hardly a word was spoken throughout.

Lastly Clapper drew several ampoules of blood from a vein in my arm. He asked for the urine sample. I produced it with a flourish, and held it out for him to take.

"Place it in the kidney dish," he said, indicating a steel bowl. "That's all. You can get dressed now."

"Did I pass?"

"Pass?"

"Isn't it a test?"

"Don't be facetious," he said.

This was my first intimation that the practice of Union might turn out to be more undignified than we had been led to expect.

We returned to our study with a sense of anti-climax.

"I feel a bit low," said Purkis, dropping onto his bed. "This bloody Union business is getting on my nerves." The melancholic side of his nature, never far from the surface, had been much to the fore over the last few weeks.

"What else did you expect?"

"I don't know," he admitted. "An end to discontent, perhaps. A feeling that life might at long last be starting to deliver."

"Deliver what, exactly?"

"I don't know, Riddle," he said forlornly. "I just want to *belong* for once."

5

There were four agents, and forty candidates. As it happened my name was called early, within the first half-hour. My interview was held in the Deputy Head's office. I tapped on the door and was instructed to enter.

The man behind the Deputy Head's desk was young and neatly groomed, with pale blue eyes and a chiselled face – he looked a bit like an actor. He wore a grey suit and a grey shirt and a blue tie. None of this was at all remarkable, but he had an unusual presence. He was the sort of person you would think twice before insulting.

"Riddle?" he asked, rising and holding out his hand.

"Yes."

"Francis Weston."

"Hello."

"Take a chair, Riddle."

I did so. He sat behind the desk, and took up a clipboard. He looked from me to the clipboard and back again, as if checking my attributes against an inventory. The effect of this intense scrutiny was rather like having an ant crawl over your bare chest when your arms were pinned to your sides. To add to my discomfort, the pants of my white outfit were straining at my crotch. I wriggled, fighting off the urge to dive a hand down the front and adjust the position of my testicles.

"William Oliver Riddle," he read from his list. "Born November 9th, 465. Son of Professor George Riddle, inventor of the Riddle Suction Cleaner. Educated Glenlockie Middle School, Gillie Vocational Middle School, Cantleford Tutorial College, Bune College. Majoring in Art, Anglian Literature, and History. Something of a clown."

I felt alarmed. Was this some kind of test, to see if I could keep my temper? Or had Porter primed him to destroy my self-confidence, to make sure that I was rejected as a candidate?

"Is that what it says?" I asked.

"Broadly speaking, yes. Are you disputing the judgement?"

"There's no point."

"It's always possible to register a protest. Do you want to do that?"

"No."

"As you wish." He lightly drummed his fingers on the desk, then leaned forward. "It's my job to evaluate you as a candidate for Union. What do you know about Union, Mr Riddle?"

I started to come out with the responses I had learned from Counsellor Joyce, but he held up a finger to stop me.

"Forget all that," he said. "What do you really know?"

"For certain? Nothing."

"Why is that, do you think?"

I shrugged. "Because no one will talk about it."

"Correct. No one will talk about it. That's because Union is a private matter, Mr Riddle. It is a confidential matter between you and the state. You don't discuss it with anyone who hasn't taken it, and you don't discuss it with anyone who has."

"All right."

He cocked his head on one side, with a twist to his mouth and a curious glint in his eye. "Well? What do you think?"

"Sorry?"

"You agree with that? Once you have taken Union you will never speak about it to a living soul?"

"I suppose so."

"You suppose so. In other words, you well might, if you thought you could get away with it."

"That's not what I meant," I said defensively.

"Really? What's to stop you discussing it? The fact that I tell you not to?"

"My word of honour," I said firmly.

"And what would that be worth?"

I shrugged. "That's not for me to say."

He tweaked his nose, watching me keenly. Then he placed his clipboard on the desk, swivelled it towards me, then swivelled it back again. "How do you like it here, Mr Riddle – at Bune College?"

"A lot."

He nodded. "Bit of a change for you, I imagine, when you came here from the wilds of Alba? Back then you were nobody. Here, suddenly people were interested in you, admired you, gave you their time. Like your tick-master, Mr Nevis."

The name affected me like a blow. "That's right," I agreed. "I was his tick in my first year."

"Tell me about that. How did Mr Nevis treat you?"

I shrugged.

"Nothing to say on the topic?"

"Not really."

"You don't sound too enthusiastic. Did Mr Nevis punish you, by any chance?"

"Once or twice."

"For what reason?"

"My cooking, mostly. And cleaning."

"And you thought that unfair?"

I shrugged again.

"You don't think you deserved punishment?"

"Perhaps I did. It's just that––"

"Yes, Mr Riddle?"

"Well, he caned me. Every evening."

"Because you didn't improve?"

"Because he *wanted* to."

"I see. You think he had it in for you?"

"Yes."

He picked up the clipboard, turned over a page, then looked back at me. "And yet it says here that Mr Nevis did his very best to help you settle in. Helped you with your pronunciation, for example; helped you to get fit; bought you some luggage, and some clothes – is that right?"

"I actually had to pay for those. Or rather, my father did."

"Which is fair enough, surely? You didn't expect Mr Nevis to buy you things simply out of the goodness of his heart, did you?"

"I didn't expect anything."

"You didn't offer him anything in return?"

I blinked. "No."

He looked back at the file. "Sexual favours, for instance?"

"No."

"What about oral relief? Did anything like that take place?"

I went fiery red "What did he say?" I asked wildly.

"He said it did take place. Rather frequently. Well? Did it or didn't it?"

"All right, yes. But it wasn't my idea."

"Really?" He consulted the file. "You didn't tell him, for example: 'It's OK Nevis, I won't tell anybody. I like doing this.'"

"No. That's not how it was."

"How was it, then, Mr Riddle?"

"He abused me. First he flogged me, then he made me do things to him. It was horrible."

"So what you're saying is, *Mr Nevis* initiated these acts? Not you?"

"Yes."

"Mr Nevis says differently."

"Then he's a liar."

"Is he? I have his sworn deposition here," – he tapped the file in front of him – "saying that you threw yourself at him, and he was too weak-willed to resist. The way he tells it, you were practised in sexual acts he had never heard of, learned from the urchins you consorted with in Glenlockie. Far from *him* abusing *you*, he says that *you* abused *him*. What do you say to that?"

"It's not true."

"So you keep saying. Tell me, Mr Riddle, did you ever report this alleged abuse to anyone? A friend, perhaps, or one of the masters?"

"No."

"Why not? If it was as bad as you say?"

"No one would have believed me."

"That's right. They wouldn't have believed you, and the reason for that is that it wouldn't have been true."

This went on and on: probably just for another five minutes, but it felt like a lifetime. When he finally stopped, tears were streaming down my cheeks.

"All right, Mr Riddle, that'll do. You're thoroughly ashamed of yourself, I can see."

I couldn't deny it. What I had done would be broadcast to the world – to Purkis, to my father, the whole school. I would have to leave Bune. I would have to go somewhere where no one knew me, and bury my shame, and work at a horrible job, and hide away from the world for ever.

He placed the clipboard face down on the desk. "Anything you want to ask me?"

"What's going to happen now?"

"What do you want to happen?"

"Nothing. I don't want anyone to know."

He leaned back, smiling. "Well, Mr Riddle, there's no reason they *should* know."

I stared.

"The fact is, whether we like it or not, everyone's got something they'd rather keep dark. With some it's this, and with others that, but generally speaking sex is at the bottom of it. It's human nature, I'm afraid. It's the way we're made. That doesn't disqualify you from Union. In a way, it makes your candidacy all the more credible. It means that there is something you're ashamed of. That's why people keep quiet about Union, Mr Riddle. Nothing to do with serving the Anglian nation-state or the NAC, nothing to do with taking an oath of silence. People keep quiet because they're afraid of *being found out.*"

He turned a page, took out a document, wrote something in an empty box, and added his signature. He looked up. "All right, Mr Riddle," he said, "you are now eligible to receive Union."

6

I went out into the mid-morning sun, not sure whether I was angry or cowed or delirious with relief. My secret was known, but not to all the world. These people knew it, but they couldn't use it, because if they ever used it they could no longer hold it over me as a threat. So long as I didn't discuss Union with anyone – which I couldn't, I wouldn't dare – my secret was safe. And so was I.

I still didn't know what Union was, however. It must be something pretty bad, I reasoned; otherwise they wouldn't go to such lengths to keep it secret. So what could it be?

7

Purkis had gone in to be interviewed. I went as instructed to the Medical Centre. My heart was thumping against my ribs, as if trying to break out and flap off into the sun. Union was about to take place. I hoped that nothing violent would be involved, nothing to do with knives or blood or screaming, things I couldn't bear. I hoped that I would strong enough to deal with whatever was going to happen. I caught sight of myself in a mirror: my face wore an ashen petrified expression. There were other boys waiting in the foyer: they all looked the same as me.

Everyone's got something they're ashamed of...

I wondered what that something was in the case of these other boys. I wondered, but I did not really want to know. My own shame was quite enough.

8

I was shown into a small curtained cubicle. There was a narrow padded bed on a metal frame. Beside it on a steel table rested a plain white tray, on which were arranged a number of articles, and a glass of brown liquid. There was also a black box, like something from my father's workshop, with various dials and knobs and gauges.

As instructed I removed my Union tunic, put on a white gown, knotted it at the neck, and lay down on the bed.

The Union Practitioner swished aside the curtain: a tall white-coated man carrying a black briefcase. His eyes were dark and soulful, set into their sagging sockets like two black olives in a matching pair of canapés. Opening the case, he produced a soft helmet like a large bathing-cap, with two wires covered in white plastic sprouting from the sides. He plugged these into a black box beside the bed.

This was starting to feel like a routine from a bad horror film.

"I hope this isn't going to hurt," I said, with an attempt at humour.

"Let's not have any conversation, if you don't mind.'

"OK. You're the dentist."

He frowned. "Lean forward, please."

I leaned forward. With quick practised movements he pulled the helmet over my scalp and pushed two earplugs into my ears. Now I could no longer hear anything: only a kind of muffled roaring, the far-off sound of the sea. Turning to the tray, he selected the glass of liquid and held it out.

"What's this?"

He said something – his mouth opening and closing silently– and then mimed the act of drinking. Taking the glass, I took an experimental sip. It was strong and sour, a bit disgusting. He wagged a finger, then tipped an invisible drink straight down his throat. I followed suit. It was in fact easier to get it down that way: just as nasty, but safely down the hatch before you could start to gag.

He drew down the top of the helmet, blocking my vision. His hands smelled of lavender soap. They pressed my head back against the pillow. Iridescent patches of colour swarmed shimmering in front of my eyes. I sensed him bending over me – the musky scent of body-ointment – then there was a *click!* and my wrists were fasted to the two rails running down the sides. Another *click!* and my ankles were fastened. A strap went round my neck. He tightened it.

I was now helpless.

Music started up in the background: a hypnotic underwater throbbing without any discernible melody. Something odd was happening to my brain. My mind was bogged down in a kind of heavy treacle, but my senses, to compensate, had sprouted all over the place, like a great gaudy plant, or an octopus with a surplus of raw nerves instead of tentacles. As things progressed, everything started to focus around the central core of my body. My first thought was one of disappointment: *so this is what it all boils down to – that fucking idiot Nevis, violating me all over again*. But everything with Nevis came down to pain and humiliation and the exercise of force and friction. This *thing* I was now experiencing was the absolute opposite: a drawing of self out of self, as if I was being skilfully turned inside-out like a pair of tights. Things were happening to me simultaneously on several levels. I was being bathed in warm milk: I was beached and breathing on warm sand; I was being licked from top to toe; I was floating on a rough sea; I was swimming underwater naked in a tank of scarlet jelly; I was flying amazingly over threads of roads and fields like postage stamps and forest-clumps like heads of broccoli, upwards, towards the sun. Below all this, in a green glade, improbably beautiful dancers were performing acrobatic feats for my entertainment, coupling, tripling, quadrupling. I was consumed by a ravishing kaleidoscopic geometry of elastic globes and yielding folds and creases, constantly melting and reforming into fresh arrangements of succulent flesh and flowering hair.

The tension mounted unbearably.

There came a point where I could no longer hold back. White light blossomed, and a soundless explosion that went on and on and on; and for an unmeasurable passage of time I was incapable of thinking or perceiving anything at all.

9

"Feeling better now?' asked the Practitioner, standing over my bed.

I had been wheeled into another room. There were other beds alongside mine, all empty. "Is it over?" I asked dully. I was still coming to terms with what I had just experienced

"All done and dusted, yes. You're free to go."

"Go where?"

"To your party. Better get dressed first, though."

"Where are my things?"

"Behind the door."

Sitting up I discovered an uncomfortable feeling in my bottom. I just made it to the flusher in time. Quite a lot of stuff gushed out. Half-standing, I looked into the bowl. All I could see was a kind of colourless mass. When I wiped, a gobbet of translucent jelly fell out.

I fetched my things and put on my cotton underclothes and then squirmed into the tight white pants. Something crackled in a pocket. It was a note, folded as small as a postage stamp. I unfolded it.

The message was in Purkis's handwriting. *Was it good for you? – P.*

I folded the note up again, and buttoned it into the breast pocket of my waistcoat. Then I put on the white belt, and my soft leather boots, and my tunic, and last of all set the white cap on my head. A full-length mirror was fixed to the wall. Reflected in it was a grotesque figure, a mock military dandy with an ashen face. There were two spots of colour on his cheeks.

I swung up my hand in a salute.

10

The party was a boring affair with lots of back-slapping and mutual congratulations and larks. It was held in Tap, normally the preserve of the Fifth and Sixth years, but open on this occasion to those seniors who were making Union. Several types of beer were served, but they were all so weak that you had to drink enormous quantities of the stuff in order to feel in the least bit drunk. To keep up with the demand every table was crowded with huge glass jugs which were periodically topped up by a team of envious ticks, eyeing us in our white tunics as if we were gods. The flushers were in constant use; the corridor leading to them was jammed by a long queue of jiggling boys anxious to take their turn at the stalls. Music played, and a few couples danced. A few members of Crow lounged in a roped off corner of the bar, ignoring our proceedings with lofty disdain.

Later, as the weak beer began to take effect, the floor grew crowded with Unionists intent on showing off. Boys pranced and capered, deliberately bumping into the boys behind them, doing their best to send one another flying. Some idiot careered into a table loaded with drink, and the brimming jugs slid off and went crashing to the floor. A couple of ticks were despatched to find mops and brushes.

The acrobatics continued. Caps were thrown in the air. Someone stood on a table and attempted to sing, before being dragged down and sat on. Scuffles broke out.

By now most of our white uniforms were stained with beer: a matter of no real consequence, as none of us would ever have to wear them again.

Just as the party looked like turning into a riot, the Crow Leader, a boy named Tarbutt, intervened: first by ringing a bell, and then climbing on a table. Everyone went quiet. Flicking back an unruly lock of hair, he launched into a long boring speech about how his own Union was one of the fondest memories of his school career; how we would all go on to greater things, Praetorship, and even Crow, and then the great world outside, but would always look back at this as "the night the party began".

"Did you ever hear anything so bogus?" I asked Purkis, who was standing next to me, flushed and sweating, his uniformed soaked with beer, his up-combed haystack of white hair collapsed around his ears.

"Everything's bogus, Riddle," said Purkis, turning to follow the progress of some youth he was currently interested in. "Haven't I always told you that?"

11

There was only one more week to go, then it was the end of Pagan, and the long vac. As always, the prospect extended before me as a waterless desert, devoid of either Malcaster or Purkis. My depression at the thought of those three months of boredom was only alleviated by the news, received two days before we broke up, that Purkis and I were to become Praetors.

TEN

Afternoon Tea

"It's very odd," mused Wisley, pulling on his old briar for all he was worth.
Rattle looked up from his newspaper. "What's odd?"

"Fate," said Wisley. He ran his tongue around his thin lips, collecting
a few stranded morsels of breakfast past. "People think they're safe and
settled for life: nice little job, big house, plenty of cash in the bank, han-
ky-panky whenever they feel like it...while all the time there's something
lurking among the flower-beds: a great savage beast, waiting to leap out
and devour them."

"Mad," muttered Rattle, returning to his perusal of the racing statis-
tics. "Utterly mad."

'Good Riddance', from *The Infected Pistol and Other Stories* by H O
Minty and F R Trumper (Privately printed, 480).

1

At the beginning of our Fifth year Purkis and I, now Praetors, were
permitted to move into a room together, in the Old Stables. This
was a decidedly irregular arrangement: usually boys roomed with
others of the same group. Purkis of course was an Equestrian, and
if anything his affinities should have been with the Patricians, so
an exception had to be made. I think Sir Roger must have put in
a word; he had considerable influence with the school governors,
having at that time just been appointed Minister for Home Affairs.
The tacit assumption (it could never be spelled out; the school
maintained a policy of turning a blind eye to such matters, exactly
like every other educational institution I have ever attended) was
that Purkis and I were in a stable 'relationship', which it would not

be helpful to break up. This was both right and wrong. Our friendship was indeed a close one – we told one another everything – but for sex we went elsewhere. We never discussed the possibility of having sex together directly, but we both made it clear that our friendship was too valuable for us to put it at risk, particularly as we didn't fancy one another in the least.

The experience of acting as low-level members of the school's disciplinary squad proved in practice less entertaining than either of us had imagined. As Fifth-year Praetors we were forced to act as the dogsbodies of the system. The stuff we were given to do was relentlessly trivial: taking roll-calls for country runs, and making sure everyone made it back, grumbling at slackers and smokers and scruffs, lecturing trainee bullies, quietening riots in the dorms, policing the dress code and so on. This was tedious work that exposed you to a good deal of ridicule and won you no plaudits whatsoever: the upper echelons only took note of your efforts when something went wrong. The only punishments we were permitted to administer ourselves were lines and detention: if we wanted anyone flogged we had to get someone from Crow to do it. In fact all the really glamorous business was reserved for Crow. They frequently stood in for masters who had something better to do; they read out the morning lesson; they directed and acted in the school's annual performance of a Wagstaffe comedy. A low wall was reserved for them to sit on – it was called Crow Row – at the end of Bellarby's Piece. If any non-Crow so much as approached one of these precious perches they were driven off with kicks and blows. Crows were allowed to stroll about with furled umbrellas, which were commonly used as duelling-sticks. The younger boys treated them with reverence bordering on hero-worship. Compared to them we were nothing.

The sole benefit of our Praetorship was to be allocated a tick of our own. Worsley, the boy in question, was very small and slight, in spite of which he proved more than capable of the tasks we set for him. Despite his eagerness to please, there was something mulish in his expression that reminded you of the children of the lower orders: the sort of ragamuffins that call you 'sir', and then make a rude gesture once your back is turned. This hint of rebellion was more an aftertaste than a definite impression, but it hung around long after he had quit the scene.

2

Worsley stuck his head round the door. "Riddle!" he sang out, quite a bit louder than was necessary.

This was early in Pagan, toward the end of our first year as Praetors.

"I'm not deaf, Worsley. What do you want?"

"You have a gentleman caller, sir. Claims to be your father."

"Why would anyone *claim* to be my father?" I said irritably.

"It was a form of words, Praetor. Do you want me to send him up?"

"Yes."

Worsley left at speed.

"I wonder why Worsley is so very accommodating," I mused. "His almost superhuman efficiency goes well beyond the call of duty."

"I believe he has a father in what he calls 'the hospitality industry'," said Purkis languidly. "Worsley was brought up to follow in his footsteps. It seems that his training involved cleaning every flusher in his father's hotel every day for three years."

"Really? How do you know that?"

"From the tick's own mouth. Unlike you I show an interest in the lives of boys less fortunate than ourselves."

"How very virtuous of you. Tell me more."

"Apparently his father's business has gone from strength to strength. He now operates a chain of identical establishments, all marketed under the brand name of 'Rest Assured'."

"An inspired choice. Though come to think of it 'Rest in Peace' might have been more fitting."

"'Cheap Sleep' might be more fitting still. The chain's mission, Worsley tells me, is to offer comfort, cleanliness convenience and consistency at a modest price. Each room is to a standard size with identical appointments, down to the toothbrush holder."

"Are you quoting from an advertisement?"

"They are Worsley's own words. Anyway, what's your pa doing, turning up on the doorstep without warning?"

"I don't know. It's most unusual behaviour. Probably wants to take me to task over something or other."

"How unlike my own dear parent, who indulges me in everything. I expect it's all for your own good."

"You think so? – Hello, Pa!" I said, as the door opened and my father's head looked round.

"William ... Paul." He shook hands, first with Purkis, then with me; then stood about in his usual awkward way while Purkis cleared some books off the spare chair, and placed it near the fireplace.

"Not in the middle of anything are you?" he asked me, once he was seated.

"No tutorials today – half-hols."

"Right. Right. That's what I thought." He took out a pipe, examined it, then replaced it in his jacket pocket. "Just called in to see how you were faring."

"I'm doing well."

"Good. Good. I thought we might go for a drive."

"That would be fun."

"Maybe lunch in a teashop somewhere."

"Excellent! Purkis could come with us."

"Ah – yes, of course!" he said, not very enthusiastically.

Purkis was never slow to take a hint. "Actually I can't, Riddle, I'm afraid," he said. "I have this stuff to finish off."

"Is that so?" My father's relief was palpable. "Pity. Next time, perhaps."

Purkis made his excuses, and left.

"Impeccable manners, your friend," said my father, his tone changing as it always did when there was just the two of us. "Gets it from his father, I suppose."

"He means well."

"What – Purkis senior? He's out for himself, like all the rest. He's an expert at disguising the fact, that's all."

This was pretty much the way it always went. First my father would have a go at my friends and their fathers, then finally get around to having a go at me.

"How are things with you, anyway, pa? Are you working on anything interesting?"

"Ha! I couldn't explain it to you if I was. You don't have the vocabulary."

"Because I don't know any maths, you mean."

"Well you don't. And you should. Everything worth studying turns into maths sooner or later. Having said that, calculations of the sort I work with call for computers, if they're not going to take forever. They built one recently, to my design. Big as a bank vault, but faster and more powerful than anything else in the country. The irony is they won't let me use it. Not even for five minutes. Mind you, they call me in quick enough it if needs fixing. But even then someone stands over me all the time, in case I take a peek at their precious secrets. Ridiculous!"

"Must be irritating."

"You've no idea. Technology's been at a virtual standstill for the best part of a century. Take energy now. Great concrete power stations that gobble up coal at one end and fart out smoke at the other. Windmills that cost more to run than the electricity they generate. Solar panels that only work when the sun shines, which is roughly one week in fifty. Steam-powered carriages that weigh more than a team of horses and consume more vegetine than a chip shop. Where's the sense to it? Why drag a cannonball down a hill when you could simply stand back and let it roll? Look at hydrogen, I told them; it's cheap, it's everywhere, and it's crying out to be developed. Or better still, look at the stuff we're made of. Imagine you could harness the atom! Sounds absurd, I know, but so did electricity before some bright spark found how to make it. And think of the potential! Unlimited amounts of energy, for a start – enough power in a thimbleful of water to power a city. Make a bloody fine bomb as well, if anyone wanted such a thing. What an opportunity! All that's needed is the funding. And can I get it? Can I buggery!"

"That's ghastly," I said, without enthusiasm.

He gave me a look. "No interest, eh?"

"Not much."

"You'd rather we talked about you, is that it?"

"Maybe for a couple of minutes. Then you could go on about your work again."

"All right. Anything happening in your life, William?"

"Not much. Won an art prize, but I don't expect you want to hear about that."

"You won a prize? For some sort of painting, was it?"

"I don't do paintings anymore."

"Some sort of sculpture, then? No? Something else?"

"I can't explain it in words. You'd have to see it."

"Lead on, McDougall."

"I wouldn't bother."

"Don't make me pay with blood, William. Show me the thing – whatever it is – and I'll tell you what I think."

3

The art zone was occupied by a couple of Third-year boys, who were painting clumsy great portraits of one another in oils. They looked curiously at my father. He is not a particularly prepossessing man, with his tweed suits and unruly red hair and wild red beard, and I saw the fact reflected in their expressions. He stopped to look at their paintings, and cleared his throat in what came over as a critical way.

My portfolio was kept under a table in the Dutch barns. It was large and cumbersome. I hauled it onto the painting table, and untied the ribbon holding the boards together. Inside was a collection of sketches, photographs and notes proposing the construction, at some time in the future, of a life-sized replica of The Bune Bookstop, the scene of the original conception of Malcaster.

"At first glance," I had written, *"the shop looks identical to the original, but a thorough search by the right sort of person will reveal various significant points of departure. Squashed into one of the wobbly wire spinners is a well-thumbed copy of* The Mystery of the Missing Penknife,

holding an illuminated bookmark that reads, 'Without Great Endeavour
There Can be No Enlightenment'. Those who take this instruction to
heart will eventually uncover a tiny door, hidden behind a dummy book-
shelf, which leads by way of a steep rickety staircase to a bare windowless
room, furnished only by a moth-eaten carpet. Lift the carpet and examine
the floorboards underneath, preferably with the aid of a powerful mag-
nifying-glass, and you may just make out a faint bloodstain, scrubbed
almost to the point of invisibility, which bears witness to a crime which –
because it can only be reconstructed in your imagination – is as horrific
or as inconsequential as you care to make it."

My original idea was to have the room occupied by actors playing a group of The Malcontents, who would be surprised in the act
of conducting their midnight congress, but out of consideration
for Mr Trotter (whom I liked as a person, however hopeless he was
at painting) I thought it best to leave that detail out. In the event I
rather preferred the censored version; it was more subtle.

A number of other details of the plan were contributed by
Purkis. For example, the bookmark in the copy of *The Mystery
of the Missing Penknife* would have marked the page I was reading
when Purkis and I first met. He also specified that the contents of
the wire spinner should include a copy of *A Guide to Bune College*,
defaced at various places by someone with a grudge against the
school, and that a small poster should be taped to the door advertising the imminent publication of *The Infected Pistol and Other
Stories*.

The intention, of course, was to recreate the Malcaster of our
stories in a plastic medium. Knowing what Porter thought of my
artistic endeavours, I never thought that anyone other than Purkis
– and perhaps Mr Trotter – would have any time for it. To my
surprise the portfolio had received high (if somewhat perplexed)
praise, and led to my being awarded the Walter Sidney Art Prize
at the end of Vernal.

Now that I was showing it to my father, however, the whole
thing seemed suddenly inept: a silly private joke that had nothing
to do with art. It embarrassed me to look at it.

My father spent about five minutes looking through the

portfolio, his eyes flitting from one page to another, alighting nowhere for more than a second or two.

"And you won a prize for this?" he asked dryly, adjusting his spectacles to peer more closely at a list of bookshop stock, with notes detailing the precise physical condition of each item.

"The Walter Sidney Award for the Best Work of Art by a Senior Scholar."

"Really? What were the other entries like?"

"Rather more conventional."

"Well congratulations are in order. You've given Bune precisely what it likes best: an art based on private jokes, disguised obscenities and near total impenetrability."

"I gather you don't think much it."

"It all seems rather trivial, if you don't mind me saying so."

I did mind him saying so. "Perhaps you don't get the point."

"I get it all right. I don't think it's enough to sustain a work of art, that's all. It lacks depth.'

"Well, other people think differently."

"Which is why I have to speak my mind. You mustn't harbour any illusions about this sort of stuff."

We went back into the art room. The Third years were grinning furtively: I think they must have heard his verdict.

"Lunch?" asked my father.

4

The town of Bune is well served for teashops and restaurants, more for the benefit of visitors than the school. Some of them are very grand and very expensive; my father typically opted for the humblest. 'Ken's Place' was pokey and dark, with crumbs and dirt trodden into the carpet and cobwebs in the corners. The window panes were small and square with a thick swirl of glass in the centre, through which the sunlight street outside looked weirdly distorted.

It seems to be a rule of these places that you are served by someone whose appearance matches the aesthetics of the establishment. The man who took our order – you could hardly call him a waiter – was a dirty fellow with a limp and a lazy eye, possibly Ken himself. My father ordered gammon, egg and chips; I a steak and kidney pie and chips.

"It's a bit scruffy," said my father, "but I don't see the point of spending a fortune on a meal, do you?"

Actually I did. The previous week Purkis's father had come up for the day, and taken us for lunch at the Ancient Hermitage. No cobwebs and dirty carpets there: the decor and the food were equally stunning. It didn't matter what you chose: every dish was equally delightful, and unexpected, and satisfying without being absolutely filling, so there was just enough room left for what you knew would be the sweetest and lightest and most flavoursome of puddings. Under a palm tree a pianist softly stroked the keys of an enormous white grand. Immense gold-framed paintings of dramatic landscapes decorated the walls. A surfeit of uniformed waiters hovered discreetly in the background, ready to glide forwards to top up your glass of wine or hold a flame to your cigarette the moment you placed it between your lips.

My father, of course, would have found all this profoundly irritating, particularly the business with the wine and the cigarettes. "Good service be buggered," he would have said. "They only want you to tip it down quicker so you can buy another bottle. What's more, I prefer to light my own fags, *thank you very much*; and wipe my own arse too if it comes to that." We were by no means poor, but he hated extravagance, and would have considered the price of a meal at the Ancient Hermitage a shocking waste of money. That would have been my view as well, before I went to Bune; now I found it absurd. Anyway what was the alternative – gammon and chips at 'Ken's Place'? My father grumbled about that too. But with him there was only one side to any argument: he was never going to be in the wrong, whatever I said.

5

My father ordered a glass of red wine with his gammon. I ordered tea. The wine arrived almost immediately. He took an experimental sip.

"The usual cat-piss," he said, pulling a face. "Shall I order a glass for you?"

"No thanks."

"Please yourself." He gulped down the rest of the glass, and called to the waiter to bring another. "Has it ever occurred to you, William," he went on, "that the Universe may be something of an illusion?"

"It's occurred to lots of people," I said.

"Locked in a walnut shell, I count myself
The emperor of infinite space..."

My father looked annoyed. "What's that?"

"Andrew Wagstaffe, the first century dramatist. *Tarquin, Prince of Antibia*. You should read it."

"Why in the world would I do that?"

"You might learn something."

The waiter plonked down a second glass of wine, spilling some on the tablecloth. My father picked up the glass, pulled a face, and took another gulp – it was like watching someone swallow down a draught of some particularly unpleasant medicine.

"Wine all right, pa?" I asked.

"Disgusting. Going back to poetry: there's nothing I could learn from that form of discourse that isn't better said by a few simple mathematical equations. But people involved in the arts are always trying to teach the scientist his own business. Telling us for example to take another look at the bloody Alchemists, on the grounds that they anticipated all the ideas of modern Physics. What utter nonsense!" He took another swig of his wine. "Where's that waiter gone?" he demanded, twisting round in his seat.

I wondered if he was a little drunk. "This food's taking a long time," I said.

He shook his head irritably, as if reacting to a bothersome fly. "There's a reason for everything. All you have to do is puzzle it out. Or wait for it to puzzle you out. Not taken Union yet, have you?"

It was typical of him not to know. "I'm in the fifth form, pa. I took it last year."

"Don't believe all you hear, that's all."

"People don't really talk about it."

"I don't wonder. It isn't a particularly edifying activity, lifting the stone."

"I suppose not."

"You ever wonder what this is all about? How we got in this mess?"

"Is it a mess?"

"You don't feel ... powerless?"

"Not really."

"Thanks to Bune, eh?"

"I suppose so."

"There he is!" he exclaimed, as the waiter appeared from behind a curtained doorway. He raised his hand to his lips, and mimed the action of drinking. The waiter raised a finger, and disappeared behind the curtain. My father grimaced sourly. "Small business, eh?" he observed. "If only there were some better way of running things."

"Sometimes it helps to spend a bit more money," I said dryly.

"Well it shouldn't. Money isn't everything. People should take a pride in what they do. Instead they seem to delight in making things as unpleasant as possible." He shook his head grimly. "That's by the by. Have you ever wondered, William, what school is for?"

"How do you mean, pa?"

"Not just school. Education in general. What is its function? Why is it *there?*"

"Um – to teach people, I suppose."

"To impart knowledge?"

"Yes."

The third glass of wine arrived, served as ineptly as before. My father took a quick gulp. "Well that's what people say," he continued. "But if that was really what schools were for, they'd be an abject failure. No one in this society learns a thing until they've *left* school – not about the subjects they're supposed to be studying, at any rate. The main function of a school is to serve the requirements of the state not the individual. I'm not speaking about the Artisan institutions, where they teach you how to use a screwdriver or a saw; I mean the normal run of schools most people get to attend. Nursery schools, for example, are there to keep little boys out of mischief while they're still too young to look after themselves. The common or garden variety of Middle schools, like the one you attended in Glenlockie, focus on implanting the notion of obedience and respect for authority, so that when their pupils enter the world of employment they will do what their masters order them to do without questioning it. Schools like Bune, on the other hand – the schools of the ruling classes – are designed above all to give the boys who go there a sense of unshakeable superiority and self-confidence that will stay with them for the rest of their lives. The object is to get them to slot effortlessly into positions of authority, where they can run things, and keep their inferiors in order, and generally make sure that the machine functions as it's meant to. Every school, in other words, is an instrument of social control. One way or another. Do you follow?"

"I can see you don't approve of Bune. Which is odd, considering you sent me here."

"It is, isn't it? But you know what they say: the best place to hide a cuckoo is in a quarrel of kites. Not that that's proved particularly true in your case, more's the pity. The world's a dangerous place for misfits, William: sooner or later their natural enemies contrive to smoke them out and pull them limb to limb. I'd hate to see that happening to you."

This was all a bit puzzling. "Nothing's happening to me, pa. I'm happy – for once in my life."

"Fine, fine. Best change the subject, I fancy. Tell me, Will, do you recall, by any chance, our going on holiday once, when you were a boy, to the Western Islands?"

"Yes, I do. We went on a boat trip, to a deserted island."

"That's right. Another world entirely. Happy times, wouldn't you say?"

"Yes, I would. Where is this all leading to, pa?"

He took a second gulp of his wine. "I just wondered how you saw yourself a few years down the line – in ten years' time, say? Will you be one of those who do what you're told, or one who does the telling? An alumnus of Glenlockie, or an old Bunian?"

"If that's the choice, I'd rather be an old Bunian, obviously."

"Well there's my answer. Nothing more to say, really." He drained his glass to the dregs. "I'm proud of you, my boy. You're going to be a useful member of society."

Eventually the food arrived. His gammon was burnt, the fried egg was cold and rubbery, and the contents of my pie were like stewed boot-leather. The chips were coated with a strange orange crust and smelled of garlic. Both dishes came with a portion of drab green peas that must have come straight out of a tin.

"What's wrong with this bloody thing?" said my father, shaking the sauce bottle vigorously over his gammon and chips. "They should try making them out of soft plastic, then you could squeeze the stuff out like toothpaste. – Oh hell!" he cried as a great gobbet of red sauce came loose and spattered all over his hand and the sleeve of his jacket.

I fetched some flimsy paper napkins. "Thanks, William," he said abstractly, dipping one in his glass of water, and scrubbing at his sleeve: making the mess even worse than it was already. "Why is eating out always such a bloody disaster?"

"I don't know, pa. Why do you think it is?"

"Haven't a bloody clue. – Have you ever noticed, William, that people always choose to talk about the most trivial things? I mean, they never think to address the really big questions, thing that are so glaringly obvious that you have to adopt a sort of willful blindness in order to ignore them. And yet people do ignore them – all the time. It's almost as if they're afraid to do so."

"I suppose you're talking about science again," I said.

"Not this time, no. What I had in mind is sex."

"Sex?" My face reddened. Sex, in my view, could only be discussed with the most intimate of friends – certainly not with one's father.

"Think about it," he continued, blithely oblivious to my reaction. "Here it is, the most crucial aspect of our lives – without which we wouldn't *have* lives, there wouldn't *be* any life – and we just take it for granted. Doesn't that strike you as absurd?"

"I never thought about it, pa."

"Time you did, then."

Another silence. Then he said: "But you're enjoying yourself here, aren't you? At Bune. With your art and so forth. Now that you're a senior."

"I'm looking forward to next year, certainly. I'm hoping I'll get elected to Crow."

"Well, stranger things have happened. I'd stick with it, if I were you. It seems to suit you. Couldn't stand it myself, but that's just me." He signalled for the bill. "That wasn't so bad, was it? I'll bring you here again." His tone was odd. Probably the drink had a lot to do with it. But one thing was clear: I was a disappointment to him, and not just because I lacked aptitude in mathematics.

ELEVEN
Goodbye to Bune

GOODBYE TO BUNE
Bune made me what I am,
Shaped my frame from boy to man,
Helped me bear the pangs of youth,
Fed me wisdom, taught me truth.

The Rt. Hon. Oliver Wooten-Smedley MP (Bart.) (362–425)

Wisley bared his mossy teeth in a wolfish grin. "You misunderstand the true nature of happiness," he said. "The whole point is to put the gullible off their guard, much as a meadow of lush grass is designed to conceal a loaded mantrap."

'Sentiment and Sentimentality', from
The Infected Pistol and Other Stories by H O Minty and F R Trumper
(Privately printed, 480).

1

The foregoing account takes me up to mid-Pagan, 484. Looking back from that point I felt I had good reasons for self-congratulation. I had been a pupil at Bune for four-and-a-half years. My passage had not been easy or straightforward but I had survived it with my spirits and reputation intact. My origins, in so far as they were remembered, were no longer held against me. Above all, I was secure in the affections of a boy who belonged among the elite. I was a Bunian, one of the favoured few, destined to be one of Albion's ruling men, its arbiters of taste and opinion. My future

145

life rolled out in front of me like a golden road leading into a radiant landscape of high status and great possessions.

The weather, as Wisley once observed, is always at its most lovely immediately before a thunderstorm.

2

My last day at Bune started in unexceptional fashion with a bracing cold shower, followed by a generous helping of bacon and eggs, served by Worsley on large blue and white china plates. Outside the sun shone on the dazzling playing fields and the golden stone of the school's venerable study blocks. Malcaster and all its works seemed very far away.

Purkis that morning was on particularly good form.

"You are a paragon, Worsley, do you know that?"

"I'm not sure what the word means, Purkis."

"It means, ignorant youth, that you are a wonder-tick. You perform your duties in exemplary fashion, and without a murmur of complaint."

"Thank you, Purkis. I think you're exaggerating a bit, though."

"Not at all. You are far and away the best of ticks. Of course it must help enormously to have tick-masters as nice as me and Riddle. We never ask you to do anything unreasonable or humiliating. But is that sufficient incentive?"

"For what, Purkis?"

"For your apparent devotion."

"Sorry?"

"Do I have to spell it out? What's your *price,* man? A blind eye if you ever (perish the thought) transgress? Possibly even *cash?*"

"No, Purkis" said Worsley, colouring. "I don't expect anything like that."

"Don't lie. No one does anything for nothing. Basically people are just out for themselves. They can't help it. It's human nature."

"Purkis-nature, you mean," I chipped in. "Worsley is a different breed of dog altogether. Servility in his case appears to be its own reward."

Worsley continued to clear the table with an air of absorption.

"Settle this for us, Worsley," I said. "Purkis is right: your conduct as a tick is rather too good to be true. You actually appear to *enjoy* your duties, even the most menial of them. That is very odd. Explain."

"I do enjoy them, actually, Riddle," said Worsley. "My father has taught me from an early age that the greatest fulfilment comes through serving others. That is our business philosophy, and my experience is that it works equally well in all other spheres of life. – Is it all right for me to go now?"

I was fighting hard not to burst out laughing. "Go, Worsley, go!"

The door closed behind him. Purkis and I looked at one another.

"I wonder if the Worsley family has a heraldic shield," I said. "Perhaps I should design one for them. Crossed bedpans over a scrubbing-brush rampant – that sort of thing."

"Perfect. And underneath, the family motto: Nobility through Abasement."

We laughed for some time.

"What's really funny," said Purkis, "is the idea that we're expected to take the boy's servility at face value".

"I have no problem with it. Worsley is the product of an industry that elevates service above human dignity, in the pursuit of profit. He is the modern version of the faithful slave."

"You're so fucking trusting Riddle. Worsley watches everything we do: every letter, every conversation, every time one of us so much as farts in the bath."

"That would be you, in fact."

"Trust me, Riddle: I know all the signs. He's a spy."

"I don't give a toss either way," I said. "He won't find anything worth reporting."

"Speak for yourself."

"Been up to something, have you?" Purkis was always trying to sell himself as being heroically promiscuous, like his hero Lord Percy, but his appalling complexion – the sore red eruptions that encrusted his face and neck – meant that the opportunities he got to misbehave were pretty infrequent, and hardly anything to boast of.

"Possibly."

"I know how fond you are of photographic studies of the unclothed youth. That's hardly a hanging matter, even here."

"Perhaps you don't know me as well as you think."

"Perhaps not. Good luck to you, if you have something worth concealing for once. I know I don't. My hands and heart are as pure as trodden slush."

3

The Headmaster was sitting at his desk, massaging the palm of his left hand with the thumb of his right.

"Sit down, Riddle," he said, indicating the Interrogation Seat.

I sat. A game of sticks was in progress, somewhere out of sight. Faint cheers drifted through the open windows.

There was a painful silence. The sourness that marked our last encounter had if anything intensified in the time between. Neither of us had any inclination to ameliorate matters. The feeling that flowed between us was pure undisguised loathing.

"I have some bad news for you. It concerns your father." He steepled his fingers, raised the construction so that his index fingers were touching the end of his nose, and his thumbs resting on his chin, and regarded me over it like a giant peering over a steeply pitched gable-end.

"What about him?"

"When did you last see him?"

"About a month ago."

"Did he give any indication that anything was amiss?"

"Such as?"

Porter cleared his throat. "He never told you he was under investigation?"

"By the police?"

"By our security service. Under the direction of the NAC."

"What's he supposed to have done?"

"The precise details of the allegations against him have not yet been divulged," he said, tasting each word as if it might be tinctured with arsenic. "The suspicion is that he has done something *treasonous.* Anything more than that I am not at liberty to discuss."

My father had been in trouble before, usually for refusing to take no for an answer, but this sounded more serious. "My father isn't interested in politics. He's a scientist. There are books written by him in the school library."

"One book," he corrected me. "The volume you refer to has been on our shelves for ten years; the last time I checked the pages were still uncut. Your father is chiefly known for his development of a labour-saving household appliance – hardly the most spectacular achievement I can think of. It certainly does not entitle him to break the law; nor would it offer him any protection in the event of his doing so." The tip of his tongue peeked out, and then withdrew.

"It's a mistake," I asserted, with more confidence than I felt.

"Well, we shall see. If it's any comfort to you, the NAC is not known for recommending people for prosecution without just cause. If your father is innocent he will be given ample opportunity to clear his name."

His words, as he intended, offered no comfort at all. My father had instilled in me a profound distrust of the NAC. At the same time he had always impressed on me the need to keep this opinion to myself.

In the heat of the moment I threw caution to the winds. "This is stupid," I blurted out.

"Stupid? A ruling of the NAC?"

"That's what I said. They're not infallible are they?"

Porter studied me like an insect that has landed on his plate. "Arrogant words, Riddle; the words of an arrogant youth. It was a controversial decision, admitting you to Bune. I was opposed to it. I see that my misgivings were right." The tip of his tongue moistened his upper lip. "You realise of course that you will have to leave?"

There are harmless taps, and there are bruises, and there are sledgehammer blows, and you never know which they are going to be until they land.

"Leave? Why?"

"We can hardly keep you here under the circumstances."

"That isn't fair. What have I done?"

"This is precisely the sort of thing I mean. You have been given a determination, and you treat it as an *opinion*. Instead of accepting and obeying, you *argue the toss*. I can't continue this conversation any longer. Collect together your possessions, and be ready to leave within the hour."

"So that's it?" The words spilled out in an unseemly rush. "Three years of my life – wasted!"

"You have been given every opportunity at Bune. If your time has been wasted here that is no one's fault but your own."

"You know what I mean. I've only been a Praetor for five months. And next year I could get elected to Crow."

"Frankly it was touch and go whether you would make Praetor at all – I certainly didn't support your candidacy. As for membership of Crow, Bune may tolerate a variety of opinions, but we're not so open-minded as to give a fox the keys to the hen-house."

I sent him a look of hate.

"I'm interested to see," he continued, "that you appear to be less concerned about the fate of your father than the loss of your place at Bune."

I reined back my anger. "What do I do now?"

"An Officer of the State will come for you."

"And take me where?"

"A corrective facility, most probably. Some institute where you can be taught to show a modicum of respect."

A wave of fury rose up in my chest and came crashing out of my mouth. "You don't deserve my respect, you pompous lackey," I said, rising from my seat.

Porter stood up and walked over to the door. "I will note that remark on your file," he said coldly. "It will pursue you wherever you go." He opened the door, and waited for me to leave.

4

Purkis was sitting in one of our two armchairs, puffing away at his briar, and looking thoughtful. Friend or not, at that precise moment I couldn't stand the sight of him, if only because I was being sacked and he was not. I turned my back to him, and began pulling stuff out of a cupboard.

"What's all this? You're not leaving?"

"Don't pretend you don't know."

"Know what?"

"About my pa – getting himself jugged up."

"How would I know about something like that?"

"How indeed?"

"You're being paranoid. What has your pa done?"

"Porter won't say."

"Must be something unspeakable, in which case. Are large dogs implicated, by any chance?"

That is the way you dealt with things at Bune. Any misfortune, however awful, was met with an airy quip. Pointed jabs and down-right insults had to be taken on the chin. It was not done to show emotion; in fact the worse you had been hurt the more rigorously you were expected to control your feelings. If you took offence you had no sense of humour. If you broke down you were a weakling.

"It's no joke," I said.

"I can see. Tell me more. NAC involved?"

"Yes."

"It's serious, then."

"I'm not worried. They can't get away with this. He's not some pathetic nobody, you know. He's a top scientist."

"That's true. Only scientists don't count, unfortunately."

"What do you mean?"

"Riddle, old chap, I thought that by now you knew how the world works. Scientists and academics are roughly equal in the pecking-order to flusher attendants."

"Thanks, Purkis, that makes me feel a whole lot better. You fucking shit."

He looked at me thoughtfully. "You know, I could always put in a word with my pa."

"Ah, the great Sir Roger. What the fuck could he do?"

Before he could reply there was an efficient double rap on the door.

"Who is it?" I snarled.

The door opened, and a man entered the study. He wore a long belted raincoat, somewhat crumpled and grubby; it had obviously been slept in on more than one occasion. A dented felt hat was squashed down over his head, pushing out the tops of his ears. Along the lower edge of his lip ran a thin black moustache. His profession – that of the secret policeman – was as laughably obvious as if he had been dressed for the part in a play.

"Which of you young gentlemen is Riddle?"

"There's your man," I said, pointing at Purkis.

The man advanced on Purkis. "Special Police Constable Jarvis. I'm here to–"

"I'm not Riddle," said Purkis.

"Don't try it on," said Jarvis. "Your Head warned me–"

"My name is Purkis."

"Purkis?"

"You recognise the name, I take it?"

"I know of a Sir Roger Purkis. He's a Senior Government– "

"That's the one. He's my father."

Jarvis did something involving his tongue and his upper lip. "I assume you have proof of that?"

"Of course," said Purkis, rooting around in his pockets.

"Don't worry if you can't find it," I said. "I could always ask my pa to put in a good word for you."

"Cheap shot Riddle," said Purkis. He pulled out a grubby leather wallet, extracted his college pass, and handed it over.

Jarvis too his time examining the pass: looking from the photograph to Purkis and back again. "Thank you, Mr Purkis." he said, handing it back, "It seems I owe you an apology."

"Not at all. You weren't to know."

"No. So the real Riddle, I take it, is this other gentleman?"

"Right second time," I said, holding out my own pass.

Jarvis took it from me and gave it a cursory glance. "That's a low trick," he said, "trying to drop your roommate in the sewage."

"It was a joke."

"A joke, was it?"

"Bang the bugger up," said Purkis. "He deserves it, pulling a stunt like that."

Jarvis pocketed my pass, frowning. "I'll keep hold of this, if I may," he said. "Right, Riddle, get your stuff together."

"That'll teach you to appropriate my name without permission," said Purkis.

"Fuck off, Purkis."

"Mind your language," said Jarvis severely. "I thought this was a school for the sons of gentlemen."

"That's how they talk – the sons of gentlemen," I said. "It's how their fathers talk too, if it comes to that. It's 'fuck this' and 'fuck that' all the time. The only people who see any virtue in civility are the lower classes."

"Like me, are you saying?" asked Jarvis, with a sharp jerk of the neck.

I shrugged, and got on with my packing.

"Hey," said Purkis. "Taking that bubbler with you?"

The bubbler in question was made of brass, and quite bulky. I had found it in a curiosity shop in Ensor, in the shadow of the castle. I only bought it for show, and in fact smoking it made me feel ill.

"Do you want it?"

"If you have no use for it."

"It's yours."

"Ta very much."

There wasn't much else. My collection of waistcoats weren't going to be much use outside of Bune: Purkis could have those too. Not that he needed them; he had enough of his own.

"That's it, then, Purkis," I said, picking up my suitcases so that we wouldn't have to shake hands. "I doubt we'll meet again."

Purkis made no reply. I'd like to think he was too choked up suddenly to trust himself to speak, but very probably he was glad to see the back of me. I blame The Bunian Code. No one ever said what they felt; it was all guesswork, and walking on eggs, and if you did really like someone you had to pretend the exact opposite.

5

Outside we ran into Worsley.

"Riddle!" he cried, running up to me. "Is it true you've been expelled?"

"Something like that."

"What lousy luck."

"Thanks, Worsley. Shit is what I'm used to."

"And who are you, sir?" asked Jarvis.

"Thomas Worsley. I'm Riddle's tick."

"A 'tick'. That's some kind of servant, right?"

"Something like that," I said.

Jarvis ignored me. "How is that spelled, sir – W-U-Z-L-Y?"

Worsley corrected him.

"Much obliged." He wrote it down in his notebook. "I'll be returning in a few days to make further enquiries. I may have some more questions for you at that time."

"That's fine. So long as you understand I'm not going to rat on Riddle."

Jarvis perked up at this. "You know something incriminating, then, do you?"

"I didn't say that."

"It's all right, Mr Worsley. Anything you tell me will be in the strictest confidence."

"There's nothing to tell."

"I understand perfectly. I won't detain you any longer."

Worsley walked away. Reaching David and Jonathan he turned and raised a hand. There was something oddly furtive about the gesture.

"One of the new boys, is he?" said Jarvis.

"Yes."

"Young and impressionable, in other words?"

"You could say that."

"And their duties, these *ticks*, what are they exactly, may I ask?"

"They make toast, run errands, polish your boots – that kind of thing."

"So what they do, in short, is attend to your personal needs?"

"In a manner of speaking."

"He seems very fond of you, young Mr Worsley."

"Well you know how it is."

"No, I don't sir. Perhaps you should fill me in."

"I don't think you'd understand."

"I wouldn't be too sure of that. You know the penalties for corruption of minors, I suppose?"

"Don't be idiotic."

"Idiotic, am I?" he said. For a moment he seemed to be on the point of landing me one. Instead he grabbed my arm, and steered me over to an exhausted black steamer saloon slumped in the drive. He opened the boot, and gestured for me to put my cases inside.

I did as he asked.

"Hop in, now."

I climbed into the passenger seat. A fuggy smell came off the upholstery, of fried food and sweat and cigarette smoke. Jarvis got in beside me. When he slammed his door the smell intensified.

"Nice steamer," I said, with a sniff.

He leaned his face close to mine. "Drop the lip, Riddle," he said. "You've had it nice and cushy up to now, what with your servant boys and your private rooms and pretty waistcoats and shiny toppers. Well those days are over. You've left your corner of privilege behind. You're on my territory now. You do what you are told. You eat what you are given. You speak when you are spoken to. Is that clear?"

"Perfectly."

He pressed the starter button. The steamer wheezed and coughed, then leapt into life with a sudden fury of hammering pistons and puffs of steam from the boiler. The pressure counter inched towards the green. Jarvis threw the machine into first. With an outraged *harrumph*, the abused machine lurched into motion, and began its lumbering progress along the gravelled drive.

The midday sun was streaming down over Bune. A thick film of grime covered the windscreen, blurring and distorting the golden scene. A line of Crows lolled on Crow Row, watching as two of their number, flaunting waistcoats of emerald green and primrose yellow, duelled with furled umbrellas. I would never now be one of them.

I took a last look at the stone towers and the shady arches and the bright trees and the boys in their flowing tails and and tilted toppers racing across the lawn to witness my departure. It was the same world as I had woken to, some six hours earlier, but I was no longer a member of it.

The insensible steamer rumbled past the vivid scene, expelling sulphurous chuffs of steam. I turned in my seat. The great west front of Bune College dwindled in easy stages to the size of a toy fort. We came to a pair of ornamental gates – they were standing open – puttered through, rounded a green bend, and it was gone for good.

TWELVE

Welcome to Cromwell House

Lockwood Hall emerged from the mists, a grey crumbling pile of masonry, over which a thick growth of ivy had fastened itself like the disfiguring marks of some terminal disease.

Jason Hardcastle by WC Collins, (Ludden 384)

WR is a 17-year-old youth from a working-class background who has acquired a bit of polish as a result of his education at the famous 'Bune College'. Expensive suit. Face covered in freckles, unruly mop of ginger curls in need of a good trim. Smarmy manners. Not half as clever as he thinks he is. Accent a bit 'put on', as often the case with people who have risen above their station. Likes to stir. Inveterate liar.

From the notebook of DCI Horace Payne,
Wednesday June 8th 484

It's not as if the boy is a real aristo, not that I care for any of that but when someone's dad is arguably the lowest form of pond life it's hardly likely his spawn will be much of an improvement (illegible) swanning about with his little freckled nose tilted aloft (illegible) doesn't convince me (illegible despite all that I bet you five-pence to a quid that your average man-in-the-street who can't see beyond a topper and a waistcoat will take the little fake at face value, as an honest-to-goodness (illegible). Beats me how the (illegible) ever got into Bune School in the first place. Three years sucking up to the sons of the great and good, wangling his way into their good graces in the hopes of future advancement in the world outside. They wouldn't do that for (illegible) boy. (illegible) how completely useless they are even at the few jobs they were born for (illegible) inherited fortunes, they also get paid cartloads of filthy lucre for doing SFA and as if that's not enough they've still got to lie and cheat and perjure so they can milk the common man of countless more thousands, and when they get caught with their fingers in the till which is rare but it does sometimes happen usually when some interfering so-and-so gets to know more than is good for him their only punishment is to hang their heads in shame for a week or two until the next scandal comes along (illegible) found guilty of thieving that much cash would be slung into clink along with the rest of the rubbish like rapists and subversives and workshy (illegible) there's no such thing as justice but whoever (illegible) man is just as bad as the next or would be if you gave him half the chance, the only difference being (illegible) in less than five minutes he'll be grafting and swindling and fiddling as to the manner born without a hint of shame. I don't care, it's my job to police the system not criticise it, but fair is fair that doesn't mean opening the floodgates to anyone who can wriggle (illegible) bottom line the boy is weak. (illegible) enough to bring tears to his eyes, which makes you wonder what a bit of real (illegible) might wring out of him only that isn't going to happen, worse luck, thanks to a big fly-in-the ointment, the less said the better.

From the Notebook of SPC J Jarvis, Thursday June 9th, 484

1

We drove for ages through a succession of shabby towns, each as depressing as the last; until suddenly the urban desolation gave way to a great drab plain as borderless as the ocean, across which a fierce wind blasted relentlessly, unhindered by any wall or hedge or dwelling-place. My depression deepened. I could die out here, I thought, and no one would notice, apart from the foxes and badgers that picked over my bones.

It was getting dark when I got my first sight of the asylum, rearing up from the otherwise featureless plain like a clump of toadstools on a billiards table: a nightmare muddle of steep gables and turrets and leaking drainpipes and rusting fire escapes, topped by a massive grey smokestack, towering high above the lot, pumping toxic fumes into the yellowing sky.

We lurched down a drive of broken tarmac pitted with ragged potholes. Jarvis was cursing under his breath. He was one of those drivers who are perpetually at war with their vehicles, with other drivers, with the very road itself. This struck me as peculiar. The man had a reasonable job, considering his talents, and presumably he possessed some kind of status in the world he inhabited. Clearly it wasn't enough. Something was making him bitter, and bitter people are dangerous.

He pulled into a small car-park alongside the concrete foyer and parked in one of the many spaces available. A flaking sign read:

CROMWELL HOUSE
ASYLUM CENTRE
PROPERTY OF THE GOVERNMENT OF ANGLIA
THESE PREMISES ARE ALARMED AND
PROTECTED AGAINST TRESPASS
RISK OF DEATH BY ELECTROCUTION

The reception area was a square single-story erection of stained crumbling concrete, grafted onto the main building like an inadvisable afterthought. Through the huge plate-glass window, I could see a tubby man in a light-blue uniform slumped behind a desk, his oily hair gleaming under the floodlights. A chequered pattern of green and purple carpet tiles covered the floor. Long sagging sofas of ripped black vinyl lined the walls. The open spaces were punctuated at regular intervals by a regiment of identical plastic aspidistras, each of them sprouting from a massive black cube filled to the brim with small bean-like pebbles. The ghostly traces of martial music leaked out into the night.

Jarvis reached over and opened my door. 'Out,' he said.

I stumbled out and collected my cases from the boot. My bum had gone to sleep on the cold metal seat. I was so stiff I could hardly walk. Ignoring my complaints, Jarvis steered me across the carpark and through the plate-glass doors.

The music met us at full blast, like a thunderous headache. We approached the reception desk.

"SPC Jarvis,' said Jarvis briskly to the man in uniform behind it. "Liaising with DCI Payne."

The man's head was bent over an open appointments book. His eyelids were lowered like blinds. Looking closer, I saw that he had pulled open a drawer in the desk, and was resting his elbows inside.

"Do you think he's dead?" I asked.

"Did I say you could speak?"

"Not in so many words, no. Only– "

"You speak when I tell you to, and not otherwise. –*SPC Jarvis!*" he repeated loudly. *"Hello!"*

"No need to shout," said the receptionist, stirring resentfully into life. He pushed the drawer shut. "Who'd you say you were – Jarvis?"

"SPC Jarvis. Reporting to DCI Payne."

He pointed a brown stained finger at me. "And who is this?"

"Name of Riddle. New admission."

"You'll have to sign him in. And yourself." He pushed an open book towards Jarvis. "That your steamer out there?"

"Yes."

"You can't park there. You'd better move it quick, unless you want it clamped."

Jarvis gritted his teeth. "Where can I park, then?"

"Round the back, where it says 'Staff and Visitors'."

"Is it far?"

"That depends. Ten minutes max, on foot. If you know your way."

Jarvis looked at me. "You wait here," he said.

"No he doesn't," said the man quickly. "He's your responsibility."

"Then what do you suggest I do?"

"Not my problem, mate."

"Can we leave the suitcases here, at least?"

"No unattended luggage or packages of any kind."

There was a longish pause. Jarvis muttered something, shaking his head. I could see his problem. In order to play this by the book he was going to have to march me and my suitcases back to the steamer, then start up the steamer again – hardly the simplest of procedures – and drive around until he had found the other steamer park; and even after that he would still have to find his way back to the foyer in the dark with me stumbling along beside him with my suitcases. The whole set-up was a neat illustration of the self-defeating nature of bureaucracy. With one or two embellishments it would make a good subject for a Malcaster story. Except that there weren't going to be any more Malcaster stories, I thought sadly: not then, not ever. Malcaster, Purkis, Bune: that part of my life was gone for good.

"Where will I find DCI Payne?" asked Jarvis. He was making an effort to sound fully in command of himself, but his hand – still clamped on my upper arm – was shaking.

The receptionist reached for a blurrily printed diagram, and drew a clumsy circle with a blunt pencil. "That's Payne, you're here. If you want light you'll have to keep pressing the buttons. You've got ten seconds between one end of a corridor and the next. What about the steamer?"

"Clamp it," said Jarvis. "The NAC will foot the bill."

"Don't bet on it."

"What's your name again?" asked Jarvis.

The receptionist scowled. Jarvis leaned forward, read the man's name off his badge, and wrote it on the leaflet, with the air of someone scoring a small but decisive victory.

2

Payne's door had no name on it, just the number: a tarnished brass 5 hanging from a single screw. Jarvis knocked. We waited for a few seconds.

"Must have gone out," I said.

"What did I say about speaking?"

"Oh – right. Forgot. Sorry."

The door opened. A man in a brown cardigan peered through it. His brow was creased with deep horizontal lines. He wore half-moon rimless glasses. The crown of his head was perfectly bald; in order to disguise this fact the hair on one side of his head (lifeless, grey) was combed up from a parting just above his ear and stuck down on the opposite side. Like Jarvis he had a moustache, only his was a full grey walrus.

He looked at Jarvis, then at me, and then at Jarvis again. "Special Police Constable Jarvis?"

Jarvis nodded. "Detective Chief Inspector Payne?" he countered.

"Correct. And this must be Mr Riddle."

"It is indeed."

"Welcome to Cromwell House, Mr Riddle."

"Thank you, Inspector," I said, putting out my hand.

Payne looked at it. "We won't shake hands, if you don't mind," he said. "This isn't a social occasion."

"I was just being polite."

"Well don't be. You won't win me over that way, and I dare say you won't win over SPC Jarvis either."

"I wasn't—"

"I'm not asking your opinion. Come in, stow those cases in the corner, then sit down and wait to be spoken to."

"I told him that," said Jarvis. "He's—"

Payne held up his index finger. Jarvis's face was stony, but he swallowed back his words. I was beginning to understand why he was so angry all the time.

3

Payne's office reeked of cigarette smoke. A naked lightbulb hung from a tangle of exposed wires in the middle of the ceiling, alongside two lengths of twisty flypaper mottled with the black bodies of hundreds of flies. The walls were painted bottle green to chest height, and cream above. There were lots of cracks, some as wide as your finger. The floor tiles were of brown plastic, printed with a crude approximation of woodgrain; they were scuffed and needed a good mopping; in places they were lifting from the concrete.

There was only one window, its small panes pasted over with creased squares of brown paper. A grubby meat-safe stood against a wall, with a grimy gas-ring on top. A square table occupied the centre of the room, half of its surface taken up by a hulking reel-to-reel tape recorder, the rest covered with the usual debris associated with administrative work: used polystyrene cups, puddles of spilt coffee, balls of crumpled paper, broken pencils, bent paper-clips, dog-eared notepads, and an overflowing ashtray as big as a chamber-pot. A far corner held a square sink. The tangle of plumbing around it looked like the excavated remains of some archaic wind-instrument. The tap – there was only one – dripped with a just-audible beat.

"Coffee?" asked Payne, holding up a dented tin kettle.

"Yes please, Chief," said Jarvis.

"How do you take it?"

"Milk and two sugars, please."

A stray fruit-fly drifted around the region of the table. Payne's hand shot out like the tongue of a chameleon, and then returned to the table.

"Will you join us, Mr Riddle?"

"I won't, if you don't mind."

"Not posh enough for you, Riddle?" asked Jarvis.

"I would recommend that you steer clear of the personal tone, Jarvis," said Payne. "It tends to confuse matters."

Jarvis tightened his lip. "You're the boss," he said.

"I am. You'll find all the gubbins in the cupboard,' added Payne, pouring water into two cups.

Nodding, Jarvis went over to the meat-safe, and removed a half empty jar of brown powder, a bottle containing about an inch of milk, and a damp packet of lumpy sugar.

"Now, Mr Riddle," said Payne, "SPC Jarvis and I are going to have a little chat." He opened another door. "You can wait in here until we're ready for you."

The room was tiny: about ten feet by four. No window, and the only furniture was a low slab of concrete topped with a grubby foam-rubber mattress. A tin bucket stood in the corner. The room, as you would expect, smelled of whatever the bucket was used for.

"All mod cons, as you see," said Payne. "Regrettably I've no reading material to offer you, unless you're interested in a collection of leaflets on topics to do with public health."

"It's OK," I said. "Really, don't trouble yourself."

"There's no danger of that, I can assure you. There's a garment on the bed. You'll need to change into it."

The garment in question was a one-piece overall of yellow cotton flannel, like something a very large baby might wear. I held it up. "This?"

"Do you see any other?"

"No."

"So what conclusion are you led to?"

"This is it."

"Correct," said Payne. "All the inmates have to wear one, not just you. Helps to identify you if you ever leave the premises. You can think of it as the Cromwell House uniform. There's also a plastic bag for your personal effects. SPC Jarvis will get you to sign a chitty, so that it'll all be waiting for you when we let you go. If it still fits by then."

"What about my cases?"

He gave them a glance. "Fancy. Not short of a bob or two, your father, then?"

"I suppose not."

"Let's hope it stays that way. You can leave those here. We'll go through them. If there's anything you can keep you'll get it back – eventually."

He closed the door. I heard a key turn in the lock.

I sat on the bed. I collapsed my topper, took off my shoes, and my striped trousers, and my tails and waistcoat and shirt, folded them neatly, and put everything in the carrier bag provided; then I put on the hideous yellow one-piece jumpsuit. I was now officially an inmate of Cromwell House. It did not feel good.

Having nothing else to do I climbed on the slab and curled up like a snail. There were no pillows. The foam rubber was perished and grubby and smelled pretty rank, but when you are tired enough you hardly notice that kind of thing. In fact it gets to be weirdly comforting, like your own smells under the covers. I fell asleep.

I woke to see Jarvis standing in the doorway.

"We're ready for you now," he said.

4

The interview was in essence a duel between Bune and official-dom. Given a level burly-field there should have been no contest. But the burly-field in this case was far from level. I had the advantage over them in terms of sophistication and intelligence, but they held all the power.

Payne switched on the tape-recorder, and tapped the micro-phone a few times. "Hello," he said into the fat black baton. "DCI Payne. DCI Payne. DCI Payne." He played it back. The recording was muted and so muffled and overlaid with hiss and crackle you could barely recognise the words or the voice of the speaker. *"DCI Payne,"* it said harshly, *"DCI Payne, DCI Payne."*

"Sound as a bell," said Payne.

The lead for the tape-recorder, I noticed, was a bit short: it ran over to the wall-socket at ankle height, like a trip-wire.

Payne switched back to record. *"Date: 8/6/84. Subject: William George Riddle. Interview conducted by: DCI Herbert Payne. Also present: SPC Ronald Jarvis. Time: 10.45 p.m."* He turned to me. "How's the uniform, Mr Riddle?"

"Fits like a glove."

"Excellent. Mr Riddle: do you know why you are here?"

"Not really. To answer your questions?"

"That goes without saying. But yes, to answer my questions. Do you know on what subject?"

I pretended to consider the matter, scratching my head, creasing my forehead, and putting my hand up to my mouth. "Not really," I said finally, shaking my head. "Something to do with my pa, is it?"

"Your 'pa', yes, there's a good place to start. Tell us about your 'pa', Mr Riddle."

"You can call me William, if you like."

"I won't, if you don't mind. I was asking about your father."

"What do you want to know about him?"

"What do you want to tell us?"

"What can you tell *me?*" I said. "Where is he, for a start?"

Payne and Jarvis exchanged glances. "No one's told you?"

"Told me what?"

"Where he is?"

"I was told he'd been arrested."

"By whom?"

"Porter."

"You mean your Headmaster. *Dr* Porter."

"That's the one."

Payne switched off the recorder. "A word, SPC Jarvis please," he said. They left the room for a few minutes. I looked at Jarvis's ring-bound notebook, but it was covered with neat but unreadable symbols. Some kind of code, I supposed. Payne had taken his notebook with him. I looked at the mess of charred tobacco in the ashtray: it made me want to smoke. I started wishing that I had accepted Payne's offer of tea: it would have been nasty, but better than nothing.

The two men came back into the room, and resumed their seats. Payne switched the recorder back on. "Now, Mr Riddle," he said, "I want you to bring your mind back to the time of your arrest."

"You're done with my father?"

"Blast!" said Jarvis, leaping to his feet and clutching his head like a man who has just remembered leaving a pan of milk on the stove an hour earlier.

"What's up, SPC?"

"Forgot something," said Jarvis. "Would you excuse me, sir? I'll only be a couple of ticks." Without waiting for a reply, he made for the door. In his haste he tripped over the lead connecting the tape recorder to the wall-socket, and went flying, pulling out the plug as he did so. With a backwards glare he struggled to his feet and rushed out.

Payne rose heavily from his seat and plugged the lead back in with an expression of irritated bewilderment. He played back the last few seconds. *"Would you excuse me, sir?"* said Jarvis again, sounding a thousand miles away, in the middle of a thunderstorm. *"I'll only be a couple of ticks."* Payne switched back to record.

"I wonder what he's forgotten?" I said innocently.

Payne took out a pipe, and began to pack it with tobacco from an oilcloth bladder. "No doubt all will be made clear in due course. Now at the time of your arrest–"

"I wasn't arrested."

There was a long pause. Payne looked at the tape recorder, then he looked back at me. "Technically speaking you're quite right, you weren't. That's one to you, Mr Riddle."

"Thanks."

"Or should I say," Payne continued, *"That's the first nail in your coffin?"*

Payne gave me a hard stare, waiting I suppose for a reaction. I declined to provide one.

"Let's move on," said Payne, lighting his pipe. "SPC Jarvis tells me that when he asked to see your papers, you pretended to be Mr Purkis."

I shook my head. "I never said I was Purkis. All I said was that Purkis was me."

Longish pause. Puff of smoke. "I see you're a stickler for detail, Mr Riddle."

"You're the policeman," I said. "You have to get the details right."

"Thank you for reminding me of that," said Payne. "Pass the hammer."

I looked around the room. "Can't see one."

"It's an imaginary hammer, Mr Riddle. For the imaginary nail. The second one. In the imaginary coffin."

"Oh. I get it."

Another longish pause.

"I'll start again," he said heavily. "When SPC Jarvis first entered your room – according to his verbal report – he asked for you by name. Instead of owning up to who you were, you falsely indicated your roommate Mr Purkis."

"That was a joke."

"A joke?"

"Come on, now, Inspector: I'd have to be very *stupid* to think I could get away with that. For one thing Purkis wasn't–"

"Don't labour the point, Mr Riddle. You were joking. Yes. You're a bit of a joker all round, aren't you?"

"I suppose."

"You suppose. What else do you suppose? Was it a *joke* when you called your Headmaster an insulting name?"

"Oh, you heard about that."

"I hear everything Mr Riddle. Nothing escapes me."

I felt my advantage slipping away from me. "That was a bit stupid, I admit."

"Yes, it was." He shook his head pityingly. "We'll come back to that later. Tell me now about this smoking apparatus of yours. Your, ah, *bubble-pipe.*"

"What about it?"

I had forgotten about the pipe. Purkis and I had puffed away at it every night, stuffing it with whatever we could get our hands on. Our chief supplier had originally been Nevis. Most of what he sold us was pretty disappointing: the sort of muck you suspect of being basically just meat powder mixed with dried herbs. It was only occasionally that we struck lucky, and got to smoke the real stuff. At such times our heads filled with extraordinary visions. We made wild plans to blow up the school, kidnap the Headmaster, run away and join a circus. We would talk through the night, about everything under the stars, so long as it had something to do with Malcaster.

"Apparently," said Payne, drawing heavily on his own pipe, "you gave the pipe to Mr Purkis, as a parting gift".

"That's right. He asked if he could have it."

"So I understand. And you obliged. Possibly because it was not so much a *gift* as a *plant.*"

"What do you mean?"

"What was the pipe used for, Mr Riddle?"

"Smoking."

"Smoking what?"

"Tobacco."

"No other substances?"

"I don't know. Other people used it, not just me. I can't say what people smoked in it when I wasn't there."

"By 'people' are you referring to your close friend, Mr Purkis?"

"Among others."

"You're being evasive. What I'm suggesting, Mr Riddle, is that giving Mr Purkis your pipe was a ruse to cover up the fact that you had used it for the ingestion of forbidden substances. A way, in short, of putting the blame on him."

"I wouldn't do that."

"So you admit that there were substances smoked in the pipe of an illegal nature?"

"No."

"I think you did, Mr Riddle. I'll play back the recording."

He rewound it, and played back the exchange. He switched back to record. "As you see, Mr Riddle," he said, pausing to suck on his pipe, "you don't deny that you used the pipe for an illegal purpose. That means you're tacitly accepting that you did."

"I don't see that."

"Do you want me to play it again?"

"It's up to you."

"Well, we haven't got all day. Here's where we are on this one. Mr Purkis asked for the pipe, and you gave it to him. SPC Jarvis told me the story soon after you arrived. I immediately under-stood its significance, and rang your Headmaster. I asked him to confiscate the article. He has now done so. Fortunately no one had used it since your departure. So whatever substance is detected there will be laid at your door."

"What if it's clean?"

"I doubt very much that that will be the case." He leaned for-ward to knock out his pipe in the ashtray. "There's also the issue of young Mr Worsley."

"What's Worsley got to do with it?"

"SPC Jarvis feels that you may have been exercising an unhealthy influence. Abusing your privileges as a senior scholar to procure personal favours."

"That's outrageous," I said indignantly. "Does Worsley say I did that?"

"I'm not at liberty to divulge that information."

The door banged open. Jarvis stood on the threshold, looking sweaty and wild-eyed. Payne regarded him satirically. "Decided to rejoin us, SPC?"

"Yes," muttered Jarvis. "Sorry." He advanced into the room,

"What on earth is the matter, man? You look like you've seen a ghost."

"They've clamped me," said Jarvis bitterly.

"Clamped your vehicle? That's ridiculous. Where were you parked?"

"By the entrance."

"In the Governors' Car Park? No wonder! I'd take this up with Denis, the receptionist, if I were you. He should have warned you not to park there."

"He did," said Jarvis dolefully.

"Oh, he *did*? In that case you've no one to blame but yourself. They take their parking entitlement very seriously here. All very petty, but I'm afraid it'll land you with a thumping great fine."

"I'll explain the situation."

"It won't do any good. They won't let you off. Not if Denis warned you in advance."

5

The questioning resumed. They went over the same points, many times: what happened when Jarvis asked which one was me ... the bubble-pipe ... Worsley ... when Jarvis entered the room ... illicit substances ... Worsley ...

It was like being slapped across the face with a wet towel: *slap, slap, slap,* without let up.

Finally, when they had badgered me for more than an hour, Payne stood up, massaging his back. "That'll do for now," he said. "We'll resume tomorrow morning, after breakfast. In the meantime SPC Jarvis will take you to the residential warden, Mr Pope, who'll get you to fill in a few forms, and then allocate you a bed."

"How long will I have to stay here?"

"Oh, that depends. The rest of your life, if tonight's little performance is anything to go by. That's a *joke*, you know – I can tell them too, you see. Joking aside, Mr Riddle, I've no interest in prolonging any of this if I can help it. Once you start cooperating you'll be out of here in a flash. We'll talk about that tomorrow. All right, SPC: Take him away."

Jarvis pushed back his chair. "Follow me, Riddle," he said. "Bring that bag with you – with your clothes. You'll need some toiletry materials too."

THIRTEEN
Misdirections

"This man is one of the inmates," said Wisley, bending over the recumbent form, which was clad in Wormwood Hall's distinctive scarlet overall. "And this" – he rolled the body to one side to reveal a gaping wound, from which fresh blood was still leaking in profusion –"shows that he was murdered."

"That's appalling," said Rattle. "This was supposed to be a holiday."

The Asylum, by H O Minty. (Grubstop Press, 485)

1

Cromwell House was a miserable place, as these places are meant to be: cheerless and down-at-heel, rather like an old men's retirement home. A few years earlier it had been a hospital, and very little had been done to adapt it for its new purpose. I was allocated a berth in what had once been a ward, with twelve iron beds separated from one another by sets of translucent plastic curtains embossed with a cheerless pattern of yellow and purple circles and triangles.

Mr Pope, the Head Warden, was a flushed toothy man with the false heartiness of a leader of the Woodland Patrol: possibly one who had been dismissed for the usual sort of misconduct. He wore a whistle hanging round his neck, presumably in case any of the inmates became violent, or tried to escape. I wondered how often that happened, and what other security there was.

He showed me where my bed was and asked if I wanted anything to eat.

"What have you got?"

"I'll see if we can rustle up a bowl of soup."

"Thanks."

"Will you need a pill? To help you sleep."

"I might."

"I'll bring a couple with the soup."

The soup when I got it was pale green and slimy, and tasted of onions. There was also a heel of bread, as dry as a biscuit. I ate what I could. The overhead lights were dimmed. The other occupants of the ward were already in bed, their curtains drawn. Reading lamps illuminated some of the plastic tents like lanterns; others were dark. I used the washroom: brushed my teeth and did the usual stuff. The water tasted foul, like water scooped from a stagnant pond; as it ran down the plughole it released a stench of sewage. I had been provided with one towel, a threadbare rectangle of washed-out cotton that soaked up water like blotting paper. I returned to the ward. A pair of frayed yellow pyjamas were folded on my bed. I closed the plastic curtains – they were clammy to the touch and smelled of disinfectant – changed into the pyjamas, and climbed into bed. The sheets and blankets were tucked as tight as bandages. I felt terribly alone. It felt weirdly like my first few nights at Bune, except that here I didn't have a book to read.

I switched off the light.

It was only now that I got to thinking seriously about my father. Where was he now? Would I ever see him again? Payne and Jarvis were obviously hiding something: they couldn't ask me too much in case they gave the game away. In the morning, I thought, I would start to fight back. There had to be a few serious agitators in here, people dedicated to overthrowing the system. I imagined myself sharing cigarettes with them, benefitting from their knowledge, helping to organise a mass break-out.

All around me I heard groans and mutterings and the creaking of bedsprings: the sound of people trying unsuccessfully to get to sleep. At first I thought I would have to take one of the sleeping pills, but before I knew it the curtains around me were grey with the light of morning.

2

I joined the queue to the washroom. Like me, everyone was wearing yellow pyjamas. My towel was still damp from the previous night's ablutions. The other men eyed me curiously. One asked my name, and where I was from. Lying I thought might well complicate things, so I answered that I had come straight from Bune College. His eyes widened, and after a minute or two he made some excuse to get away. At first I thought he had found my story intimidating; later it occurred to me that he had assumed I was lying.

For breakfast we had another version of the previous night's slimy soup, only this time it was grey. The absence of any flavour was somewhat mitigated by the copious addition of salt. This was served together with some crusts of bread that were even drier than the previous night's offering, and a mug of lukewarm brown liquid of uncertain provenance.

We all ate together at a long table at the far end of the ward. Up to that point I had been hoping Cromwell House might be harbouring members of what I vaguely thought of as 'the resistance'. One look around this dormitory was enough to cure me of that illusion. My fellow inmates belonged without exception to the company of the defeated. One main topic of conversation was the food: what was on the day's menu, what might be served up in the future and the fact certain dishes were coming up rather too often. Sporadic attempts were made by one man or another to interest the table in the condition of their health (frequency of bowel movements, acute indigestion and its causes and remedies, headaches, colds coming on, and so forth.) The weather was also discussed, though in a rather lacklustre fashion – I got the impression that most people spent as little time as possible out of doors. Some inmates looked shifty, it's true, but more in the way of a serial shoplifter than a man with a bomb in his pocket.

After breakfast we went into what passed for a garden. There were benches and a square of brown grass, bordered by weedy flower-beds. I sat on a bench, and looked over at a line of fir trees mouldering on the skyline. It was hot. The air felt depleted of some vital component, the sun scorched my skin. I watched a bumble-bee hovering expectantly at the open trumpet of a purple flower. A scream was building up inside my head. I had been awake for only three hours or so, and already I was terminally bored. The only bright spot on the horizon was the thought that in the next day or two I might be subject to a further interrogation.

A young man sat next to me. His skin was pale; stray wispy clumps of hair sprouted from his cheeks like weeds.

"Michael," he said, offering his hand for me to shake.

"William Riddle."

"Hello, William. Do you mind if I don't reciprocate?"

"Sorry?"

"Tell you my other name, I mean? "

"Not in the least."

"It's not that I don't trust you. It's the other people here. They're desperate to know your business."

"Some people are a bit nosey. I don't like it myself."

"Nosey isn't the word. One of them is a spy."

"Who?"

"I can't tell you that. He might find out."

"Well, of course."

"Why of course?" he asked suspiciously.

"You said it. He's a spy."

Concern became agitation. "How do you know?"

"You told me he was."

"I see. I see." He screwed up his eyes for a second or two, clench-ing his teeth at the same time; I had the impression that he was performing some kind of mental gear change. "I see you're an edu-cated young man."

"I have been educated, yes. On and off."

"Are you wondering how I knew?"

"Not particularly."

"I can tell from the way you speak. I am too – educated, like you. I'm a schoolmaster. Qualified to teach Grammar and Mathematics to level three."

"So why are you in here?"

He was looking agitated again. "Why do you ask?"

"Just making conversation."

He lowered his voice to a whisper. "A pupil of mine reported me."

"For doing what?"

He delved a hand into his pants and started scratching his groin. This seemed to reduce his agitation to some extent. "I don't know. Someone said it was something to do with misusing school stationery."

"Did you do that?"

"What's wrong with writing a few letters?" He brought his hand up to his face, sniffed it, and then replaced it in his pants. "It's not as if I was complaining about the system; just the behaviour of *certain people*."

"That sounds very unjust."

"No, you can't say that. The authorities have been very fair. They're looking into the whole business. They'll soon get to the bottom of it, don't you worry. They'll find out that that boy was telling lies. He'll be punished. He might even end up in this ward. I'll point him out to you."

"Please do."

He looked alarmed. "Did he report you too?"

"Not as far as I know."

"Then why are you so interested?"

"I'm not, really."

He thought this over, rocking back and forwards in his chair. A moment later he was stalking away. He made straight for one of the alleged nosey-parkers, and started muttering to him in the same confiding way, glancing over at me every few seconds, as if to check I was not a figment of his imagination.

Minutes later his place was taken by a tall man in his late thirties. His upper body was developed out of proportion to his lower, as a result I would guess of too much time spent in the gym. His lean jaw ended in a bony lump like a new potato. His name, he said, was Eric Calvert.

Obviously something was preying on Eric's mind. He began by

making the usual roundabout enquiries, but virtually everything he said returned to the question of how he had ended up as an inmate of Cromwell House. Eventually he told me the whole story, or at least his version of the story.

Until last summer he had been a medium-ranking civil servant with responsibility for the transport of the peripatetic workforce from one part of the country to another. One day a trainload of some five hundred agricultural labourers intended for the rape-fields of Bissex was diverted into a siding. The weather was unusually hot. The men were housed in boxcars; after a couple of days they ran out of water. About two hundred died.

"I don't understand. Why did they stay in the car, if it was so hot?"

Eric was fidgeting. "The cars were locked. As a security measure."

"Who ordered that?"

"It's standard procedure." His voice took on a note of pleading. "What you have to understand, Bill, is that in government you have a chain of command. The further down it goes, the more people are involved, and the possibility of accidents happening increases accordingly, if only because the lowest echelons are by definition – how can I put this? – people of low intelligence."

"Yes, but someone–"

"I'm not pointing the finger, Bill. The men who locked those carriages were only doing what they were told. The problem is, they didn't use their initiative when things went wrong."

"There must have been some sort of supervision, though, surely?"

"That's something that remains to be established. It's no good your allocating blame until you know all the facts. The authorities have launched a public enquiry. That's the proper way to go about it. When they're done I expect to be fully exonerated. Until then I'm being housed here to guarantee that I'm available if they need my assistance."

"Is anyone else being held?"

"One or two. People from middle-management, like myself.

And roughly twenty of the guards. Not here, in other centres, spread out across the country."

"I take it they don't want you to talk to one another?"

"Not at all – solely a matter of administrative convenience.

"I see."

"I don't know if you do," he said. He was starting to get irate. "The thing is, Bill, things like 'responsibility' and 'negligence' are a legal fiction, when you get down to it. Before an accident like this all the talk is about 'efficiency' which is basically a matter of cutting costs wherever possible. So the man who can cut the most costs is praised for doing a great job, and the man who wants to add to costs gets shunted downwards, and if he doesn't shut up he eventually gets dismissed. It's only afterwards that people start talking about regulations and public safety, and who did what and who didn't."

"That sounds all wrong."

He looked at me askance. "Wrong? Why is it wrong?"

"Well according to you –" I began.

"No, no, I said nothing of the sort. There's nothing wrong with cutting costs. You can't go spending public money as if there was no tomorrow."

"But if that leads to accidents–?"

"Who said it leads to accidents? Accidents happen. It's a fact of life. You must see that?"

"All right," I said. "So no one was responsible. The system worked the way it was meant to. Except that it didn't."

He sniffed. "You're a dreamer, Will. You want to be careful about that." He stood up. "Fancy a trip to the gym? Helps to stay in shape when you're in here. Saves you from getting depressed."

"I'll come another time," I said.

"Suit yourself."

After he had gone Michael came sidling over.

"Hello again," he said.

"Hello, Michael."

"Saw you talking to Eric."

"That's right."

"Nice chap."

"Seems to be."

"He's a mass-murderer, you know. Did he tell you that?'

"He did mention something along those lines."

"He always does, sooner or later. They'll never let him out, you know."

"Well, it's a serious business."

"He didn't say anything about me, by any chance?"

"Nothing that I recall."

"But something?"

"No."

He nodded disbelievingly, and went away.

3

Two weeks passed, during which I heard nothing further from Jarvis and Payne. Eventually I concluded they must have found enough evidence against my father to proceed against him without interrogating me further. This made me miserable, but there was nothing I could do about it.

Cromwell House had a library of sorts, but there was no fiction, just practical books on subjects like building and joinery and plumbing and marketing, none of which interested me in the least. To make up for this, the gym was quite well equipped, with a couple of bikes and a rowing machine and a weight-bench. Eric was usually in occupation, lifting mighty weights, or rowing as if his life depended on it. Every time I came in he called me over, and did his best to explain why he was in no way responsible for anyone's death. After a few such conversations I learned to avoid the place.

The recreation room was furnished with a tinky-tonk table, and a selection of board games and some large boxes of complicated jigsaw puzzles, each consisting of several thousand pieces. The wireless was permanently tuned to a station playing the sort of jaunty music that makes you feel like killing yourself. This room also had its regular resident, a stout elderly fellow with a great curved scythe of a nose, and a bird's nest of wild white hair, permanently open flies, and food stains all over his waistcoat. The other inmates referred to him as 'the Jigsaw Man'. Whenever I went in there I found him working on of one of the enormous jigsaws, using the tinky-tonk table as a base for his endeavours. One corner of the table was reserved for small piles of loose pieces sorted into groups of sky, foliage, water and people, the remainder for the framework of the puzzle. Purkis's father, I remembered, was also a keen puzzler. Watching the Jigsaw Man patiently fitting one piece of sky into another I began to understand what its appeal might be to someone whose working life involved stressful predicaments and snap decisions.

Eventually, more out of boredom than curiosity, I engaged him in conversation. This involved some determination on my part. For a while I stood watching him without venturing a comment. Apart from briefly glancing up when I first went over, he continued fitting one piece into another as if I did not exist.

"That looks fiendishly complicated," I said finally.

He made no reply, other than a low grunt.

"Have you done this one before?" I asked, after a few minutes had elapsed.

"Five times. It's a crying shame what's happened to it. When it first came in it was perfect, but once they let the criminals loose in here pieces started going missing. Eighteen altogether, by my count. That makes it quite a challenge to complete. Still, one should never give up without a struggle."

He returned to his puzzle.

"Have you been in here long?" I asked, after a silence of some minutes.

He put down the piece of puzzle he was trying to fit onto a corner of sky, removed a silver timepiece from the pocket of his stained waistcoat, and studied it for a minute or so. "I wouldn't say 'long'," he said patiently. "Roughly some two hours and sixteen minutes, if my chronometer is correct. Since eight-thirty-two this morning."

"I mean here, in Cromwell House. In residence."

"Cromwell House! Is that what they call it now? It used to be known as 'The Retreat' when I was a boy."

"You first came here as a boy?"

"I've *always* been here. This is where I live."

"Why actually are you here?" I asked, after another long silence.

He looked surprised. "To finish the puzzles, of course. Someone has to do it. They won't solve themselves, you know."

"I never thought of that," I said satirically.

Looking up, he bent forward, narrowing his eyes as if seeing me for the first time. "Might I offer a word of advice, young man?"

"Please do."

"You need to find yourself an occupation. Something challenging."

"Like doing jigsaws, you mean?"

"It doesn't matter what it is, so long as it passes the time. Otherwise you could easily go mad."

"Oh, right," I said. "Thanks. I'll keep that in mind."

4

I felt very alone. The truth is I was missing Purkis. If he had been there with me it would have been different. Cromwell House was not unlike Malcaster, though on a meaner scale. We could have pilloried its staff and elaborated on the crimes of its inmates. This at least would have passed the time.

For want of anything better to do, I spent most of the day in the recreation room, playing myself at squares, or presiding over the work of the Jigsaw Man. Sometimes we would enjoy a short conversation, usually a harmless exchange about the day's breakfast, or I would assist him by completing a patch of choppy ocean. As soon as I had quit the table he would invariably dismantle my effort, and return the pieces to the appropriate pile.

My thoughts turned inwards, and what I saw I was not likeable. I began to despise my personality, my appearance, what I had made of my life. All this time I had been picturing myself as a rebel, but the truth is I had never really rebelled against anything in my life. At Bune I had allowed myself the luxury of sneering at the establishment, while enjoying the privileges that same establishment made possible. And now those privileges had been taken away from me, and I didn't like it. I couldn't even form a bond with my fellow victims. If anything, I rather despised them. My father was right: Bune had turned me into a snob, and I had done nothing to stop it.

Depressed and lonely, I occupied myself by penning one more Malcaster story. Floater and Toadflax persuade Rattle that Wisley has become a danger to himself. Believing himself to be acting in his friend's best interests, Rattle gulls him into becoming a 'guest' at a private lunatic asylum called Wormwood Hall, on the pretext that it is a hotel where 'health cures' are administrated to the out-of-sorts. Wisley is placed on a diet of pea soup and boiled artichokes. When several of his fellow 'guests' are found dead in the hotel's shower-room, Wisley begins to suspect that the hotel is in fact a camp for the disposal of social undesirables, and takes refuge in the Hall's bat-haunted attics. Two policemen going by the names of Cain and Gamble – thinly disguised versions of Payne and Jarvis – apprehend him, and hand him over to the Hall's chief psychiatrist. He is restrained and heavily medicated on the grounds that he is a dangerous lunatic. Rattle departs, leaving Wisley in a straitjacket, weeping and shouting for help. Later that day, Wormwood Hall is burnt to the ground. Wisley is presumed to have died in the blaze. I called the story 'The Asylum, or Malcaster Victorious'.

5

One morning after breakfast Mr Pope called me to his office and told me to expect a visitor. Not just any visitor, but the Minister for Communications himself, Sir Roger Purkis.

"I had no idea you were acquainted with anyone in the government," he said worriedly. "I knew you'd been to Bune, of course, but really: *Sir Roger Purkis!* I mean to say, who's next – Lord Haverhill?"

"I know him too," I said.

"You do? Well, this is most extraordinary. I trust you'll give Sir Roger a good report of your treatment here. You haven't any complaints, have you? If so, you must let me know."

"No complaints at all," I said. "I've stayed in expensive hotels which aren't anywhere near as comfortable."

"Really? I'm very glad to hear it. What about the food?"

"The food is excellent. Wholesome, fresh, and consistently delicious. My compliments to the chef."

"I'll pass that on. And you'll say all this to Sir Roger, will you?"

"Absolutely."

A shadow of anxiety darkened his face. "You won't be *too* complimentary I hope. Cromwell House isn't supposed to be a holiday-camp, you know."

"Don't worry," I said. "I shall be strict but fair."

6

Sir Roger was waiting for me in the foyer. He was armoured against the autumn chill by a magnificent camel overcoat, which he wore over a grey double-breasted suit and a starched shirt of some iridescent blue fabric. This stunning ensemble was completed by a pair of dark red brogues and a bright floral tie. His long fair hair was combed back from his forehead and fell to his shoulders in smooth tailored waves. He was a bit pink in the face.

Seeing me descending the staircase in my yellow rompers, he did a double take. "William!" he said, rising to his feet and holding out his hand. "How nice to see you, dear boy!"

I was inclined to be grumpy. "What are you doing here?'

"Paul asked me to look you up. I promised I'd see if there was anything you needed: books, blankets, that sort of thing. He's worried about you: feels that you might blame him for what's happened, in some way."

"Well, I don't."

"Thank goodness for that. I'd hate for you two to fall out. We Bunians stick together, you know, through thick and thin. We don't let our friends go down the drain if there's anything we can do to help out."

"Pleased to hear it."

"You sound a touch bitter. I can understand that. You must be feeling pretty fed up."

"I am, yes."

A group of inmates brushed past us, talking excitedly to one another, and making clumsy gestures. Sir Roger watched them go with a look of concern. "You shouldn't be in here with these hopeless cases," he said in a lowered voice. "A Bunian like you."

"Well I'm not here by choice."

"I know that. Look, why don't we go for a bit of a walk? I'm sure the Warden won't object to that. Pull on something warm, if you have it. If nothing else it'll save me having to stare at that atrocious romper-suit they've got you wearing!"

7

We sat together on a curly iron bench, and stared at the flat horizon. The weather had turned chilly. An unruly wind untidied his hair, which he kept pushing out of his eyes. My own hair had been shaved close to the scalp by one of the guards; it was a precaution, they told me, against head lice.

"Treating you all right in here, are they?" he asked.

"Well, you know. The place is a dump, the food is terrible – but what else can you expect?"

"Grin and bear it, eh? Very sensible. There again, I supposed you're used to 'roughing it' where you come from?"

Paul had obviously given him a less than glowing account of our cottage in Cantleford. The rich have very little idea of how most people live. "The worst thing is the boredom," I said.

"Boring, is it? Perhaps I could send you a couple of big jigsaws. Excellent for taking your mind off things, I find."

"Thanks," I said, wondering how the Jigsaw Man would take the arrival of some fresh puzzles. He was pretty set in his ways; I had the feeling it might cause him distress.

"I gather you've run into two characters by the name of Payne and Jarvis," Sir Roger continued.

"Yes."

"Payne's all right. Old school, good manners, knows his place. Jarvis is another type of dog altogether. Ambitious, pushy, resentful. He's the one to watch out for."

"I can't say I care for either of them."

"That's understandable. Things look different when you're on

184

the receiving end, I should imagine. Ask you about your pa, did they?"

"Actually no. They were more concerned about Bune stuff. They made out that I seriously tried to pretend that Paul was me. It's obvious that was just a joke."

"Policemen and jokes don't mix. And that kind of joke could easily be misinterpreted. Has been, in fact."

"That's stupid."

He shook his head. "Never underestimate the simplicity of the official mind, William. They take everything literally. Unlike at Bune, where exactly the reverse is true. No one ever means anything they say – even when it's a declaration of love."

The word seemed in this setting shockingly indelicate. I quickly changed the subject. "It gets worse. Jarvis has been quizzing our tick Worsley. He seems to have the idea–"

"I know what idea he has. Way off the mark again. It's a very special relationship, the tick and his tick-master. You can't expect a policeman from the underclass to comprehend that."

"Can't someone put him right?"

"There wouldn't be any point. They're just looking for a hook to hang you on – something that will hold up in court. Any old hook'll do, so long as it's got your name above it. The trouble with mud is that it sticks. Take this business of your bubble-pipe."

"What about it?"

"They've done an analysis. Traces of a certain *substance* have been found."

"So what? Everyone uses that stuff at Bune."

"Not everyone at Bune is in your position." He was silent for a few seconds. Then he said: "Look, William: Jarvis and Payne are coming back again tomorrow. This time I want you to handle things a bit differently. Stop being obstructive. Stop trying to score points. *Give them what they want.*"

"What *do* they want? I don't know."

"Nor do they, as a matter of fact. But they'll know it when they hear it. Trust me, William, I've got a nose for these things. Somewhere inside that charming head of yours you're sitting on something frightfully valuable. It's the proverbial diamond in the rubbish-dump. All you have to do is dredge it up. Be open with them. Tell them everything, every little detail; even if it seems of no account."

"Why should I?"

"Because if you cooperate all of these charges will be dropped. You'll be set free." He stared at the horizon, then swivelled in his seat and fixed me with his pale blue eyes. "You could have your place back at Bune, William. This time next year you could be a member of Crow."

I stared at the elasticated cuffs of my yellow romper suit. They were very grubby. Something furious and violent was happening inside me, like a storm in a sealed dustbin.

"What about my pa?" I asked.

"Come on, William, you have yourself to think about. Your father's an adult: he can look after himself."

I agreed with this in a way. In another, it was terrible, despicable, the sort of idea that can wreck your life. If I did as he suggested the little shit I carried inside me would overcome, and what remained of me – the true me, the William who loved his father and his friend – would disappear.

8

The next morning, as Sir Roger had predicted, I was summoned for a further session with Payne and Jarvis and their stupid tape-recorder.

Since Sir Roger's visit I had been mulling over what he had said – particularly the bit about the diamond in the rubbish tip. I didn't think there was a diamond, personally. But I might be able to convince the two men that they were on the point of finding one, even though I was feeding them nothing but rubbish. I didn't quite know how I was going to manage this, but I was going to give it a try.

9

Payne set up his tape recorder, making use this time of a lengthy extension lead. As before he took charge of the questioning, while Jarvis sat watching the proceedings with ill-concealed impatience.

Sir Roger's summing up of their opposing characters had been astute. Payne, I now saw, was an officious old relic who had risen through the ranks by virtue of his unassailable dullness. Jarvis was a bit more dangerous. He wasn't exactly clever, but he made up for that with the single-minded determination of a foxhound. Give him a scent, and he would follow it to the ends of the earth.

Give them what they want, Sir Roger had advised. That was out of the question, if only because it would inevitably mean betraying my father. Instead I would offer them the exact opposite – something that would send them in the wrong direction entirely. I wasn't sure yet how I was going to accomplish this feat, but I had a vague idea of the general direction.

"I believe," began Payne, "that you had a visitor yesterday."

"That's right. My friend's father."

"Your friend being, in this instance, one Paul Purkis? The friend you attempted to pass off as yourself?"

"That's the one."

"The friend on whom you also endeavoured to plant a brass pipe bearing, as we now know, traces of narcotics?"

"If you say so."

"You're admitting guilt?"

"I'm accepting that that's your view of the matter."

"You realise that these are offences with which you could be charged in court? Number one, wilfully and with malice misleading an officer of the law; number two, possessing and making use of substances proscribed under the law. Not to mention endangering the health of other persons subjected to the fumes resultant upon such use."

"I am aware of that, yes. Are you charging me now?"

Payne looked crafty. "That depends on the extent of your cooperation."

"OK. I'm cooperating. What do you want to know?"

Payne bit his pipe; Jarvis looked up at the ceiling.

"Let's talk about your father."

"Right. Fire away."

"We've established that you last saw him six weeks ago, when he paid a visit to your school."

"Yes, on a half-holiday."

"What was the purpose of this visit?"

"Just the usual father-son stuff, you know."

"Nothing particular to impart?"

"Not that I recall. What kind of thing were you thinking of?"

Payne looked at Jarvis. Jarvis said: "He doesn't visit you very often, does he, your dad? Once a year, if that. So for him to come at all was unusual in itself, wouldn't you say?

"It must have been the annual duty-visit."

"Duty rather than pleasure?"

"Well, my pa isn't one for sentiment, as a rule. And as you know, he's a pretty busy man."

"Tell me about that day. What did the two of you do together?"

"Nothing out of the way. He arrived, we chatted, had lunch, then he went. I could tell you what we had for lunch, if you like. He had gammon and I had a steak and kidney pie. This was in a cafe called–"

"We know where it was," said Jarvis.

"OK. It's just that Sir Roger insisted I should tell you everything."

Jarvis looked at Payne. Payne said: "During this lunch did he seem at all agitated?"

"Why would he be?"

"He didn't mention anything to do with his work?"

"We never talk about his work. Touchy subject."

"Why is that?"

"He's a scientist, I'm an artist, no common ground – that kind of thing."

"But you remain on friendly terms?"

"Yes, if we avoid certain topics."

"He would tell you, for example, if he was in any trouble?"

"Not necessarily. He's actually a very private person. Doesn't talk much about personal things, not to me at any rate."

Jarvis leaned forwards. "If I may, DCI Payne."

Payne sighed. "Go ahead, SPC."

Jarvis fixed me with his eye. "You say you're an artist. What kind of art is that? Painting landscapes?"

"No, sorry, not much good at that I'm afraid. I prefer to build things. Like a stage set you can walk into. My last piece, for example was a mock-up of a murder scene, set in The Bune Bookstop. Not the real Bookstop, though – a replica."

"What was the point of that?"

"Well, if you don't see a point, then for you there isn't one."

Jarvis moistened his upper lip with his tongue. "So what you're saying," he proposed dangerously, "is that I am fundamentally incapable of understanding this ingenious confabulation of yours?"

"No, not at all. It's more that it isn't the sort of thing that *can* be explained. I'm not working with words, so words won't make it clear to you. You have to work it out for yourself."

"If you can be bothered to do so."

"Well, yes, obviously."

He sniffed. "And they encourage this at Bune, do they?"

Payne was tapping his fingernails on the table: he had been doing so for some time. "I'm not sure that's relevant, Jarvis. We're not here to evaluate the educational methodology of Bune School."

"I was interested to hear that Riddle here thinks himself an artist. I was wondering what sort of art that could possibly be."

"Well, the point has been cleared up now, I think. Can we move on?"

"Absolutely." Jarvis continued to stare at me. "I just wondered–"

"Yes?"

"What *did* you talk about, the pair of you? During this visit. Did you discuss your 'art', for example?"

"I told him I'd won a prize."

"You won a prize?"

"Yes."

"And he was pleased with that, was he?"

"Not really, no. He thought I should be doing something a bit more serious. Like science."

"So there was a quarrel?"

"Absolutely not. We're past all that."

Round and round it went: covering the same old boring ground, getting nowhere. It was time, I thought, to introduce a red herring. I waited for the right opportunity.

Payne started asking me about my father's friends. He didn't have any, I said, only colleagues.

"No particular friend?" pressed Payne. "No one he's specially attached to?"

I hesitated. "Not really."

"Not really? Or not at all?"

"He used to know someone in Gillie."

"Where you used to live?"

"I didn't live there with him – I was at Glenlockie first."

"But you met this man?"

"Sort of. You see, when I was little my pa used to take me off for a week or two in the summer. And some of the times we would stay in a place called Drumfyn."

"Drumfyn. Funny little town. My dad used to take me there, in the summer, when I was a boy. Freezing cold. Rained all the time. Nothing whatsoever to do. Go on, Mr Riddle."

"Well, he had a friend there. They used to go off together in the evenings. For a drink. And he wouldn't get back until late."

A lie was beginning began to construct itself: small at first, and fairly simple, but sprouting multiple branches as I continued.

"Can you describe him, this friend of your father's?"

"He had a black beard, I think. He always wore a bonnet, though, so I don't know if he was bald or not."

"But you were introduced to him?"

"Not by name. Pa said, this is my son William, and we shook hands, and I went back to my book."

"How many times did he come round, this chap?"

"Every night, I think."

"Did you ever see them, ah, embrace?"

"No."

"Say or do anything that might have led you to suppose they enjoyed an, ah, *physical* relationship."

"No. That's not my father's style."

"He doesn't go in for physical relationships?"

"I've no idea. It's not the sort of thing we talk about."

"You stayed in a guesthouse, you say?"

"That's right. I don't remember what it was called, but it was halfway up a hill. I remember the cobbles, and some steps. And it was painted white, I think…"

Payne asked me to describe the owner of the guest house. He wasn't old, I said, but he wasn't young either … but there was something odd about him…

"In what way?"

"He had this very black hair, very thick and sort of solid, like an animal's pelt. It used to slip sideways, when he picked up the breakfast tray, and he had to put the tray back down to straighten it."

I went on elaborating my tale, adding extra floors and annexes, mapping out a tropical garden, introducing an insignificant contradiction or two. Once the lie was launched it more or less told itself. I enjoyed the process immensely; it was like eating a stolen pie that was all the more delicious for belonging to someone else. I described breakfasts of porridge and salty brown kippers, and my father getting back one night so drunk I had to help take his boots off. Unfortunately, I had to wash out one of the boots afterwards, because he'd been sick in it.

This last detail might have been a little too colourful, because at that point I noticed Jarvis's eye flicker in my direction, then go stony. He refrained from challenging me on the point, but the information imparted by his face was a warning to me to tone things down a bit.

"Well now," said Payne, "at last we seem to be getting somewhere. Drumfyn, guesthouse, white front, cobbles, hill, wig – they shouldn't be too hard to track down. I'll let you do the spadework, SPC Jarvis. You could do with a bit of a break, and the Western Isles are very pleasant at this time of the year. You can start off tomorrow morning. A train leaves Middleton around midday. Two changes will take you to Gillie; after that you get a bus to Rad na Glen, then a taxi to Ardowhyll, where you can get a ferry directly over to Drumfyn. Two boats a day, one first thing in the morning, the other at seven at night. You'll be gone about a fortnight, I should think."

"I shall enjoy that," said Jarvis, glancing at me as he spoke. He wasn't going to contradict Payne, that was clear; he would go off and do as he was told; but I was a little apprehensive about what would happen when he came back.

FOURTEEN

Escape from Cromwell House

The tourist industry in Anglia is strangled by a surfeit of red tape and a mountain of unnecessary paperwork. Every movement is recorded, every visit to a national monument, every conversation, every cup of tea. Agents even report on how often a visitor uses the flusher.

Dead Ends: The Scandalous Condition of Our Economy,
by H Shaftesbury (Embankment Press, 468)

1

As soon as I was back in the ward, my feelings of apprehension grew stronger. I started devising the usual anxious scenarios about what would happen when Jarvis got back from his wild goose chase in the islands of Western Alba. Within two weeks he would know for certain that there was no white-painted guesthouse halfway up a cobbled hill in Drumfyn with a wig-wearing owner, all pointing to the conclusion that my Alban story was a complete fiction. I had manufactured too many identifying details, that was the trouble. Next time I would be far less specific. Except that there wouldn't be a next time: Jarvis and Payne were never going to give me a second chance.

What would they do when Jarvis came back? Charge me with deception and drug-dealing, most probably. My ambiguous status as a 'person of interest' would be replaced by that of a 'convicted criminal.' I would have to serve a sentence, probably of indefinite length. This was something to be avoided at all costs. I would have to escape.

Escaping at first looked easy. Security at Cromwell House was practically non-existent. Some evenings there were only three guards on duty in all ten dormitory blocks. The main doors to the outside were locked at night and connected to the alarm system, but for anyone who knew the building there were plenty of ways you could get out without being spotted or setting off an alarm. There were only two roll-calls: at 8.00 am and 10.00 pm. The yellow jumpsuit was the main problem, because it made you so easily identifiable as an inmate. If I could find a civilian outfit – a suit, or even just a long overcoat – there was a good chance I could break out without anyone noticing me, particularly if I left mid-morning.

Perhaps, I thought, I could overpower a civilian and steal his clothes. Then I could lock him up somewhere, or knock him out, or drug him and then get on with my getaway.

Realistically, of course, that wasn't going to happen. Theatrics like that call for a Nevis: someone ruthless; someone who is at home with violence, and unafraid of its consequences – not someone like me, who preferred to leave the heroics to other people. For a second or two I found myself wishing that I could be a bit more like Nevis, even if only for an afternoon. But trying to emulate someone you despise is a tricky proposition, like trying to hold onto a slippery fish-like creature which keeps mewing and trying to wriggle free, and looks and smells disgusting into the bargain. Like it or not, the thing you always end up with is yourself.

Briefly I considered trying to get hold of a guard's uniform. But they were kept in the staff quarters, under lock and key, and in any case all the guards knew one another – there was no way I could pass myself off as one of them.

Even supposing I did manage to get hold of some clothes and get out of the building, what would I do next? Cromwell House was in the middle of nowhere. The nearest town was a good twenty miles away. Within ten hours the search parties would be out looking for me. I had no cash and no ID, and no map. I didn't even have any decent shoes: the soft-soled canvas slip-ons we all had to wear would hardly get me across a muddy lawn let alone a ploughed field. And what if it rained? It was coming on for winter, and the land was flat and marshy. I would need a waterproof coat, and gloves, and a sleeping bag, and something to eat.

I found myself wishing that I had paid more attention to Woodcraft Training. The College unit of the Woodland Patrol formed every Friday afternoon for drills and training. There were courses in survival skills – anyone who aspired to be a Pack Leader was sent off after Pagan for a fortnight to the Western mountains, to learn how to light fires and build a shelter and live off wild berries and the odd dead weasel. I had always lazily insisted that the whole business was silly and childish. Now that I needed those skills, I began to appreciate how useful they might be.

On top of all that, I remembered the notices plastered all over Cromwell House warning 'electronic devices' that could cause 'injury and death.' I had assumed to begin with that these were bogus threats, with no working system to back them up. But what if they weren't?

The more I thought over at the problem, the more complicated it seemed. Security at Cromwell House, it seemed, was not so lax after all.

2

The Jigsaw Man, when I next saw him, was in a state of feverish agitation. He waved at me from the pocket-ball table with rapid jerky stabs of the arm, as if trying to batter an elusive fly with a knock-ball racket.

He started shouting as soon as I entered the room. "Have you seen what the silly buggers have done now?" he wailed. "They've only gone and sent *two new jigsaws*, for heaven's sake! Great lumbering boxes of two thousand pieces each. 'Storm at Sea' and 'Rapefields in July'– can you imagine the complication? How do they think I'm ever going to find the time to tackle stuff like that? I've got my work cut out as it is!"

Feeling somewhat responsible, I offered to help.

"You?" he said scornfully. "Don't make me laugh! You couldn't solve a slice of toast if it was cut into two and fed you on a plate!"

3

My anxiety mounted in daily increments. It was like the House of Horrors at Ensor Fun-Fair, which I had visited once with Purkis – he was keen on that sort of thing. One of the rooms in the Dungeon of Demons had walls which gradually closed in on you: only a few centimetres at a time, but enough to scare the life out of you. Just as you thought you were going to get crushed to death a flap in the wall flipped open and tumbled you out onto a mattress.

Here, however, there would be no flap to release me. The walls would go on closing in until they were pressing on my back and my chest, and the ceiling would come down over my head, and I would be compressed into a cube of squashed Riddle like an old steamer at the scrapyard.

Like all the best solutions, the right one came unbidden, when I was thinking of something else. As I was sitting at the dining table one evening, waiting for the soup to be served, a memory popped into my head: of plates of mashed potato passing along at eye level, one after another after another. I felt myself twitch. There was a feeling of vacancy, as if nothing was real. My body went rigid. My neck jerked, once, twice, three times, rhythmically. Then my arms and legs joined in.

"Bloody chameleon!" said my father irritably, somewhere in the back of my head.

4

I chose my moment, during supper, when it was too late to call in a doctor. The plates passed along the table, and I began to twitch. There were a few worried glances, but no one did anything. My twitches grew more violent. People stood up, drew back, reached towards me. I threw myself about on the chair, knocking over glasses of water, sending bowls and spoons crashing and tinkling to the floor. Finally I let my chair fall backwards, with me still sitting in it. I had practised this a few times in the recreation room. Most of the time I had got away unscathed; once or twice I bumped the back of my head. Doing it now, I threw in an extra backwards jerk, flew off the chair, and smashed my head against the floor.

196

That was bad luck, but at least it made my act look convincing. My head hurt, but I kept up the thrashing around. A froth of foam gathered on my lips. Something odd was happening to my eyes: they were open but I couldn't see. I heard cries of alarm. I was putting up a pretty convincing show.

Rather than getting an ambulance, Mr Pope called in security. Within half an hour Payne – worse luck – was standing over me in the warden's office. I lay on the floor twitching from time to time.

Payne got on the telephone. I heard him through a fog. I had a thunderous headache from the bump on the head, and my body ached all over. From time to time I lost consciousness.

Payne's voice chuntered on at a far distance.

"Yes. He could be faking … I don't know. I'm not a doctor."

I twitched violently.

"We could just let him sleep it off. If you want to take the risk. Well, I thought I should check. You want me to do that? SPC Jarvis isn't here. Yes, I agree. Yes, Cantleford DH. Yes, a big place. What about security? Yes. I won't let him out of my sight."

The headache drummed on ferociously. My eyes closed of their own accord. Odd sinister visions came into my head: Porter, Worsley, Nevis, Counsellor Joyce cavorting stark naked in a glade infested with big black flies. For a time I must have passed out, because when I opened my eyes I was lying flat on my back, rattling over the cobbled yard on a trolley. I kept still, closed my eyes again. There was a bump, and a slam, and a light came on above me, and I felt someone fastening a mask over my nose and mouth. Straps were secured around my chest and legs. A siren started up. I was in an ambulance.

The ride took a long time: possibly an hour. I dozed off several times on the way.

5

A blur of lights overhead.

"Stand aside, sir. You're in the way."

"I'm a security officer. He's in my charge."

"He's my patient. He's at serious risk."

"I'll explain it to you, shall I?"

"Terry, take this end of the – sir, you're going to have to wait in the seating area."

My main advantage was the fact that everyone – except possibly Payne– thought I was unconscious. If Payne would only get lost it would be relatively easy for me to slide off the trolley and sprint off down the corridor.

Hold on, I thought. Pick your moment.

My jumpsuit was peeled from me like a banana skin. A light cotton gown was draped across my chest and legs, then they moved me onto my side to fasten it on the back. A cold metallic disc pressed against my chest. Someone gripped my wrist. Something was wrapped around my upper arm. I felt it swell like a balloon. Someone read out some numbers, some medical mumbo-jumbo. The trolley trundled down a corridor – bars of light passing like plates, flash, flash, flash – then took a turn and stopped. A curtain swished aside. The trolley moved again.

"Count of two. One – *two!*"

On 'two' I was jerked into the air and dumped down onto a padded platform. Paper rustled under my back.

Through half-closed eyes I could see that I was in a small cubicle. Orange plastic curtains on three sides. Various machines sat in the corner. Dials, wires, bottles. A chair. A small window.

A shadow fell across my face. "What happens now?" asked Payne, sounding rather closer than was comfortable.

"A doctor will come and see him."

"When will that be?"

"When one is free. There's no hurry – he's in no danger."

Payne sat heavily in a chair next to me. A reek of pipe tobacco wafted across the space between us. He wheezed slightly as he spoke. "Is this going to take all night?"

"It might. We're busy."

"I haven't time for this. Is there a phone I can use?"

"In the waiting-room. There might be a bit of a queue."

"You must have one closer than that."

"Hospital staff only."

"This is state business."

"Can't let you use it without authorisation."

"I can get you authorisation. All I need is a phone."

"In the waiting-room," said the nurse, with a note of quiet satisfaction. "May be a bit of a queue."

Payne made a strangled noise in the back of his throat. "I can't leave him."

"That's up to you."

"He's in my custody. Can you find some restraints?"

"I can't authorise that. You'll have to wait for a doctor."

"He might be faking." The pipe tobacco smell drew close. Payne touched my cheek, wheezing, then took a fold of flesh between his fingers.

"Don't do that. You could set off another seizure."

"Let's see, shall we?" He pinched my cheek, hard.

I conjured up the plates. One after another they passed in front of me. I twitched, and twitched again, then started thrashing.

"He's seizing! Stand back!"

"He's faking." His tone was suffused with a kind of malicious certainty. "Hold him still and I'll prove it."

Another voice: "DCI Payne?"

"That's me."

"There's a phone call for you. Sir Roger Purkis."

"Have you explained the situation?"

"I'll let you do that."

"He's a tricky little bugger. What if he tries to escape?"

"Where's he going to go? The doors are all locked."

"One of you will have to watch him."

"We'll keep an eye on him," said the nurse, with a touch of sarcasm. "We'll let you know if he makes a run for it."

"If he gets away," said Payne, "I'm holding you personally responsible."

Shuffling sounds, then silence. I left it another few seconds, then half opened my eyes. The view through my lashes indicated that I was alone.

I sat upright. I didn't have much time. I opened a slot in the curtain to the left, and peered through. An ancient man was sitting on a blue plastic seat, naked to the waist, a tube leading from his arm into a bag of colourless liquid. He regarded me balefully, but without interest.

"Sorry." I closed the curtain, and separated the one to the right. Another cubicle. Empty this time. Clothes folded over a chair – grey wool, mostly. A pair of black leather shoes.

I yanked off the hospital gown, and began pulling the shirt over my head, and struggling into the trousers. No time for shorts or socks. Shoes next – they slipped on like canoes – then the jacket. There was something bulky in the breast pocket.

I pulled back the curtain, and shuffled out into the corridor, my feet sliding about in the over-large shoes. The loose jacket gave off a smell like vegetable soup. The cuffs covered my hands. The pants, without a belt, were slipping off my hips; I had to stick my hands in both pockets to hold them up.

At the end of the corridor a man in a white coat was punching a number into a keypad. I followed him through, and found myself in a crowded waiting area. No one took any notice of me.

Over by the reception desk Payne was complaining into a black telephone. I walked past him to the door. My back felt vulnerable, like a target. At any moment I expected to hear Payne's shout, and running feet, and a hand closing on my arm.

I pushed open the swing doors. A blast of cold air hit my face, and swirled about my sockless ankles. I kept walking.

Ahead of me was a bus stop and a small queue of people. As I shuffled towards it a bus pulled up. I reached into my breast pocket. The bulky thing was a fat wallet, stuffed to bursting. I opened it, took out a ten-shilling note. Joined the bus queue. Climbed on board. Acres of empty red seats. Sat down.

"Where to?" asked the conductor.

"Railway station?"

"That's one and six."

I handed over the note.

"Nothing smaller than that?" he asked.

"Sorry."

Grumbling under his breath, he wound out a ticket, and handed it over with a fistful of change.

The bus moved off.

It was almost too easy.

6

There was no point in heading for the country. A childhood spent in Glenlockie had taught me that in a village or a small town anyone unfamiliar sticks out like an erection in the showers, and attracts just as much opprobrium. I decided to catch a train to Ludden. There at least I would not be the only stranger in town. I had only visited the city a few times, but knew it for a dirty, noisy, crowded place, marked by extreme contrasts: grand houses and filthy shelters; extreme wealth and extreme poverty; beauty and ugliness, people of immense importance and people of none whatsoever. Other than this, I had gleaned a certain amount from the novels of WC Collins. My best bet would be confine myself to the haunts of the poor, where the only people I was likely to come across were the dregs of society, the unemployed, the homeless, petty criminals, drug addicts: people not unlike the inmates of Cromwell House. Within that milieu, I conjectured, I might be able to uncover a cell of rebels who would give me shelter and help me work against the system.

The idea was hollow, unconvincing. I was by no means sure I wanted to find such a cell. Even if I could, I doubted I could pass myself off as a rebel myself. The rebels of popular imagination had high ideals; they were brave, and capable of dedicating themselves to a cause, for the benefit of the greater good. I just didn't see myself in that light. I had too much of the Bune veneer; I had absorbed too many of its values.

Somewhere in the back of all of this hovered the indelicate word Sir Roger had used when we were sitting on the bench, but to me that was as delusionary as the hope of making a better world through revolutionary action. Why did people always set themselves such impossibly high goals, I wondered? Didn't they see they were just asking to be disappointed?

All I could hope for in my present situation was to find a bolt-hole, and hide myself away, and hope for things to improve: for my father to be rehabilitated; for the charges against me to be dropped. Then I might be able to find a job, somewhere: making things, perhaps, in a rural setting.

Even to me that sounded pathetic. The truth is I was lost. Practically speaking, all I could do was surrender to the current, in the vain hope that it might carry me into something like safe harbour. I was aware, of course, that I was far more likely to end up trapped in a den of thieves and murderers, but I tried not to let that worry me.

7

Close to the station was an arcade full of shops, mostly catering to the poor. The goods were all of inferior quality, many not service-able, so I had to be quite fussy about what I bought. I chose a pack of black underpants, a pack of socks, a scribbling tablet of coarse grey paper, a pack of pencils, some cheap razors, a toothbrush and a jar of toothpaste; also a small trolley-bag to carry them in. This last item used up a great deal of the cash in my stolen wallet, but knowing how suspicious hoteliers are of people who arrive with-out luggage, I reckoned it to be a necessary investment.

I hid in a small park until it got light, then went into the station. People milled about, taking no notice of me, but I remained tense, anticipating the worst. Trains for Ludden left every hour. I bought a ticket. The station clock read 10.45.

I got into a carriage full of young people.

For a while I dozed, waking with a hammering headache and a mouth like furred kettle. A young man opposite was looking at me curiously, his mouth hanging open. I stood up and went out into the corridor, where I watched a deserted village whizz past, fol-lowed by drab fields of brown stubble, and long linked lines of iron towers, and the occasional lonely clump of rusting trees.

Where could I go? The remaining money in my wallet would not last more than a day or two. I had a horror of sleeping on the streets or begging. Under other circumstances I might have approached one or another of my father's colleagues; as it was, they were more likely to turn me in than give me shelter.

The stations followed one another in dull succession. Some of the names were familiar. I took a look at the line plan. We were about twenty miles from Ensor.

'Ticket sir?'

I handed the man my ticket, and he punched it routinely.

"Does this train stop at Ensor?"

"This is for Ludden."

"Thought I'd look around the castle."

"I wouldn't bother. One small wing open to the public. The rest is all offices."

I was still undecided. I thought about Purkis. Where did his loyalties lie? He had never held back from jeering at the school establishment. But when it came to matters of government, the NAC, Sir Roger himself, he had always been refrained from voicing any judgement. I remembered how odd he had been about Union: how insistent that we took it seriously. Friend or not, Purkis was part of the system, by family if not by inclination. I could hardly expect him to choose me over his own father.

The train slowed, and the sign for Ensor slid into view. We pulled up at the platform.

8

Ensor station was as always decked out in the traditional style, with scalloped wooden palings hanging over the platform, and flowers – artificial at this time of the year – in wooden troughs, and a bright blue pillar post-box. Everything was spick and span. The woodwork was freshly painted. Tasteful posters advertised excursions to surrounding attractions: Ensor Woodcraft Centre, Shadlock House with its water gardens, Rugglesford Abbey, Bune College, Masham Towers Amusement Park.

It was still early in the morning. A uniformed porter sloped discreetly in a doorway, trolley to hand, permanently on the watch for a traveller with a heap of luggage. Other than him, the platform was deserted. I was the only one getting out.

On the train I had stuffed my shoes with newspaper, to make a tighter fit. This worked up to a point, but my toes felt squashed against the leather, and hurt when I walked. I was acutely aware of how loosely my suit hung over my shoulders, how my pants flapped around my legs and threatened to slide off my hips. If anyone was looking for a fugitive I would be the obvious suspect.

I handed in my ticket, and limped down the hill towards the town. There was no point in turning back now. I was desperately tired; I needed a place to stay.

Below the castle was a row of guest-houses: 'Ensor Lodge', 'Phildon House', 'Castle Corner', 'Roger's B & B', 'Herman's Hideaway'. Signs advertising 'VACANCIES', variously decorated and in wildly contrasting styles of lettering, hung in every doorway. 'Castle Corner' was in a poor state of repair, with leaking drainpipes, peeling window frames and cracks in the grey stucco. 'Phildon House' was discouragingly fussy, with an abundance of fake ornamental details and two perfectly manicured bay trees flanking the steps. 'Roger's B & B' looked like the sort of place where long-distance steamer operators might congregate.

On balance the Lodge was possibly my best bet. It was scruffy, but not too scruffy. With any luck, I thought, it would be relatively cheap.

I pushed open the door. There was a small reception desk, and the usual raked display of leaflets. A plastic plant straggled upwards from a tarnished brass pot. Overhead a ceiling tile was missing, exposing a tangle of electrical wiring and lagged pipes. The green flocked wallpaper was peeling away from a water stain on the wall. Behind the desk was a reproduction of a painting of a ragged street urchin with molten black eyes. An overlarge tear shone on his cheek.

On the desk was a brass bell. I pinged it.

A very small man appeared, seemingly out of nowhere, wearing an oddly formal grey suit with high wing collars. I knew how ridiculous I looked in my capacious suit, with my cheap suitcases. I fully expected him to refuse me a room.

"Do you have a single?"

Without replying he consulted a book on the desk. His lips moved silently, as if completing a complex calculation. "How many nights?" he asked.

"I'm not sure. How much is it?"

He consulted the book again. Keeping his eyes fixed on whatever was written there, he named a sum. It was outrageously high. Paying it would exhaust most of the cash in the wallet. But fugitives can't be choosers: not unless they want to forfeit their liberty.

"Does that include breakfast?"

He paused, making a further soundless calculation. "Express," he said. "Full Saxon is an extra five."

"OK," I said, doing my best to keep my own tone as neutral as his. "I'll have the full Saxon, in that case."

"Any ID?"

"Actually no. I–"

"Cash in advance."

I fished my last pound note out of my wallet.

He swivelled the register and pushed it towards me. I signed my name as Thomas Rattle, and my address as Waterford Place, Ludden. He swivelled back the book, and read what I had written.

"Filthy place, Ludden," he said. "My old dad used to take me on the odd day trip, as a nipper. You wouldn't see me dead there now."

"It's certainly busy."

"Busy with filth."

He handed me a small key attached to a heavy brass fob.

"Do I get any change?"

"Change?"

"I gave you a pound note."

Without replying he rummaged in a drawer and selected a small number of coins. He counted them into my hand slowly and deliberately.

"Thanks."

Removing a brass-tagged key from the board, he reached for my bag. I held onto it tightly. "I can carry it myself," I said.

"That's my job, if you don't mind. Management rules."

He reached for the bag a second time. We stood there for a

second or two, locked in a silent battle of wills; then I pushed him it sullenly towards him, mentally calculating how small a tip I could get away with.

There was a lift, but it was out of action. Swinging my cheap case as if to illustrate its inadequacy, he made for the stairs. I followed behind.

The dusty carpet was embellished with swirling patterns in rust and green, which matched the queasiness I had been feeling all morning. My room was number 14: next door, I noticed, to number 12. The door was coated with a lumpy dark brown varnish. The area around the lock was scarred and splintered, as if someone had recently forced an entry.

The man turned the key in the lock, and pushed open the door with his shoulder. He placed my case on the bed, and stood beside it, waiting. I stuck my hands in my pockets.

"My name," said the man, after what seemed an age, "is Jimmy. If you need me and I'm not there, ask for Jimmy. Or if there's any services you require: ask for Jimmy."

"I will."

Jimmy waited another second or two, more, I would guess, to make a point than in any expectation of a last-minute change of heart, then turned on his heel and left, closing the door a little more firmly than was strictly called for.

9

The room held a single bed, a bedside table, a large battered wardrobe and a sink. There was no room for anything else. It smelled of confinement, of hurried private acts and spilled milk and unwashed socks and a long accumulation of unriddled dust. For ornament there was a clumsy print of a ship; for entertainment a small grey plastic wireless. A handwritten sign read:

GUESTS KINDLEY TAKE NOTICE

NO FOOD TO BE CONSUMED IN THE ROOM
NO VISITOR'S TO BE ENTERTAINED IN THE ROOM
DO NOT USE THE SINK FOR WASHING SOX ECT

ENSOR LODGE OR ANY OF IT'S SERVANT'S OR AGENT'S WILL
NOT BE HELD RESPONSIBLE FOR INJURY, DEATH OR LOSS OF
PROPERTY ATTENDANT UPON FIRE FLOOD EXPLOSION OR ANY
OTHER EVENT
WHETHER ACCIDENTAL OR WITH MALICIOUS INTENT
<u>WITHOUT EXCEPTION</u>

FULL LAUNDARY/VALETTING SERVICE AVALABLE
AT VERY REASONABLE CHARGE ENQUIRE AT RECEPTION

<u>Guests ignoring any of these directions
will be forcibly removed from these premises
forthewith,
such removal incurring full nights
charges without redress</u>

Thanking you in advance for your cooperation
THE MANAGEMENT

I removed the shoes and the enormous jacket, and lay down on the bed.

10

Someone tapped on the door. I was awake in an instant, my heart racing. For a moment or two I had no idea where I was, or even *who* I was. I couldn't be *William Riddle,* surely? Riddle the escaped prisoner, son of a disgraced father, the boy who had been expelled from Bune College... Oh please, let me not be *him!*

Whoever it was tapped on the door again, bringing the world back in a rush. My mouth was gummy. The ghost of the awful pie I had eaten at the station lay on my breath.

"Yes?" I said. "Who is it?"

Whoever it was tried the door handle.

"What do you want?"

"Sorry – am I disturbing you?"

The accent I recognised as belonging to a working-class youth, probably a native of Ensor or somewhere nearby. There was a time, not so long ago, when I would not have applied the designation 'working-class' to the sounds I heard, but Bune had taught me to appreciate these subtleties.

"I'm awake now," I said crossly. "What is it?"

"Can I come in?"

There was a weak quality in the voice, a note of pleading. I opened the door. A tall spindly youth stood there, with a long nose and thin fair hair combed back from his high pimpled forehead.

"Can I come in?" he repeated.

"What do you want?".

"You're new here, aren't you? I thought you might need a few pointers."

By this time he was inside the room.

"Errol," he said.

"Rattle," I said curtly.

"Funny name."

"Thomas Rattle," I clarified.

"Come from Ludden, Tommy?"

"Going there."

"Smart man. Just back from there myself. Ran out of the ready – not surprisingly. You can spend a lot of cash in Ludden."

"I can imagine."

"I'm looking for employment. Build up a bit of dosh, so I can go back again. Anything'll do, bricklaying, catering, stress relief. You wouldn't happen to know of anything, I suppose?"

"I'm afraid not."

"I'm not proud, I can turn my hand to anything. I met a rich old boy in Ludden, sort of gent who like to help boys out, if you know what I mean."

"Useful."

"It was. This old boy helped me out for a while, then turfed me out. So I was living rough for a bit. Not a good situation to be in."

"I sympathise."

Errol, I noticed, had terrible teeth, the front pair almost transparent with decay. A smell of dustbins rose from his baggy garments.

"I don't have too much dosh myself," I said, noting with irritation that I was aping his accent and vocabulary, but powerless to stop myself doing so.

"That's funny. Going by the sound of your voice I would have said you were loaded."

"I've fallen on hard times."

"Tell me about it." He pulled a rolled-up comic from one of his baggy pockets. "Take a snit at this. Bought it in Ludden."

The comic was called *Rump* and turned out to feature the sort of activities which Purkis was fond of describing in his contributions to the Malcaster stories. Multiple penises abounded, all equally enormous, showering copious gouts of semen. Multiple pink bottoms were offered by legions of young men, lined up on all fours. The 'hero' of these adventures strode through this jungle of ripe flesh, sowing his seed in all directions.

A rhythmical chaffing noise drew my attention downwards, to where Errol's fingers were busily rubbing in the region of his fly. Desire can take many forms, but its complete absence leaves no room for interpretation. Blank-faced, I rolled up the comic and handed it back.

Errol's face registered disappointment. He removed his hand from his fly, and stood up.

"You can borrow it, if you want," he said.

"No thanks." I went to the door, and held it open.

"Please yourself."

I said nothing. Errol left.

I went over to the stained sink, and splashed some rusty water on my burning face. Taking a spare pair of paper socks from my suitcase, I lay back on the bed, and attempted to get some relief. It was an uphill struggle. More than once I was tempted to call it a day. As I finally came – quite painfully, for some reason – it occurred to me that I might have misjudged Errol's motives. What he had come to my room for wasn't dosh but company.

I wiped myself with the socks, pulled up my paper underpants, and plunged headlong into a deep sleep haunted by guilty dreams: multiple versions of the same scenario, in which I had committed an unspecified but abominable crime.

FIFTEEN
Gratuities

DI Ernest Rattle was feeling hot. The sun beat down from a cloudless sky, making him sweat profusely within the straining confines of his prickly tweed suit. As always when crossing Bollingford Bridge he experienced a sense that he was leaving the ordinary world of beer and sandwiches for somewhere vastly more dangerous: a place of secrets and disguises, of dark intentions and darker deeds.

'Next Time Keep Your Trap Shut' from *The Infected Pistol and Other Stories* by H O Minty and F R Trumper, (Grubstop Press, 485)

1

When I woke it was already dark. I had no timepiece, so switched on the wireless and had to endure five minutes of light music before the idiot presenter read out the time. It was seven-thirty. The day was nearly over. I had wasted the afternoon sleeping when I should have been trying to contact Purkis. To make matters worse, I had used up virtually every penny of my funds. Tomorrow I would have nothing other than the price of a stall at the flushers and the unexpired portion of my ticket to Ludden.

I pulled on the jacket and the painful shoes, and limped down the stairs. Jimmy was on sentry duty behind his desk.

"Going out?"

"Yes."

"Would you mind leaving the key with me?"

I considered answering in the negative, but it did not seem worth the inevitable battle. I handed over the key, and hurried outside.

The streets were empty. Ensor is only busy in high season; for much of the autumn it is generally deserted. There are two good restaurants, and a few interesting pubs, and far too many tea shops, and a small cinema, and the Elysian Fields Dance Hall, and that's about it. Bune, although much smaller, has more facilities for visitors because of the college. I made for the bridge. From a distance I caught sight of a field of tall toppers, swaying above a bright flare of waistcoats – azure, canary yellow, hunting pink. I halted. I had been gone from the school for less than a month, and yet it was as if a huge bank of time had elapsed: years, decades, a short lifetime. It was staggering to think that the Pagan Half in which I had been expelled was not yet over. In two days' time the school would break up for the long Festival holiday. Tests were already taken; by now the results would have been announced. The end of term parties would be in full swing.

A gush of bile soured my thoughts. I should have been at those parties; I should be looking forward to two further years at the school, and possible elevation to Crow. Instead I was an outcast: an escaped prisoner. The thought stopped me in my tracks. Suddenly I was breathless, my face liquid with sweat. What was I thinking of – coming back to Bune, where everyone knew me? What if someone alerted the police?

I was paralysed by indecision. I wondered if I should give Bune up for a bad job, go back to the Lodge, and catch the train to Ludden in the morning.

"Riddle!"

I turned, recognising the voice.

"It really is you!" said Worsley, in an awed whisper. "Whatever are you wearing?"

He looked as small as ever. His topper – I had never seen him wearing one before – seemed intended for a much larger head: the brim sat on a level with his eyebrows.

"I look like a clown, I know. Look, Worsley–"

"Are you looking for Purkis?"

"I suppose I am," I admitted. I had been hiding this fact from myself; now it was unavoidable.

"He didn't say you were coming."

"That's probably because he didn't know."

"Right, I see," said Worsley, nodding. "Actually he's at a party. Crow are looking him over."

"Lucky him," I said jealously. "He must be pleased."

"Very. You should have been there with him, Riddle."

"Nice of you to say so. But I would never have made Crow in a million years."

"That's rubbish, if you don't mind me saying so. The only reason you won't make it is because you were expelled, and that wasn't your fault. Your father must have done something pretty frightful for this to happen."

Coming from him, this was appallingly presumptuous. "You know nothing about it," I said.

Worsley's face fell. "You're right, of course. Sorry, Riddle."

I felt like giving him a good kicking, but now was not the time. "Don't worry about it," I said coldly. "How are you, anyway?"

"Grand, actually, thanks. I'll be a Praetor myself, in a few years, if I play my cards right."

"Looking forward to that, are you?"

"Who wouldn't be?" he asked cheerily. "Are you here for long, Riddle?"

"Just the night."

"Staying locally?'

"Yes."

"Might I enquire where?"

"It's called the Ensor Lodge."

"O dear!" he said, pulling a face. "That is not a very reputable establishment, I'm afraid. It's a pity you didn't get in touch with me before making your booking. My father could have found you somewhere far more comfortable in one of our own establishments, at a fraction of the price."

I had forgotten about 'Rest Assured', the Worsley family business. Once I had found the concept sneerworthy; now that I had sampled the eccentricities of the Ensor Lodge I was better able to appreciate it. "Unfortunately I came here at rather short notice,"

I said. "And the fewer people know about my whereabouts the better."

"I absolutely understand. For future reference, my father is the very soul of discretion. Many of our guests check in under assumed names. Guaranteed anonymity is a highly valued commodity in the hospitality industry."

"I suppose it would be."

He nodded energetically. "Riddle," he asked in a confidential whisper, "do you want me to fetch Purkis for you?"

The whisper was an affectation: there was no one close enough to hear us. "That would be kind," I said curtly. I was impatient to move things along. In any case, the evening chill was beginning to get to me. I had forgotten how vital socks are to the insulation of the feet.

"Not at all. I'll go at once."

"Off you go, then."

He left at the run. He was an odd creature: quaint and artificial, like a boy in an old storybook. I had never quite believed in him, and neither had Purkis.

I sat by the banks of the Ajax and waited. Lights glittered on the water. Bats flitted about, half-invisibly. I shivered. It was the hour when Malcaster came to life.

Purkis appeared in the distance, insubstantial, wraith-like. He raised a hand. I stood up to greet him. He had taken, I noticed, to covering the spots on his cheeks, chin and forehead with some sort of flesh-tinted lotion. In places this was dry and crusty. It made him look like a burns victim.

"Hello, Purkis," I said coldly.

"Hello, old man. How's tricks?"

"There aren't any. I've done a bunk."

"So I hear."

Presumably his father had told him this: another source of irritation. "You would know that, of course. Cromwell House is one of your pa's prisons."

"Cromwell House?" said Purkis steadily. "That's not a prison, it's a looney-bin. Cat D: harmless lunatics and social misfits. They put you there because they didn't know what else to do with you."

I had already worked this out for myself, but had suppressed the information, as you do with stuff that paints you in a less than flattering light. Purkis, as usual, had seen through me. Another win for the prosecution. "That'll make a fine story at Bune," I said bitterly. "You can have a good laugh at my expense."

"Don't be silly. Have you been charged with anything?"

"Not yet."

"There you are then. All they want is information."

The conversation felt very strained: too many things were standing in the way of complete openness. It was not the first time I had felt estranged from Purkis, but in the past we had approached our differences as equals. Now he had the upper hand. That was galling, whether he cared to take advantage of it or not.

He kept looking around him. It came to me that he was ashamed to be seen in my company. I was a pariah, and he had a reputation to keep up.

"I hear Crow's taking a sniff," I said, failing to keep the jealousy out of my voice.

"Yes, did Worsley tell you?"

"He did. Should I offer you my congratulations? Or is that a bit premature?"

"It's just a preliminary look-over. It may not come to anything."

"Either way, you can't afford to be seen with me."

"Probably not. I'm not going to throw you over, all the same."

"If you say so."

He looked away. "You don't think much of me, do you Riddle?" he said in an odd voice.

"I don't have think much of anybody at the moment."

"I'm not surprised. Let's go somewhere a bit more private. Where are you staying?"

"B & B, near the station. It's a bit of a dump. Anyway, shouldn't you get back to your party?"

"It'll wait."

We agreed that Purkis should follow me at a distance. I slopped back to the Ensor Lodge Hotel, looking behind me every so often to make sure he was still following.

Luckily Jimmy was nowhere to be seen. I took the key from the board. Purkis came through the outer door. I pointed upstairs, one finger on my lips. He nodded.

I limped upstairs, and unlocked the door. Purkis followed.

"I see why you chose this place to hide out in," he said once we were safely inside. "It's pure Malcaster."

"There's no safety in Malcaster, except for Malcastrians. Anyone else gets turned in to the authorities."

Purkis was reading the handwritten notice. "'Guests must not entertain visitors in the room.' How peculiar. I've never come across that rule before."

"You never stay in this kind of place."

"Well that's true enough." He sniffed. "They don't want you washing your socks, either."

"Fortunately mine are made of paper."

"How disgusting. That suit's a bit unfortunate too. Couldn't you find anything more dashing to escape in?"

"I had to take pot luck."

"Pot luck, eh? That never pays. The question is, Riddle, how am I going to help you?"

"That's up to you."

"I expect you're going to need some moolah."

I turned away. This is precisely what I had been hoping for, but now that he had volunteered it I felt angry, as if he was patronising me.

"Don't worry. I can manage."

"If you could manage you wouldn't be staying in this smelly dump."

This could not be denied. For the second time that day I felt my eyes water. "It's not your responsibility, even so," I forced out.

"It's the least I can do. And the most too, probably. Here – take this for a start, in case you need anything tonight." He held out a ten-shilling note.

"That's awfully generous. I–"

"Pipe down." He pressed it into my hand. "I wish I could do more."

I slipped the crumpled note into the warm envelope of my trouser pocket.

"OK then – thanks," I said grudgingly. I hesitated, screwed up my eyes.

"What is it, Riddle?"

"Purkis, I'd rather you didn't tell your pa about this."

"Wouldn't dream of it."

There was a tap at the door. I tensed, fearing the return of Errol, and what Purkis would make of it if it was.

But it was only Jimmy. "Mr Rattle?" he called through the door in a voice saturated with righteous indignation.

Purkis frowned. "Friend of yours?" he asked in a low voice.

"It's the bloody management," I mouthed back.

The man knocked again, insistently. "Mr Rattle, I know you're in there. And I know you've got a *visitor* in there with you."

Purkis sniggered. I too was finding it hard not to laugh.

"Guests are not allowed to have visitors in their room. It states that clearly, both on the noticeboard and in the room."

"He isn't staying the night," I said loudly, "if that's what you think".

"I've told you the rule – *No Visitors*. Open the door now, please, or I shall have to call the police."

"Better do as he says," said Purkis ruefully. "Pity – I was intending to seduce you."

"Some hopes."

"Oh, quite," he said. "I'll come back tomorrow morning with some more cash, right?"

"Thanks."

Jimmy beat thunderously on the door, making the entire room tremble.

"Just a minute," I called.

"You've had your minute. I'm calling the police now."

I unlocked the door. Jimmy barged his way in. Purkis looked down at him from a Bunian height. "Manners," he said.

Jimmy stared at his topper and waistcoat. "Are you a college boy?"

217

"That's none of your business."

"It is my business, as a matter of fact. You can't come here–"

"Silly little man," Purkis said, pushing past him and making for the stairs.

"Well *you're* one to talk about manners, aren't you? Perhaps your headmaster would be interested in hearing of this adventure."

"Farewell Rattle!" called Purkis, from the foot of the stairs. Jimmy gave me a parting glare, and hurried after him.

Closing the door, I lay down on the bed. Angry thoughts raced around in my head like worried sheep. Purkis was going back to his friends in Crow. They would be carousing until dawn. It's very hard to like someone when you feel viciously jealous. The fact that Purkis had given me money didn't help in the least. Instead of making me grateful, it made me furious. It put me under an obligation, and because I couldn't return the favour, it made me a sponge. Why should Purkis have both money and freedom – and get to make Crow into the bargain?

The reason he's so keen to help, I thought, is because he feels guilty: perhaps with good reason.

I wondered why I hadn't told Purkis about the episode of Errol and the comic. That was the kind of thing he relished. I had kept it dark deliberately, I realised. Was that because I was ashamed of what had happened? Or was it simply that we were no longer close enough to share that sort of confession?

2

It was hard to get to sleep. The mattress was incredibly hard and lumpy, and the blanket smelt of old sweat. I dozed for a few minutes, dreaming that my father was being hanged in front of me. He stood on the scaffold with a noose around his neck, then the platform gave way with a faint click, and he began to fall.

I sat bolt upright, my heart racing. *My father was in danger.* What if I never saw him again? The thought filled me with terror. He was the one true thing in my life: the only person who had never lied or compromised or sucked up to people he didn't like. I couldn't afford to lose him.

I lay down again, and tugged the foul-smelling blanket over my head. It was important now to sleep. Tomorrow I would set out to find my father. If I couldn't rescue him, I would share his fate, whatever that happened to be.

3

I woke up early, feeling hungry. I hadn't eaten anything for more than twenty-four hours, unless you could count the bad pie I had bought at Ensor station. The smell of frying bacon drifted up from the bowels of the Ensor Lodge. This is normally one of the most appetising smells on earth, and not even the seediness of my room and the thought of having to see Jimmy again could detract from its power.

I washed quickly, and made my way downstairs.

The breakfast room was in the basement. The bacon smell had been strong two flights up; within that confined space it was overpowering.

Jimmy was standing at the door with a pink hand-towel folded over his arm.

"Mr Rattle!" He spoke with elaborate formality, tinged with a smear of malice. "I trust you slept well, sir!"

"I did indeed." I looked around. Fortunately Errol was nowhere to be seen. One of the tables was taken by a mousy couple in identical brown corduroys; apart from that I had a choice of six. I took one close to the door. Like all the others, it was topped with a pink tablecloth, over which was stretched a weathered covering of yellowing transparent plastic, secured to the table-edges with red plastic clips.

Jimmy approached me with a little pad in his hand.

"Full Saxon breakfast, I think you said, Mr Rattle."

"That's what I've paid for, yes."

"Tea or coffee?"

I ordered coffee.

"Help yourself to–" he began. He broke off. For a moment he remained fixed in position, open-mouthed, wrestling with whatever it was that was preventing him from finishing his sentence. I waited, not very patiently, feeling less hungry with every passing moment.

The issue resolved itself: he struck his forehead playfully with his open palm. "I wondered why it was so quiet! I'll be forgetting my own self next!"

He marched over to an object suspended on the wall: a kind of shallow box with a glass front. Inside was a rural scene, with a lake, a boat, a clump of trees and an agricultural labourer with a spade. Jimmy operated a switch at the side, and immediately the scene sprang to life. A large bird flapped awkwardly overhead, the boat staggered across the lake, the leaves of the trees stirred violently, as if in the grip of a furious wind, the labourer frantically applied his spade, like someone trying to dig a way through to the antipodes. All this was accompanied by a distant tinkling sound, not unlike music, and the creaks and groans of exhausted machinery.

Jimmy stood back with a proud look on his face. The mousy couple applauded soundlessly.

"Amazing!" I said.

"I'm glad you like it, Mr Rattle. The Eldon Lodge is famous for its 'living landscape'. It's mentioned in all the guidebooks. So silly of me to forget to switch it on!"

4

The full Saxon was a sad disappointment. Every ingredient was compromised, in terms both of texture and flavour. The grilled tomato was watery and tasteless, the beans were sickly sweet and stewed to a pulp, the fried mushrooms bore no resemblance to anything organic. The bacon was particularly hateful. It was a peculiar shade of dark red, with a white foam of salt along the edge; it was tough as boot leather, and rancid, with a worrying aftertaste. I say it was disappointing, but I must have been mad to expect anything else. My father and I had breakfasted in many cheap establishments, but had never been offered anything quite this bad.

I stood up.

"Not leaving us already, I hope, Mr Rattle?"

"I am, I'm afraid. I'm all packed; I just have to collect my case."

"I'll bring it down for you."

"No need."

"No trouble at all."

He scuttled past me, and rushed up the stairs. Sighing, I climbed the narrow stairs up to the lobby, rummaging in my pocket for small change. Apart from the crumpled note Purkis had given me the previous evening, I only had coppers left, but even those I begrudged him.

Jimmy came down with my case. "All present and correct," he said triumphantly.

Thanks," I said, holding out my hand. Jimmy looked down at it. I followed suit. To my horror, Purkis's ten-shilling note, folded neatly into four, had become accidentally wedged between my fingers.

I watched in dismay as the note vanished into a distant recess of Jimmy's apparel. "Thank *you* sir," he said, rubbing his hands, and deforming his face into a caricature of gratitude. "That's *very* kind of you. Very generous indeed."

I was speechless.

"By the way, sir," he went on, "I must apologise for what occurred last night. I hope you weren't too put out by it. I was expecting a visit from the General Manager, you see; if he had found a *visitor* in your room: well, to be frank, I could have lost my situation."

"I see. Well, we couldn't let that happen."

"It's good of you to see it that way, sir. Incidentally, sir–" He leaned forward, lowering his voice. "It might be to your advantage if you left as soon as is convenient. What it is, sir, we receive a daily inspection by the Aliens Regulatory Office, to ensure that every guest has the documentation required by law. They send a man round every weekday, shortly after nine. That's when they start work, of course – nine. They never come any earlier."

I looked at the clock above his desk. It was five to.

"I'd better go, then," I said. "Thanks for the warning."

"It's a great pleasure sir. I do hope you'll come and stay with us again, the next time you are visiting this neck of the woods."

"I'll certainly consider it."

"One other thing." He placed a solicitous hand on my arm. "With regard to your friend, the young gentleman from Bune College: the next time you do stay, would you please assure him he can visit you *whenever he pleases*."

"In that case," I said, "I'll definitely come again."

"Please do sir. And thank you very much. Thank you."

Still uttering variations on the same theme, he escorted me to the door. I hurried out, almost colliding with a man with a briefcase, wearing the obligatory soft felt hat and cheap blue suit of the low-level bureaucrat. He stared after me, but made no attempt to follow.

5

We met as arranged at 'Merry's Muffins'. I was furious at the loss of the ten-shilling note. Purkis, by contrast, was highly amused. "You're such an innocent, Riddle," he said. "Most people live or die by cash – it's all they ever think about. Grease a few palms and they'll treat you like a Lord. You don't do it just to be nice."

"I'd better get hold of some, then. That half quid was all I had."

"It's a lesson you had to learn. What's more it saved you from getting a grilling from the TP. *And* it only cost you half a measly quid! I call that a bargain! Talking of moolah–" He removed an envelope from his breast pocket, and slid it over. "This is all I could rustle up in the time. If you let me have an address I'll send you some more."

I hardly knew what to say. I felt both grateful and irritated, without knowing which emotion to go with. I knew I should be making some grand gesture, embracing him, or saying something memorable, but I couldn't bring myself to do it.

Purkis stood up, we shook hands, and that was it. We parted outside the cafe. I slopped up the hill to the station in my too-big shoes. I did not look back.

SIXTEEN
The Fig Leaf

Foxton Street earned its nickname 'The Magic Mile' in the last century, an era of big stores and big profits. Until the last twenty years or so the mere possession of a Foxton Street address was a guarantee that a business had earned its place in the super league. It is still a first destination for visitors from all parts of the country, but these days, thanks the greed of landlords and the city authorities, the street has degenerated into a hotchpotch of businesses of the very worst sort: vast department stores selling fake copies of expensive branded goods; cut-price traders in crudely printed leisure-wear; fly-by-night outfits selling leases for stays of one week per year in unbuilt holiday apartments on the coast; sandwich shops; long narrow snack-shops for people prepared to eat and drink standing up; mysterious shops with forbidding names and blacked-out windows; public auctions of boxed goods that turn out to be rubbish.

These last outlets are invariably held on a temporary licence. Anyone who wants to complain (i.e., virtually anyone who makes a purchase) will come back with their pathetic bag and worthless scrap of receipt, only to find that the shop has been replaced either by an empty unit hidden by graffiti-covered hoardings, or (more probably) a similar shop with a sim-ilar range of worthless goods but a different name. Even if the shop from which they made their purchase does still exist the would-be complainant will be met with a wall of resistance: no manager is available, there are forms to be filled in, in triplicate, ID has to be produced, and checked an out-of-date register, and so on. At the end of the process someone without a name assures them they will be contacted within five days: a contact which naturally never takes place.

It is of course always an option to report the seller to the Commercial Police. Unfortunately that invariably involves queuing for hours in a crowded office to be interviewed by a harassed official, filling in forms all over again, and (yet again) waiting weeks for a reply that in most cases will never come. It is impossible to find out who owns these businesses – the records name a confusing tangle of holding companies and associates, most of which turn out (if the investigation ever gets that far) to be dummies with non-existent directors and fake addresses. Once you have parted with your cash, you never get it back.

The LCA claims to be taking action against rogue traders, but nothing ever gets done. The cynical view is that the revenue derived from these businesses is so great that the authorities cannot afford to take any more than token action against them. An even more cynical view is that officials all the way up the ladder are given huge bribes to keep these traders in business.

Dead Ends: The Scandalous Condition of Our Economy
by M Salisbury (Embankment Press, 468)

1

Far from discouraging sex-pests, my ill-fitting suit seemed actually to attract them. On the train to Ludden I was propositioned twice. The first proposition was made in the dining car, where I was drinking tea, by an elderly gentleman who should have known better. I left, and edged down the train looking for an empty seat, only to be propositioned again: this time by someone of about my own age. He was an artisan – an electrician – and a sports fan, so we had very little in common to talk about, but it was flattering all the same, and for a minute or two I was quite seriously tempted. He gave me an address, scribbled on the back of a timetable. Once he was gone I crumpled it up and threw out of the window: an act I was later to regret. By following it up I might have earned myself a couple of nights' free accommodation.

The envelope Purkis had given me contained twenty pounds in one pound notes. Judging by the price of my night's stay at the Ensor Lodge, I calculated that this would last me about a week at the most; and even then I would have to live on bread and pink spread. I certainly wouldn't be able to afford a full Saxon breakfast.

The train terminated at Empire Cross. Like all big railways stations it was surrounded by establishments catering to the lowest of tastes: knocking shops, fast food outlets, gambling dens, and twenty-four hour cinemas offering a diet of cartoons and simulated erotica. There was also a scattering of cheap hotels, all of which reminded me of the Ensor Lodge. I left the area by foot as fast as I could.

For some time I wandered aimlessly through an area of leafy streets and small squares of overgrown grass guarded by rusty railings. Presently I drifted, like a canoe caught in an increasingly swift current, into a busier thoroughfare, which carried me irresistibly on to Foxton Street. Knowing this celebrated boulevard by its reputation as a prime destination for shoppers from all over Anglia, I was somewhat surprised to find it lined with bargain shops of the vulgar cast. From a Bune standpoint these were the kind of establishments you should go out of your way to avoid, but the perilous state of my finances meant I was in no position to turn up my nose at bargains, and I spent a good hour or so adding to my bagful of shoddy items of clothing.

Halfway down, the pavement was blocked by a crowd of people spilling out from the interior of a shop where some kind of public auction was taking place. The plate glass window had been moved to one side, exposing a temporary platform, on which there stood a skinny boy of no more than twelve, holding above his head a succession of expensive-looking articles: glittering crystal bowls and decanters, sets of heavy silver cutlery, fine jewellery boxes of inlaid jet and walnut, domed barometers with mechanisms of solid gold. A fierce-looking growler with suspiciously black hair and yellow teeth, stood over the boy, waving his arms about in a theatrical fashion.

"It's your lucky day, gennelmen," roared the growler. "I can't say which of these precious articles you're going to get, but at this price how can you afford *not* to make me an offer? I'm not asking ten pund. I'm not asking five pund. I'm not asking four pund ten. *I'm not even asking three pund nineteen shillings and sixpence!* Two pund fifty! Can you believe it? I'm giving it away! I'm bankrupting myself! Who wants one? –That gennelman there. Hand him a parcel, Nigel. Make sure it's one of the heavy ones, they won't last for ever. And another. And there's another! Gennelman in the high hat, Nigel. And another!"

Something happens to one's normal ration of common sense when one is presented with the prospect of getting something valuable for next to nothing. If the articles in the boxes were even half as good as the ones on display, I reasoned, I could sell them afterwards at a much higher price. I was just checking that I had three 'pund' notes in my wallet, when a hand gripped my arm.

"I'd put that away, if I were you."

I turned, in some alarm, expecting to see a policeman. Instead it was someone I knew.

He favoured me with a pleasant smile. "William, isn't it? William Riddle?"

"Yes – and you're Ronnie."

"How flattering that you recognise me. Just got to town, have you?"

"That's right. Only this afternoon."

"Thought as much. Dear boy, you're not about to *buy* from these rascals, are you?"

"I was thinking of it. Two pounds fifty doesn't seem much of an outlay."

"Far too much to pay for bloody rubbish. It's a swindle, Billy-boy. It's not one box, it's half a dozen, one inside the other. Open the last of them, and all you've got is a soggy ball of newspaper crumpled round a plastic dog-bowl."

Now that I thought of it, this sounded horribly plausible. "Isn't that against the law?"

"Not in the least. What were you promised? Nothing. And if you were, how could you prove it? The whole of bloody Ludden is an elephant-trap for innocents, Bill. You have to know your way around or you won't last a day."

"Oh. Well, thanks for telling me. I'll have to be more careful."

"You will indeed." He still had hold of my arm; he was drawing me away from the auction, in a friendly, avuncular way. "As it

226

happens, Bill, I was just on my way for a quick snifter in my club. It's not far from here – Barrel Street. Select little venue. Members only – and their friends. Care to join me?"

2

Ronnie steered me down a narrow side street, and into a very different area: a quarter of small pubs and glum little cafes, of boys loitering in dirty passages, and pink neon signs, and shop doorways festooned with strips of multicoloured plastic.

By now it was getting dark. Malcaster – or its Ludden equivalent – was waking up. Cigarettes glowed and faded in the shadows; men in black overcoats brushed past us, murmuring.

We passed a brightly illuminated theatre fronted by a long queue of tourists. The advertised show was called *Handsome*: it described itself as the country's longest running musical. Snatches of music caught at us as we passed it like thorny branches on a woodland walk. From all directions we were bombarded by the smells of the city: frying onions, disinfectant, stale beer, ground coffee. It was all rather exciting. I felt that I was on the verge of experiencing something forbidden. It was a relief to think that there was no one there to know or care what I saw or did, unless you counted Ronnie, which for obvious reasons I didn't.

You could easily have passed his club, The Fig Leaf, without knowing it was there. All there was to advertise its existence was a dirty metal plate set on the wall next to a purple door.

Ronnie pushed a button set into the plate.

A tinny voice came seemingly out of nowhere. "Yes?"

Ronnie set his face against the metal plate. "Captain Francis. And friend."

A buzzer sounded. Ronnie pushed the door open. Ahead of us was a dimly lit corridor decorated with red flock wallpaper. There was a shabby black desk, and behind it an array of coats and an elderly man with a white beard.

"Who's your pal, Ronnie?"

"This is Mr – who are you today, old boy?"

"Tommy Ransom."

The man pushed an open book towards us. "You'll have to sign him in."

Ronnie did so with a flourish.

"Coats, gentlemen, please."

We handed them over.

"Mind settling your tab, today, Ronald?"

"Not at all. I'll see Freddie about it."

"You can settle it with me, if you like."

"I'll see Freddie, if you don't mind."

"Suit yourself."

The club was cosy, in a stuffy sort of way. The predominant colour of the walls and furnishings was red. Small red table lamps with small red shades, and wall sconces with yellow candle bulbs and more little red shades, provided the only illumination. None of the customers could be seen at all distinctly, so the tell-tale signs of age were to some extent obscured. On the downside, their faces tended to be lit from below, creating a somewhat devilish effect.

Ronnie led me to a booth comprising two benches padded with worn red velvet facing one another across a rectangular table. I sat down, while he went to get us drinks. The bar, backed by a mirror and row of inverted bottles, created an island of relative brightness. Several customers pressed up against it, some perched on stools. The barman was a man with a white beard, pretty much the double of the individual who had taken our coats at the entrance.

Ronnie came back smiling broadly and carrying two drinks: a gin and tonic for me, and a large whisky for himself. Putting the drinks on the table, he sat down next to me. Our thighs collided, and I moved mine away.

"So, Billy boy, how are things with you?"

"Good, good," I said. Under circumstances like these it is best not to volunteer too much information. "You?"

"I get by." He patted my thigh in a chummy way. "Let's not talk about me. How is Bune treating you? Have you been introduced to the mysteries of Union?"

It was odd to be asked this, particularly by a grownup. I

preferred not to talk about it, in case it got back to Union official in charge of my confidential records. On the other hand Ronnie could hardly get me into hot water without implicating himself. I opted for the vaguest of replies.

"Yes, last summer – just before I left."

"Splendid! What did they do you for?"

"I'm not really sure."

"Knock you out, did they? Play noises in your ears, waft a scent-bottle under the nostrils? It's all a bit of a performance, I understand."

I described very briefly what I had experienced, leaving out any intimate details.

Ronnie slapped my knee. "Sounds like the buggers extracted your juice. Before you know what's hit you you'll be getting a son of your own to lead astray. Fortunate boy! All they ever wanted from me was blood. Still, I don't repine. One between two is plenty enough responsibility for Roger and me."

Some essential pieces of the puzzle clattered into place, bringing the gaps that remained more clearly into focus. Sperm, as perhaps you know, is not a particularly nice substance; it smells unpleasantly sharp, and always leaves a tell-tale stain whatever precautions you take to catch it, but the ability to ejaculate is pretty essential if you are to have any status among your peers. But what exactly was Ronnie getting at with this talk about fathers and sons? Could it be that sperm and the 'seed' which Joyce referred to were one and the same thing? This made a kind of sense, now that I came to think if it. If nothing else it explained how they could get you to make Union without cutting you open.

But why, in which case, was it all such a huge secret?

Possibly because sex was involved – the great forbidden topic that everyone knew about but never discussed. But somehow that wasn't enough of an explanation. There had to be something more to it, but what?

I would have liked to quiz Ronnie on the subject, but that would have meant exposing my near-total ignorance, and besides, he was still talking. For the moment I shelved the matter, interesting as it was. As it turned out, it was some time before I had any cause to think about it again.

"Mind you," Ronnie was saying, "I never went to Bune myself. My school was a touch on the disreputable side. The masters were either closet sadists or madmen, and the boys were a pathetic crew whose fathers were always behindhand with the fees. As was mine, needless to say. –So: what's next for you? Three Ps at Cantleford, I suppose?"

"Actually, I was thinking of taking a year off."

"Excellent plan. Don't jump before you can count the rocks below. I wish more boys would follow your example. Take Paul, for example. Roger, I know, has great plans for him. Law or Administration. But what does he want for himself? That's the important thing."

"I don't really think he cares that much."

"Really?" He drained his glass. "Another?"

"Ronnie," I said, when he got back to the table: "Would you mind if I asked you something?"

"Certainly, dear boy, as long as it isn't money you're after. In short supply, alas. Used to pick up a few bob for my acting, but that's dried up now."

"It's not about money. It may, um, sound a little odd."

"Fine by me. I like being asked odd things."

"Would you mind not telling Sir Roger that you've seen me?"

He snorted with laughter. "My dear boy, I don't call *that* an odd request. What happens between these four walls is a matter for those who are here, and no one else. Your secret is safe with me – whatever it is."

"I thought that since you and Sir Roger are partners –"

"Nothing to do with it. That's the way we stay married, as a matter of fact. He has his secrets, and I have mine. He doesn't confide in me about affairs of state. And I don't confide in him about the state of my affairs. All right?"

Some expression of mirth was called for. "Ha!" I said briefly.

"Contrary to what people seem to think," continued Ronnie, pushing back his forelock, "you can't make a marriage work by sticking to the rules. The secret is to keep things in watertight compartments. That way–"

"Who's your new chum, Ronnie? Don't keep him all to yourself, will you?"

The speaker was a heavy dishevelled man with a face set in a scowl. His large blunt hands, I noticed, were stained with paint of many colours. There were also splashes and blotches of paint on his unbuttoned yellow waistcoat, and on the blue shirt beneath it.

"Dan, this is Tom," said Ronnie. "Tom, this is Dan. Dan is a painter."

"You make it sound like a fucking boys' first reader, Ronnie. *'Dan is a painter. Ronnie is a thespian.'* And what in fuck's name is *Tom?*"

"Tom is – yes, what are you, Tom?"

"I'm between jobs," I said carefully.

"*Riddle* jobs, you mean?" asked the painter, seating himself opposite me.

"Naughty naughty, Dan," said Ronnie, routinely. He was looking a bit put out.

Dan ignored him. "I'll give you a job, Tommy," he said. "I need a model."

"Is that paid work, old boy?" asked Ronnie.

"Of course it's paid! Rude bugger! What do you take me for?" He extracted a crumpled card from his trousers and tucked into the top pocket of my jacket. "Call me if you're interested. Some time when this awful man isn't hogging the field."

He lurched back to his cronies at the bar with a face like thunder. I watched as he downed a tumbler of amber liquid in one gulp – it was there waiting for him on the bar. By most standards he was appallingly ugly, but an alluring air of power hung over him like a portable weather system.

"Oops!" said Ronnie. "Splashed right in the sewage, as usual. Bloody celebrities – the more famous they are, the more careful you have to be."

"Is he famous?" I asked. "Should I have heard of him?"

"*Everyone's* heard of him," said Ronnie. "Bloody good painter.

231

Pity he's such a lush, but it doesn't seem to affect his work. I'd take his offer seriously, if I were you. Nice little earner, if you find yourself short of cash."

"I'll think it over."

"Do that. You won't be young and pretty for ever, you know. Another drink?"

"Ronnie," I said, when he came back from the bar. "You know my pa?"

"Only met him that once, when you came to dinner. Abrasive sort of chap. Not my cup of tea, on the whole. Gigantic brain, though, by all accounts. What about him?"

"Did you know he's been arrested?"

"Has he? Whatever for?"

"That's the thing – I don't know."

"Well it's no good asking me, dear boy. No one tells me *anything*."

"All I want to know is where they're holding him. In prison? Or what?"

Ronnie stroked his nose thoughtfully. "Depends on what they want to know. There are strict rules and regulations governing these procedures. Tend to slow things down. Interfere with 'the free flow of information', to quote the official jargon. Sometimes a man gets carted off to Evelyn, if they want to bypass the process."

"Bypass the process?" This sounded worrying. "How do you mean?"

He shook his head. "Do me a favour, will you? Just forget I said that."

"Of course."

He sighed. "No wonder Roger doesn't discuss these matters with me. I start rambling on, and the stuff just flies out." He slapped my knee affectionately. "Just as well *I* don't hold public office, eh? I'd bring the government to its knees in a weekend."

"I expect I'd be the same."

His hand descended on my knee, and gave it a squeeze. "You take things too seriously, Bill. Fancy worrying about your dad, at your age! You should be off somewhere having fun. Going to parties, indulging in a few dangerous adventures! Leave us old crocks to fend for ourselves."

This felt like a prompt. Circumstances being what they were, I felt obliged to oblige him. "You don't seem old to me, Ronnie."

"That's very sweet of you, my dear. Anyone would think you were trying to get into my pants." The hand worked away at my knee, squeezing and stroking and pinching. "Where are you staying tonight, if it's not a rude question?"

I hesitated. I was pretty exhausted. I still had the money Purkis had given me, but I needed to make that last. I didn't fancy Ronnie in the least; on the other hand he didn't exactly disgust me.

Practicality won the day. "I don't know. Where would you suggest?"

The hand paused. He drew back, gave me an appraising stare. "Bit of a problem, is there?"

"Yes, actually. I don't have any papers."

"No papers?" He blinked, and his expression changed in some indefinable way. "That's bad. You go checking into a hotel without papers, first thing they'll do is get on the blower to the DHS. Before you know it, you'll be getting a call from a gentleman in a belted raincoat."

"That's what I'm afraid of."

You could see his mind ticking over. "Are you AWOL by any chance?"

"Something like that."

"Which is why you don't want Roger to know your whereabouts. Right?"

I nodded.

"I might be able to help you with that. The papers thing in particular."

"Do you mean forgeries?'

"Forgeries! What an absurd idea! Nothing speaks to a person's guilt like papers that don't check out. You're better off with no papers at all, quite frankly. No, what I was thinking of was getting you back on the books. The real thing."

"Is that possible?"

"Anything's possible if you know who to ask. I'm thinking of someone you already know."

"Do you mean Sir Roger?"

"Absolutely not! That would be the end of everything, if I brought Roger into it. No, I'm thinking of someone with rather more clout. Lord Haverhill, no less."

I said nothing.

"What's up? Face like a weekend in Yarborough. Something about Haverhill, is it?"

"No. I'm not sure if he's the best person to ask, that's all."

"Nonsense. Haverhill is a first-rate man – take my word for it. He's come to my aid any number of times, when I was in hot water myself. I mean, fair enough if you'd rather not risk it, but I do think you're being a bit foolish."

"Perhaps so," I agreed, thinking that I would rather spend a year being tortured by Jarvis and Payne than appeal to Haverhill for help.

"Well, don't dismiss the idea out of hand. You don't have to decide straight away. I'll give you his number – how about that? Sound him out beforehand."

"Thank you. That's very kind."

"Thank him, not me – provided he helps you, of course. Not that I have any doubts on that score. Now regarding your current predicament: there's no way you should be looking for bed and board in the current state of play. Tell you what. I keep a useful little bolthole not far from here. You can stay there."

"Are you sure?"

"Absolutely."

"That's incredibly generous of you."

"Not at all. We irregulars have to look out for one another. You never know: I might be asking *you* to put me up, one of these days."

We left the club and walked through the small streets towards the Lighthouse Building, the great tower at the intersection of Foxton Road and Elton Cross Street – Ronnie's 'bolthole'; was on the twenty-ninth floor. I already knew the Lighthouse from photographs in books about architecture, where it was heralded as a fifth-century landmark. I recognised it from half a mile away, rising above the surrounding urban muddle like a giant white plastic harmonica. It swelled in size as we approached, gobbling up one building after another, until it towered over us, blotting out the sky.

The entrance was via an ill-lit underpass, smelling of piss. A group of men stood facing the wall, smoking and conversing in low voices.

"Hello lover-boy," said one, as we went past.

"Not today," said Ronnie tartly, and hurried me past.

3

The foyer was noticeably dilapidated, with lumpy fabric wall-coverings and smelly rucked carpets. Several of the spotlights set into the ceiling were dark. There were two lifts, one of which was sealed with striped tape.

"The Lighthouse was the first of the really big buggers," said Ronnie, as we waited for the lift to descend. "Bit of a museum piece now, but very serviceable all the same."

The lift landed in front of us with a thump. Inside it smelled of air-freshener, and some ghostly traces of whatever the freshener was applied to eliminate.

Ronnie examined himself in the mirror on the lift wall, touching his moustache, and smoothing back his wayward forelock. His skin, in the harsh overhead light, had a grey tinge. Afternoon stubble darkened his cheeks and chin. I looked from his reflection to my own. My hair was standing on end, my lips looked very red, my cheeks were blotchy, and my eyes were so wide open that the brown balls of my pupils were surrounded by a leaf-shaped lake of white.

The lift juddered to a halt at every floor, sliding the steel doors open and shut, then launching itself upwards again. By the time we reached Ronnie's floor I was feeling a bit nauseous.

Ronnie disappeared into his little bathroom – to 'wash his hands' he said – giving me a chance to look around. There was a kitchen, a sitting room and a bedroom: all of them shoehorned into the smallest space possible. The best thing was the view: a glittering vista of multiple towers, lit from within by countless points of blue and white light. Other buildings existed in pockets of darkness. Lines of orange streetlights streamed in close-packed parallels towards a point of convergence beyond the horizon.

Ronnie reappeared, looking somewhat refreshed and smelling of aftershave. He had taken off his jacket and was wearing a red silk dressing-gown.

"Great view," I said.

"It's all right. Not so great once you've seen it a thousand times." He lowered the blind. "I prefer to keep it covered. That way I don't have to think of jumping out."

"Is it that bad?" I asked, with an embarrassed laugh.

"Only joking, dear boy."

He put a record on the turntable: a brooding piece of orchestral music, with long mutterings of horns and passages of strings that alternately wailed and grumbled like an argument between two mental patients. He patted the seat next to him. "Come here, laddie."

I did as he asked. He placed one hand caressingly on the back on my head, drew me towards him, and put his lips on mine.

His mouth tasted minty, with a dark undertow of whisky. I put up no resistance. Presently his head went to my lap.

I was hoping that matters could be concluded quickly. This was not the case. After a minute or so Ronnie came up for air. He looked me in the eye. "Do I detect a certain lack of enthusiasm?"

"No, keep going. What you're doing is very nice."

"Nice," he repeated. "Nice isn't the point, really. What you mean is, I can lead the horse to water, but I can't make it drink – isn't that it?"

"Something like that," I admitted. "Sorry, Ronnie."

"You don't have to apologise. You're young and I'm not. Cracks appearing in the paintwork, bit of a creaky back, rather too much hair in the comb every morning. Am I right?"

"Not exactly," I said, although those factors did in fact have a lot to do with it. "It's hard to explain."

"Don't bother." He rose, and poured himself a large glass of scotch. "You'll have to put on a better show than that, William," he observed from the sideboard, "if you want to make a living on the streets."

His earlier affability appeared to have deserted him. I have seen this before with very good-looking men. They get used to being admired for their looks – they come to expect it as their due. Once it stops they get seriously depressed. Either that or fly into a rage. Sometimes both at the same time.

"I'm hoping I won't have to."

"Best of luck, is all that I can say. No papers, no cash, no friends, nowhere to stay … It's hardly a promising outlook, is it?"

"Do you want me to leave?" I asked.

"Did I say that?"

"No. I just thought–"

"Well don't. Don't think, don't assume, don't do or say anything at all. Stay the night – you can have the couch – then in the morning you can just bugger off and get lost."

4

The couch pulled out into a reasonably comfortable bed. But it was hard to sleep. The room was unbearably stuffy, with the kind of heat that makes you sweat. Ronnie visited the bathroom several times. Every so often I heard him let out a muffled cry. There were other sounds: the flusher cascading, the radiators clicking and gurgling, an abrupt fart, the intermittent roaring of the boiler.

Eventually I must have fallen asleep, because when I opened my eyes it was daylight. Bars of light and shadow slanted down the wall. The muffled sounds of traffic – a low rumble punctuated by occasional hoots – rose from the streets below.

The flusher crashed like a controlled explosion. Ronnie emerged from the bathroom, wrapped in a towel, his toothbrush still busy in his mouth.

"Still here?"

"Sorry – yes."

He dabbed at the white foam at his lips. "Owe you an

237

apology. May have been a bit of a pain last night. Gets me that way sometimes."

"That's all right. No offence taken."

"That's because you don't care. Bit of a cold fish all round, aren't you?"

"More like a fish out of water, actually."

"That's just a fancy way of dodging the bullet. Not that it matters to me. I feel sorry for Paul, that's all."

"What do you mean?"

"The poor boy is madly in love with you. Don't you know that?"

I was staggered that this should be his opinion. "It never occurred to me."

"Must be blind, then. Or stupid."

"I think you're wrong, actually."

"Not a chance."

I washed, cleaned my teeth, put on my newly purchased outfit, got ready to leave.

"No hard feelings, I hope," said Ronnie. "If you need me for anything, you know where to find me."

"Thanks."

I descended to the street in the jerky lift. Outside I remembered Ronnie's offer to put me in touch with Haverhill. I was glad now that I wouldn't have to take it up. Contacting that beast was strictly a last resort. I couldn't see myself ever doing it.

The thing about last resorts is that you usually get round to using them sooner or later.

SEVENTEEN
Friends and Lovers

"You speak of 'an uneasy conscience'," said Rattle, laying a sympathetic hand on his friend's corduroy sleeve. "Outside of the deluded scribblings of literary hacks, I sincerely doubt that such a thing exists. Like the concept of 'guilt', it is largely the invention of the legal profession."

'The Guilty Party', from *The Infected Pistol and Other Stories* by H O Minty and F R Trumper. (Privately printed, 480)

1

I headed for the Anglian Gallery, some half a mile away from the Lighthouse, and was propositioned three times on the way. This was now so regular an event as to be more irritating than flattering. I found myself wishing to be left alone, at least for a few minutes.

Inside the galley it was no better. I stopped, for no particular reason, in front of a picture of water-lilies. Within seconds a young man in a cape was at my elbow, casually engaging me in conversation, casually inviting me to join him for coffee, casually mentioning a film or play he had tickets for, casually offering me a place to stay for the night. Declining these offers, I moved on to a room full of first-century paintings, where I was drawn to a picture of a willowy youth being used as a target by a gang of brutal archers. Moments later a muscular middle-aged man began heading relentlessly in my direction, like a robot designed for precisely that purpose. I moved away.

Certain pictures, it seemed, functioned as magnets for people with an affiliation for the subject depicted. Weird dream-like fantasies

239

were patrolled by people with coloured beards and body-piercings. Pictures of food attracted both the obese and the half-starved. Third-century rooms, filled with interchangeable faded landscapes in misty tones of orange and brown, were the haunt of gentlemen of a certain age, who watched me carefully with fish-like eyes, waiting for a signal that it was safe to approach. And so on.

Eventually I drifted into a room of paintings by someone whose name I recognised. Most were nudes: men of all ages, sizes and conditions, reclining on sofas or piles of dirty rags. I found the card which Dan, the painter from Ronnie's club, had handed me the previous evening. It was the same man: Daniel Higgins.

Within remarkably few seconds a young man with a long nose was drawing my attention to the tension between the beauty of the brushstrokes and the imperfections of the models. His name, he told me, was Mark. Mark seemed a nice chap, and refreshingly intelligent. We had coffee in the teashop in the basement, then moved on to a large public house, where we had a mainly liquid lunch balanced by a couple of cheese sandwiches. At some point I gave my name as Thomas Bunting. Inadvertently, I also told him the name of my school.

"Bune, eh?" he said, in a tone that mixed mockery with a degree of envy. "The school where golden youths are groomed for golden futures. What happened?"

"I was expelled."

"What for?"

"The usual stuff. Lotus-eating, basically."

"Was that all?"

"That was some of it. Anyway, the head took exception to my popularity, and booted me out. Farewell Bune. Next stop Ludden. What about you?"

"Nothing much to tell. I went to Polchester, then on to Medlock. Came away with a degree in Journalism Studies. Finally managed to land a job in broadcasting."

"How did you manage that?"

"I had a stroke of luck. An uncle is one of the programme commissioners at ABC, and put in a word."

That wasn't my idea of luck, though I didn't say so at the time. "And then?"

"Then I showed I could cut the mustard, which not everyone can. Since when I've floated steadily upwards. That's about it."

The conversation came to a halt. Clearly he was not going to confess to anything personal – the sort of stuff that makes for intimacy. Nor was I, as he doubtless also realised. The main difference between us was that I was lying, he was simply doctoring the truth. That was the opening condition of our relationship, and it never greatly changed.

2

Later the same afternoon I accompanied Mark back to his flat. By that time we were both very drunk. The flat was both scruffy and chic in a style familiar to me from my father's house in Cantleford. Mark invited me to take a bath. After a few minutes he joined me, naked and carrying a bottle of red wine and two glasses. His body was as hairless as a boy's, his skin smooth and soft, and very pale. He soaped me fondly, then he drew my head towards his and kissed me on the lips. His mouth was soft and yielding. His tongue explored my open mouth. I returned all of these favours with interest. It was all very nice. Perhaps, I thought, this is it, the thing I have been looking for, the further connection that will make up for everything.

We went into his bedroom. He lay down on his back on the white sheets, and I lay on top of him. We kissed. His erection was hard against my stomach.

This was a new experience, being in bed with someone without any need for subterfuge, or any fear of being surprised in the act. I was not at all sure what was expected of me. Realising this, he folded back his legs, and then placed his hands on my bottom and encouraged me to enter him.

Kissing him fiercely, I plunged in and out three times, climaxed, and fell instantly into a short blissful sleep, like dropping into a deep well.

I woke a few minutes later. The sheets were damp with the

sweat of our mingled bodies. His sperm was sticky on my stomach. I wiped it off with a corner of the sheet, wrinkling my nose at the sharp intense smell. Mark was flat out beside me, his body laid open and defenceless. He was snoring: a quiet regular rumble. I wanted to feel tender and loving, but my main emotion was disappointment, a sense of having been taken in, not so much by Mark as by my own unrealistic expectations.

3

The next evening we went for a tour of Mark's favourite bars, and along the way I was introduced to a number of his friends. I found this gruelling in a way I hadn't expected, although I probably should have. There was a good number of these people, and more kept turning up all through the evening, so I was both outnumbered and confused. To make things worse, Mark insisted on introducing me as a refugee from Bune. No one from that group could ever have been seriously considered for admittance to Bune, so they were naturally keen to rubbish it as a school for snobs. Faced with this barrage of self-righteous opprobrium, my first instinct was to lie my way out of trouble by pretending to have been more of a rebel than in fact I was – a line of defence I had already used with Mark in our first conversation. This encouraged his friends to take the mud-slinging to extreme lengths, and before long I found myself becoming surprisingly distressed.

By this time it was impossible for me to attempt any sort of defence of the school; which meant – such is the horrid inevitability of embarking on a lie – that I was forced into a position of further exaggerating its faults. The lies multiplied, and with them my sense of guilt at uttering them: my sense that in doing so I was letting the school down.

I returned to Mark's flat smarting from this assault on my school, and from the strain of having to pretend to agree with it. It was impossible to explain any of this to Mark, since that would have meant confessing to a lie, and revealing a lot more about myself than I intended, then or ever.

Strong feelings invariably find an outlet, however, and mine was to launch an attack on his friends.

"I'm sorry," I said, "but they're all phonies."

"Oh? Why do you say that?"

"They pretend to be against the system, but really they're nothing of the sort. They're far too comfortably off to risk changing anything, like stopping corruption, or helping the poor. They're not interested in overthrowing the system, only in making fun of it." That, of course, had been my own position, right up to the moment of my expulsion, and knowing my own culpability in this area did not make me any the less passionate in my attribution of blame. Also, I should mention, I was more than a little drunk, which made the lies and confabulations flow all the more freely.

"A serious charge. Why didn't you say this to their faces?"

"Perhaps I was being considerate."

"You needn't be considerate on my account. I'd much rather you were truthful than see you sneaking around, trying to spare everyone's feelings."

"Well next time, perhaps I'll try that. See whether you like really honesty as much as you claim."

"I wouldn't like it, and nor would you. But it would be better than hearing you boasting about your revolutionary works of art, and then looking disappointed when they failed to show any interest in private jokes made in the comfort of an exclusive school art-room."

Then went on to become a full-blown row. We said a number of hurtful things, threw some ineffectual blows that turned to a wrestling match, and thence to angry sex.

4

I would say that was the beginning of the end, but in fact the end was already prefigured in the beginning. Under other circumstance we would have gone our separate ways, but my dependence on Mark for a place to stay meant that this was not immediately possible. No doubt he could have thrown me out, but he was not that kind of person. My guess is that certain experiences in childhood, to which he vaguely alluded from time to time, had left him with a disabling feeling of guilt, which manifested itself in a sense that he was somehow responsible for my immediate welfare. Either way I was placed in the unfortunate position of being obligated to someone who did not greatly like me, and whom I did not greatly like in return. He for his part had to put up with an increasingly unwelcome and increasingly hostile guest. It was hardly a recipe for comfort.

The practical outcome was that Mark made it clear to me that he would sleep with anyone whom he fancied, and that I was free to do the same. His hope was that sooner or later I would find some other person to leech off. The next few weeks were an unending monotony of casual sex and constant arguments about nothing, which after a while became a routine that was in some way comforting. It became, in short, something not too different from marriage.

It was a novelty to fuck someone different every night, without having to worry about hurting anyone's feelings. Moreover the fucking, while far from satisfactory, provided an efficient form of release, greatly superior to the hurried fumbling acts I was used to. But a distraction was all it was. My conscience was uneasy, and became increasingly more so as time went on. For much of the time the root of my uneasiness was hidden from me, but every so often it broke through the defences I had constructed to stop me examining it.

It broke through, for example, in a conversation I had with Mark about his relations with his father. "He's an old fool," I remember him saying at one point. "Stuck in the past, not an original thought in his head. I no longer see the man; it's easier for both of us. This *relationship* business is all a racket designed by the system to make us keep in line. Marriage, responsibility, fatherhood – who needs it?"

Most of this, I recognised, was aimed at justifying his own lack or real commitment. What I wanted to do was cut through all this, and talk about my own father, how different our relationship was to what Mark was describing. But I couldn't, and I didn't. When you have committed to a lie, or even just a false impression, the truth has to be avoided at all costs, even tiny portions of the truth, in case it pulls up larger truths by the roots.

Inside my head, however, those larger truths were running riot. The mental picture of my father in prison was torture. So too was the realisation that I was doing nothing to help him escape. I shied away from any contact with these thoughts, and yet I kept going back to them, sniffing at them, like a mouse returning to a loaded trap: knowing it is risky, perhaps fatal, but incapable of leaving it alone.

EIGHTEEN
Election Fever

"An attempt has been made," said Rattle heavily, "to incriminate the School's Headmaster, Dr Floater. For a time even I gave some credence to this despicable falsehood."

"Then who did it?" asked Wisley, mopping his brow with a small face-flannel he kept for emergencies like this.

"Sources that prefer to remain anonymous have supplied me with a telling piece of evidence." With a flourish, Rattle unfurled a crumpled poster the size of a waistcoat. In lurid tones of red and green it depicted the manically grinning visage of a heavily moustachioed man of swarthy complexion, under the legend: 'For One Night Only: Dr Pook's Celebrated NATURIST CIRCUS. Bune Working Men's Club, Saturday July 14th, 1406.'

"I don't follow."

"The date, man, the date!" said Rattle impatiently. "The only performance of this public display of indecency took place on the night of the murder."

"Then you think this person – what's he called – 'Pook'? – may be the killer?"

"I have never been more certain of anything in my life."

'The Guilty Party', from *The Infected Pistol and Other Stories*
by H O Minty and F R Trumper. (Privately printed, 409).

1

The weeks that followed were overshadowed by the general election, which was due to be held at the end of September. Mark and his friends in the world of radio and newspapers talked of little else.

Few of the boys at Bune held any real political views. Most, if asked, would say they supported the Lords of Folly, whose policy was to have no policies at all, arguing that such things were essentially absurd. LoF candidates displayed their contempt for the political process by dressing up as clowns or wizards or vampires or stage villains with walrus moustaches and huge furry eyebrows. In Bune mock elections they always won by a thumpingly large margin. After leaving the school most Bunians found themselves a comfortable berth in the Pragmatic Party, that being the quickest and most straightforward route to a career in the media or Law, or indeed in politics itself – a good number became Pragmatic MPs.

The Pragmatists (popularly shortened to 'the Prags') considered themselves to be the natural party of government, and the country generally speaking supported them in this opinion – in the past half-century only three governments had been formed by anyone else. Virtually every member of the Prag cabinet was an old Bunian, including the prime minister, The Right Honourable Malcolm Pooley. The main opposition parties, the Progressives ('the Progs') had to make do with men from schools of the calibre of Barrington, Redmayne and Polchester. The National Socialists ('the Plebs') recruited their candidates from the Artisans Guilds, and the wilds of Kymrie and Alban.

At this time the Prags were holding on to a narrow majority of fifteen. The Progs were the next largest party, followed by the Plebs. The minority parties – the Alban and Kymrie Independence parties, the far-right Defenders of Albion, and the far-left Workers' Party – 'the Proles' – held only fifteen seats between them.

Reading this back, it sounds as if I was quite knowledgeable on the subject. In fact most of that knowledge was acquired after I met Mark. Before that I couldn't have told you the name of the Prime Minister.

Politics was Mark's obsession; his other interests – sex, money, food – took second place. My ignorance on the subject appalled him, and he had no problem with telling me so, to the point, sometimes of humiliating me in front of his friends.

After a few days of this I resolved to acquire a smattering of information, so that I could at least avoid showing myself up in public. His flat was full of books and journals with titles like: *Fiscal Discipline, The Way of Pragmatism, The Progressive Tradition, Rebel in the Ranks: Memoirs of a National Socialist* and the like. While he was at work I trawled through this material, leapfrogging over it when I came to anything too boring. I am a quick learner: within a week I knew enough to follow what Mark was talking about. I was careful, however, not to insist my own opinions into a conversation. Mark regarded politics as his personal preserve; I knew he would resent my claiming any share in it. I depended upon him for my safety, and my position with him was perilous enough as it was.

The more I delved into the subject the more it seemed to me that there was a puzzle, an empty place at the core of everything I read and everything I heard. That empty place had a name: the NAC. The available material gave no information about its members: no names, no arrival dates, nothing about their backgrounds or credentials, or views. And yet the absence of these things was taken for granted, passed over, as if it were perfectly natural that individuals who were collectively so influential should be in every way anonymous. Discussion of the NAC was not only off-limits: so was discussion of the fact of it being off-limits. It was very strange.

Foreign policy was another curious area. We knew there were foreign countries beyond the ocean, where they spoke different languages and ate different foods, but what went on in those countries was a mystery. The coasts were rigorously guarded; for anyone to attempt to leave the country was a serious offence.

As I pondered these questions I recalled something my father had once said – I couldn't remember on what occasion – to the effect that the world as we know it might be a fake. Perhaps the truth about the NAC was that there was no NAC – that they were a bogeymen myth fabricated in order to keep us in line. It seemed ridiculous, but so too were many of the things we were taught to accept without question.

Thoughts of my father reminded me that he was still in custody somewhere, charged with a crime so appalling the authorities could not even speak its name. Guilt reared up; I had to fight hard to suppress it. Three weeks ago I had resolved to find out where he was being held, and do my best to set him free. Since then I had done nothing. This business with Mark was a diversion, a way of avoiding the issue.

2

"The worst thing about a business trip," said Mark, "is the sheer awfulness of being away from one's home comforts. The only thing worse is a holiday: two weeks of paralysing boredom spent in an unheated boarding house half a mile from the nearest stony apology-for-a-beach, constant rain, not enough books, other than a stained selection of abandoned would-be erotic bum-fests, dreadful food, and the dreariest little town full of shops selling plastic buckets and restaurants specialising in 'gourmet fish and chips'. It's even worse when you go away with someone else. A person you can only just bear for five minutes at a time becomes completely intolerable when you are forced to endure their company twenty-four hours of the day."

Much of this was aimed at me but I refused to rise to the bait. Spending two weeks cooped up with Mark wasn't exactly to my taste either, but I was looking forward to seeing a bit more of the country, and Mark had – very reluctantly – agreed to take me along as an unpaid 'research assistant'. Of course, anything interesting would be solely his responsibility; my 'research' would be confined to running errands and carrying messages and making the sandwiches. Galling as this was, it was better than nothing, and there was always the possibility that I would find a chance to shine, despite his determination to keep me under a stone.

"At least it makes change," I pointed out.

"A week in prison would be a change, and probably not that much worse. The real nightmare will be finding a decent hotel – or rather ten of them all told. You can't rely on any of the so-called hotel guides, which are all thrown together by hacks who invariably get a hefty kickback from mine host, along with free accommodation and the very best of treatment, and bugger all if they don't play ball. The only real indication of the quality of an establishment is the price; and if you go for that solution it means spending an arm and a leg wherever you go, and having nothing left over for entertainment."

Mark's rant brought back memories of Worsley and his father's chain of hotels. "Perhaps I can help with that," I said.

"You? What do you know about it?"

"A boy I knew at school has a father in what he insisted on referring to as 'the hospitality industry'. He promised to give me a discount." I stopped short: going into details about my connections might be a mistake. Mark knew little of substance about me, including my real name – he still thought I was called Thomas Bunting.

"Tell me more. Would this man be able to give me an invoice?"

"I don't see why not."

"For the full amount, I mean."

"Why is that important?"

"Don't be so obtuse. My expenses are paid by the ABC. There's no reason why they should benefit from the connection."

"I see. You'll pocket the difference."

"Of course. That's what anyone would do. What's the matter, Tom? You look as if you've swallowed a maggot."

"I'll ask the question," I said. "But don't blame me if the hotels are not to your taste."

"Why? What's wrong with them?"

"For a start they're completely lacking in character. Every room is exactly the same as the next."

"What's wrong with that? At least you know what you're going to get. I've stayed in too many ancient dumps to worry about 'character', which usually turns out to be shorthand for draughts, damp beds, and smelly flushers. What's it called, anyway, this chain?"

"'Rest Assured'," I said reluctantly. "My friend and I always referred to it as 'Rest in Peace'."

"You would, you snobby little bugger. Why do you always have to piss on everything like that? 'Rest Assured' is a perfectly good name. Conveys modern standards of comfort together with peace and quiet. Who is this 'friend' you keep referring to, anyway? One of your stable companions from Bumfellow Hall?"

"You wouldn't know him," I said. It was bad enough Mark knowing about my connection to Worsley; if he got wind that I was friends with the son of Sir Roger Purkis I would never hear the last of it.

"No one I'd *want* to know from the sounds of it. This Rest Assured man, on the other hand, sounds like a thoroughly decent guy. What did you say his name was?"

"Smith," I said reluctantly, plucking the name from the air. I had no moral objection to telling lies, particularly under the present circumstances, but I had learned by now that the fewer lies you told, the less likely you were to be called out on them.

"Smith – really? An inspired name for a hotelier – and for his customers likewise." He trotted his fingernails impatiently on a table. "Well? What are you waiting for? Are you going to get in touch with this Smith?"

"If that's what you want?"

"What I want, William, is for you to get off your insufficiently ornamental backside and make some sort of contribution. Even if it's nothing more than saving me ten bob a night on hotel charges."

3

There was a 'Rest Assured' on the Mancunian Way, close to Mark's flat: a cube of white concrete fronted by a wall of plate glass. I called in later the same day. It was immediately apparent that the Rest Assured was a cut above the Ensor Lodge. The lobby was clean and modern and totally inoffensive. The desk-clerk was similarly a cut above Jimmy: a sharp-suited young man with a shaved head and a black goatee. He was a bit frosty to begin with, but once I mentioned the Worsley name nothing could be too much trouble. He picked up the telephone, and within a matter of minutes had secured a booking for a total of fifteen nights in any of more than fifty branches of the Rest Assured chain of hotels, at a discount of 20% off the standard price.

I had been dreading having to raise the issues surrounding the billing. In the event these were handled with singular efficiency. The clerk volunteered without any prompting to make out the invoice for the full amount, without recording any discount.

"Splendid," I said. I hesitated. "There's just one other thing…"

"You would rather your name was omitted from our records, am I right?"

"Absolutely. You anticipate my every need."

"Good of you to say so, sir. We at 'Rest Assured' pride ourselves on doing precisely that."

"Well you can 'rest assured' at having done a first-rate job. Perhaps you could convey my gratitude to young Mr Worsley himself."

"I will indeed, Mr Riddle. May I also report, sir, that you will bear us in mind when making any further bookings?"

I assured him that he could. After a further exchange of compliments, I left, holding a fat booklet of vouchers for various Rest Assured services –manicures, meals, haircuts, massages, taxi-rides – and feeling slightly soiled, as one does after handling a hairbrush liberally plastered with scented oil.

Flushed with success I returned to Mark's flat. "Well done, sunshine," said Mark. (Slipping every now and then into the vernacular of the streets was one of the affectations he had acquired from his strictly minor-league school.) "There's a turn-up for the books. Someone's been taking useful pills."

'Pass the hammer', as Payne might have said. For all Mark's many uses, I was beginning to hate him: not all the time, but at odd random moments when he did or said something that jarred like a discordant note in a passage of music. Those moments occurred with increasing frequency; eventually, I knew, they would merge into one sustained discord, and I would have to leave.

4

Over the next two weeks we travelled the length and breadth of Albion, wherever a rally was being held, or a village fete, or a march, or a street protest; wherever a result was likely to be close, or one of the parties outnumbered all the others by a large margin; wherever one of the fringe parties – the purple-shirted Defenders of Albion, the red-shirted roughnecks of the Workers' Party, the fanatical advocates of Kymrian or Alban or Curwenian Independence

– could muster a visible degree of support. We visited muddy Northern hamlets inhabited by two or three gaunt labourers and a ragged flock of boys; we shivered on the brown pebble beaches of the Eastern shore, and the deserted sandy beaches of Campshire and Bissex; we took in the vast yellow rape plains of Chant, and the secretive coves of Cerwen, and the lakes and snow-capped mountains of Windwater, and finally we ventured into the grey country, the vast industrial conurbation defined by the harbour of Slurry in the West, Elmet in the east, and Arden in the south.

5

In the wealthier constituencies, the talk was mostly about how to ensure that the Pragmatic Party was returned with a decent majority. In those areas where there was a concentration of the underclass, the chief topic of conversation was the Statutory Fixed Wage, otherwise known to those who considered themselves its victims, as 'The Big Freeze'.

The SFW had been introduced by the Progressive party during one of their rare periods in office, some ten years earlier. The idea was to divide every worker into one of thirteen bands, ranging from the people like Entertainers, Cabinet Ministers and Judges (Band A) to apprenticed manual labourers (Band P). A government committee set the bands, and fixed the rates of pay that went with them, adjusting the levels annually according to what the country could afford.

At first the Artisans' Guilds had welcomed the SFW, believing it to offer their membership a guaranteed fair wage that would rise annually in pace with inflation. It was not long, however, before they discovered that this was not how it worked in practice. The first annual review saw the wages of those in bands A to H increase by 20%, and those in bands J to P by 3%. With each succeeding review the gap grew larger. According to the Progs, this 'adjusted differential' as they called it, was necessary in order to 'control inflation' and make business 'more competitive'.

The Prags returned to power three years later on a platform that included a promise to reform the SFW 'root and branch' and take 'emergency measures' to 'put the country back on its feet'. In practice this meant freezing the wage levels of everyone in band J and below – some 90% of the working population – while allowing the wages of everyone in the higher bands to increase by even larger increments than previously. These 'emergency measures', as might be expected, were widely welcomed by those workers in bands A to I. Among those in bands J to P it was cordially hated.

In seven years the freeze had never been lifted.

6

On Thursday evening Mark covered a Pragmatic Party meeting in Brackham – a decorous event at which only eight persons were present, including ourselves. Those in attendance spent the greater part of the meeting congratulating one another, and the remainder fulminating about the 'spendthrift' policies of the Progs. They were particularly incensed at the Progs' 'bribe', as they called it, to lift the freeze 'as soon as circumstances permitted': a policy which was clearly designed 'to drive business to the wall'.

We stayed the night in a Rest Assured close by the ancient Market Hall – the usual reliable room and service, spoiled only by the hourly booming of the Hall's mighty bells. Early the next morning we set off in our bright yellow steamer for Arden, travelling via Sheafton and Derwent, into the heart of what is known, for obvious reasons, as 'Grey Country'.

7

The first stage of our journey began under blue skies. Mile after mile of bright yellow fields extended to the gently undulating horizon. As we steamed along, top open to the elements, we caught the first whiff of what was awaiting us: a sharp metallic tang, with a smoky, sulphurous undertone. The smell grew worse; soon there was no escaping it. We stopped the steamer to fold out the top; we wound up all the windows. This had little effect. The sky furred over. Some few miles further on a faint blot on the horizon took shape as the iron winding gear of a coalmine, alongside a mountain of black filth. Soon we were surrounded on both sides by armies of blackened terraces marching over the black hills and silting up the black valleys. Along with the mines came the factories: as huge as mainline railway stations, only windowless, with row after row of tall chimneys belching smoke into a smoky sky. The land surrounding them was choked by more blackened terraces. Their grey back gardens hung with sagging lines of soot-spattered underclothes. The men themselves were as shy as mice: only occasionally did you catch a glimpse of one loitering hunchbacked on a street corner, wearing the trademark stained blue overalls and flat woollen cap.

The windscreen acquired a layer of black grime. Mark pressed a button, squirting up twin fountains of soapy water. The wipers swiped back and forth, stirring the filth from one side to another; eventually creating a pair of streaky crescents through which it was just possible to make out the road ahead.

The sun was now a dim grey disc, peering through a blanket of thick grey air. Our tongues and lungs and stomachs were coated. Our eyes watered and stung. The muck had somehow penetrated the interior of the steamer, coating its upholstery with a fine patina of soot. Black smuts marked my hands and my trousers. I itched all over.

As we approached the denser parts of the conurbation we were diverted onto an elevated road propped up on massive concrete pillars high above the landscape. A factory was below us, mapped out in segments like a toy farm. A whistle blew a shrill blast like a scream, and then another, followed by a great chorus of siren-shrieks and hooters. Men flooded out of the doors, swirled about the walled yard like slurry, then emptied through the open gates and down the dirty streets, a seething mass of dirty overalls and soot-marked faces and flat grey caps.

"Look at them!" said Sam. "The army of the unwashed. Another year or two, Thomas, or you could end up being one of them."

I assumed that Mark was being ironic. Irony at Bune was very much the prevailing mode of speech, and had always seemed a reasonable way of holding oneself above the fray. Now that I had left the place – or more precisely, now that the place had cast me out

– it seemed cheap and dishonest: a way of disowning a prejudice and indulging in it at the same time.

"I was one of them once," I said. "They're not that different from the people you admire. Just a lot poorer, and of course they have to work a lot harder. By the way, they don't think much of journalists either. You're the scum of the earth, so far as they're concerned."

Mark made a small mocking noise, a kind of mini-raspberry. "What's this you're saying, Thomas?" he asked mockingly. "I knew you'd been to Bune, but you never said you had a former life as a waif and stray."

"There's a lot you don't know."

"So it would seem. I'm intrigued. Tell me more about these experiences of yours. Were you by any chance one of those raga-muffins they send down the mine to see if the air is fit to breathe? If only that were true! We could write it up for publication. *My Struggle: From the Grey Country to the Golden Fields of Bune*. Followed in the succeeding issue by instalment two, *Living on My Wits: Down and Out in Literary Ludden*."

I refused to rise to the bait.

"Well?' he persisted. "Tell me more. Now that you've got my attention."

"Why should I? You'll only sneer, whatever I say."

"Then say something that isn't pretentious. Or silly. Or untrue."

"I'd rather say nothing at all, if that's your attitude."

"Good."

8

We were now running alongside an enormous cemetery, with ranks of plain wooden posts packed together as tightly as bristles on an unshaved chin. The road swooped up, and we were looking down over a confusion of railway lines, bridges, tunnels, points and signals, sidings and rolling stock and the weed-choked spaces between the rails. The grey sun glinted in the grey puddles. Another swoop, another turn, and we were running parallel with a road bordered with high walls topped with razor wire. A convoy of cyclists emerged from a tunnel, heading relentlessly in one direction. Their cycles were old and rusty, their frames as thick as scaffolding poles; each had a hefty wheeled crate attached to it on one side, big enough to take a passenger, as well as a collection of capacious baskets bolted on above front and back mudguards. The cyclists pedalled head down, with furious concentration, spared from colliding by some animal instinct for survival.

Another bend, a dip and a swoop, and yet more bicycles swam into view: thousands of them, filling the roadways, choking the routes: all of the same heavy-framed design with two or more boxes or baskets attached to them; all pedalled by the same intent crouching men in the same flat hats and overalls. The afternoon shift was over, and the men were heading home. A convoy of three heavily armoured steamers, long and black, with tinted windows and metal cages protecting their bodywork from assault or collision, dawdled hooting in the midst of the slow-moving throng, like the stranded bodies of dead cockroaches lying in the path of a remorseless procession of ants.

The buildings grew larger: we were approaching the centre of Arden. We steamed down a long avenue of giant advertising hoardings. A vast sooty collier went past, standing naked in a tin bath while his husband lathered his buttocks with Bungo's Soap. This was succeeded by another, in which a group of young men (also naked, also seen from the rear) frolicked in the spray of a waterfall, watched by a smoking gent in a white suit and straw boater.

'Springwater Cigarettes,' said the caption. 'Pure and Clean.'

We entered an area of blackened tenements, overhung by towers of grimy glass. At ground level was an endless parade of shops, most of them boarded up or shielded by grey metal shutters scribbled over with a dense tangle of doodles. Every hundred yards or so we came across the clenched fist and lightening fork of the Workers' Party.

"Welcome to Arden," said Sam. 'The Sphincter of Anglia'."

9

The room at the Arden Rest Assured was as clean and comfortable as every other we had sampled. Tall plate glass windows afforded a panoramic view of the Arden skyline, the tall angular buildings ablaze with light. Air-conditioning hummed quietly in the background. The water was hot and plentiful. Our bathroom was dazzling, with a shower big enough for two, and free supplies of Bungo's soap and sachets of Bungo's shampoo. Inspired by the Bungo's advertisement, Mark insisted on soaping my buttocks as I stood in the tub, facing away from him. Our lovemaking afterwards had an air of melancholy. For some weeks the only feeling that had motivated our embraces was anger; now even that was fading to indifference.

Presently Mark got up and started to dress.

"Where are you off to?" I asked lazily, from the bed.

"I need to soak up some atmosphere. Find out what people are thinking."

"Do you want me to come with you?"

"No thanks. I need to be alone."

So, as a matter of fact, did I. I suspected that the work Mark had in mind would turn out to be a version of Purkis's adventures in the taverns of Cantleford. Our room had a shelf of books designed to soothe or stimulate. Among them was an erotic romance entitled *Language of the Heart*, about a heart surgeon who falls in love with a publisher's editor. It was silly but comforting. Eventually I fell asleep.

10

Mark got in around three in the morning, reeking of beer and cigarettes. Fortunately the 'Rest Assured' doubles are wide enough for two people to lie together without touching.

When I next opened my eyes the sun had just lifted above the skyline, and was shining directly on my face. Next to me, Mark was snoring, face down on a pillow stained with brown crusts of blood.

I got up and walked over to the window. At night the view had seemed glamorous; in the light of day the buildings were hideous and shabby. I lit one of Mark's cigarettes, then put it out again.

Presently his alarm shrilled. He got up and spent a long time in the bathroom. He came out, dabbing at his face with a flannel. His lip was split and swollen, and one eye was a narrow slit between two puffy purple cushions of flesh.

"What happened to you?" I asked.

"I was beaten up."

"Why?"

"I don't belong to their tribe. I don't have a flat hat, I'm not covered in grime, I don't vote black-shirt, and I don't speak like a member of the Arden underclass."

11

Over breakfast he was a little more communicative. He had been attacked within five minutes of arriving in a bar. Only the arrival of the local constabulary had saved him from ending up in hospital. They took him into custody for his own protection. After leaving him for four hours in a filthy cell, they had escorted him back to the hotel, advising him to leave the city at first light.

"And are we going to?"

"No bloody fear. I'm a journalist; we don't scuttle off just because we're in danger. Anyway, I have a plan."

His plan was for me to go down into the town and buy us two pairs of overalls and two flat caps. It was time, apparently, that I started to earn my keep. First of all, however, if I wanted to avoid being beaten up myself, I would have to dirty myself up a bit.

This was not as easy as it may sound. The room had recently been cleaned; dirt of the right sort was in short supply. We rooted around under the bed and inside the wardrobe, but all we came up with was a handful of dust and fluff.

Despairing of the room, I went down to the ground floor, and out to a squalid back yard, presided over by a smoking porter. Ranged along a blackened wall was a line of red plastic rubbish bins overflowing with kitchen waste. The smell obliged me to work with haste. Levering up the lid of one of the bins, I took hold of the first item that came to hand, which happened to be a mould-encrusted carrier bag.

The porter watched these activities curiously.

"Morning," he said.

"Good morning."

"Morning constitutional?"

"Something of that sort."

"Breakfast room's inside. Down the corridor and first left."

"Thanks," I said.

I returned to the room. The contents of the carrier-bag did the job, in that it completely ruined a clean shirt and a decent pair of trousers. I studied my reflection in the bathroom mirror. Despite the stains, my shirt remained white, and my trousers were too good a fit to belong to a working-man. My hair, on the other hand, looked impressively disgusting, thanks to a liberal dressing of clotted slime. The smell was also authentically foul.

Maintaining a heathy distance, Mark doled out three pound notes from the little black purse he kept inside his belt. "Get me receipts," he said.

I took the stairs down into the lobby. The porter from the dust-bin area was lounging by a stainless-steel pillar.

"Back for more?"

"I'm actually looking for a way out."

"There you are," he said, indicating a gate set in the wall behind the bins.

"Thanks."

"Nice one, John."

I raised the latch and left.

12

The Cantleford expedition with Purkis should have taught me that attempts at disguise serve only to draw attention to those seeking to avoid it. Soon I had collected a retinue of ragged boys, who followed me through the streets, shouting insults. I ignored them.

The first few shops I came across sold old furniture and other junk. There were a couple of sordid cafes full of depressed smokers, then a long row of betting shops and warehouses selling old bikes and second-hand bed-linen. After that came some lottery ticket stalls, and the blacked-out windows of some sex shops, and a couple of gloomy taverns, and the dank entrance to some ancient flusher-stalls.

Finally I came to a shop called 'TOGS & CLOGS'. Its window was dressed with a collection of headless manikins wearing identical overalls. A hand-scrawled sign pinned to one of them read: 'Best Price 5/-'.

I went inside. My retinue remained outside.

The interior was dark and dusty. A huge bald man stood behind the counter. Behind him was a bank of battered wooden drawers.

"Yis?" he asked belligerently.

"Two pairs of overalls, please."

"Oyveralls?' he said.

His accent was a good deal more pronounced than that of the porter: it was quite a struggle to understand him. "The outfits in the window."

"Pocket-johns. That what yow askin' fower?"

"Yes please. And two flat caps."

"Stinleys," he corrected. "Tow johnnies and tow stinleys."

"Correct," I said brightly.

The door pinged, and the head of a boy looked round the jamb. "Bogger off artavit!" he shouted, raising his fist. "Not yow, chick," he added, smiling at my startled expression. "Thowse little bleeders at the do-er."

"Right," I said, once I had deciphered this. "Yes, they're a nuisance."

"Theyse a fookin' pen in y'erse." He looked from my stained shirt to my lilywhite hands. "What's yower trade thin? Boom-rintal?"

No point in taking offence. "I'm a porter," I said, supposing this to be a sufficiently menial occupation to satisfy him. "I work at the Rest Assured hotel."

"Ooh-ah?" he said disbelievingly. "Canna they find an Ardie to wit on travellin' bagmen? Get yowersen hime, chick, yower not welcome her."

261

I was reminded in some ways of the men of Glenlockie. They had a similar contempt for foreigners, but tended to be more deferential to the foreigners' faces, particularly if they suspected them of having money to spend.

"Fair enough," I said. "Can I have the 'clegs' first, though?"

"Siven and sex a-pyce the johns. En tree for the stans. Eighteen bob to yow."

"The sign in the window says three shillings," I pointed out.

"Is yow calling my a chite, yow cheekay erse?" he said dangerously. "Tree bob's the sheert, not the fookin' john."

There was no point in arguing. I handed over a pound note. He turned it over, held it up to the light, and made some marks on it with a pen kept on his counter. Finally he slipped it into his pocket. From one of the drawers he took out two pairs of johnnies. From another he removed two stanleys.

"Medium and small," I qualified.

He shook his head. "Yin size fits owl."

The proposition was demonstrably false, but I kept this opinion to myself. "Fine. Could I have a receipt?"

"Coom agin?"

I started to explain, but he cut me off. "Oy now worra 'resight' is, jimmy. Oy daint gee resights."

If I could not get a receipt, I did at least expect some change. I waited. He eyed me belligerently. Reluctantly he counted out two shillings in small copper coins. I considered asking him for a bag, but decided against it.

13

"How much did this crap cost?" demanded Mark, when I got back to the room.

I told him the sum.

"Where's the receipt?"

"He wouldn't give me one."

"You are bloody useless, Thomas, do you know that? How am I going to get the money out of ABC if you don't get a receipt?"

"We'll go back there if you like. You can ask him for one yourself."

"No bloody fear. I've got enough to do without doing your job as well."

We both put on the johnnies. Mark's, as I had expected, were far too tight, mine far too loose. The stanleys were similarly ill-fitting.

I looked at Mark, and smiled. Above the ankle the pristine johnnies made him a passable, if over-clean, facsimile of a working man; below that point his hand-made Redmaynes – crafted from heavy maroon leather, with yellow stitchwork around the soles, and patterns punched into the toecaps and around the lace-holes – stood out like a rose on a rubbish dump.

"What is it?"

"Your shoes."

"No one's going to notice my shoes."

I made no reply; contenting myself with smearing my own inferior footwear with some of the remaining kitchen slime.

14

On our way to the ABC building we attracted a good deal of attention, partly, as I had predicted, because of the distinctive nature of Mark's footwear; partly also because of the newness of our pocket-johns. Men shook their fists at us, urchins chased after us chanting the local version of the WP rallying chant: "Foyte, foyte, foyte; foyte wi' all your moyte! Trust the Wukkers Poyty to gie the fokkers shoyte!"

"Ignorant bloody Proles!" said Mark, pushing a way between the crowds. "Can you wonder the country's in such a state?"

Despite his experience of the previous evening, he was more angry than alarmed. I felt the reverse. Our disguises were useless. To make things worse, they were uncomfortably hot, and stank. The heat and the smell intensified as the day progressed. The foul air was warm and muggy, and the sun for all its dimness burned as if directed at us through a magnifying glass. Sweat gathered inside the pocket-johns, saturating my underclothes. Rivulets of sweat trickled down my chest and sides and thighs, collecting around my knees and along the band of my underpants. The stanley oppressed on my forehead, leaving a raw red mark; my hair and face were soaked with sweat. Sweat blocked my eyes; sweat dripped from my chin. The physical discomfort, the gathering crush into which we were being herded, the atmosphere of barely suppressed rage, the howling and chanting, the clenched fists and bared teeth and bulging eyes of the mob, all combined to create a feeling of unendurable oppression: of being surrounded by savage enemies who were on the point of tearing us to pieces.

15

The ABC building was surrounded by a cordon of police in combat gear, carrying guns and stun-sticks. Their glittering black helmets and padded knees and elbows and V-shaped shields made them look like a colony of giant black beetles.

One of them stood in our path and gestured with his stun-stick for us to leave. Mark waved his ABC pass. The policeman shook his head. Holding his pass up like a shield, Mark took a step forwards. A moment later he was flat on his face with one arm twisted behind his back and the stun-stick hovering about his ears.

A man in a belted raincoat detached himself from the line of policemen. Kneeling next to Mark, he took the passbook from him. He looked it over, then gave an order. The policeman stepped back, slotting his stun-stick into its holster. Mark climbed to his feet, looking shaken. The SS man handed back his pass, and beckoned for me to come forward. My heart thumped in panic.

"He's with me," said Mark.

"I gathered," said the SS man. "You gentlemen are asking for trouble, coming here dressed like that. I took you for one of the rabble."

"That was the idea," said Sam.

"Well it's a bad one. The lads are all jumpy today. Another few seconds and my colleague here would have given you an electric headache."

A policeman escorted us to the doors of the building. He spoke into the intercom, and we were admitted. Order was restored.

We were offered tea and biscuits. While we were waiting for it to arrive, Mark excused himself, and disappeared in the direction of the ABC employees suite; reappearing some twenty minutes later looking scrubbed and refreshed, and wearing a striped shirt and borrowed trousers: over-tight but freshly laundered.

"You didn't tell me you were going to change," I said accusingly.

"They offered me a change of clothing. –Sorry, Thomas," he added, smiling at my expression. "These were the only set they had."

"Nice of you to think of me, all the same," I said sarcastically.

"I don't know what you're complaining about. I have a job to do: I can't go round looking like a plumber."

"But I can, you mean?"

"Better than me, certainly."

At that point a man brought the tea in a small silver pot, along with a plate of dry biscuits shaped like little bricks. The tea was thick and green, and did nothing to quench my thirst. Nonetheless I poured myself two cups, and took one of the biscuits. It stuck in my throat, absorbing what little saliva I had left.

"Finished?" asked Mark.

I tipped up the teapot: only a trickle was left.

"I need the flushers," I said, thinking that at least I would find running water there.

"You'll have to wait. They're taking us out to the balcony. There's probably somewhere you can pee up there."

"Forget it," I said furiously. It was as if Mark took satisfaction in making my life as miserable as possible.

16

We were taken up to a third-floor balcony overlooking the square. A crowd of journalists and photographers were there already. As I had expected, there were no flushers.

On the far side of the square was a temporary stage hung with WP banners. For the moment the platform was empty, apart from a few men in black messing about with the sound system. Below the stage was a cordon of insect police with black riot shields.

The marchers had come from three gathering-points: Slurry on the west coast, Medlock in the centre, and Elmet in the north-east.

By the time the three streams converged they had swollen to a body of forty thousand. From where we stood the massed stanleys looked like a great lake of floating mushrooms. The square was now filled to bursting, and more kept packing in.

"Ahoy there, lads!"

Across the square caps tilted upwards. Two black-shirted men with ropes and harnesses had scaled the Wagstaffe Column behind the stage and were now standing alongside the stone effigy that topped it: a dapper scholarly individual wearing long flowing locks, a trim beard, a magnificent lace collar, a narrow-waisted tunic and a pair of groin-hugging tights, and holding a long roll of manuscript in one hand and a quill pen in the other.

One climber leant in and planted a kiss on the playwright's stone cheek; the other playfully fondled his stone cod-piece. Roars of laughter. Standing shoulder to shoulder, the men turned their backs – occasioning fresh roars of laughter, accompanied by some predictably lewd remarks – and made some mysterious adjustments to something they held between them; then with a sudden flutter, like a butterfly spreading its wings, a black banner unfurled, hung around Wagstaffe's delicate neck and falling to his slender cross-gartered ankles. The flag was emblazoned with the clenched fist and silver lightning-flash of the Albion Workers' Party.

Cheers rang out, echoing off the surrounding buildings like claps of thunder. At first I thought the cheers were for the men on the column; then I realised they were for something that was happening on the stage below it. A man in a black shirt and black trousers was standing centre-stage in front of the microphone, holding up his arms for silence. We were just about close enough for me to get an idea of his appearance: a slight lopsided man, with leathery reptilian features and an expression of intense anger.

"Arnold Massey," said Mark. "Number One black-shirt. Bit of a firebrand in public, but basically harmless."

Massey tapped the microphone with his finger. Three amplified thudding noises were followed by a piercing electronic squeal; then he began to speak.

His voice – what could be heard of it above the roaring of the

crowd – was nasal and rasping. I caught the words 'fellow workers' and 'coomrades' and 'bands Oy to Joy', then another ferocious
electronic squeal; and suddenly, for perhaps thirty seconds a few
phrases were clearly audible. "Yow reckon it's the bastid Pragses'
fault!" he bellowed. "Nay lads, the Prags are nobbut well-paid stow-
ges!" Roars of approval. "So are the fookin' Progs, – *and* the fookin'
National sow-called *Sowsialist Plebs.*" More roars, accompanied by
frenzied whoops, and the thin *parp-parp-parp* of the plastic trum-
pets commonly heard at kicker matches.

Massey was now in full spate, his words bouncing and booming off the surrounding buildings. "Yow wanna now his *riley* to
blame?" *Boom-squawk!* "Oy'll tell yow hie!" *Parp parp parp!* "It's the
fessless fockin' tyrants of the NA fockin' C!"

The enthusiastic shouts of the crowd drowned out his next
words. His microphone squealed again, and then died, leaving
him mouthing soundlessly like a stranded fish. Shaking his head
angrily, he bunched his right hand in a fist, and raised it high. Fists
shot skywards all across the square. The crowd began to chant:
"Dobya *Pee,* Dobya *Pee!*" Their chanting had a naked primitive force
like the hammering of pistons, or the thumping of drums, or the
pounding of blood in the runner's ear. It mounted to a crescendo.

All of a sudden the tone changed from jubilation to rage. Howls
of protest rang out, like the frenzied bellowing of a wounded
beast. Two men in belted raincoats were standing beside Massey,
taking the microphone from his grasp, taking hold of him by both
skinny elbows, hustling him away.

The crowd erupted. Men boiled all over the platform, climbing
over one another. A wedge-shaped formation of insect policemen
drove into the mushroom sea. People were trampled underfoot.
Chairs sailed through the air, smashing into the window behind
me. More screams, more roars, more flying objects. Men in caps
were swarming over the railings of our balcony, wielding bottles
like clubs. Missiles whistled past my face: stones, knives, chunks
of masonry. Men were ripping at the posts supporting the platform, swinging them like cabers, and hurling them through the
air. Sirens wailed furiously. A puff of smoke rose up, very suddenly,

in one corner of the square, followed by a silent devastating *whuff!* that sucked up all the air, creating a giant awful vacuum. There was one terrible half-second in which nothing happened at all, followed a torrential downpour of glass and brick and muck. Great jagged slivers of glass flew through the air, bursting at my feet.

17

My eyes were choked with dust. Something liquid was coursing down one side of my face. I touched it: blood. My arms were spattered with it.

Mark was nowhere to be seen. The doors to the balcony were locked. Men – photographers, journalists, waiters – were beating on the plate glass with their fists.

On the far side of the square a row of buildings were on fire. Smoke poured from the windows. In the centre of the square the insect police had formed a solid line of black shields. A mob confronted them, wielding sticks, shouting abuse. They charged, and were beaten back. They charged again.

I looked up at the dim disc of the sun. I closed my eyes.

When I opened them, some minutes later, the square had emptied, leaving a dusty litter of motionless bodies like abandoned bags of rubbish. Dust-coated men crouched over them, turning them over, reaching into their pockets. *Whuff!* Another building went up in flames.

More screams, more angry roars, and finally the repeated sound of gunfire.

18

The police who arrested me assumed from my clothing that I was a working man who had climbed the face of the building with the intent to loot and vandalise. I attempted to explain their mistake, but no one was interested. I was driven to a detention facility in the crowded cage of a secure steamer. I was then placed in a cell, also crowded with men in pocket-johns. There was nowhere to sit but the floor. My pocket-johns were torn and stained with blood, I had lost one shoe; there was a great gash on one side of my face. At some point I had lost my stanley, but I still wore the mark of it on my forehead: a raw line of sore skin, like a wound.

I wanted to discuss what had just happened, but I was shunned the minute I opened my mouth.

19

The next day Mark came to collect me.

"Look at you," he said, ruffling my hair playfully. He meant it affectionately, but it came over as patronising.

"What happened to you?" I asked him.

"I was close to the door when the bomb went off. I got inside the building and took shelter."

"But you were there when they arrested him?"

"Arrested who?"

"Arnold Massey. That's what kicked it all off, wasn't it?"

Sam's face closed up. "You're imagining things. Massey's speech was inaudible. They had some problems with the sound system, then the bomb went off. Terrible carnage. And the riots afterwards – despicable."

20

The riots had gone on for the rest of the day and much of the following night. Much of the city centre was destroyed. Many big stores had been burned to the ground. Government buildings and offices were blackened shells.

Fortunately our Rest Assured was undamaged. The police had closed off the Morris centre once the riots began, diverting the rioters into the shabbier zones, where they had run amok, according to all reports, 'like wild beasts'.

Our yellow Harris 200 was still in its underground garage, where we had left it two days earlier. The garage men had given it a good clean and polish, and sprayed and disinfected the interior.

NINETEEN
Snooper

"The explanation immediately under one's nose," said Wisley mildly, examining a crust of dried skin at his elbow, "is inevitably the one least worthy of consideration."

> 'Next Time Keep Your Trap Shut', from *The Infected Pistol and Other Stories* by H O Minty and F R Trumper. (Privately printed, 480).

1

We had intended to steam on up to Alban to cover an AIP meeting, but Mark thought it more important to return to Ludden: he had arranged to interview the prime minister about the terrorist outrage.

By this time responsibility had been claimed by a shadowy outfit called Resurgence. An attempt was made to link them with the far-right Freedom Party, nicknamed 'the purple people' because of the colour of their insignia. The Freedom Party vehemently denied involvement.

Michael Pooley, the prime minister, gave a radio interview in which he deplored the attempts made by anti-democratic elements to interfere with the democratic process. 'We may not agree with what the WP has to say," he told listeners, "but we will defend to the death their right to say it".

Later in the day most of the other party leaders – Duncan Hedger of the Progressives, Philip Sayer of the Natsocs, Jack Burns of the AIP, Kitto Trenowden of the CIP, Dai Lewis-Williams of the AIP – queued up to give voice to their horror and indignation. The one notable absence was Arnold Massey, who had been severely injured by the bomb blast as he was being escorted out of the square by police offers – for his own safety, apparently.

Besides speculating about the bomb, much of the press coverage was given up to attacking the deplorable behaviour of the rioters. They had indulged in an orgy of violence, setting fire to small businesses and humble office buildings, looting shops and private houses and setting fire to them, before staggering away with armfuls of luxury goods. These vandals were also widely reported to have rifled through the pockets of people crushed to death in the fracas, stealing their wallets and any valuables. Various other crimes were hinted at, too indecent to be reported in detail. More than a thousand men were now in custody, charged with a string of offences ranging from common theft to looting, arson and murder. The public prosecutor promised to hand down sentences appropriate to the inhumanity of their behaviour.

A total of two hundred and thirty-four people had been crushed to death in the immediate aftermath of the explosion; some hundreds more were still in hospital. "We saved as many lives as possible," said a police spokesman, "but when people act like animals there's not a lot you can do to help".

2

Mark bought an armful of newspapers, and I skipped through them while he was driving us back to Ludden. The front page of *The Warrior* featured a photo of a rioter carrying a refrigerator out of the doorway of a burning shop. "YOB RULE" ran the caption. "Bombing, looting, and rioting – do these shameless yobs represent the working men of Anglia?"

Inside were more photographs of looting and burning, and an editorial deploring the morals of the rioters. "There's only one way to beat these beasts," it concluded. "And that's to turn out on November the fifth and place your X beside Michael Pooley's Pragmatic Party."

Aside from this the paper contained a fair ration of the usual gossip about entertainers and sportsmen. Page four was given over to a photograph of a shirtless young man with the kind of physique Purkis always referred to as 'top-heavy'. The caption read: "Handsome Caspar Hawkins (22) caught during an energetic work-out at his local gym. When he's not working at a steamer repair shop, Casp likes to 'work out' with swimming, dancing and 'pumping iron'. That's not all he'd be pumping if our readers had their way!"

"Admiring the beefcake, Thomas?" asked Mark, looking over to see what I was reading. "You're a callous little bugger sometimes, do you know that?"

Pass the hammer.

3

With two weeks to go before the election, it looked as if the result was going to be close. Despite the wave of support for the Prags that followed the incident at Arden, there seemed a good chance that the Progs and the Plebs would win enough seats to form a coalition government.

Back in Ludden, Mark was booked to interview Michael Pooley at his office in the Palace of Thorneycross. I was to accompany him as his research assistant: mainly I suspect to make him appear more important. There would be technicians there to oversee the recording, so my function was somewhat obscure. Nevertheless I was glad to be included: it would give me a chance to see what Pooley was like at close quarters. My father had always dismissed him as a fool, albeit a crafty one. I was interested to see how these two qualities could exist in a single person.

4

Thorneycross is a vast ornate first-century building, with a clock tower at one end and the Hall of the People at the other. Security was very tight: a contingent of armed policemen stood shoulder to shoulder at each of the arched entrances. We both had to submit to an exhaustive and rather intimate search of our persons, before being admitted. After that an extravagantly uniformed official – I remember an excess of gold braid and feathers and a ludicrously ornamental sword – escorted us to Pooley's offices, where we were searched again, before being admitted into the great man's presence.

We were ushered into a large elegant room, lit by an ornate gold candelabra holding a dazzling array of electric bulbs in the shape of candle-flames. The furniture was recognisably antique: dark and encrusted with carved knobs and sugar-stick rods. The panelled walls supported a succession of gold-framed portraits of dull-looking men wearing costumes that varied from ruffs to high collars and ornamental waistcoats.

We waited at a discreet distance while Pooley posed for the obligatory photographs at a large rosewood desk, on which several bulging files were arranged. Behind him was a bookcase holding a long run of parliamentary transcripts, bound in identical red leathertex. He was a short tubby man with an excess of chins and pale eyes of some indeterminate colour that flicked from side to side, taking everything in. Round, steel-rimmed spectacles. A sharp little nose set in a moon-face, the mouth small and virtually lipless. His thick grey hair was oiled straight back, leaving his broad shining forehead and fleshy cheeks exposed.

The photographers departed; it was our turn to be noticed.

Mark had only met Pooley once before, apparently, but the prime minister greeted him as an old friend. "Mark Parker, what a treat!" he said. He rose from his seat and took Mark's hand between both of his own. "Good to see you again, my dear."

"And you, sir. Flattered that you remembered me."

"Well naturally I would remember a rising star of the wireless. And who is this blushing youth?"

A crease of annoyance appeared momentarily in the gap between Mark's eyebrows. "My Assistant, Thomas Bunting."

Pooley offered his plump little hand for me to shake. Rather than letting go, he drew me towards him until there was only a foot of air between us. I smelt his musty scent: opium on a bed of jasmine. Behind his gleaming spectacles his pale eyes flicked here and there, taking in every detail, every button, every stray hair, the slightest wince or twitch.

"Bunting, eh?" he said, giving my hand a squeeze. "Seed-eating bird of the family Emberizidae, closely related to the finch. Over forty varieties." He released me. "I daresay Mark will have warned you I'm what we hobbyists call a 'snooper'?"

"Sorry?" I looked to Mark for aid. He was grinning, enjoying my discomfiture.

"A birdwatcher, Thomas," volunteered Pooley merrily, "nothing more sinister than that. Birds are my passion. They must be yours too, presumably, since it is from them that you derive your family name. Am I right?"

These were dangerous waters. "Well, yes, too some extent, obviously," I mumbled.

"Obviously indeed! A Bunting has to be an expert on the bunting, if nothing else! Enlighten me, Thomas: which variety is your favourite?"

"Guess."

"Well, let me see." He studied me with his sharp little eyes. "Could you be a devotee of the gorgeous *Golden-breasted Bunting* of the eponymous effulgent plumage?"

"Close." I said warily.

"That's a polite way of telling me I've missed the mark." He stroked his collection of chins thoughtfully. "In that case I am going to plump for the amusingly dubbed *brown-rumped Bunting,* a bird whose natural habitat is the subtropical forests of the far side of the planet." He leaned forwards, twinkling at me like a mischievous uncle. "Well, Thomas? Does the brown-rumped Bunting 'fit the bill'?"

I smirked politely at the pun. "Perfectly. One hundred percent."

"Good. Excellent. What fun!" said Pooley. "What about you, Sam? Are you a bit of a 'snooper' as well?"

"I can't say that I am, sir," said Sam.

"Really? What a pity! Many of my happiest hours have been spent supine in long grass, with a pair of powerful binoculars, waiting for a rare variety of bird – perhaps even a *brown-rumped bunting* – to cross my path." He beamed happily from Mark to me, then back to Mark again. "Back to work then, I suppose. You have some questions for me, Mark?"

Mark took out his notebook.

Released from my ordeal, I opened a notebook of my own and started to sketch a chubby many-chinned penis in the formal garb of a member of the Albion House of Commoners.

The interview took place at the periphery of my attention. I remember only one exchange at all clearly.

"What was your reaction, prime minister, to the recent incident at Arden?"

"Horror," said Pooley. "Outrage. I believe you yourself were caught up in the fracas, am I right?"

"Yes, I was."

"That must have been very distressing for you. But you escaped safely?"

"Yes."

"Excellent. Many, alas, were not so fortunate. The death toll is in three figures, and rising. The mentality of people who could plot such an atrocity against their fellow workers – unimaginable! And what came afterwards – rioting at such a time, the damage to property, the looting – unforgiveable."

"Going back to the numbers of dead, prime minister, it's been suggested that if the police had not allowed so many men into the square, the fatalities would have been far fewer."

"So we're blaming the police now, are we? I'm surprised at you, Mark. You of all people ought to know what a difficult job the police have to do. Always first in the firing line, whether the ammunition used against them consists of *bricks* or *brickbats*. Who could predict that anyone could be so wicked as to set off a bomb on such an occasion? The police did all they could. With exemplary courage – exemplary. Many were injured, you know, some seriously. But their shoulders are broad. They have to be. The country depends upon them."

"How are the investigations going? Are we are nearer to finding the men responsible?"

"That I can't comment on. I don't wish to say anything that might in any way jeopardise the work of tracking down the terrorists. But depend on it: the culprits will be found. And they will be punished. With the utmost severity."

"Have you any ideas as to why they would target a Workers' Party meeting? Instead of a meeting of your own party, for example?"

"Again, it would be irresponsible of me to conjecture about these matters while the investigation is ongoing. But yes, we have theories. Were the black-shirts targeted? Or were we all? The enemies of way of life are devious, and they play a long game. Their target ultimately is democracy, the pact between the people and the state that guarantees stability and good governance."

"Speaking of good governance," said Mark, "your opponents claim that freezing the wages of bands J to P is unfair."

"They do say that, yes," asked Pooley, smiling benevolently. "The reason they can say that is because they're *idealists*, and the reason they are idealists is because they have no practical experience of being in government. In my book 'fair' is whatever is best for the country as a whole. My party's approach to this issue, as our names implies, is essentially *pragmatic*. We're not afraid of tough decisions; we're not afraid of being unpopular. Yes, the mass of workers have had to tighten their belts in the past few years: and for one very good reason. There was no other way of getting the country back on its feet."

"You haven't considered freezing the wages of bands A to I instead?"

"No, Sam, we haven't. And the reason why we haven't is because it *wouldn't work*. The sums raised would be negligible: nothing even close to anything that would make a difference. Indeed it might even result in a negative yield overall. More importantly than that, it would damage morale at the very top of the heap. Our best managers, our innovators, our wealth-creators would simply stop trying. Is that what you want to see?"

New as I was to the language of politics, it seemed to me that I had heard all these arguments before, many thousands of times, and that rehearsing them now was a pointless exercise, designed for no other purpose than to numb people into submission. In many ways it reminded me of the interminable lectures of Counsellor William Joyce, and the classroom discussions which followed them, discussions which were not debates in any real sense of the term so much as assertions and reassertions of a single orthodox point of view.

For some minutes I elaborated the penis portrait, adding shading, wrinkles, tufts of hair, spectacles and overlapping chins; then I sketched some faces from memory; then I jotted down the word ALBION and ornamented it with leaves and branches until it resembled a small copse. I began to drowse. Stray phrases penetrated my dreamy reverie like needles going through a woolly blanket: "… act of criminal irresponsibility … holding the country to ransom … hundreds of bankruptcies … mass unemployment … starvation … rioting on the streets…"

On and on went the interview, like an infinitely long serpent uncoiling from a trap-door under Pooley's desk and winding and unwinding around Mark's legs and Pooley's legs and my legs, looping us all together like a living hosepipe with a blind hooded face and a mouth like the slit in the head of a penis.

The door flung open. Masked figures arrived. Their leader removed his mask. It was my father. "Gentlemen," he said, "we have reached that part of the proceedings where nothing is what it seems. Let the Union begin!"

To my horror he removed his trousers. Other figures followed suit. Three of them I recognised: Purkis, Nevis and Worsley. Pooley by this time was standing trouserless on his desk. Mark – also trouserless – stood next to him. Mark was cradling a small creature in both hands: a ball of yellow fluff with an open red beak. He handed it carefully to Pooley, who brought it up level to the little rosebud of his mouth. He puckered his lips and blew.

"Fast asleep, Thomas?" asked Pooley. He had come round from behind his rosewood desk, and was standing directly in front of me. He lifted my notebook off his lap. It opened at the page containing the penis portrait. "I say! What is *this* intriguing fabrication?"

"It's a doodle," I said.

"A *doodle*, you call it?" he chortled. "I shall have to remember that one!" He handed the notebook back. "By the way, Thomas," he said roguishly, "I thought of one more *bunting* you might consider adopting as your personal insignia – the common 'corn bunting': a native of these shores. Some might find him a little drab for their taste, but thanks to his dowdy plumage he is skilled at evading capture by *merging anonymously into his background*. What do you say? Might there be an affinity there, do you think?"

He removed his spectacles, and looked me full in the face with his naked eyes.

"Possibly," I said warily.

"Possibly *yes*, and possibly *no*. Best to stay on the fence, I agree. That way no one can accuse you of holding anything so treacherous as an *opinion*. Well, goodbye, boys – it's been a great pleasure. I look forward to getting my copy of the transcript, Mark – as usual. I'll speed it back to you with any corrections before the week is out."

5

Afterwards Mark spent a good five minutes scolding me for my conduct during the interview. I heard him out with a blank face.

The lecture limped to a halt.

"Well?" he demanded. "Haven't you anything to say for yourself."

"Not a thing," I said. Underneath I was fuming. Mark was treating me the way a master would treat his pupil – the master of the sort of second-rate school he had attended himself.

We boarded a bus, and sat for some minutes in silence, watching the ornamental stone facades of the historic quarter drift past one after the other like the frames of a comic book.

"What did you think?" asked Mark suddenly.

The tiff, I was relieved to see, was now over. "Fine. You gave him a good grilling. He didn't get away with anything."

"I was only doing my job. I treat the Prags exactly the same as everyone else. I'd come down just as hard on Duncan Hedger if I had to interview him."

"Even if you agreed with his views?"

"Then especially. It's my duty as a reporter to be impartial. My personal opinion is something else entirely."

"Still, he's an awful old crook, isn't he, Pooley?"

Mark rolled his eyes. "What do you know about it, Thomas? You have no basis on which to arrive at a judgment. You'd hardly even heard of Pooley before you met me."

That put me in my place. I retreated into silence. Mark sat stiffly upright with primly folded arms. Seen in profile, his rosy lower lip jutted out in a way I found intensely irritating. That lip had troubled me on a number of occasions, but in the past I had ignored it, just as I had ignored my other instincts where he was concerned. Sam, I reflected, had always posed as a free-thinking liberal, a man who hated the Anglian establishment at least as much as I did, if not more. The better I knew him, however, the more likely it seemed that in the privacy of the voting cubicle he would place his cross against the name of the Pragmatic candidate.

6

The day of the election was one of feverish activity. Mark conducted a number of last minute interviews. Philip Sayer of the Proles admitted to being "very excited". Duncan Hedger of the Progs declared himself "cautiously optimistic". Arnold Massey's deputy said that whatever the result, it would do no favours to the working man.

The count went on all night. Some of the results were very close. There were recounts. Exit polls gave indications of a massive upset at Slurrywater South, at Brackham, at Chipping Medbury and Raglan. It appeared that the Natsocs had swept the board in Cerwen and Kymrie, and that the AIP had won a majority of the seats in Alban. The Workers' Party looked to have held on to their two seats in Medlock and Arden. The Progs had made substantial gains in Ludden and Windwater. The Prags held steady in their strongholds in the south and south-east, but in the north they had been virtually wiped out. We looked to be heading for a new coalition government.

7

The full picture only emerged the following morning. There had been a landslide. The only consolation for the Prags was that the opposition was too fragmented to allow any one of the opposition parties to form a government. Talks between the election's two main winners, the Progs and the Proles, went on all day. Members who had formerly declared that they would never under any circumstances compromise their conscience by working with another party so devoid of principle, were sudden eager to find common ground. A deal was done. The Proles and Progs were to form a government. Duncan Hedger was to be prime minister, Philip Sayer his deputy.

The victory party was held in 'Wigs', an exclusive nightclub in the prestigious district of Endhaven. Mark naturally enough was invited; so it seemed was I, and virtually all his radio and newspaper friends. A famous restaurant offered to provide the buffet, at a substantial discount on their normal prices. Two small orchestras volunteered to perform free of charge. There was to be country dancing until dawn.

8

The entrance to Wigs on Chaplin Avenue is narrow and discreet, with only a small blue sign to advertise its presence. It was approaching midnight: the party was just getting going. Groups of people stood outside, holding small plastic beakers of wine, their breath steaming in the sharp October air. The atmosphere, was euphoric, almost frenzied. The doorman waved us in between gulps of ale from a long bottle. We descended the stairs, pushing past one after another group of excited young people, jabbering away excitedly. The cavernous space below was crowded with happy revellers. At the far end the Moods of Midnight Dance Orchestra was playing a lively jig. Men of all ages and body-shapes cavorted together in twos and threes and fours. Many I suspected had taken to the floor for the first time in years. A great deal of alcohol had been consumed. Men of all persuasions bumped into one another, roaring with laughter, as if a drunken collision were some kind of joke. Peter Palfrey, a leading light of the Proles, had his arm around Albert Tapper of the Progs; both were having difficulty in remaining upright. Someone handed me a drink. It was red and tasted dreadful. I downed it in one gulp, and looked for more.

Mark, a few bodies away, was talking excitedly with Philip Sayer.

"… a very great victory," he was saying. "Beginning of an era. I never thought you could do it, but you have. Well done, Phil. Very well done."

"Glad you approve," said Sayer, dryly. Unlike everyone else, he appeared to be both sober and less than deliriously happy. "You gave us very little support during the election."

"Who did?"

"The ABC."

"I'm not the ABC," said Mark indignantly. "I'm—"

Something happened: a blinding white flash, followed by a soundless, sightless, irreversible obliteration of everything, like the cruel trick of a giant conjurer. One moment there was laughing and jollity and music and frolicking; the next there was nothing.

Only thick clouds of white dust, and screams: plenty of screams.

9

My leg hurt.

The dust hung sullenly in the air, swirling, like fog. It was everywhere, rimming my eyes, matting my hair, coating my mouth, clogging my nose.

Vague shapes of people blundered about like ghosts, screaming, in a white void. Others crawled, or whimpered, or lay still.

Something was pressing on me, an upside-down statue made of dusty white plaster. I tried to push it off. My leg screamed, or I did – the scream and the pain were co-existent.

I spat out part of a tooth. It landed on the statue's chest in a gobbet of blood: a cherry on a wedding-cake.

From far away came the high skirling whooping of sirens.

10

I listened to the news from my hospital bed.

Many of those newly elected to serve as members of the

Parliament had died in the blast. At some point in the future, once the situation had calmed down, a fresh election would be called. In the meantime the Progressive government had declared a State of National Emergency. A new interim Government of National Unity had been set up, consisting of representatives from all the major parties. Its leader was the Right Honourable Michael Pooley.

Pooley was addressing the nation on the radio.

"The enemies of democracy," said Pooley, "have now struck twice in as many weeks. Our sympathies are with the victims of this horrific act of violence, and with their grieving families.

"Some have commented on the apparent lack of any kind of security at the event where this appalling outrage took place. It has been alleged that emergency exits were locked, thus contributing to the large number of fatalities suffered by the celebrating party-goers.

"These matters will all in due course be thoroughly investigated, and those responsible will be dealt with in the courts. The outgoing Progressive government cannot be held accountable for organisational failings at an event held without reference to the relevant authorities.

"There is a lesson here for all of us. In future we will have to be more vigilant, more alert to the dangers posed by extremist groups who have at the heart of their agenda the destruction of our way of life. From a government perspective, many more resources need to be put into guaranteeing the security of the state. Like it or not, we are all going to have to sacrifice some of the freedoms we have previously – perhaps too easily – taken for granted."

One of the listening nurses began to applaud. My fellow patients looked at one another questioningly, and then joined in.

TWENTY
The Prince of Indecision

The Anglian people are seen at their best in a time of adversity. It is only when they get too comfortable that they start complaining and demanding higher wages and a change of government.

Memoirs III: A Richer Dust
by the Rt Hon Michael Pooley PM (Ludden, 484)

1

In the country things rapidly went back to normal, or what passed for normal. For week or so people went about staring anxiously at parcels left unguarded for more than a minute or two, and staying away from crowded nightclubs and public meetings; then when nothing further happened they began going out again in the evening, and talking about subjects other than national security and subversive groups out to destroy the very foundations of democracy. The Government of National Unity was generally regarded as a necessary thing, and Pooley as a 'safe pair of hands'. The GNU received a further boost in popularity when it raised the wage rates of workers in bands J to P by 2% across the board in recognition of "the extraordinary sacrifices made by the nation's artisans in the national interest".

2

I had been lucky; Mark had shielded me from the worst effects of the blast. Mark himself had suffered a head wound, broken ribs and a leg broken in several places. He remained in hospital; I returned to his flat to think things over and await his return.

I occupied my time doing nothing: lying in bed, mostly, with a dull book, worrying about what I should do next. The two outrages I had witnessed were of course appalling, but they seemed to have nothing to do with me or my father.

While I waited for Mark to be discharged the weather started to turn. By late October it had become bitterly cold; the arrival of November heralded the beginning of an early winter. My seventeenth anniversary was on Thursday November 9th. I celebrated it alone, with a cheap thriller, a box of luxury caramels, and a bottle of red wine from Cantlefordshire. I had imagined myself getting quietly drunk, possibly to the point of passing out. In the event I managed to down one glass, then left the unfinished bottle to gather dust in the kitchen, in preparation for Mark's return.

3

Mark was discharged with his leg still in plaster; he had to use two crutches in order to get around. His friends came round to celebrate his return. By the end of the evening a great deal of wine had been drunk, including the remains of the bottle I had bought for my anniversary. That night a new friend – a trainee sound technician – kept him company; I slept on his couch. I rose at first light to find the street outside transformed by a thick layer of snow.

4

One of my special subjects at Bune was the works of Andrew Wagstaffe, the celebrated first-century dramatist, commonly known as the 'Bard of the Grey Country'. Wagstaffe was Anglia's most famous writer; his childhood home at Fossford, some twenty miles south of Arden, was a prime destination for tourists, and his plays – particularly the tragedies – were set texts for anyone studying Anglian Literature. A further aspect of his fame was his well-documented penchant for young men of the labouring classes. This factor had led a number of scholars to speculate that his name was a pseudonym adopted to conceal his identity as a member of the Anglian aristocracy, the favourite candidate being Arthur Lord Avon.

A new production of Wagstaffe's *Tarquin, Prince of Antibia* was opening at The Angel in New Foxton Street. The radio company had given Mark had two tickets for the first night. The trainee technician had been offered the chance of accompanying him, but he had declined for reasons Mark did not make public. I was going in his stead.

I had never seen a professional production of any of Wagstaffe's plays and was unsure what I would make of it. When you read a text on the page, you can interpret it how you like; a staged version dictates an approach predetermined by the director according to his particular intellectual qualities, or lack of them.

"Modern dress," I said, looking at the programme. "What's the point of that, exactly?"

"Apparently it 'underlines the relevance of Wagstaffe's plays to our modern situation'."

"I already know his plays are relevant to our 'modern situation', as they put it. I don't need to see actors wearing suits and ties to tell me that."

"All right, Thomas, why do *you* think they're using modern dress?"

"Could be a gimmick, to distract attention from the poverty of the staging."

"What makes you think the staging will be poor? You haven't even seen the play!"

Before long the discussion had become a row, attended by insults and recriminations. That was typical of what was now happening between us. We could no longer agree on anything, even in areas where we shared common ground.

5

The actors wore capes and black leather pants bristling with zips and chains, like the patrons of a Torture Club. The stage design dispensed with the usual tacky backdrops and shaky partitions in favour of a collection of black wooden boxes and pyramids and cylinders that could be rearranged in seconds to suggest a park or a hallway or a graveyard or a bedroom. Everything was left to the imagination. This sounds rubbish; actually it was splendid.

Equally splendid was the way the production illuminated the meaning of the text. It's funny how you can know a play back to front (I could recite huge chunks of *Tarquin* from memory) and yet only really understand it when you see it on the stage.

You probably know the plot. It's a kind of a murder mystery, with an incompetent detective who can't see the solution even when it is staring him (and the audience) in the face. Tarquin, the son of Fabbio, King of Antibia, is a student of Philosophy at the University of Hellestand. Learning that Fabbio has died suddenly in suspicious circumstances, he returns to Antibia and to his depressed lover Olivier, determined to find and punish his father's killer. It takes a visit from his father's ghost to convince him that everyone has been lying. It is at that point that he speaks the famous soliloquy in which he denounces himself as useless: dim, gullible, cowardly, and worst of all indecisive.

Familiarity has made the speech meaningless, a kind of cliché, but to hear the well-worn words mumbled by a skinny wild-eyed Tarquin on a stage deserted except for a black column topped by a black sphere, was devastating, like hearing of the death of a friend.

> *Prince of Antibia! The Prince of Indecision, rather,*
> *Who staring at a broth of pitch, declares it potable*
> *For want of resolution. There are villains here,*
> *Yet pusillanimously I stay my hand. Guilty or not*
> *Of my dear Father's death, not one deserves to live.*
> *The tiger in me jibs, must burst its cage*
> *Dispensing universal woe without remorse*
> *Till all Antibia is a mess of blood and bones,*
> *Which cleared away, leaves us an empty stage*
> *Purged of all pestilence, all guilt and pain.*

Tarquin of course never acts decisively: he just blunders from scene to scene, causing incalculable damage, both to those he despises and those he loves, and ends up being killed in a duel by his stepfather – his father's murderer.

I watched on the edge of my seat as Tarquin's lover Olivier spoke his requiem:

> *... farewell my lovely prince.*
> *Honour and truth and love: farewell.*
> *Antibia's rose is plucked. We that remain*
> *Will never look upon his like again.*

The curtain went down to a great crash of applause. I clapped until my hands hurt, but inside I was feeling thoroughly confused.

6

The curtain calls ended, the audience started filing out. Mark climbed to his feet, impatient to leave. Our seats were at the end of a row, so that he could stick his leg – still in plaster – in the aisle. I remained slumped in my seat. A procession of impatient men squeezed past my knees, on their way to the one or another of the many little bars offering post-theatre entertainment.

"Stir yourself, Thomas," said Mark, prodding me with his crutch. "I'm thirsty."

We went to a bar. Hot food was being served, and on a small platform a comedian was delivering a rant about supermarket shopping. Mark bribed an usher to find us a comfortable perch. A server brought us two glasses of red wine.

"You're being very silent," said Sam.

"Am I?"

"Yes. What's the matter?"

I was done with pretending. "I was thinking about my father."

"Not this again! If you want to make up with your father, Thomas, go home and apologise. He'll forgive you: fathers always do."

I made no reply: just stared around the half-empty seating area. One of the blurry faces caught my eye. I blinked, looked again. It was Jarvis. He was sitting on his own, a few tables away, cradling a half measure of beer. He nodded at me, and gave a faint smile.

I stood up. "I've got to go."

"We just got here," said Mark, who had his eye on a young man at the next table.

"You stay."

"Don't be so bloody silly." He looked up at me with an exasperated expression. "Where are you going?"

"Goodbye Mark," I said.

7

I walked out into the chill of the evening. A few white flakes were drifting through the air, as light as ash. The pavements were slippery with a thin layer of fresh snow. Halfway down the narrow street the flame of a lamp post glowed in a misty dazzle of light like the head of a dandelion. Directly beneath it a figure was standing: a man in a felt hat and a long green belted raincoat. The upper part of his face was lost in shadow, but something about his shape and posture was unmistakeable. It was Payne.

"Evening, Riddle," he said.

He walked towards me. He was holding a pistol: a neat little thing that would fit inside a coat pocket. I looked back up the street, towards the bar. Mark was hobbling towards me on both crutches. Jarvis was there too, a short distance away.

"Don't interfere, Mark," I said. "This is none of your business."

"Hands and knees now, Riddle, if you please," said Payne.

Mark hobbled past me. His crutch cracked down on Payne's wrist, sending the gun flying, and the crutch with it. Confusion followed. Payne squared up like a prize-fighter. Mark stabbed about in the snow with his remaining crutch, struggling to regain his balance. Payne threw a punch. Mark dodged the blow, then slid sideways, crutch whirling helplessly. He crashed into Payne. Both went down together.

Jarvis headed for them, treading with exaggerated care. The abandoned crutch lay in his path, concealed in a furrow of snow. Jarvis stepped on it, windmilled for a second or two, and went slithering headlong into the tangle of bodies.

The gun landed at my feet. Without thinking, I picked it up.

By the time I looked back at them Payne and Jarvis had Mark face down with his arms braced behind his back.

"Let him go," I said, waving the gun.

"Hand it back, Riddle," said Payne "You're only adding to your list of misdemeanours. And now you're getting your friend in trouble too."

"Why am I in trouble?" said Sam. "All I've done is disarm a robber."

"You two," I ordered. "Let him go."

Sighing, Payne relinquished his hold on Sam's arm. "Come on, SPC Jarvis," he said. "This gentleman is of no interest."

After a moment Jarvis also let go.

"Right," I said. "Now start walking. If you stop I'll shoot you."

Jarvis was unsteady on his feet; he appeared to have hurt his ankle. He clutched at Payne, nearly bringing them down again.

Mark made no attempt to get up.

"Coming with me?" I asked.

"You must be joking."

"It's your choice. Well, thanks anyway."

"Glad to be of help."

Jarvis and Payne watched from a distance of some twenty yards. Turning my back on them, I headed off, hampered by the slippery snow. I rounded a corner, skidded down an alley, crunched across a small park. Some way behind me someone shouted a curse, and smashed into something with a mighty thump. I hurried on, slithering and crunching through a labyrinth of streets and alleys.

Running in snow, I discovered, can be as exhausting as a half-mile sprint. I came to a halt, and bent double, wheezing, getting my breath back. My lungs were raw. Long threads of snot hung from my nose.

There was an unfamiliar weight in my hand. I was still holding the gun. I flexed the trigger, stupidly, and the thing exploded, catapulting me backwards.

I landed on my back in the snow.

I thrust the gun in my pocket: time to go. I started to lever myself to my feet. My right shoe touched down, and I yelped with pain. I stumbled, grabbed hold of a nearby lamp post, and lowered myself to the pavement.

My shoe, when I finally managed to prise it off, was full of blood.

There were lights up ahead: a main thoroughfare. I limped towards them, groaning. A taxi approached, puffing gouts of steam. I raised my hand, and it pulled over. As I reached it, he started to accelerate away, but I already had my hand on the door handle. I wrenched it open.

"I need help."

"Not my problem. This isn't a fucking ambulance."

"I've got cash." I yanked out my wallet, pulled out a pound note and waved it at him.

He wrinkled his nose. "Where to?"

"Do you know The Fig Leaf club?" It was the only thing I could think of.

"Wait." He rummaged in his glove compartment and took out a plastic bag. There were sandwiches inside. He took them out: for a moment I had the wild idea that he was going to offer me one. Instead he put the sandwiches into his glove compartment and handed the bag to me. It was sticky, and smelled of fish.

"What's this for?"

"Put it over that fucking foot. I don't want you bleeding all over the cab."

8

I got out at The Fig Leaf. The steamer moved laboriously off, leaving wet parallel tracks in its wake. I pressed the buzzer, then put my face close to the grille.

"Yes?"

"Is Mr Tempest in tonight?"

"Who wants to know?"

"I'm a friend of his. I was here a few weeks ago."

"Are you a member?"

"No, but Mr Tempest–"

"Mr Tempest isn't here."

"Are you expecting him in later?"

"Why?"

"It's urgent."

"Not my problem, chum."

I had a sudden inspiration. I rooted around in my pocket. The card was still there.

"What about Mr Higgins?"

"What about him?"

"Is he there?"

"Who wants to know?"

"My name is Thomas Bunting. He offered me a job. As a model."

"There's a surprise."

"He gave me his card. Will you tell him I'm here?"

There was a short silence. Then: "Hold on."

This time the silence went on a long time.

A different voice. "Yes?" – brusquely.

"Mr Higgins?"

"This is he."

I explained who I was. After a long pause he said: "I remember you. Ronnie Tempest's little pal."

"That's me."

"What do you want?"

"You offered me a job."

"Taken your time, haven't you?"

"I was busy."

"All right," he said. "Come on up."

"That might not be a good idea."

"Why is that?"

"I've shot myself in the foot."

He roared with laughter. I heard him speaking to someone else – the words 'shot himself in the foot' were repeated several times, generating each time a further ration of merriment. I rested my weight on my one good foot, and jigged up and down to stop myself shaking.

Higgins appeared in the doorway, massively bulky, in an expensive green coat. One of the two scrofulous whitebeards – Teddy or Freddie, I couldn't say which – was with him. I leaned help-lessly against the icy wall, incapable of walking or even standing upright. A taxi pulled over and Higgins and the whitebeard loaded me inside. Money changed hands. Higgins got in next to me, and patted my knee in a companionable way. The plastic bag rustled over my foot. I felt the weight of the pistol in my pocket, pressing into my side. I was keeled over sideways. I might be going to vomit.

"Know any quacks, Freddy?"

"Charlie owes me one."

It was getting hard to think. I had no idea where they were taking me. Higgins was asking me questions. I couldn't reply. I could no longer see. My foot hurt like mad. Everything came down to that: the pain in my foot. Nothing else mattered.

The taxi pulled up outside a tall terraced house of dark red brick. Somehow, with Higgins's help, I managed to hobble up three flights of steps. No stair carpet, the wallpaper peeling off the wall, cobwebs, unshaded light-bulbs. The last flight was completely unlit. Higgins unlocked a door, and got me inside, and onto a low settee. The room smelt of paint. I closed my eyes.

9

"Don't move."

The voice was peremptory. This was an order. Disobedience was not an option.

I opened my eyes, cautiously, onto an extraordinary mess. Smeary canvases everywhere. Every surface covered with drips and splatters of paint, like multicoloured pigeon droppings. Jam-jars stuffed with flat-ended paintbrushes, their bristles hardened with pigment. Paint-stained rags. The smell of turpentine and lin-seed oil.

I realised suddenly that I was naked.

"Keep 'em shut."

I closed them, though not before I had taken in Higgins, paint-brush in hand, and clad in a long paint-spattered t-shirt, measur-ing me with an upright thumb from the back edge of a huge canvas.

"Where am I?"

"I'd rather you didn't speak. I have one more bit to get right, then you can take a rest."

The toes of my right foot felt strange. I reached down, and met bandages.

"Disobedient fucker, aren't you?" growled Higgins. "OK, that does it for now."

10

Lucky again: the bullet had lodged itself between the first and second metatarsals, chipping one bone, but otherwise leaving the foot more or less intact. I had to wear a bandage while it healed, and walked with a limp for some time afterwards.

At first I feared that Higgins might turn out to be a sexual predator: much like Nevis, only more powerful and more perverse. But what interested him was not sex but painting. He was obsessed with it, determined to complete as many paintings as was possible in the time left to him. To this end he drove himself like a man possessed. Around ten every morning he would appear in the kitchen in grubby unbuttoned pyjamas, and drop groaning into a chair, clutching his head with both hands like a man tormented by spiteful demons. Gagging with disgust, he would gulp down a foul drink of powdered egg, aspirin, and milk, followed by several cups of strong black coffee. After five minutes he was ready to start painting again.

Nudes were his speciality: his studio was littered with canvases depicting naked bodies of every sort and shape: wiry, obese, lanky, dwarfish, handicapped, mutilated, twisted, contorted. His cold merciless brush captured every vein, every fold, every mole and hair and blemish and wrinkle. He worked quickly, stroking and scrubbing and bullying the paint into place with brush and fingers and the occasional rag or sponge or toothbrush. The illusion thus created was magical. From a few yards away the rendition of flesh and the texture of material were detailed with pinpoint accuracy. One step closer and the detail dissolved into a mess of smears and smudges.

The painting went on without a break until four in the

afternoon, at which point he would stop point blank, as if the circuits that governed the activity of painting had been abruptly broken. Brushes loaded with paint would fall to the floor. He would push back his thick greying hair with paint-clotted fingers, and make for the bathroom, emerging some half-hour later clumsily shaved, dishevelled, and smelling powerfully of cologne. A taxi would take us to The Fig Leaf, where the night's drinking would begin. Around two in the morning a taxi would bring us back. I would put him to bed, and then lie down on the couch and fall asleep.

He was not greatly interested in other people. Politics bored him, as did possessions. He had no interest in food or wine. In his view the purpose of alcohol was to get him drunk as quickly and efficiently as possible. He knew a certain amount about literature – like Purkis he was a great fan of Lord Percy – but he was fantastically knowledgeable about painting. He knew everyone there was to know in the world of the Arts. Most of them he wrote off as fakes and charlatans. X was a greasy little prick who would have made an obscenely successful journalist; why he chose to be a painter was a mystery, and it was an even greater mystery why anyone would want to buy one of his appallingly pretentious daubs. "Except that they don't, of course. *Galleries* buy him, because he's brown-nosed his way round every art critic in the land. Tell the public he's what he says he is, and they'll swallow it wholesale. None of them know any better. So what if it's a waste of cash? Shove the shit on the wall and forget it." Y couldn't paint for toffee, "He draws like a spastic four-year-old, and people call his shit 'uncorrupted by technique'." Z was technically accomplished, in a boring, pedantic, really quite despicable way: "His nudes are like illustrations from an anatomical manual, painstakingly accurate and completely lifeless."

"I paint myself, you know," I told him once.

"Really? Tell me more."

I described my own artworks. He listened with his mouth hanging half open, like a trapdoor on a hinge.

"That sounds absolute shit," he said, when I had finished.

"Really?" I wasn't expecting this.

"Please, Tommy, as soon as you've finished this little adventure of yours, promise me you'll go back to Bune and destroy every one of these fucking *abominations*. If you don't, I will."

"I won a prize," I said feebly.

"Yes. The Bune Art Department should be closed down as a public health hazard. I only hope it doesn't catch on with the Art Schools. Otherwise we're all fucked."

It seemed a bit harsh. Apart from anything else, he had never actually laid eyes on any of my work. But Higgins was undeniably a real artist, and his judgements were not open to question. Glumly I realised that I would probably never make a work of art again.

11

As you may have gathered, Higgins had zero interest in money. No doubt if he had lost it all he would have felt its absence, but because he had cash to spare – his paintings sold for hundreds of pounds each – he paid no attention to it. Bundles of notes were everywhere: in drawers, under pieces of furniture, stuffed into books. He had no idea how much was there, and made no attempt at counting it. Occasionally I helped myself to the odd bundle. It never amounted to much – two hundred pounds at the most – so I didn't feel too guilty about it. He never noticed, and I don't believe he would have cared if he had. When we went out, either to a restaurant or to The Fig Leaf, everything went on the slate. I was never expected to pay my share; in fact there was no machinery for me – or any other of his friends – to do so. This suited me fine. When you live with someone like Mark, money rules your life. When you live with someone like Higgins you can forget that such a thing even exists.

The constant drinking was another matter. I was incapable of keeping up with Higgins and his cronies; any attempt to do so made me ill. As a result I was always the most sober member of the party, which rendered me something of a drag on the proceedings. Starting in The Fig Leaf, we would move on to a restaurant – there were three he patronised, all expensive, and all very tolerant of his behaviour – then go on to a string of public houses, constantly gathering new companions, and drinking enough in each place to make any ordinary person pissed to the point of paralysis. As the evening progressed Higgins, encouraged by his friends, would become noisy and capable of anything – walking down Foxton Street in the buff, taking a crap on the steps of the Anglian Gallery, commissioning a quick riddle in the doorways of restaurants, and other similar antics – while I trailed glumly behind, waiting for the evening to end as it always did with him passing out, so I could get him back to the studio in a taxi and go to bed.

12

By now I was finding these jaunts increasingly tiresome. One evening I asked Higgins if he would mind if I stayed at home for once – I pleaded that I was coming down with a cold.

It was virtually impossible to get a white lie past Higgins. "High life proving too much for you, Tommy-boy?"

"I don't have your stamina, I'm afraid."

"That's booze, not stamina. I'd soon start flagging if I had your measly capacity. But you stay in, Tommy, if that's how you want to play it. Anything I can get for you – woolly night-cap, bed-socks, hot-water bottle?"

"No thanks, Dan."

"My taxi's waiting. Have fun."

Left to my own devices, I made myself a hot drink, and settled down with a book. His tastes in fiction were a bit strange – the experimental ravings of drug addicts, obscure works of third-century pornography, fourth-century horror novels – but he had a fantastic collection of art books. Some were about people I'd never heard of, like Walter Pears or Matthew Grade; others dealt with artists I knew existed, but whose works could only be found, if at all, in the collections a very few private individuals. Reproduction of their paintings in any form was forbidden in law, but for anyone with unlimited funds at their disposal it was possible to get hold of copies, if you knew the right dealers to approach.

One such artist was Gary Tealboom – the name was a pseudonym – whose best work had been done in the early years of
the century. Neither I nor anyone I knew had ever seen any of
his works, but they were reputed to be shocking, disturbing,
mind-blowing, and so on. Normally I am distrustful of works of
art described in these terms – they never quite live up to their reputation – but I was interested in seeing a few Tealbooms, so I could
judge for myself.

Higgins owned a slim monograph on Tealboom's work, which
I found upside-down on a high shelf. I opened it at random on a
picture entitled 'The Beast in the Bedroom'. The scene – painted
realistically in great detail – was a lavishly furnished boudoir,
complete with velvet curtains, silk carpet, ornate stained glass
lamps, and a magnificent four-poster bed. One the bed stood an
animal – presumably the 'beast' of the title – the size of a small
steamer, and enormously bulky, with a piebald coat, and a strange
deformed appendage – a kind of bulbous bag adorned with a profusion of knobby extrusions like pencil-ends – hanging below its
belly. Clustered around it were a number of white bearded men
wearing blindfolds, each of them using his hands to explore a different part of the animal – the tail, the snout, the hoof, the dan-
gling appendage. The painting obviously referred to the famous
fable of the blind men who set out to identify a bicycle by the same
means, and failed to agree as to its characteristics. So much was
clear, but what exactly was it trying to say? I had no idea.

The door opened, and Ronnie Tempest entered, supporting
Higgins, who was in his usual end-of-the-evening state of near
collapse. I helped Ronnie ease him down onto the couch, where he
threw back his head and began to snore.

I had not seen Ronnie since leaving his apartment two months
earlier. "Thanks, William," he said, dropping into a sagging armchair covered with a paint-spattered sheet. "He's overdone it a bit
tonight, poor devil. Copious quantities of white powder and clear
spirits, enough to fell a weightlifter. What's that you've got there?"

I showed him the monograph.

"Ah, Tealboom," he said. "He's taking a risk, keeping this on his shelves! Still, I suppose he can afford to pay off the coppers if he ever gets caught. Take this, for example." He tapped 'The Beast in the Bedroom'. "That animal, you will be interested to hear, is a called 'a cow'. They're used for milk production, believe it or not. You won't have seen one; they're confined to huge multi-storey animal husbandry facilities in the wilds of Alban, and other similarly out-of-the-way places. I only know what it is from an illustration in one of the files Roger brings home sometimes. Shouldn't really poke my nose into them, should I?"

"It's just an animal. Why is it such a big secret?"

"Yes, why is it? Your guess is as good as mine. All I can say is, going by this painting it's hideous enough to give anyone of delicate sensibilities a heart-attack. How are you, anyway, dear boy?"

"I'm fine," I said.

"You don't look too fine, if I may say so. Higgins treating you all right is he?"

"Absolutely. Incidentally, Ronnie, Dan thinks my name is Tommy Bunting. Do you mind–"

"No problem whatsoever, old chap. My lips are sealed. You're still on the lam, I take it."

"Yes. With no end in sight, I'm afraid."

Grinning boyishly, he smoothed back his unruly forelock. "What do you intend to do?"

"Find my father, for a start."

"Really? Mine always gave me the opposite problem: I could never get rid of the old bugger fast enough. But presumably your pa is a different proposition." He placed his hand over his eyes, in an actorly pose suggestive of thought. "Did you ever think of contacting Haverhill? He would know where he was."

"That's what you said before. But would he help? He'd just turn me in."

"Perhaps. You never know with people like that. If one appealed to him in the right way..." He pulled strenuously on his nose, as if trying to shape it into a parsnip. "Here's an idea. We could get Higgins to paint him. I could it set it up for you."

"Could you do that?"

"Easily. He loves Higgins's work – he'll jump at the chance. Once you had him as a captive audience, you could, I don't know: go down on your knees and beg. A little gentle persuasion. He'd enjoy that. What do you think?"

I remembered the gun: that was the sort of persuasion I would need. "Good plan. But what about you? I mean, this might get you into trouble."

"Oh, don't worry about me. I can weather any storm. As long as you don't tell anyone it was my idea."

"I wouldn't do that, of course."

"That's settled them. He's a busy man, as you know, so it's probably best if you and Higgins go there, to his residence in Ludden. Wonderful piece of architecture, the opposite side of the square from ours. Finer in every way, I have to say. I keep telling Roger he should get somewhere more suitable, now he's what he is, but he doesn't want to move. He's probably right: the bigger the premises, the lonelier it makes you feel."

He promised to speak to Haverhill the following day. As promised, he would leave my name out of it. In the meantime, he said, I should work on Higgins to get him to agree – he didn't always accept commissions from the great and good.

I said I would.

He put on his hat, turned up his collar and left. I looked at Higgins, fast asleep on the couch; then I went into what passed for my bedroom and lay down, staring at a brown stain in the ceiling, above which a poisoned mouse had bled to death some weeks earlier. Tackling Haverhill in his mansion would be like stepping into the jaws of a trap. But it had to be done.

TWENTY-ONE
The Condition of the Flesh

The primary subject of the nudes is the condition of the flesh: the process of aging, the marks of disability and disease. Conversely his formal portraits focus on the inner qualities of his sitters, and particularly their weaknesses. Pride, ambition, cruelty, deviousness, concupiscence, parsimony: whatever Higgins sees in the individual's face, dress and bearing is set out like the evidence of wrongdoing, without any attempt at amelioration. Take for example the famous 'Portrait of Young Man with Bandaged Foot' (c. 480) in the Anglian Gallery. The naked body of the eponymous youth is relatively flawless, apart from a certain slackness of the flesh around the hips, a narrowness of the chest, and the transparent whiteness of the skin. The face in contrast is suffused with a species of self-regard more unbecoming than any deformity.

The Art of Daniel Higgins by Pearse de Blaby (Ludden, 493)

1

The sitting was scheduled for Gifting Eve, that being the only day on which Haverhill was free. Higgins didn't mind: he had no time for Festivals like Gifting, and hardly even noticed they were taking place.

Haverhill's House was in Macclesfield Square, not far from the house where Purkis lived with his father. I had been there only once, on the occasion of the dinner party I had attended with my father three years ago. It was a bit of a shock to be thrown back mentally to a time when things were on the up, and my only worry was whether my father could manage to remain polite in polite company for the duration of a single evening.

I was interested to see if I could recognise Sir Roger's house. The remnants of a recent fall of snow, grimy now from the partial thaw and the constant procession of cars and carriages, at first confused me, but eventually I spotted it on the far side of the square: an elegant flat-fronted terraced house constructed of white stone, four stories high, with delicate sash windows, a portico with two slim white columns, and a black iron railing fronting the pavement topped with gilded arrowheads.

Haverhill's house, directly in front of us, was bigger and grander, though in a rather overpowering way: a long facade of white stone, topped with an immense pediment, with a balanced array of arches and tall windows defined by slim stone pillars and surrounded by an abundance of weighty detail. In style it looked more like a museum or a town hall than a domestic dwelling.

"Pompous bloody place," said Higgins, climbing out of the cab. Between us we lifted the great easel onto the snow-dusted pavement. I got on with unloading the rest of our stuff – two large canvases and an immense carpet-bag containing his painting equipment and a few items of my own, purchased earlier in the week – while Higgins, bundled up in a huge camel overcoat, his collar turned up against the biting wind, mounted the flight of steps and rang the bell.

The door was answered by a servant, an elderly wrinkled man in a tight red uniform. Another servant – small, balding, bandy-legged – was summoned to help me bring in the equipment. Piece by piece we lugged it into Haverhill's library, where the sitting was to take place.

It was an enormous room, filled with light. The ceiling was high, its cornices heavy and overburdened with detail. A chandelier boasting a dazzle of candle-shaped lightbulbs hung flickering from an elaborate plaster rose, crowded with fruit, leaves, flowers, and cherubs. A cavernous brick-lined fireplace held a selection of lazily burning logs balanced on an ornamental grate; the whole performance framed by an immense white marble mantelpiece. The walls were hung with clusters of gilt-framed paintings of fine looking horses, along with some craggy landscapes, and a couple of aristocratic looking gentlemen showing off their best velvet clothes against a sketchy background of pale foliage. There were shelves displaying sets of books in uniform red and green leather binding, their spines and titles picked out in gold. Silk carpets covered the floor. A Gifting Tree, glowing with gaily coloured baubles, towered over a mountain of gifts, wrapped mostly in gold and silver paper. At the far end of the room a great bow window overlooked a snowbound garden, descending in levels to a tiny frozen lake.

My eye was drawn to an antique globe sitting in a rosewood stand like an oversized egg in a fancy wooden egg-cup. Dr Porter, I remembered, had a modern replica of this article in his office. In fact the entire room was a perfect example of the kind of effect Porter had been aiming at, the difference being that everything here – the chairs, tables, the paintings, the fresh flowers in the vivid ceramic vases – radiated authentic antiquity and infallibly good taste. Noting the fact, I struggled to prevent myself from liking what I saw. Hating Haverhill as I did, I wanted his house to be full of vulgar rubbish, the better to despise the man. But the place was magnificent, and I was unable to deny it. I had felt the same way about Bune when I first got there: I had set my face against it, but ended up being seduced.

We waited for Haverhill to come down. I started getting in a bit of a state, wondering whether the man would remember me. On the face of it, there was no reason why he should. He had hardly so much as glanced at me during the dinner party – for a man of his sort children, like servants, are only visible when they cause a nuisance. What is more, the dinner at Sir Roger's had been three years ago, and I had changed quite a bit since then. My hair was a lot longer, I had grown a small goatee, and instead of my Bune smarts I was wearing the traditional uniform of the art student: loose black shirt and baggy black trousers. Rationally I should have had nothing to worry about, but I went on worrying nonetheless. What would Haverhill do if he did recognise me? Call the police? Wrestle me to the ground? I fondled the small pistol in my pocket. It felt snug and warm and capable. I didn't know how many bullets were left, but just having it my pocket made me feel a different person: tougher, colder, capable of anything.

"Dan! What a treat seeing you here!"

Haverhill, splendid in a red silk dressing-gown, advanced towards Higgins with one hand outstretched. I dipped my head into the carpet bag and started checking the contents. "This is Tom, m' assistant," grunted Higgins. I straightened up, bracing myself to meet a stare of recognition. Haverhill looked blankly in my direction, gave a brief nod, and returned to the job of buttering up Higgins.

Buttering up it was, with a vengeance. Until this moment I hadn't fully appreciated how famous Higgins was, or the extent to which Haverhill would be prepared to suck up to him because of it. Getting Higgins to paint your portrait was obviously a huge coup for Haverhill, putting him in the same category as Lord Trumpington and the film actor Donald Dewhurst. It had its risks, all the same. Higgins's paintings were known for never flattering the sitter, however rich or famous. But people like Haverhill don't let things like that deter them. Supposing the painting made him look a total shit, he would put that out as evidence of his open-mindedness, his dispassionate appreciation of great art. "Puts the knife in, doesn't he, the old bugger," he would say, posing proudly under the finished portrait. "That's how you know the thing's a genuine Higgins."

Higgins was anxious to get started. "I'm going to sit you against the big window," he said. "Make the best use of the light while we have it. Good wintery background, I can do something with that."

"Any particular chair? Unless you want me squatting cross-legged on the carpet?"

Higgins made a faint grunt. "Sit on that," he said, pointing. "Next to the whajoumaycallit. The little fancy armchair."

"The Cameron Giddings? – splendid choice. Been in the family for centuries. Anything special you want me to wear?"

"I'd rather you chose for yourself."

"You don't want me in the buff, then?"

Higgins gave a token snort. "Not this time, no."

"I was thinking of donning my Woodland Patrol uniform – I'm Grey Wolf, as perhaps you know –but it's rather plain, and exposes the knees. Other than that I have a ceremonial smoking jacket I'm rather fond of."

"That sounds about right – the smoking thingy."

I busied myself erecting the easel while Haverhill went off to change. He came back after about ten minutes in a jacket of red velvet with gold piping, and a pair of tight black trousers. "Fancy a tipple to help you along?" he asked, settling uneasily in the small armchair, which like a lot of antique furniture was not really designed for comfort.

"Not while I'm painting."

"Would you mind if I did?"

"As long as you don't keep sipping at the fucking thing."

"In which case, perhaps I won't."

"Up to you," said Higgins, squeezing some burnt umber onto one of his well-used palettes. He selected a paintbrush.

"Any particular position you'd like me in?"

"Whatever's most comfortable."

Haverhill crossed and uncrossed his legs a number of times, and finally lounged back with legs extended, resting his elbow on the arm of the chair, and touching his cheek with the tips of his slender fingers.

"Is this all right?"

"Absolutely fine." Higgins loaded his brush.

"I'm a huge fan of your work, you know."

Higgins looked up, with a fiercely cocked eyebrow. His brush was poised in mid-air. "So Ronnie said."

"I particularly like the early stuff. The little portrait–"

"Would you mind awfully if you didn't speak? Interrupts the flow."

"Fair enough. Might doze off, is the only problem."

"Be my guest."

Haverhill sniffed; the brush descended.

Higgins worked at speed, and with great accuracy. One twiddle of the brush, and Haverhill's left eye stared out coldly from the canvas, like the eye of a fish. Another twiddle captured the haughty tilt of his chin. A projecting ear sprang into place, together with a flared nostril and angled eyebrow. The red velvet smoking jacket accumulated colour and texture.

In the snowbound garden the light began to fail. Higgins laid down his brush. "That'll have to do for now."

"Just as well," said Haverhill, stretching. "The cheeks of my arse are as numb as a frozen turnip."

Far away a doorbell chimed. I started dismantling the easel, while Higgins cleaned his brushes.

"Compliments of the season, Nigel. We come bearing gifts."

The voice was one I recognised. Three figures stood in the doorway, loaded with silvery parcels. Sir Roger was one, Paul Purkis another, and the third was Worsley. Paul's arm, I noticed, was resting across Worsley's shoulders. I turned away, but Paul had already spotted me.

"William!" he said. "I thought you were dead."

"Well, I'm not."

"So I see. Interesting haircut. What are you doing here?"

"You know these people, Tom?" asked Higgins, giving me a bewildered stare.

"He knows us; we know him," said Haverhill, vigorously massaging his buttocks. "William's an old pal of ours."

"His name is William?"

"I fear he hasn't been quite straight with you about that – about a number of things, if truth be told. –Don't look so dumbstruck, William: I recognised you the moment you pitched up."

"You didn't say."

"I thought it best to hold my fire. Not everyone likes to be reminded of his origins. Particularly if he has something to hide."

"I don't have anything to hide," I said, producing the gun. "You're the one who's hiding things."

"What a terrifying piece of equipment," said Haverhill. "Do you intend to use it?"

"If I have to."

"You probably won't manage it, when push comes to shove. You need to be tutored in violence in order to apply it with any conviction. Enlighten me, though: what is it you think I'm hiding?"

"The truth about my father."

"Too broad. Specifically?"

"Where is he now?"

"I've no idea."

"Don't lie. Your gang arrested him."

"By 'your gang' I assume you mean the Security Service."

"Same thing."

"Well it isn't, as a matter of fact, but that's by the by. The SS hasn't arrested him. He hasn't been arrested, period."

"You're a liar."

"And you're being unpleasant. Who told you he'd been arrested?"

"Porter."

"Dr Porter isn't much of an authority, I fear. A capable enough administrator, perhaps, but perfectly useless in this kind of affair. Let me say it once more. *Your father is not in state custody.*"

I shook my head. "How can you say that?"

"Let me ask you a question. What do you think he's done?"

"I don't know. Treason, according to Porter."

"Once again Porter's got it wrong. The charges against your father are rather more serious – not to say shameful -- than that."

I was gripped with a feeling of dread. "What are they then?"

"Well, let's start with abduction of a minor."

For a few seconds I was struck dumb. "What?" I managed finally.

"He's abducted a child of twelve."

"Rubbish!"

"There's more. The child's parent is a member of the NAC."

I shook my head. The onion had shed a layer, but the layer underneath was meaningless, nonsensical. Forget the onion: it was more like opening a pie, and exposing a nest of open-beaked birds. "You're making it up."

"Why would I do that?"

"I can't imagine."

"Think about it, young man. Blood and feathers in the hen-house, and the fox off on his travels. What does that tell you?" Haverhill turned to Higgins. "You're a man of the world, Higgins. What do you think?"

Higgins had slumped down on the sofa, a picture of gloom. "People do all kinds of things," he said. "My own father was a shit of the first order. Capable of anything, particularly if sex was involved. Or cash."

Higgins's father was of no interest to me. I turned back to Haverhill. "You had me in custody for three weeks. Why am I only hearing about this now?"

"The NAC wanted it kept under wraps. They're understand-ably protective of their private lives, if only from the point of view of security. If it started getting about that one of their own can be abducted, other maniacs might be encouraged to repeat your father's crime."

The gun felt slippery in my hand, temperamental, as if it might go off at any second. "My father isn't a maniac. He's not a criminal either."

"It's not how he comes across, it's true. It's an enormous pity. He's a brilliant man, possibly the most gifted scientist Anglia has. Stubborn and opinionated, yes, but he's made a huge contribu-tion to society over the years. If he'd done anything else; if he had abducted a child of the lower orders, say – anyone, really, rather than one of the NAC – we might have been able to ah, handle the matter more discreetly. Reorientation, chemical impulse-manage-ment, and so forth. But *this* ... You can see the problem."

Inside my head the words had begun to rattle, like nuts bounc-ing round the walls of a tin. Nothing made sense.

"This is deep shit, Riddle," said Purkis.

"It's somewhat unfortunate, Paul, you're right," said Haverhill. "But you needn't worry too much on William's account. He's done nothing so very bad – so far. Running away from a state facility, waving a gun about ... all of it very small beer. At first we feared he might be implicated in his father's misdemeanours. But if he's not – and so far there's no evidence to the contrary – then nothing very much will happen to him. A course of counselling, perhaps; some monitored treatment using guilt-by-association therapy. After that, who knows? He might even be allowed to return to Bune."

The prospect of returning to Bune was what Sir Roger had dangled under my nose some weeks earlier at Orwell House. Then it had seemed tempting; but in the intervening weeks Bune had rather lost its attraction.

"Oh fuck off," I said.

Haverhill smiled. "This bravado of yours is all very well," he said. "But what I must impress on you is the urgency of the situation. The child has been missing for several weeks. In matters like this the first twenty-four hours are crucial. We've already gone way past that point. By now we may well have a homicide on our hands."

The thought that my father might be a murderer was so intrinsically ridiculous that it wasn't worth considering. The fact that Haverhill could suggest such a thing only made me hate him even more. "I can't take this seriously," I said angrily.

"Well, you may have to, if we don't find them in time. Didn't your father say anything – anything at all – that might give us a clue as to his whereabouts? Some place he thought of as safe, that only you and he knew about?"

Something clicked in my head. "No," I said stoutly.

"That's hard to believe. If you're lying – and I think you are, you will have to take the responsibility for the consequences."

"Fine. –Worsley: come here."

Worsley perked up – he had been looking rather left out. "Yes, Riddle, what can I do for you?

I pointed to my holdall. "Open that bag, will you?"

"This one?"

"Yep. See a plastic bag in there?"

He rummaged about. "'Chains of Love'. Is this the one you mean?"

"Yep. Open it up."

Worsley took out the contents, one by one. It was the kind of equipment you can buy in the bondage shops of Ludden: an assortment of black leather restraints decorated with sharp silver studs, various chains and padlocks, some zippered rubber face masks, and several red and white ball gags with black leather straps.

"Fascinating!" said Purkis. "I didn't know you went in for this kind of thing, Riddle."

"You – Haverhill," I said. "Sit."

"Must I? I've been sitting all afternoon."

"Do it."

He sat.

"Hands behind your back."

Sighing, he did as he was told. Worsley, without having to be asked, buckled his wrists together with some leather straps, did the same for his ankles, then fastened him to the armchair with a generous application of jolly-tape. He was surprisingly good at this; anyone would think he'd done it before. But then he was a keen member of the Woodland Patrol, where you learned how all sorts of practical things – how to make fires, build shelters, set traps, skin animals, and so on – so perhaps it wasn't all that surprising after all.

"I must say, William, you seem to have thought of everything," said Haverhill, as Worsley wound a final length of jolly-tape around his wrists. "You've been one step ahead of us all the way. I'm really impressed."

"Thanks."

"Well, praise where praise is due. I mean: first you escape, then you find shelter, and pick up some new togs and a spot of cash, and even get hold of a pistol. That can't be all luck, can it? And now this! Bondage gear – who would have thought of that?"

"How's that, Riddle?" asked Worsley.

I tested the bonds.

"It'll do."

"What really impresses me," said Haverhill, "is the way you seem able to inspire loyalty in virtual strangers. Your friend Mark, for example. He took a big risk, helping you to get away from Detective Chief Inspector Payne."

"All he did was disarm someone he thought was a robber. Nothing criminal in that."

"That was his argument too. The justice system, unfortunately for him, takes a different view. He's been sent to your old stamping ground, Cromwell House, you may be interested to hear. Indefinite term of residence. But that's the price of loyalty to the undeserving, I fear. It doesn't come cheap."

"You've got it all worked out, haven't you?" I said. "You and Pooley and all the rest of you. Anyone you want to shut up, you have them arrested, like Arnold Massey. If you don't like an election result you let off a bomb, and then declare a state of National Emergency."

This came out in a fierce rush, like an unblocked drainpipe. I had been mulling over my suspicions for weeks, alternately discounting them, and then reconsidering them again. They were implausible, I knew, and yet they would not go away. Besides, in Massey's case I had the evidence of my eyes to go with. What I had witnessed directly contradicted the official account. No difference of interpretation was involved: the authorities were lying, about that if nothing else.

Haverhill's expression was mirthful, derisive. "I've no idea what you're talking about. Massey – is that the agitator fellow? Died in the explosion at Arden. Nothing to do with us, I'm afraid. As for the bomb in 'Wigs'!" He shook his head. "Have you any idea how difficult it would be to carry off that sort of thing? How many people would have to be involved? How could we ever get away with something so outrageous?"

"You can't," I said, with more conviction than I felt. "Because I know the truth."

"The truth?" Haverhill smiled. "What *is* the truth, William?"

"The truth is what really happened."

"And who's to say what 'really happened'? Certainly not you. No, William: the truth is whatever people believe it is. The truth is what people read in their newspaper."

"Newspapers print a pack of lies."

"Nonsense! Ask your friend Mark: he'll tell you. You'll be seeing him soon, no doubt – back at Cromwell House."

Something made me glance at Higgins. He was staring at Haverhill with an expression of intense loathing, as if he would happily have strangled him. Catching my glance, he widened his eyes fractionally, then let his face go blank. All of this happened in a flash – blink and you'd miss it – but it made a definite impression. It meant something, I was sure: something important, but I had no idea what.

"Ball gag, now," I said. "And then the leather mask."

"Of course. This is rather fun."

"Must you–?" began Haverhill, but before he could finish his sentence Worsley had popped a red ball into his open mouth and tightened the straps behind. The face mask went on last: he wriggled it down over Haverhill's head like a rubber sock. He stood back to admire the effect.

"Who's next?" he asked brightly.

I pointed at Sir Roger. He rolled his eyes, glanced at his son, and nodded with world-weary resignation. "Go ahead," he said.

Paul watched Worsley trussing up his father with a worried expression. "Should you really be doing this, Riddle?" he asked me quietly.

"What choice do I have?"

"I don't know. Give yourself up?"

"What would be the point?"

"What's the point anyway? You're not going to get away, are you?"

"Why not? Anglia's a pretty big place."

"Show some sense, old chap. They only–" He broke off, shaking his head.

"What?"

"Never mind."

"Do you want me to do this man now, Riddle?" asked Worsley, indicating Higgins, who was lounging back on the sofa with an expression of boredom. I wasn't sure what to reply. It was bad enough having to truss up Sir Roger, who in spite of everything had always been pretty decent to me. Now that it was Higgins's turn I felt even worse. The man had rescued me, and given me the run of his studio, and left cash around for me to help myself to; what is more, he was an extremely good artist.

"Oh, for fuck's sake, man, get on with it!" said Higgins. "Why should I miss out on all the fun?"

"Now what?" asked Worsley brightly, once his work was complete.

"Now I leave."

"By yourself?"

"Worsley, I'm not taking you with me."

"We're both coming," said Paul. "We're all Bunians, remember? We stand by one another."

What he was saying was absolute shit, and we both knew it. But I was too tired to argue with him. What did it matter anyway – what did anything matter? There was no point in threatening him and Worsley with the gun: they both knew that I would never be able to use it on them. Purkis was right: I was never going to get away. The SS were bound to catch up with me sooner or later. All I could do was delay the thing for as long as possible.

"I've just thought of something," said Worsley, as we crossed the hallway.

"Enlighten me."

"We haven't finished dropping off the gifts."

"So what?"

"So the Sceptre is still waiting outside."

Hope flared briefly, like a match striking in the dark. "I can't drive. Can you?"

"We don't need to. There's a driver. You can make him take us anywhere. You can threaten him with your gun."

"This is *our* bloody steamer you're talking about, Worsley, thanks very much," said Purkis irritably. "And the driver in question–"

He broke off. Haverhill's servant was striding towards us from the end of the hallway, his crumpled face a picture of outrage. Worsley dragged open the front door, letting in a gust of snowflakes and frozen air. He and Purkis brawled their way into a whirling white blizzard. I followed close behind. Running was out of the question: the pavements were slippery with fresh snow. The servant, a silhouetted stick-man with one raised fist, shouted at us from the bright rectangle of the doorway. A long black steamer – a Prebble Sceptre 200 – sat throbbing at the kerbside in a great cloud of steam. Worsley was already trudging doggedly towards it. Pistol in hand, I followed him.

"This isn't such a good idea," panted Purkis, catching up.

Ahead of us, Worsley was climbing into the front passenger seat.

"Come on, Purkis," I said. "What's the worst that can happen?"

"Well, sudden death for a start."

"Always the pessimist," I said. We were alongside the car. Purkis opened the rear door, and gestured for me to climb inside. I did so. He got in beside me, and slammed the door.

The driver turned round. "How's tricks, Jimmy?" he asked, grinning.

My heart sank. "Hello Nevis," I said. "Good to see you, old man."

TWENTY-TWO
Gifting

The Festival of Renunciation was originally a time of fasting and contemplation, during which the citizen was expected to donate a portion of his wealth to charity. These days the occasion is used as a celebration of community, and a giving of thanks to everyone with whom one enjoys a relationship, both in the public and the private sphere.

December 25th, Gifting Day, marks the culmination of Renunciation. Family and friends hold variously extravagant dinners, according to their purse and the number and status of their close friends.

The day begins with an exchange of gifts. The etiquette regarding gift-giving is necessarily strict: retailers are required to grade gifts according to a range of values from 'a' to 'o', 'a' being the most desirable, 'o' the least expensive. It is bad form to give anyone a gift from a category lower or higher than their status demands. For example, if you yourself have a status of 'g' and your employer is status 'e', you are expected to give him a gift from the category below your own, i.e., 'h'. He in turn will give you a gift from the category above yours, i.e., 'f'. The system has been evolved over many years, and is of great practical use. In the case of employee/ employer exchanges it eliminates any question of partiality or its lack, and protects all parties from any suspicion of bribery. It also ensures that Gifting cannot be interpreted as an expression of discontent, dissatisfaction or dislike, unless the Giver deliberately intends it to be.

To avoid duplication, employers with a large number of employees will lodge lists of acceptable gifts with large multiple retailers. As an item is bought it gets removed from the list. To avoid receiving a large number of worthless objects, many employers use the list to accumulate a gift with multiple aspects, for example a fine set of china – even the lowliest of employees can afford a saucer. For the sake of convenience, leading employers give identical gifts to all workers in a particular group. Thus all 'g' status employees might receive an alarm clock, and all 'f' employees a sylkon scarf.

Between lovers the etiquette is a little more relaxed: a lover is expected to buy his loved one the most expensive present he can afford. Failure to do this is often taken as a signal that the affair is on its last legs.

The commercial sector relies upon Gifting Day to produce the year's profits.

The Meaning of Gifting by H Lofthouse, (Ludden, 468)

1

My first impulse was to use up a valuable bullet, and be rid of the bastard for good. What I actually did – as dictated by the Bunian code – was smile, and greet Nevis like a long-lost friend.

For Nevis to be discovered working in such a menial position, even for a boss as grand as Sir Roger Purkis, was a surprising comedown for someone of his class and education, and I allowed myself a bit of spiteful glee on that account. From the way he talked, however, anyone would have thought the occupation of a chauffeur was something to be proud of.

After a few brief enquiries about my situation, and a few token commiserations about the perceived misdemeanours of my father, he filled me in on his career since leaving Bune. He had started off reading for a degree in Business Ethics at Cantleford, but it hadn't worked out. "Got in with the wrong set, never studied at all, other than swigging the hop and rolling the dice – cards, marbles, ant-racing, you name it. Naturally I crashed my half-year exams, but the worst of it was I ended up owing a sewage-cart of big ones to the kind of asswipe who won't take 'No' for an answer. Come Pagan I scarpered – fresh start well overdue. Tried to enlist with the Prags as the shoe-in candidate for Shithole-in-the-Marsh, somewhere North of Beeston. No dice. Try the Progs, they said – they're not so fussy by half. Or come back in a generation or three, when the name of Nevis has a tad more form. Bugger that for a lark, I said: I shall enter the city. They're not interested in who your grand-pa was, only whether you can stack up the moolah in record time. Ran into the revered Dr Porter at his club in Ludden, threw myself on his mercy – touching scene – and he kindly fixed me up with a berth in the city working as a broker for a tidy little outfit called Corporal Finance – CF to the uninitiated. Now the great thing about CF is that they have a *very* select clientele. And huge capital reserves: most of it, at my point of entry, invested in the sort of mind-bogglingly boring stock that never loses value, and never gains very much either – basic commodities, iron, coal, rapeseed-oil: that kind of crap. Absurdly out of date in other words, and quite unaware of the fact – had to be dragged kicking and screaming into the fifth century. 'Buy bad debt,' I told them. 'As much of it as you can get hold of. Forget the risk – the returns are fabulous!' 'Show us how,' they begged. So I did. Made a shitload of bullion for the buggers in a matter of weeks. 'Ta very much, Nevis,' they said, 'you're bloody brilliant! Never seen anything like it!' Flavour of the month for a good six weeks. Then one day, as fuck would have it, I backed the wrong pigeon, not to mention the wrong pigeon's brother, uncle and first and second cousins. Overnight the big smiles dry up like piss in the desert sand, leaving yours truly standing directly in the firing line. Arseholes in grey suits with fat notebooks nosing through the filing cabinets like rats at a dustbin. Questions to be answered. Answers not satisfactory. Five thousand squid is the number I was down for. CF somehow kept it dark, in case it 'threatened confidence in the company's financial competence,' as they put it; but there was no way the cock-chafers would keep me on. Two months on and I'm wearing out the bones of my arse in a cut-price hovel-shark at the Balls Lake Junction. As luck would have it the Good Sir Roger rode to the rescue. 'Can't have this happening to a Bunian,' he said. 'Work as my driver to begin with, and I'll find you something more salubrious when times improve.' Naturally I jumped at the chance. Fantastic steameroos, the pick of the bunch – this Sceptre is just the luggage-coolie – and I get to drive them for free. And because it's a government post you get ten days off a year, and a handsome pension at fifty-five, if you last that long.

Couldn't think of a better job, other than breaking in the rent-boys at a nobs' knocking-shop. Drive yourself, do you Riddle? No? You should learn."

And so on.

2

For the first hour or so we made reasonable progress. The snow had not been falling long, and we reached the Great North Road about seven in the evening. After that it was impossible to travel at any speed. The road was knee deep in snow, and all you could see out of the windows was black night and a swirl of fat grey flakes and the puffs of white steam rising from the Sceptre's vast boiler.

The Sceptre is in no way 'sporty', but it is supremely comfortable, and even in these terrible conditions it inspired a powerful sense of security and wellbeing. The great tyres rolled silently over the deep snow, the feed-pumps thumped with a regular hypnotic rhythm, like the blood coursing through your veins, the wind whistled plaintively around the vehicle's massive radiator and mudguards, thousands of miles away, and I began, despite myself, to understand something of Nevis's pride in his occupation, the simple pleasure he derived from being the master of a machine so powerful and so obedient to his every command.

Nevis fell silent. A man like that needs an admiring audience, and the only one of us making the right noises was Worsley, who didn't count. A sullenness settled over him. Pleasantries gave way to put-downs. Outside of Bune, it seems, the code only holds good for the first hour or so, after which it reverts to enmity. Nevis barked the occasional order to Worsley – pass the water, wind down the window, find some music on the wireless. Our former tick, true to form, was only too happy to oblige. The boy was a phenomenon. His appetite for humiliation was insatiable. You had to wonder, sometimes, if he was altogether human.

Purkis, next to me, said nothing. His face was set in a grimace: presumably because I had made Worsley truss up his father.

"What's this thing with Worsley?" I asked.

"What thing do you mean?"

"You seem very good pals all of a sudden. Is he staying with you?"

"It was Sir Roger's idea," piped up Worsley, turning around. "He knew I had nowhere to go for Renunciation, so he invited me down for a few weeks."

"He helps out with the cooking and cleaning," said Purkis.

"How very convenient."

Purkis leaned close. "I know what you're thinking," he muttered.

"I'm not thinking anything. None of my business."

"He's a useful chap to have around. That's all there is to it."

"I believe you."

For a while everyone was silent. The atmosphere in the car was getting increasingly oppressive. Hot air pulsed constantly from the rattling heater. Everyone was cross and sleepy. Worsley started to whistle, tunelessly – a jaunty seasonal tune, to do with the joys of Gifting – and was promptly ordered to shut up, which he did. The car crept on through the deepening snow.

I drowsed off for a few minutes, waking to find Nevis pulling into a layby.

"I need a wazz," he said, opening his door.

"Stay where I can see you," I said.

"Feast your eyes, sweetie," he said, climbing out, and unbuttoning.

"I need to go too," said Worsley.

So did Purkis. In the end the three of them they stood side by side, pissing into a snowdrift, while I stood guard over them. Nevis pissed with the force and volume of a fireman putting out a blaze. By this time I needed to go myself, quite badly. I chose another snowdrift, unbuttoned myself with difficulty – I still had hold of the pistol – and added my stream to the consensus.

Next thing I knew, Nevis was standing next to me. "Hello, old pal!" he sniggered, looking down. He placed his arm around my shoulder, and leaned on me, heavily.

My blood boiled. I was shaking with rage, and the pistol in my hand made it impossible to control what I was doing. Piss sprayed everywhere, soaking one leg of my trousers. Nevis pointed, guffawing. I felt both furious and humiliated, with the fury feeding the humiliation and vice versa. It was ages since Nevis had left Bune, yet here he was, lording it over me again, as in the days when I was his tick and he my master. The gun, which should have made a difference, actually made things worse, because it demonstrated that Nevis's ascendancy over me was an elemental condition of my existence. Even with a weapon in my hand I couldn't get the better of him.

He climbed back into the driver's seat. When I got in behind him, he turned round, sniffing loudly and wrinkling his nose.

"All right, Nevis," I said. "I pissed myself. Let it go now."

"I need something to take my mind off that stink. Have we any grub?"

"We've got Sir Roger's seasonal gifts," said Worsley. "They're in the boot – tons of them."

"Hang on, chaps," said Purkis. "Those gifts belong to my pa. You can't just help yourself, just because you're feeling a bit peckish."

"Your pa isn't here," said Nevis. "Get the gifts, tick."

Worsley looked at Purkis enquiringly. "Purkis?" he asked.

"What do you think, Riddle?" asked Purkis. "You're the man with the gun."

I wasn't up to taking a stand against Nevis just then. "Nothing to do with me," I muttered.

Worsley scrambled out and went to the boot. He returned with a slippery stack of red and gold packages wedged between arms and chin. "There's lots more, if these are no good," he said, unloading them into the seat.

Nevis picked one up: it was obvious from the shape that it was a bottle of something. "Glen McLockie malt," he said, ripping off the paper. "This is better than grub."

Worsley unwrapped another parcel, carefully picking off the tape. "It's some kind black stuff," he said, folding the wrapping paper into a neat square. "In a jar." He popped open the lid. "Smells of fish."

"Fucking thieves – the lot of you," said Purkis. He sounded on the verge of tears.

"Here, Riddle – take a swig," said Nevis, passing me the bottle. I took it from him, and drank. Fire coursed down my throat, and settled glowing in my belly. I took another swig.

"You're a rotten shit, Riddle," said Purkis, pushing open his door. He climbed out, and stood shivering in the snow, a picture of misery. I felt a momentary pang of guilt. But I couldn't see what all the fuss was about. Yes, they were his father's gifts, but so what? Sir Roger could afford to replace them. I took another swig of the malt.

"Brandy-laced chocolates," said Worsley. "Some very smelly cheese. And raw ham. And biscuits."

"Get a few more parcels," said Nevis.

Worsley hurried to do his bidding. While he was outside, rooting around in the boot, Purkis climbed into the empty front seat.

"Come to join the grown-ups, sweetie?" said Nevis.

"Wait till my pa hears about this, Nevis."

"You can't blame me," said Nevis carelessly. "I'm not the fucker with the gun."

I took a long swig of malt. Nevis was right: everything would be blamed on me. But I had other things to think about: a great wet burden of worries, spilling out in all directions, leaving no room for anything else. But I didn't want to think about them. I didn't want to think about where we were heading, or what I would do when we got there. I didn't want to think about my father, or what he was charged with. I didn't want to think about anything.

Just thinking about thinking about these things was a huge weight on my heart.

So I didn't.

3

I woke, shivering. A pale light filtered through the grey layer of snow-crumbs coating the windscreen. The world outside was entirely white: white sky, white road, white fields, white trees.

The car stank of fish-paste and stale piss and whisky. A collection of bottles lay spilled on the carpet, uncorked, and half-empty. Ripped fragments of red and gold wrapping paper were strewn everywhere. The floor and seats were littered with pots and jars and boxes and cartons, all opened and sampled and chucked aside.

Worsley lay slumped against me, burbling quietly in his sleep. Purkis was doubled up in the front passenger seat. Nevis, at the wheel, lay back, mouth open and snoring.

Purkis straightened up and turned round. "This is all your fault, Riddle," he said, eyeing me accusingly

"Sorry."

"You could have stopped it."

"I had to tie him up. He would have raised the alarm."

"Stopped them opening the bloody *gifts* is what I mean. Have you any idea how long my pa and I spent getting that stuff ready?"

"Forget it, Purkis."

Nevis made a honking noise, half-way between a choke and a snore, and came awake with a start. "Fuck," he said. "Fucking headache." He stared around him at the ripped paper and the discarded gifts, letting go of a short fart as he settled his buttocks. "Fucking whisky." He looked out the window, through a hole in the snow-crust. "Fucking snow."

I tapped his shoulder with the pistol. "Do you think we could get a move on?"

"You're the boss," he said satirically, pressing the ignition button. The motor turned over complainingly once or twice without getting anywhere, then the feed-pumps got going, the steam got up pressure, and we chugged off into the universal whiteness.

"Hey, chaps!" said Worsley, sitting up and rubbing his eyes. "It's Gifting Day! Happy Gifting, one and all!"

No one returned his greeting. We crawled on northwards, towards the borderlands of Alba.

4

The sleep had done me good. Mercifully a lot of stuff had sorted itself in my head. I had been too fatalistic: too ready to listen to the voices – Payne, Haverhill, Purkis – telling me I didn't stand a chance. I *did* have a chance, slim though it was. I even had a destination. I had made Nevis drive north without really knowing why.

But some sort of reasoning must have been at work. The North was the direction of Alba, the scene of my earliest memories. It was where I had spent that first enchanted holiday with my father. It was a region I knew better than any other – better, I reckoned, than my pursuers. Once I got to the coast I would buy or rent or steal a small boat, and take off for the uninhabited islands of the Sperides – there were thousands of them, scattered along the ragged Western coast like the discarded pieces of a complicated jigsaw puzzle – leaving Purkis & Co to find their own way back to Ludden. No doubt Haverhill and his gang of cronies would go on looking for me, but I doubted they would put much effort into the search. It was my father they wanted; I was of no importance to anyone.

"So where exactly are we heading for, chief?" asked Nevis.

"North."

"Any particular reason?"

"No."

But there was a reason. Initially the North had been an instinctive choice – somewhere as far from Ludden as possible. But there was more to it than that. Something was calling me, memories of my rough childhood in Glenlockie, memories of my father, memories of a trip we had taken together when I was a boy. I remembered glaring rape fields extending to the horizon, and a one-eyed giant, and a hired motor-boat. There was a small uninhabited island – my father had reminded me of it the last time I saw him – where we had stayed two nights in a deserted cottage high up on the cliffs, overlooking a pebbly crescent beach. Wyrd.

All the pieces flew together of their own accord. My father was on Wyrd. He had mentioned the place deliberately, so I would know where to find him.

A wave of joy crashed through my body, rushing outwards to the tips of my fingers and my toes. My father hadn't deserted me. He had left me a clue; he had wanted me to know his hiding place.

The gritting carts had been out early, and for an hour or two we were able to make good progress. We stopped at a fuel station to fill up. An elderly man wearing a maroon beret worked the pump.

Nevis unpeeled a wad of vouchers, and I handed over two five-pound notes. Nevis said he needed another piss, then Purkis and Worsley said they did too. We all trooped off to the flusher, a line of cracked porcelain stalls, open to the elements and stinking to high heaven. Nevis, the beast, arranged it so that he stood next to me a second time. I fumbled with the gun – I was trying to point it at the three of them – and managed somehow to whack myself in the groin. Nevis pointed with two loaded fingers. "Hands up, chaps, or the cock gets it!" he barked, setting off an outbreak of giggles.

Naturally the piss went everywhere again.

"You're stinking out the car," he said, when we got back in.

5

As we travelled further north it got colder. An endless tailback held us up for a couple of hours: a juggernaut had collided with two steamers, completely blocking the road. It began to snow again: thin mean flakes at first, then big grey chunks like fat moist insects, swirling through the afternoon sky and exploding against the windscreen. Cloudlets of steam drifted backwards from the boiler. The feed-pipes throbbed, the wipers thumped from side to side. The heater hummed, pumping a constant blast of hot air directly in my face. Worsley prattled away about some trip he'd gone on with the Woodland Patrol: what fun they'd all had, singing songs and toasting bangers and riding the rafts over the white-water rapids.

My trouser legs were stiff with drying piss. Nevis kept sniffing loudly, and pretending to vomit into his hand.

"Black steamer," said Purkis suddenly.

"What?"

"Behind us. I've been watching it in the mirror. It keeps falling back and then catching up again."

"Someone's tailing us?"

"Obviously."

"When did you first notice it?"

"While ago."

"Fuck," I said.

"Want me to lose it, boss-man?" asked Nevis.

I debated how to reply to this. "If you can," I said, finally.

"Oh, I can all right. Watch this."

Nevis swung out into the far lane. Steamers heading towards us blared and swerved away, bumping over the verge to avoid a collision. He overtook two wagons, then four or five steamers, then threw the Sceptre into a violent left. We skidded on a patch of ice, but he steered out of it. We bounced for some yards along a pot-holed country road, took another left, then swerved through an open gate into a frozen field. Churning mud, we skidded past a startled sheep, then left the field as suddenly as we had entered. The road here was only just wide enough to take one car at a time. A dirt-track led into a small wood: he swung into it, and came steaming to a halt.

Worsley was sent to the boot again. He returned with a cake and two bottles of liqueur. This time Purkis didn't object. The drink was sickly sweet, and tasted of plums. We finished one bottle then started another.

"I'm fucking sick of this," said Nevis, starting the Sceptre. He took a left and then a right, keeping his left hand on the thin stem of a bottle, and swigging from it every few minutes. Within a few minutes we were turning onto the main road we had left half an hour earlier.

"Any sign of that car?" I asked Purkis.

"No."

"You think we've lost them?"

"How would I know?"

6

Evening came on. The road, as we approached the Alban border, became narrower, with numerous rough patches and potholes. We started climbing. The road twisted from side to side like a snake. Pale ghosts of mountains hung beyond the horizon. Frozen forests loomed up on either side. We crossed a narrow bridge, suspended on metal girders high above a silver river.

Worsley suggested we sing some songs. He launched into a medley of Woodland Patrol favourites – 'The Green Woods', 'I am a Hunter', 'Men of the Mountain Trail', and so on. After a few minutes of this a minute or two Nevis drowned him out with a rousing rendition of 'The Gambler'. This is a song about a man who takes a seat at a gaming table and is joined by a comely young lad, who asks if he can toss the dice for him. As you would expect, virtually every phrase has a double meaning.

> *Take 'em in your hand, me lad,*
> *Fondle them at leisure*
> *Seal the bargain with a kiss*
> *And toss them for me pleasure.*

He sang raucously, occasionally gripping Purkis's knee, or diving a hand down to his groin.

"Lay off, Nevis," said Purkis angrily. "You're not such a stud as you think."

"Lighten up, old fruit," said Nevis. "You're being a prick."

"Hello!" said Worsley. "Obstacle ahead at twelve o'clock."

Nevis bore down on the brake.

The obstacle was a long grey Fenman estate, slewed across the road at a diagonal, blocking our way. A blur of steam hung over it like a private cloud. The front wheels rested against a low bank, below which the road dropped steeply towards a snowbound clump of trees. Two vague figures stood in the steam like ghosts, growing by degrees more substantial: a tall man in a broad-brimmed hat and long brown overcoat, and the slight figure of a young boy, his pale elfin face framed by a raised hood.

They'd better not fucking ask us to help," said Nevis.

Purkis meanwhile was crouching forwards, peering hard at the two figures. "Riddle," he said. "I think that's your pa."

"What?" said Nevis indignantly. "That fucking child-fucking fucker?"

The man moved towards us, raising his hand. Purkis was right: it was my father. His beard, I noticed, was streaked with grey.

"Get out the way," said Nevis, more to himself than anyone else. He jammed his foor on the accelerator. "Get out of the fucking way, you fucking fool!"

The Sceptre shot forwards.

What happened next was a muddle.. I saw my father's hand drop and his mouth come open, and heard a sharp yelp from the boy next to him. Purkis screamed something; then then he leaned across and wrenched at the wheel. We slid sideways. Nevis's feet pumped frantically first on the brake then the accelerator, but we went on sliding. The Sceptre spun round in a half-circle, and then drifted inexorably towards the bank. Nevis let out a roar: a blend of rage and frustration, metamorphosing suddenly into terror. There was a moment of weightlessness as we hung above the frozen landscape, with the immense grey sky all around us, and the seats no longer supporting our weight: then we fell, very suddenly and with tremendous force.

We smashed into the hillside, bounced, turned upside down, and hurtled at terrible speed towards the trees at the bottom.

TWENTY-THREE
The Second Gender

The true challenge, for a public servant, is to put all personal consider-ations to one side, in favour of the greater good.

Safety of the State: A Memoir by Antony,
Lord Haverhill, (Ludden, 485)

1

Steam hissed deafeningly. I saw everything through a dense mist of steam. My mouth was full of blood. I was jammed up against bottles and wrapping paper, and broken glass. Everything was upside down. The steering-wheel hung from the ceiling; the roof of the steamer was flat against my face. Purkis was moaning. He hung awkwardly from his upside-down seat; there was something odd about the way his limbs were arranged. The windscreen was shattered. Poking through it were the scuffed leather soles of a pair of shoes, toes pointing upwards. These belonged, I realised, to Nevis. The shoes were vaguely attached to a pair of trousers; the rest of the mangled body hung out-side the car. The bonnet was embedded in the snowy trunk of a tree, and speared by various bits of wreckage. I closed my eyes.

There was a white interval, during which my head started to throb, intolerably.

The boiler gave a long whistling sigh, releasing a fresh head of steam.

Next to me the door came open. Someone leaned in and caught hold of me, wrapped his arms around my chest, and started drag-ging me out by the armpits. I protested – I was stuck – I hurt too much to free myself.

"William. *William!*"

It was my father's voice. I struggled to focus.

His face was close to mine.

"You have to help me get you out of here."

I braced my feet against something soft and squishy. My knee squealed in agony, but something in the tangle of bodies and wreckage and misplaced seating had shifted for the better. I braced again – more agony – and this time felt whatever was trapping me collapse sideways. One more heave, and I was out, drinking in the cold air.

I was turned over, then I was dragged over snow, then the dragging stopped, and I was staring upwards at the treetops and the sky.

Two faces swam into my vision. My father was one, the boy another. He had narrow freckled features and slate-grey eyes. He looked to be about twelve years old.

"William!" said my father. "You have to get up. We have to go!"

"I'm not sure I can move."

"I'll help you. We haven't got much time."

He bent down and drew me towards him, and my legs straightened underneath me, supporting most of my weight. I was like a wonky deckchair someone was putting up the wrong way round, but at least I was upright, and could place one foot in front of the other.

Together we stumbled and crunched and staggered up the bank towards the ridge.

2

The boy had gone up ahead of us, and was standing by the grey Fenman. My father opened the back door, and lowered me onto the seat, half in, half out. My right foot was wet and freezing cold. I was missing a shoe.

I grasped my father's arm. "Who's this boy?"

The boy turned, and looked at me with his odd expressionless eyes.

"This is Beth," said my father.

"What is he doing here? Haverhill says you kidnapped him."

He looked pained, as if I had asked him to explain something that should have been obvious. "Beth is your sibling."

It seemed an odd choice of words. "He's my brother?"

"Not exactly. We'll discuss it later. Let's get you into the car."

He helped me back to my feet.

A moment later Worsley came over the ridge, white-faced and bleeding. He was holding my pistol.

"Oh thanks, Worsley," I said gratefully, reaching for it. "I'd forgotten that."

He pointed it in my direction, then wiggled it a few degrees to one side to include my father and Beth as well.

"Give that to me," said my father. He started moving towards Worsley, and the pistol spurted fire.

"Learned the lesson now, Riddle?" said Worsley.

My father was clutching his arm. Blood leaked between his fingers.

I looked from him to Worsley. "What lesson?"

"That was all you had to do."

"What?" I said again. I had no idea what he was talking about.

"To stop Nevis. It was that simple."

I looked at him, then I looked at the gun, then I looked at the blood on my father's arm. Everything had a new meaning.

"Right," I said. "Yes, I should have done that."

My father had slumped against the side of the car. His arm hung uselessly by his side, like a broken branch. I noted the blood dripping from his fingers with an odd feeling of detachment. The boy was standing next to him, his eyes glittering, his face twisted with anger. My knee was hurting again, and so was my head. I sat down in the snow.

"This was a bad idea," said my father.

The boy shook his head and looked away.

A few things were starting to make sense, in a weird topsy-turvy sort of way. Worsley, for example – Purkis had always said he was a spy, so I had no business being surprised that that is what he was. But then I had always considered him beneath my notice – practically invisible, in fact. So much for my understanding of the world of spies and the identity they create for themselves. I looked at him now, hoping to understand the mystery that had been under my nose all this time. He was standing with levelled pistol a few yards away. His face was completely empty of emotion. It was like looking at a stone.

3

Time passed, uselessly.

Presently a black Harris pulled up, belching steam like a locomotive. Payne and Jarvis got out. They were wearing identical black overcoats, and both were carrying guns. Payne put his gloved hand on Worsley's shoulder, and drew him aside, while Jarvis waved his gun at my father and me. We were made to kneel down in the snow so that he could get us into handcuffs. Payne went over to the boy. They exchanged a few words, then he led him to the Harris, and held the door open while the boy got into the back seat. He sat there woodenly, facing straight ahead, his face hidden by the folds of the hood.

Another Harris arrived. It waited, steaming, behind the first. No one got out.

After some more discussion, Worsley and Payne climbed over the verge, leaving Jarvis behind to watch over us.

They returned a few minutes later, looking grim. Blood was running down Worsley's cheek from a gash below his ear. Payne led him, limping, over to the second Harris. Reaching it, Payne extended his arm. At first I thought they were going to shake hands, but all that happened was that Worsley handed over my pistol, which Payne then slipped into his pocket. Fair enough, I thought: the pistol was Payne's to begin with, so it was only right he should have it back at the end.

Ambulances arrived – sirens, flashing lights – followed by a fleet of yellow police steamers, and a couple of police transporters. The ambulance men scrambled down the bank, carrying stretchers and green boxes.

The second Harris drove the boy away. The Fenman remained slewed sideways in the road, quietly steaming.

Jarvis bundled my father and me into the back of a transporter. He got in front, in the passenger seat, and the three of us sat in silence, waiting for a driver. A panel of steel mesh divided us, converting Jarvis into a kind of dark blur, but I could tell from the posture of his neck that he was pleased with the day's work. He didn't so much as look in my direction. It seems I had forfeited any right to an acknowledgement.

EPILOGUE

FROM: Deputy Leader and Chief of Security M. C. Panks, National Advisory Council of Greater Anglia.

TO: Field Intelligence Operatives 1215, 4509, 1894.

You are hereby authorised to take any measures appropriate to the investigation of the following categories of offence, as defined by the Protection of the Rights of Subject Populations Act, Section 25 c., paragraph (iii): Permitted Methods of Obtaining Information in Extraordinary Cases.

Disclosure of information vital to the maintenance of public order.

The normal stipulations and penalties apply with regard to confidentiality, deniability, etc.

I trust that the above extraordinary authorisation will assist you in bringing your enquiries to a speedy and successful conclusion.

MCP

Clearance level: Named Agent Only
Message security rating: EXTRAORDINARY
From: Tan Most, Chief Security Officer, Milasian Galaxy.
On behalf of: The most Excellent, the Munificent Impellan Bossard, CBCn.,
DD., Xpn, Supreme Leader of the Universal Council of Elders.
To Agent 3501, Sector 156:147:869, 211c
LD: 01:01:485

Take Note:

The recent incidents which have disturbed the former relative tranquillity of
Greater Anglia are matters of grave concern.
Unrest on this scale points to serious failures of both governance and intelligence.

We refer to your communiqué (12.10.484) which pleads that this state of
affairs results from the 'indisposition' of the elected leader of the Subject
Council.

Be assured that a Subject NAC is responsible for whatever happens under
its governance as a body, and that the failure of any one of its members, not
least of all its leader, reflects badly on the Council as a whole, and on those
operatives who oversee its conduct.

The UCE is unshakably committed to respecting the autonomy of its Subject
Councils. For this reason it has decreed that matters relating to the fitness of
an individual member of a Subject Council to perform his or her duties must
be resolved in the first place by the Subject Council itself, assisted where
necessary by the appropriate intelligence operatives in the field.

In cases where a Subject Council fail to exercise its duties under this decree,
the UCE is required to take whatever measures are necessary to restore stability and public confidence and ensure the security of the individual and
the federation of national councils.

Said measures to include where necessary permanent removal and replace-
ment of all offending parties.

A team of officials of the UCE will in due course visit your sector to monitor and assist with your operations.

Authorised (His retinal seal),

Bossard

APPENDIX A
The Infected Pistol and Other Stories

The Malcaster Stories exist in a limited edition of ten copies privately printed by William Riddle in 485, using a hand printing press used by the former Grubstop on the Finchester bypass for printing leaflets.

The source document is a typewritten manuscript in the possession of Sir Roger Purkis, sometime Minister for Communications in the Greater Albion Government of National Unity.

Stories 1 to 15 are the work of both authors, using the aliases H O Minty (Riddle) and F R Trumper (Purkis); the final three appear to have been written by Riddle alone.

The stories appear in the following order, which is also, so far as can be determined, the order of their composition.

The Infected Pistol

Wisley and Rattle meet for the first time, and Rattle's murder investigation is abandoned in the wake of an unfortunate accident. The story concludes as follows:

The two men stood over the broken body.

Wisley glanced up at the belltower overhead. For a fraction of a second he saw something. It might have been a dark, hooded figure, peering down. It might have been a bat, or a master's gown, flapping bodiless in the wind.

"Pity, that," said Rattle. "Another few minutes and I would have arrested him. Sadly there's no accounting for accidents."

"An accident?" said Wisley scornfully, "My dear Rattle, there's no such thing as an accident."

Next Time Keep Your Trap Shut

The story opens as follows:

DI Ernest Rattle was feeling hot. The sun beat down from a cloudless sky, making him sweat profusely within the straining confines of his prickly tweed suit. As always when crossing Ensor Bridge he experienced a sense that he was leaving the ordinary world of beer and sandwiches for somewhere vastly more dangerous: a place of secrets and disguises, of dark acts and darker motives.

A body had been discovered spread-eagled naked beneath the lectern of the Bune College Congregational Hall, and Rattle was on his way to find the perpetrator of this dastardly crime. The body had been identified as that of Martyn Midway, an art master at the College, who had been reported missing two weeks earlier. One detail stood out: a cryptic phrase scrawled with a chiselled black marker across Midway's pink hairless chest: NEXT TIME KEEP YOUR TRAP SHUT.

What did it mean, exactly? And whom was it addressed to? Not Midway, clearly: there would be no 'next time' for him. A friend of his, perhaps? Another master? One of the boys?

Rattle was, in the idiom of his home town, Little Hemroyd, 'raht flummoxed'.

Rattle discovers that the perpetrator was the school librarian, a member of the outlawed 'Crucifixion Cult'. Wisley comes up with a counter-explanation too absurd to be taken seriously.

The Innocent Boy

The startling beauty of a new pupil named Peter Acorn brings him to the attention of the Malcontents. His sublime innocence leads him to mistake their many would-be seductive overtures for common politeness. At the story's climax Dr Floater confronts Acorn in the deserted swimming pool. He unbuttons his long black overcoat. Underneath, he is stark naked, his monstrous penis hideously engorged. Mistaking Floater's self-exposure for an unfortunate accident, Acorn averts his eyes, dives in at the deep-end, and swims away to the safety of the changing-rooms, leaving the Headmaster too stunned to press the point.

The Midnight Congress

The midnight congress is a weekly event in the Malcaster calendar. Every Saturday night the Malcontents meet together on the stroke of midnight in the College's Congressional Hall. The doors are locked and bolted; black velvet curtains are drawn over all the ground-floor windows. In the light of flickering candles, the votaries lead out the boys selected for recruitment into their obscene rituals. Blindfold and naked, they are made to perform callisthenic exercises, specifically designed to test their fitness for the tasks to which they were to be assigned. In the course of investigating what he believes to be a burglary of the school's ornamental silver candlesticks, Rattle interrupts the congress at the climax of the ceremony. Belch explains the incident away as a rehearsal of the school's Dramatic Society's forthcoming production of a harmless farce called *The Bottom Line*.

Alien Invasion

An account of one night in the life of Dr Horatio Floater, told by the doctor himself. After an evening spent guzzling cheese and red wine from his personal vineyard, and gossiping maliciously about his pupils, the narrator lapses into a drunken coma and has to be put to bed by two of his minions. Barely conscious, he hears them exchange derogatory remarks about his character and personal habits. He falls into a deep sleep, and has an extraordinarily vivid dream in which he is transported by aliens to a space-station orbiting around the earth, and subjected to an intrusive and very thorough physical examination. After the dream has reached its climax he wakes to find his sheets soaking wet, and his bedclothes stained with vomit.

The New Bicycle

What appears to be a flagrant case of promiscuity is shown to have a perfectly innocent explanation.

Pure Vitriol

A vampire chooses Dr Floater as his victim, and dies. Poison is suspected.

The Cascara Overdose

The school's physician Dr Pincher attempts to silence the Geography Master Mr Willey permanently by prescribing him an overdose of cascara. Confused by Pincher's atrocious handwriting, the pharmacist erroneously gives Willey's cascara tablets to Wisley, and Wisley's indigestion tablets to Willey, with unfortunate consequences all round.

The Guilty Party

Dr Pook's Naturist Circus is implicated in the murder of one of the boys. The investigation is hurriedly abandoned when it emerges that Dr Pook (an alias) is one of the school's most generous benefactors.

The Second Gender

The longest of the Malcaster stories, written by Riddle and Purkis towards the end of Vernal Half 484.

In the course of investigating a series of mysterious sightings of what appeared to be a family of hideously deformed monsters housed in the school dungeons, Wisley discovers that for the past several years Floater and Toadflax, aided by the school's science department under the guidance of the deranged Professor Dancemaster, have been working on a plan to develop a 'second gender' in order to add to the number of sexual permutations it is possible to enjoy.

After a number of botched experiments, they succeed in manufacturing a creature of superhuman beauty named Gangri. The Headmaster and his Deputy become infatuated with this creature. Maddened by jealousy, they quarrel and fight. Their battle rages from the clock tower to the F Block classrooms and finally to the sewers running deep beneath the servants' quarters. Floater is victorious: Toadflax is shot in the groin and borne away on a river of ordure. Floater now has Gangri to himself. For a single week he enjoys a sexual extravaganza of explosive intensity, at the end of which he has become the creature's slave.

Emboldened by its newfound power, Gangri refuses the Headmaster any further rights of congress. Floater sinks into a deep depression, from which he is rescued by the reappearance of Toadflax, who has survived his submersion in the river of ordure, gaining power and status in the process. Toadflax disposes of Gangria in a manner made possible by his enhanced powers. At the end of the tale his ascendancy over Floater is assured.

The authors' notion of a manufactured being owes a great deal to the celebrated fourth century novel *Krauthammer* (397) by Hollis Bell (361–415). For the benefit of those readers unfamiliar with the story, it concerns the attempt of Professor Adrian Krauthammer to create a perfect human being. His experiment goes badly wrong, and what results is a monster lacking in any sense of morality or decorum and incapable of restraining his basic urges. Escaping from captivity, the monster goes on a wild rampage, and is finally captured and burned alive by a mob of frenzied villagers. Literary critics see the figure of the Krauthammer monster as a metaphor for Bell's one-time lover Lord Percy.

Poetic Licence

Percy, Lord Roberts, a modern descendent of the historical Earl, is discovered naked in Bune's subterranean servants' quarters. The many victims of his abuse line up to accuse him. Percy produces a bundle of scented love letters tied in violet ribbon. The head porter is dismissed.

The Lost Plot

Bune College finds itself embroiled in the investigation of a murder with no apparent victim and no visible suspect. Wisley surmises that they have strayed by accident into the plot of an erotic novel. He introduces Rattle and himself as characters. The original participants all discover that they have urgent appointments in other works of fiction, and exit before the orgy that was planned to be the story's climax can take place.

The Fatal Cure

Mr Mallard, the Physical Fitness Instructor, visits Dr Pincher, asking to be treated for obesity and gout. Within two days he is dead. Wisley discovers a half-used box of tablets beside his bed, and feeds one to the Headmaster's dog, Butcher. The dog dies, and Rattle is obliged to arrest his friend on a charge of cannicide.

Secret of The Desert

The body of the proprietor of 'Ken's Place' is discovered stuffed into the chimney of his seedy café. Wisley recognises the fragrance clinging to Ken's body to be 'Secret of the Desert,' a deodorant habitually applied by Dr Floater before the weekly midnight congress. Prepared from a formula of his own devising, it comprises a mixture of crushed wormwood, skullcap, rose-petals, ginger, ear-wax and pure alcohol. Wisley convenes a meeting of the suspects and publicly accuses Floater of the murder. Floater comes up with a watertight alibi: at the presumed time of the murder he was attending a meeting of the school governors.

The Scapegoat

This story exists only as a title. In the printed copy of the collection the title is followed by ten blank pages.

Union

Wisley interrogates Floater and Belch about the nature of the arcane ritual known as 'Union'. He is invited to witness the ceremony for himself. He is blindfolded, his trousers are removed, and he is made to taste various disgusting substances, before being thrown into the school swimming pool. He vows to report the Malcontents to the police. Before he can do so he is accused of lewd behaviour. A policeman interviews him, and lets him go with a caution.

The Asylum or Malcaster Triumphant

The Malcontents lure Wisley into becoming a 'guest' at the Wormwood Hall Lunatic Asylum on the pretence that it is a hotel where 'health cures' are administrated. They are assisted in their deception by Rattle, who has become convinced that his friend is going mad. Wisley is placed on a diet of artichokes and bean soup. When several of his fellow 'guests' are found dead in the hotel's shower-room, Wisley starts to suspect that the hotel is in fact a camp for the disposal of social undesirables. The hotel's doctor has him restrained and heavily medicated. Rattle departs, leaving Wisley in a straitjacket, weeping and shouting for help. Later that day, the Asylum is burnt to the ground. Wisley is presumed to have died in the blaze.

APPENDIX B
Bune College for Beginners

A detailed explanation of the organisation of Bune in 484 is afforded by the following extract from a contemporary document:

Most boys at Bune College will have previously attended the nearby Bune Preparatory School between the ages of twelve and fourteen. In recognition of this the forms at Bune College proper are numbered from three to six.

Boys entering the College are inducted into one of three groups, according to the nature of their entitlement to admission. The groups are: Patricians (boys of noble family); Equestrians (boys whose fathers are extremely wealthy or hold high offices of state); and Scholars (boys who have won a scholarship by the school because of their high academic or sporting achievements). More rarely, a boy may be admitted to the group of Scholars by way of a special dispensation made for individuals of promise from a difficult background.

Patricians are accommodated for their first two years in the historic Red House, a tenth-century building next to the Congregational Hall, where each boy has a small study of his own. **Equestrians** comprise some 50% of the school intake, and are consequently split into two Houses, Equestrians I and Equestrians II. Equestrians I share two-bedded rooms within The Stables, which as the name implies, is a converted former stable-block on the far side of Bellarby's Piece. Equestrians II also share two-bedded rooms within the rather grander but shabbier accommodation afforded by The Old Wing, which is attached to the main school building. **Scholars** are housed in ten-bed dormitories within F

Block, a new concrete and steel construction overlooking the back parts of the school, with a view of the River Flux and the meadows that border its banks.

From their fifth year on boys are permitted to share a study with a friend of their own choosing in one of a number of out-buildings (Willow Cabin, the Lodge, etc.). Their roommate will normally be a boy from the same group, although exceptions are occasionally made for unusually close friendships which the school body accepts to be conducive to study and good discipline.

The governing body of the school – effectively the Provost, the Headmaster and the Senior Masters – selects some forty senior boys in the fifth and sixth forms to be 'Praetors', a position which gives them the duty of governing the daily routines of the younger boys. Praetors are not allowed to flog, but they can request that a member of Crow (q.v.) flog a frequent transgressor on their behalf. Each pair of Praetors is allocated one Third-year boy – known as a 'tick' – to act as their assistant at set times of the day and at weekends. The 'tick' is expected to attend to their daily needs – doing their laundry, fetching coal, cooking their breakfast, etc. Praetors can also call upon such 'ticks' as are available to run errands for them.

Every year the school body appoints twelve seniors – four Scholars, four Equestrians and four Patricians – to form the Inner Circle, commonly known as 'Crow'. Although the power of the Praetors is considerable, it is trumped by that of Crow, who effectively control the day-to-day management of the younger boys, and administer all the punishments, from detention to (as a last resort) flogging. A member of Crow is allocated a room of his own and can call upon the services of a number of 'ticks' of his own choice. The boy selected to be Head of Crow is a figure of dizzy eminence, as powerful in some ways as the Headmaster himself.

Modern Bune: a Guide to the Customs,
Traditions and History of an Ancient School in the Fifth Century,
penned by Various Hands, Gannet Press, 470.

APPENDIX C
'Why Religious Studies?'

The following is the text of a talk given by Councillor Peter Joyce to the boys of Bune School on the morning of Sunday September 14th, 478.

Boys often come to me and ask: Counsellor Joyce, what on earth is the point of religion? No one believes in it anymore, and yet the subject still continues to find a place on the Bune curriculum.

Well, first of all, there is more than one way of 'believing' something. You can believe it in an open-minded sort of way, as a guide to conduct, and as an example of some of the typical situations that we confront in life: situations which men have confronted through the ages, and I dare say will continue to do so for the rest of time. And alternatively you can believe that every word is unalterably true, and every decree binding, for all people and all times.

Incredible as it may seem, there are people alive today who still believe in the old-fashioned second way. For example, followers of the Cult of the Cross – they call themselves 'The Fishermen' and worship a man called Hehsu – can still be found in various pockets of the world, where the system of education is by our standards somewhat primitive. Some, amazingly enough, even exist in remote corners of England and Ayreland. It may shock you to hear this, but my own grandfather often spoke of his 'Saviour Hehsu', particularly in his final days, when the present had ceased to interest him, and only memories of the distant past had any meaning.

Hehsu, we are told, was born some two thousand years ago in a far-off country beyond the Middle Sea. A poor man, the son of a joiner, he grew up a rebel, a subversive, an intellectual terrorist. He taught that no one was superior to anyone else, or had any right to tell another man how he should behave; that statesmen and educators were no better than traitors and criminals; that business in all its manifestations was immoral, and that everyone in a position of authority was a hypocrite. He said that there was no obligation on the citizen to work for a living – the Maker of Everything would look after him whether he worked or not, just he looks after flowers by the side of the highway. (That's rather like the boys who neglect their studies, in the belief they can pass an exam without actually learning anything.) He encouraged men to give away all their possessions. He said that although a man was sometimes obliged to pay lip service to the rule of law, no one had any right to stand in judgement over anyone else. He insisted that meeting violence with violence was wrong, and that all wars were immoral, however virtuous the cause. Weakness is strength, surrender is victory, poverty is wealth. He said – I am paraphrasing here – that if someone takes your boots you should give him your shirt. If someone punches you in the face, you must let them kick your bottom. I can't see that working too well at Bune, can you?

Given the subversive nature of Hehsu's teachings it is hardly surprising that he soon fell foul of the local religious establishment, as well as the officials of the empire that governed that part of the world. So much so, in fact, that they felt obliged to charge him with treason and once he was found guilty to execute him in a peculiarly barbaric way, by nailing him to a large upright post, using a cross-piece to support his arms. Ironically, this 'crucifix', as it is called, was eventually to become the defining symbol of his cult.

That was peculiar enough, but what happened next was more peculiar still. Once Hehsu was safely out of the way, the same empire that had put him to death promptly adopted the religion he founded, set up an establishment called 'The Church of the Crucifixion' and used it to impose upon its people a form of tyranny unique in the history of the world. Not only did they wage war in his name – something his teachings strictly prohibited – they also used the people's credulous belief in his divinity as a way of controlling their behaviour. They claimed that Hehsu knew everything about you – every little thought, and every little deed, particularly the ones you were most ashamed of. As if that wasn't bad enough, they said that everyone had to tell their secrets to one of their agents once a week or face the most terrible punishment imaginable. That sounds a bit irrational, when you think about it: I mean, why should you need to tell Hehsu everything you'd done if he knew it all already? But rationality and religion, I'm afraid, are not the most comfortable of bedfellows.

Poor Hehsu: the travesty that's been made of his life and his teachings over the years should be enough to make anyone turn in his grave – an event, incidentally, which his followers claim actually happened. They believe that directly after his execution he came back from the dead and walked around the world, until he finally chose to float up to some kind of vague Universe beyond the Universe and take his seat alongside his Father, the Maker of Everything.

The point I am making is that the teachings of Hehsu, like those of every other religious leader throughout history, were turned upside down. Their core message – splendidly idealistic, but hopelessly impractical as a guide to living in the real world – was either ignored or twisted into its exact opposite. Instead of bringing about freedom they were used as an instrument of tyranny and repression. This is why our National Advisory Council, four centuries ago, decided that religion should no longer be tolerated let alone sponsored by the state. The Church was discredited as a corrupt and parasitic institution. If people wanted to worship someone like Hehsu they had to do so in their own time and at their own cost. Holding religious beliefs also made them ineligible to vote or own property or hold any office of state. That soon put a stop to it. And it put a stop to much more at the same time. Wars became less frequent. Bigotry became a thing of the past. People got on with their lives, without thinking all the time about some great Spy in the Sky, watching their every movement.

So why religious studies?

We have a duty not to repeat the mistakes of the past. In order to comply with that duty we need to know what those mistakes were, so we can avoid repeating them. A well-balanced and humane society like ours is a huge achievement, which needs and deserves to be properly valued and protected. Ideologies which have failed in the past, which have led to evils like social discord, prejudice, discrimination, injustice, and the form of mass-murder known euphemistically as 'war', have to be exposed for what they are: failed belief-systems which didn't deserve to survive. The only belief-system we as educators can safely endorse is one which offers us stability and security and peace: which allows man to live happily and harmoniously with man. Only when we have succeeded in this aim will the kind of society Heshu would have approved of stand any chance of becoming a practical reality.

APPENDIX D
A Bune Glossary

A

Ajax: The river which runs past the school, continuing on to Ludden and thence to the sea. A bridge over the *Ajax* separates *Ensor* from Bune.

Argument: The weekly session when a Tutor sees his pupils.

AWA: (pronounced 'wah') Absent without authorisation. House masters conduct regular AWA checks within their houses.

B

Back-stabber: someone who prefers the active role in a sexual act. Cf: *Supplicant.*

Bellarby's: The extensive western half of the playing fields.

Brain: A Scholar

Blot: If a boy does an extra bad piece of work, his Tutor may give him a *blot*. After four *blots* the boy is sent to account to himself to the Headmaster.

C

Calendar; A booklet published each half containing a complete list of masters, a complete block-by-block list of boys giving details of each one, as well as the year's Rote.

Congregational Hall: Originally a place of worship, it is now used for gatherings of the entire school, including the weekly Meeting.

Counsellor: A senior master, generally the Deputy Head, in charge of morale and morals, conduct etc. Where a boy is having emotional difficulties, suffering from bullying, hopeless crushes, family problems, etc. he is expected to go in the first place to the Counsellor, who thus fulfils the duties of a guidance counsellor, care-worker or psychiatrist.

Chalk and Cheese: A test once taken by new boys after a few weeks in the school to ensure that they had learnt their way around.

Charge: Lessons not part of the school curriculum, and therefore charged as an extra, for example anything involving drama or music.

Cream: The academic élite of the school: the top fifteen Patricians, Scholars and Equestrians.

Crow: The elite club of school praetors, properly known as *The Bune Society.*

Crow Row: A low wall bordering the cobbled yard, upon which supposedly only members of Crow are allowed to sit.

Curfew: The time of day every evening when boys have to be back in their houses.

D

David & Jonathan: Two entwined oak trees felled by lightning on the eastern fringe of Bellarby's.

Dawn Chorus: A lesson before breakfast, usually given to boys in forms B and C.

Duty: (familiarly *Screw*): work set to be done *out of school*.

Dutch Studios (*Splosh):* A group of classrooms housing the Art and Craft department.

Doffing: Acknowledging a master when passing him out of doors.

E

Equestrian (familiarly **Nob or Toffee)**: A fee-paying pupil, generally a boy whose family has a tradition of attendance at the school. It is noteworthy that acceptance at the school depends upon the judgement of the Governing body, and cannot be guaranteed to any boy, however wealthy his family.

Horsebrain

An Equestrian who has distinguished himself academically; Equestrian scholars receive no financial benefit, but have ES after their surname in school lists.

Elevenses: A mid-morning break of twenty-five minutes when boys return to their houses for elevenses, and masters gather together, normally in School Hall. The final ten minutes provide boys with a convenient opportunity to buttonhole individual masters.

F

Free: A day on which there is no regular work whatever.

Field of Ajax: A grassy area on the banks of the Ajax from which rowing and swimming activities can be viewed.

G

Grub-hut: A school-run shop selling food and non-alcoholic drinks.

Grape Garden: A sheltered patch of grass near the Bune boundary wall often used as a place of assignation

Gobbler: Lunch.

Gong: If a boy does an extra good piece of work, his *division master* may give him a 'gong'; the boy has the work signed by his house master and tutor.

H

Half: A term, e.g., *Vernal Half, Pagan Half, Renunciation Half.*

Helping Hand: Mutual masturbation.

High Patrician: selected from among the academically most distinguished Patricians, he ranks immediately below the Captain of the School. Although the High Patrician is constitutionally the Head Boy, for most purposes the president of Crow has more power.

House. On entering the school, boys are put into one of four houses: Patricians, Equestrians 1 and 2, and Scholars. The houses compete against one another at sports. One they enter the Fifth

House divisions cease to be important, and boys make their own arrangements as to accommodation.

Houseman (familiarly *Drudge*) The matron assists the *houseman* in running his house; he has particular responsibility for the health of the boys and the administration of domestic affairs.

I

Immortalised: A boy whose work in a subject is outstandingly good may be 'Immortalised'; he shows the Head Master or Lower Master a sample of his work, which is then lodged in *College Library*.

Innebriates: a club of senior boys – normally members of *Crow* – who enjoy fine wines and practical jokes.

The Inner Circle consists of ten Praetors, five Scholars and five Equestrians, elected by the Provost, the Headmaster and the Senior Masters, and known commonly as *Crow*. About twenty out of fifty fifth-formers are selected to become sub-praetors.

J

K

L

Late Book: Unpunctual boys have to sign Late Book in *School Office* for a few days before breakfast.

Long Walk (The Plank): The corridor leading to *The Scaffold* (the Head Master's Office).

M

Meeting: The Counsellor addresses meeting every Saturday morning, sometimes with a talk on some matter to do with morals or conduct. Sometimes boys from the school are invited to address Meeting with observations, grievances etc. The system is very democratic: anyone can say anything with impunity. Whether their views are ever acted upon is another matter, but at least they can be aired. Meetings are in Bune Hall the morning on Sundays. Familiarly known as *Bullshoot*.

Bune is a village on the outskirts of London, separated by a river from *Ensor*, and *Ensor Palace* the seat of the former King of Angland.

The Bune Mouthpiece: A monthly magazine edited by senior boys. Familiarly known as *The Mouth-organ*.

Mop Jockey: A Janitor. Mop Jockeys clean the boys' rooms and oversee boys' tea.

N

Novice: A boy during his first two or three years in the school.

Number One: Head of Crow.

O

Orphan: This is pejorative, denoting a lack of class, wealth, status, or ability. If a boy is neither a Patrician, and Equestrian or a Scholar, he will often be labelled an *Orphan*, particularly by those who dislike or disapprove of him. William Riddle will have often been referred to as an *Orphan*, both to his face and behind his back.

Order Card: A card issued to each boy in the lower school (Third to Fourth) every two or three weeks by their personal Tutor, detailing how well the boy has been doing; the boy has the card signed by his house master and then returns it to the Tutor.

On Call: Masters (*Board*) take it in turns to be *'On call'* to administer or oversee minor disciplinary matters: breaking up fights, admonishing bullies, supervising detentions, and monitoring floggings (*Stripes*).

P

Patrician: One of noble family. *Patricians* have their own *House,* as do *Equestrians* and *Scholars*. Also known as *'Swells'*.

Praetor: A boy who has been given responsibility for discipline. There are thirty praetors out of a total sixth form roll of fifty boys.

Postbox: A place in a house where messages etc. can be left, and where boys tend to congregate.

Prescription If a boy misbehaves, he may be given a *Prescription,* which means that *Crow* is required to administer some appropriate punishment, for example *Clink* (detention after lessons), *Kneeling* (cleaning duties, particularly humiliating for one who has had formerly been responsible for a *tick*) or *Stripes* (flogging). Failing that he will be disciplined by the Headmaster, either by reporting him to his father (*Booking*), Suspension (*Hanging*) or as a last resort Expulsion (*Firing*). *Stripes* can only be administered by a full *Praetor*, although a *Sub-Praetor* can request it of a praetor for anyone for whom he has responsibility, including a tick.

Private Business: The weekly session when a specialist tutor sees his pupils.

Procession of Boats: An event on the fourth of June when the best oarsmen in the school of all ages, dressed in festive fourth-century naval uniform, row past the crowd of parents and masters assembled on the bank and salute them by raising their oars and standing up (which sometimes results in their capsizing, to the huge delight of the crowd).

Punishment/Trials/Ordeal/Sentence: End-of-term examinations.

Q

Quack: A master, i.e. teacher.

R

Rainbow Stripes: A severe flogging.

Remove: The Fifth form, in which responsible boys can be appointed sub-praetors

Rote: Bune's basic academic timetable, determining who does what when; it is shown at the back of the Calendar.

Rough: Rough is Bune's special game, a cross between *kicker* and *toss-ball,* and far older than either. It is played by boys of all ages in the Vernal Half.

S

Punishment Cell: A classroom.

Riddle: A vacuum cleaner (n); to vacuum (vb); vulgarly, fallatio.

Signed Off: Excused school owing to illness.

Solo: A solitary act of masturbation.

Stripes: *Flogging.* The severity of any particular flogging was left to the judgement of the *Praetor* who administered it. The least severe floggings would consist of two or three blows on the bottom with a gym-shoe; the most severe would involve being struck on various parts of the body with a stout stick known as an *Arden Cudgel*. Riddle's tormenter Nevis possessed an armoury of sticks of a variety of lengths and weights, and was known to rain blows on the arms, back, head and testicles in the course of a particularly savage beating.

It was the custom after a flogging for its recipient to offer his hand to the flogger and thank him for pointing out the error of his ways. Any perceived insincerity in the performance of this custom would merit a more severe flogging than the original

T

U

V

W

X

Y

Z